Pen
Pendergrass, Tess.
Colorado shadows

$ 25.95

Colorado
Shadows

Colorado Shadows

Tess Pendergrass

Five Star
Unity, Maine

Published in conjunction with Martha Longshore.

First Edition, Second Printing

Cover photograph by Joan Raven

April 2000

Five Star Standard Print First Edition Romance Series.

The text of this edition is unabridged.

Set in 11 pt. Plantin

Printed in the United States on permanent paper.

Library of Congress Cataloging-in-Publication Data

Pendergrass, Tess.
    Colorado shadows / Tess Pendergrass.
      p. cm. — (Colorado series ; bk. 1)
    ISBN 0-7862-2372-3 (hc : alk. paper)
    1. Ranch life — Colorado — Fiction.   2. Colorado —
Fiction. I. Title. II. Series.
PS3566.E457 C6 2000
813′.6—dc21
                                      99-089979

Colorado Shadows

Chapter 1

Maggie Parker clutched her handkerchief to her nose, but her shallow breathing still pulled in more dust than air. The passage of countless vehicles during the long, hot July days had ground the soil of the road to a fine powder which rose in clouds around the rocking stagecoach.

There wasn't much to see through the window, but Maggie kept her eyes firmly on the swirling dirt outside rather than face the knowing leer of the white-bearded man sitting opposite her. She wished she had something more substantial than her black lace shawl to wrap across her chest.

She'd worn the most daring gown her mother had allowed her to pack, a forest green silk with black ruffles that exposed her shoulders and dipped revealingly down her bosom. Though it was perfectly respectable for a Lexington ball, she'd hoped the dress would create something of a sensation in small-town Colorado. Based on the icy silence of the two other women on the stagecoach and the surreptitious glances of their male traveling companions, she'd more than succeeded.

She had planned the dress to be the first of the surprises she would throw at Cousin Lucas and his wife. She felt confident she could scandalize her frontier relations into sending her home to Kentucky within the week.

The stagecoach bounced, jolting her forward. The old man's hands reached toward her hopefully. Maggie jerked back onto her seat, wrapping her shawl more tightly around her. Apparently Langley had told the truth when he'd said her body was shapely enough to distract a man from her defects.

Almost unconsciously, Maggie traced a finger along the scar that marked her face. She had little enough reason to want to return to Lexington, but she couldn't allow her stepfather, Stephen Casey, to exile her to the end of the earth—and judging from the scenery, that pretty much summed up Oxtail, Colorado.

Her green-flecked eyes, slitted against the dust, darkened as she remembered her stepfather's satisfaction when he had informed her he was sending her to live with her mother's relatives. He could afford that smug smile. He had convinced her mother the fresh air and wholesome surroundings would be good for her.

"Oh, Meggsie," her mother had sighed. "You'll like it in Colorado. From what Lucas says, it's beautiful country. I would go with you if I could travel."

Her gentle, faded mother had suffered from fainting spells for more than a decade. Maggie suspected Lynette would outlive them all, but she couldn't fight her, as Stephen well knew. Which left her few options for escaping her impending exile.

She'd even gone to Langley for help. She flushed at the memory of that horrible encounter. To think she'd thought she loved him! And now, three weeks later, here she found herself, riding a crowded, smelly stage to nowhere.

Not for long. She would be home by the end of the month. She couldn't wait to see the expression on Stephen's face when she showed up on the doorstep like a bad penny.

The stagecoach lurched to a reluctant stop.

"Oxtail!" the driver bellowed.

The other occupants of the stage didn't exactly make a rush for the door. Maggie finally opened it herself. Her elderly admirer angled his neck to get a better view of her cleavage, but offered no help as she jumped awkwardly to the street below.

A quick glance at her surroundings made clear to Maggie why her fellow travelers were reluctant to disembark in Oxtail. The place inspired fears of being accidentally left behind. The town consisted of one dusty street lined with dusty looking businesses—a general store, a stable, a church, a hotel, and two saloons. Several large houses and some less pretentious shacks proved people did actually live in Oxtail, but Maggie couldn't fathom why.

She could only conclude that the rest of Colorado must be equally bleak or Oxtail's denizens would have all stampeded to somewhere more congenial.

"Your luggage, miss," the driver grunted, dropping her carpet bag onto the trunk he'd already unloaded from the top of the stage.

"Excuse me." She stopped him as he turned away. "Where's the office?"

The driver, a burly fellow with a look of perpetual disinterest, kept his eyes on the two stable hands changing his horses. "Ain't no office, miss. No need for one. The Colonel takes care of tickets at the hotel."

Even this unsatisfactory answer seemed to tax his patience, and Maggie had to follow him back toward the horses to ask her next question.

"I mean, where do people wait for the stage?" She glanced again up and down the street, but except for the two grooms and a boy who had come running from the general store to fetch a depressingly small mailbag from the stage, Oxtail appeared deserted. Perhaps Cousin Lucas hadn't received the telegram announcing her arrival. After all, Maggie reflected grimly, her relatives were frontier farmers. They probably came into town no more than once a month for supplies and the exciting social life.

"Beg your pardon?" The driver glanced at her in irritation.

"My cousin, Lucas Penny, was supposed to meet me," Maggie explained, straining to remain polite in the face of such deliberate stupidity. "I don't see him," she added, to make the problem perfectly plain.

The driver shrugged, casting a doleful eye over the horses as though doubtful that the grooms, who had disappeared as mysteriously as they had come, were to be trusted in their harnessing of the fresh team.

"You might try The Rose," he suggested. Then, apparently considering his duty toward this bothersome passenger fulfilled, he heaved himself up into his seat. With a jangle of the reins and a loud "Hi-yup, there!" the stagecoach moved off down the street, leaving Maggie choking in the billowing dust.

Fighting panic as her only link to the civilized world rolled away, Maggie turned to examine the nearest saloon. "The Golden Rose" was printed above the door in a color that had, presumably, once been gold. In the silence of the now deserted street, she could hear sounds coming through the swinging half-doors of the building—men's voices, the clinking of glass, a short burst of laughter. Piano music wafted to her ears, a short lilt of an Irish ballad, then a rousing dance tune, a warm-up for the evening ahead. Four or five horses stood tethered out front, but it was early yet, too early for the place to be wild.

Maggie looked down at her luggage. The way this journey had gone so far, her things would be stolen if she left them behind, but she couldn't carry them all with her into the saloon. Sighing, she picked up the carpet bag.

"Keep an eye on my trunk for me," she instructed the

10

nearest horse, a swaybacked, responsible looking gelding. A wistful brown eye looked her over, then turned back to the saloon door.

Lugging the carpet bag, Maggie stepped onto the wooden sidewalk and up to the saloon. Over the top of the door, she could see several men sitting at the bar. They didn't look dangerous. With a deep breath, she marched into the Golden Rose.

A long, low wolf whistle greeted her.

"Hey, look what just come in. Tell me I'm dreamin', Hank."

Flicking a glance sideways, Maggie saw a group of ragged cowboys sitting around a table that had been hidden from the doorway. The best of them looked as if he'd made an attempt to wash his face before coming into town. She suspected the worst hadn't bothered to change clothes in over a week. But each of them had the same look in his eyes as they stared at her.

"Well, sweetheart, you shore is a sight for sore eyes."

"Ain't she though."

"Whoo-eee!"

Ignoring them, Maggie continued toward the bar, but now the men sitting on the bar stools had seen her, and the one right in front of her leaned forward with a leer. A big man with a red-veined nose and a bird's nest of a beard, he reeked of a variety of animals she could smell from a yard away.

"Stay back, boys. I get her first," he growled at the men sitting at the table.

"That ain't fair, Shelby," one of them argued. "I seen her before you."

The bearded man lifted two huge fists. "I say it's fair," he said. "You gonna argue, Dutch?" His face relaxed into a smile. "Besides, I ain't greedy. There's plenty to share." His eyes fixed hungrily on the front of Maggie's dress.

For just a moment, his words shocked Maggie speechless. No one had ever spoken to her like that before. No one in Lexington would have dared, no matter what they thought of her.

As the man's gaze wandered over the rest of her figure, her tongue loosened.

"Put your eyes back in your head," she said tartly. Her eyes found the bartender, who sent her a black look as he wiped a glass with a rag that appeared less than clean.

"Are you the owner of this establishment?" she asked, irritation sharpening her voice.

"I ain't lookin' for any more girls."

A flush suffused Maggie's cheeks. Her dress might be daring, but it was entirely acceptable. She didn't look like *that*.

"Don't be that way, Sam," the bearded man, Shelby, pleaded, never taking his eyes off Maggie. "Just look at her. This one's somethin' special. I'll give you double the usual to have her first."

He rose from his stool, and Maggie felt a prickle of something that might have been fear if she'd acknowledged it. Shelby was none too steady on his feet, but he was big.

"Hell, I'll give you fifteen dollars to be first, Sam," said a voice from behind her. Glancing quickly over her shoulder, she saw it was the man with the clean face. He looked a little more sober than Shelby, and it made her even angrier that he, too, seemed to think she was a saloon girl.

"I'm looking for my cousin," she announced, but no one seemed to hear her.

"Twenty!" Shelby said, glaring at the other man.

"Twenty-two," he countered immediately.

"You ain't got that kind of cash, Dutch."

"Sure I do," Dutch answered, angry at being doubted.

Shelby's hands balled into fists again.

"Hey, hold it right there," the bartender interrupted, taking his first interest in the proceedings. Maggie felt a brief second of relief. "I won't have any violence, boys. We'll do this civilized. You gonna offer me more than twenty-two dollars to take her upstairs first, Shelby?"

"That's enough!" Maggie shouted, outraged. "No one is taking me anywhere!"

The bartender shot her a glare, but Shelby slammed his hand on the bar. "Twenty-five!" He swung on Dutch, his eyes narrow. "You cain't beat that, Dutch."

Looking into Shelby's face, Dutch decided the price had indeed gone up too high.

"Well, I'm second," he mumbled.

But Shelby had already turned to smile at Maggie, a big, drunk smile that showed most of his yellow teeth.

"C'mere, honey." He reached out a hand. Maggie shied back, but the big man caught her wrist and held on tight as she tugged to get away.

"Let me go, you big idiot," she snapped, fighting down a spasm of fear as she realized she wasn't nearly strong enough to break away. "I'm not a . . . a prostitute, and I'm not going with you. I'm looking for my cousin."

In desperation, she looked to the bartender, but he'd gone back to polishing the glassware. Most of the other men in the bar still watched her, but they showed no inclination to interfere.

"C'mere." Shelby accompanied this order with a tug on her arm. Maggie stumbled against him. He grabbed the hair behind her hat, and, tilting her head, brought his mouth down on hers. His breath smelled of whiskey and rotten teeth. Strands of hair ripped from Maggie's head as she twisted to avoid him.

She couldn't quite believe this was happening. Couldn't believe this horrible creature was pawing at her, obviously intending to take her upstairs whether she agreed or not. Stephen had sent her west to keep her out of trouble!

Shelby had managed to step on her skirt when she stumbled, so she couldn't free the knee she wanted. She settled for a quick punch in his gut. He didn't let go of her wrist, but his mouth pulled away from hers long enough for her to yell, "Lucas! Lucas Penny is my cousin! Please, someone get Lucas Penny!"

The girl's desperate plea brought March Jackson's head up with a snap. He was sitting at the bar, but his mind had been floating somewhere hazy where he didn't have to think, didn't have to know, didn't have to be.

It took him a second to remember what had brought him out of the reverie. A girl had asked for Lucas. Shrieked was more like it. Had the stage come already? He hadn't heard it.

He turned to look for the girl and realized that he'd seen her when she first came in. Sam's whore was looking for Lucas? But she had said she wasn't a whore. She wore no paint on her clear, fine features, not even over the scar that ran, white and thin, from her right temple almost to her jawbone.

Now her scar stood out starkly against skin mottled red with fury and fear, as she tried to wrench herself from Shelby Brennan's grasp. Everyone else in the bar had frozen when she'd said Lucas's name. They were staring at March now, but Shelby was too drunk to notice and too hot to care.

March rose from his stool, teetering slightly. "Brennan! Let her go, now. Let her go."

Shelby didn't seem to hear his reasonably voiced request, but the girl did. She glared at him with suspicion, her

14

green-flecked eyes dark and wild as Shelby took a step toward the stairs, dragging her with him.

March stumbled after them, shocked to discover that he was almost as drunk as he was pretending to be.

"Brennan, let her go, man."

Shelby ignored him, though between his drunkenness and the girl's struggling, his progress was slow. March wavered with indecision, cursing the fog that clouded his brain. Just how many whiskeys had he downed?

But in the second he hesitated, his choices disappeared. The girl was hiking up her skirt, showing a shapely calf, but it was the glint of steel in her high boottop that caught March's eye. She had a knife.

The thought of what Shelby would do to her if she tried to stick him overrode the alcohol in March's system. In one swift motion, he crossed the barroom floor and hacked the side of his hand across Shelby's wrist. Shelby dropped the girl's arm, and she fell heavily to the floor. As Shelby turned toward March, his eyes red and small as an angered bear's, March's left fist caught him full on the chin.

The big man staggered, but though his eyes refused to focus, he swung back.

The satisfying thump of his own fist striking home had lit a fire in March's brain. As he dodged Shelby's clumsy attack, he jabbed the other man's stomach. Shelby's grunt of pain brought a grim smile to March's face. The heat of the whiskey, and his anger, and the fierce pain and guilt that had been sitting in his gut for the past month seared through his arm, and his next blow caught Shelby in the nose, stunning him. March hit him again, in the ribs. Shelby fell.

Only Dutch Bates' hand on his arm kept March from falling on his opponent and pummelling him where he lay. He swung around, shaking with a sharp desire to hit Dutch, too, and anyone else within range.

"March, hey, he's down."

March stepped back, his breathing ragged, and fought for control. As his vision cleared, he saw Shelby lying uncon-scious on the floor, surrounded by the other men in the bar. He looked down at his hand, and though it hurt, the blood on it wasn't his. Spatters of Shelby Brennan's blood decorated his shirt.

Bile welled up in March's throat. "Is he going to be okay?" he asked thickly.

Sam, the bartender, looked up from where he knelt by the big man's head. He shrugged. "He'll have some aches when he wakes up. No worse'n he usually does when he drinks."

March turned his head and spat on the floor, but he couldn't get the taste of rage out of his mouth. If he'd wanted word to get around that he was drinking too much, that he was out of control—and an easy target—it surely would now. He would have laughed, but he felt too sick.

"I didn't mean to hurt him," he said, mostly to himself.

"Hell, March, none of us blames you," Dutch Bates said. Several of the other men shook their heads in agreement. "He shoulda let her go when he heard she was Lucas's cousin. Horny or not."

The girl. March had forgotten her in his desire to hurt Shelby Brennan, to punish him for March's own failures. He swiveled to find her leaning against the stair balustrade, one hand clutched around a tiny, gleaming dagger, the other hand balled into a fist. She was obviously frightened, but her chin tilted up in defiance, and he was sure she'd use that dagger on him if he tried to get near her. Never in a million years would he have recognized this spitfire as Lucas's cousin.

Yes, he'd noticed her when she came in. First that hair,

dark and red under her green hat, the ringlets against her neck pointing to the expanse of white skin across her front, drawing his eyes down to the soft curves of firm breasts. Below that, her waist pinched to nothing, and her hips looked saucy even standing still.

Hell, Lucas's "baby cousin" was a full-grown woman, and one March wanted no part of. From what Lucas had said, he'd expected a rebellious tomboy, not this shapely creature who dressed like a whore and carried a dagger in her boot.

Well, he'd be rid of her soon enough. She'd be back on that stagecoach tomorrow, headed for home where she'd be safe. He wasn't going to fail Lucas this time.

"Meggsie?" he asked, feeling foolish.

Maggie put her left hand on the balustrade to steady herself and took a good look at the man standing before her. Though he appeared to be the cleanest of the bar clientele, his wiry figure taut and ready as a mustang's from the fight, he was not particularly prepossessing. His dust-brown hair was unkempt, his clothes worn and stained, and he hadn't shaved in days.

"You're not Lucas Penny," she said, keeping her dagger poised where he could see it.

"No, miss, I'm not," he admitted. "I'm March Jackson, Jane Penny's brother. I'm Lucas's brother-in-law."

With an eye on her knife, he cautiously put out his hand. Maggie shrank away in disgust. The man flushed and yanked the bandanna from his neck, wiping away the blood.

"I came into town to meet your stage," he said, pushing the offending hand into his jeans pocket along with the stained neckerchief.

"You missed it," Maggie observed acidly. The adrenaline from her encounter with Shelby Brennan was wearing off, and she lowered the dagger to her side to keep her hand from shaking.

March's jaw twitched. "I've found you now. Let's get out of this saloon."

Maggie's fingers clenched in response, but she hiked her skirt back up to put her dagger away—noting with bitter amusement that all the men's eyes politely glanced away now that they no longer thought her a prostitute. All eyes, that was, except March Jackson's, but his mouth was so grim and his gaze so distant that Maggie felt a sudden, unexpected flash of modesty. She quickly dropped her skirts and, ignoring the now surreptitious glances of the bar's patrons, marched over to her carpet bag, saving one cutting glare for the bartender before heading for the door.

She heard March fall in behind her as she pushed through the swinging doors and crossed the sidewalk to where she'd left her trunk. She breathed deeply, trying to gather her wits about her. She knew she should question this stranger more carefully about his identity and why it had taken him so long to come to her aid, but the saloon encounter had so shaken her that she needed all her concentration just to put one foot in front of the other. At least her trunk was still there.

"That yours?" March asked, sounding as awkward as she felt.

Maggie nodded, stepping aside as he lifted the heavy trunk easily to his shoulder. She noticed he was no more eager to make eye contact than she.

"This way." He led her down the sidewalk toward the hotel, a boxy, two-story building with an elaborate three-story facade, its bright whites and greens faded by sun and dust. A patient-looking gray mare stood tethered in front. March dumped Maggie's trunk into the wagon bed behind the horse, alongside the bags of oats already loaded there.

Still without a glance at Maggie, March took her carpet bag and tossed it beside the trunk. Then he moved to the front of the wagon and offered her a hand. He heaved her up onto the seat, more as though she were a sack of flour than a woman, then swung himself up beside her.

"Giddyap, Pamela!"

They moved down the dusty street, taking a left-hand turn before they reached The Golden Rose.

Maggie kept her eyes straight ahead as they passed the last ramshackle buildings behind Main Street and rolled out of Oxtail across the plain. Two dusty wheel ruts ran west through dried grasses that billowed like a sea of gold in the light of the late afternoon sun. If she shaded her eyes, Maggie could make out the mountains beyond, hazy blue-green and white in the distance. In the illusory distances of the prairie, they seemed hardly nearer than they had in Greeley, where she'd left the train for the stagecoach this morning.

Without turning her head, she knew the silent man beside her was sitting straight and still except for an occasional signal to the mare. If she hadn't been so exhausted, she might have been frightened, riding off into the sunset with a taciturn stranger she'd just seen fell a man almost twice his weight with three solid blows.

He moved beside her, easing his position on the seat, and his voice broke the silence of the plain. "Just for my own information, girl, what the hell did you think you were doing, walking into a saloon dressed like that?"

Maggie's exhaustion and embarrassment evaporated in a blaze of anger.

"What?" She turned on him in astonishment. "What was *I* doing? I was looking for my mother's cousin Lucas, who apparently had the bad judgment to send an idiot drunkard out to meet my stage! What the hell do you mean, what the hell was I doing?"

March's face twisted with what looked like pain. "A lady would have waited outside."

The censure hit home, and Maggie lashed back without thought. "What would you know about ladies, you lousy hayseed? You and all those damn louts in the saloon."

"My apologies." March's words were sharp as knives. "I should have known you were a lady right off, from your language."

Shaking with fury, Maggie twisted away from him, just as the wagon hit a rock in the road. The shock unbalanced her, sending her tilting off the narrow board seat toward the mare's solid rump and the crushing wagon wheels. In desperation, she caught the back of the seat with her left hand, but her feet slipped off the footrest beneath her. She yelped as a sharp pain shot through her shoulder, but she didn't let go.

A strong arm caught around her waist. The breath whooshed from her lungs as March heaved her from imminent danger. He fell back on the seat, and Maggie found herself draped unceremoniously across his lap. Somewhere in her mind, she knew he'd just rescued her from certain injury and possible death, but this last indignity put her beyond rational thought and she struck at him wildly, gasping for breath, raining her fists on his shoulder, the only part of him she could easily reach.

"Hey, there, you little brat!" he yelped. He pulled the mare to a stop before pinning her arms to her sides. "You want to get us both killed?"

Maggie couldn't answer. Her struggling had turned to violent shudders that she couldn't stop. Sobs interrupted her breathing, wracking her lungs. The tension and anger and exhaustion of the past three weeks, coupled with the jolting fears of the past hour, finally overcame her, and even the humiliation she felt at her weakness couldn't stop the tears from pouring down her cheeks.

"Miss Parker?" the voice came much more quietly from above her. "There now, girl, are you all right?" The bands of steel holding her softened, freeing her arms as he rubbed one hand along her arm. "There now, don't cry. You're all right. Hush now. You'll be fine."

Surprised by the sudden gentleness of his voice, Maggie clutched at the soothing tones like a lifeline. A moment ago she'd been desperate to get away, but she couldn't stop shivering, and he was so warm and solid beside her . . . She leaned against him, letting her sobs subside under the flow of his words. As she slowly gained control over her frazzled nerves, she realized that he was speaking to her exactly as she would soothe a frightened colt. Unable to help herself, she giggled.

"What's so funny, girl?"

The voice was mild, still calming, but the nearness of it made Maggie suddenly conscious of her position. She was sitting squarely across the lap of a complete stranger, his arms wrapped firmly about her torso. Her hat had fallen back in the struggle, and his chin rested on her hair as she buried her face in his chest. He smelled of sweat and horses and whiskey and the open air, a scent as dangerously masculine as the hard muscles of his arms and thighs so close to her. And yet it was the first time she'd felt safe since before leaving Lexington.

Gently he loosened his hold on her, lifting her to the seat beside him.

"Miss Parker? Can I offer you a handkerchief?"

Maggie bit her lip to prevent another hysterical giggle. She risked a glance up at the man beside her to find him smiling back at her, a quizzical, shy smile, at odds with the hard, violent man she'd seen in The Golden Rose. And she learned something else about him in that glance. She'd been wrong when she'd thought his looks plain and nondescript. But then, she'd not had a good look at his eyes before. Blue eyes, with a hint of green, like the reflection of a cottonwood tree in a fresh-running stream.

"It's Maggie," she managed to mumble.

She took the scrap of clean white cotton he offered, wiped her eyes, and blew her nose. If she had been angry with him before, her tears and his unexpected kindness had washed it away.

"Thank you," she said quietly, embarrassed at not having said it before. "For catching me just now, I mean, and for saving me from that awful man in the saloon."

He frowned and glanced away, his whole body tensing. "No need to thank me. You were right. If I'd been outside waiting when the stage came in, you'd not have been treated like that, and I'd not have had to knock Shelby Brennan down. You were right to be angry; I've no call to blame my failings on you."

He picked up the reins, chirruped to the mare, and the wagon began to roll again, into the blazing yellow of the sun hovering over the mountaintops.

Maggie glanced at him. She wanted to ask why he hadn't been waiting outside to meet her, but she held her tongue. The grim line of his mouth said he was sorry for it, and she didn't want to set off another confrontation.

Instead she asked, "So, do I look halfway presentable?" She handed him back his handkerchief.

March turned to look her up and down, and that quizzical smile briefly touched his lips again. "Not particularly."

Irritated at herself that his answer should bother her, Maggie tilted her hat back on her head and brushed futilely at the dust on her skirt. She'd planned to shock her cousin and his family. Now, wouldn't she just!

22

"How much farther to Cousin Lucas's farm?" she asked, trying to see past the blazing sun before them.

"Not far. And we call them ranches out here." Something in his voice made her look over at him. He was gazing fixedly at the gray mare's ears, his eyes desolate, empty. "I'm not taking you to Lucas's ranch. I'm going to leave you with the Culberts. They're the nearest neighbors."

"Why not Lucas's place?" Maggie asked sharply.

"Things have . . . you can't stay here in Colorado. You have to go home."

Maggie ought to have felt elated. That was exactly what she'd wanted. But she couldn't think past the old, half-buried pain of being shoved aside and the cold certainty that March was not being totally honest.

"Lucas told Stephen he'd take me in," she said, her voice rising again. "The hell you'll take me someplace else! Take me to Lu—"

"Maggie!" March cut her off harshly, pain darkening his eyes as he turned his gaze on her. "I can't take you to Lucas. He's dead."

23

Chapter 2

"*Dead?*"

March said nothing, his eyes once again focused on the mare's ears, but he could sense the fight draining from her as she absorbed his words.

"Oh." She sounded almost like the lost little girl he'd expected to meet at the stage today.

His throat clogged with guilt and self-disgust. "It happened nearly a month ago. I would have sent word, but I forgot you were coming until your father's telegram arrived yesterday."

"He's my stepfather." She passed up the opportunity to remind March he'd forgotten her today, as well. "I'm sorry. I didn't know Lucas at all, you know. Mama says I met him when I was very young, when he was still a Texas Ranger, but I don't remember."

"He remembered you," March told her. Lucas had fairly glowed talking about his beautiful cousin Lynette and her adorable little Meggsie. "He could hardly wait for you to get here, saying Jane could use some female company."

The memories cut him like shards of broken glass.

"Lucas wanted me to come? Stephen must have lied through his teeth about me in his letters."

At the longing and bitterness in her voice, he lost his concentration on Pamela's ears. The corner of his eye caught her wrapping her flimsy shawl more tightly about her shoulders despite the lingering heat of the early evening.

When she saw his glance, her chin tilted up. "I don't

24

blame your sister for not wanting strangers visiting, but I would at least be company for her. When we got word that my father had been killed in the war, my mother couldn't bear to be alone, even for a minute."

The bile rose higher in March's throat. "Miss Parker, I'm sorry I—"

"You don't need to fob me off on the neighbors," she rushed on past his words. "I can promise you I wouldn't be in the way. I've looked after my mother for a long time, and I know when to fade into the background. I—"

"Maggie!" His shout broke her chain of words, disappearing without an echo across the prairie. "I didn't make it clear . . . I . . ." His mind balked at saying the words. "Jane, she was killed, too. And their son, Logan. We . . . We'd been having trouble with rustlers. They attacked the ranch at dinnertime."

She didn't need to know the details, the images that would haunt his dreams for the rest of his life.

"Oh," she whispered.

He thought for a moment she meant to put a hand on him in sympathy, and he didn't think he could bear it. He spoke quickly, "There isn't anyone at the ranch to chaperone you, so I arranged with the Culberts to have you stay there. They're good people, good friends."

He pointed up the dirt track they followed. "That's the turnoff to their place, about a quarter mile on. It's just through the break in that hogback there. Lucas's place is about a mile more on this road."

And a good thing, too. The bar fight and the memories had soured the whiskey in his gut, and each jolt of the wagon brought a sick sweat to his forehead.

"You had the measles?" he asked, talking to keep his mind off his stomach.

"No." She twisted on the seat to look up at him. "Why? Are you sick?" She scooted away from him. "You don't look very well."

He shook his head. Big mistake. He swallowed. "I'm not sick," he said. "The Culberts' middle boy, Daniel, has got the measles. They'll probably put you up in their bed instead of the loft with the kids to keep you away from him."

"You're planning to leave me in a place where they've got the measles?" she asked incredulously. "You're just going to throw me off on some neighbors who have a sick child to deal with? You'd just leave me there to get sick, too? I could die!"

Her voice rose, the strident tones cutting through his desperate concentration. His stomach rolled.

"Oh, for heaven's sake," he snapped, turning to stare at her. "Do you have to attack everything I say? I'm not dumping you on my neighbors; I'm trying to protect your reputation. Hell. Nobody dies from measles."

"My brother did."

She had to be making it up, but real fear chilled her hazel green eyes. March groaned as his stomach twisted.

She leaned toward him again, urgently. "He was only five. My mother got sick taking care of him, and she's never been well since. You can't make me stay with those people, with that sick boy." Her voice shook. "What if he dies?"

March could only stare at her, half hoping the pain in his gut would kill him so he could escape this mess. If she were a spooked horse, he'd know just what to do, but he didn't have the same experience with women, certainly not with women like this one.

"Daniel's not going to die." He tried to soothe her. "And neither are you. It's only for one night; you'll be back on the stagecoach tomorrow. You can't come home with me. It's too dangerous. Your repu—"

"You don't have to worry about my reputation," she broke in. "Why do you think my stepfather sent me out here, anyway?" She tossed her head and tried to laugh. "Being the guest of a man who's practically my cousin wouldn't even be living up to my reputation. Besides, nobody back home will ever know."

She was more mule than horse. March glared at her. "That's the stupidest thing . . ."

The wagon hit a rut in the road, snapping his mouth shut and ending rational thought. He brought the mare to an abrupt halt.

"Here." He thrust the reins at the girl beside him, hoping she knew enough to hold on to them. "I . . . just a minute."

"Are you okay? You look awful. Mr. . . . March? Please, are you all right?"

"I just need . . . to walk it off . . ."

He rolled off the wagon seat, collapsing to his knees. With a desperate push of strength, he managed to get to his feet and lurch away from the wagon, too sick even to be humiliated by the fact that he couldn't hide his illness from her.

Maggie watched him stumble away, fighting a sudden terror that he might die and leave her all alone in this strange, empty, violent land.

He was drunk. Drunks got sick. He wasn't going to die. She turned away when he started retching, repeating that to herself over and over again.

He's not going to die.

When she finally believed it, the anger returned. He'd called her stupid for not wanting to stay with his friends and their son, who might even now be dying. He hadn't seen Brian, almost unrecognizable with his red, puffy skin, eyes flickering with fever. It had taken only a week for the beautiful, healthy little boy, the darling of his mother's eye, to burn up and die. Her mother had never recovered, and Maggie had lost her last link to her father.

She still remembered the smile on Papa's face when he'd left to join the Confederate army. He'd pinched her cheek and said, "There, big girl. Don't cry. You take care of your brother for me."

Maggie shut off the memory, bringing herself painfully back to the present. She was not going to watch another little boy die.

She turned to glance at March. He was on his knees, breathing deeply, probably only now sharing her conclusion that he wasn't going to die. Still, she couldn't rely on him to listen to reason in his state. He intended to take her to the Culberts regardless of her wishes.

The mare before her shifted restlessly, impatient to be home. March had said the Penny ranch wasn't far down the road. She glanced back at him. He hadn't moved. He'd said himself he wanted to walk off his drunk. It certainly wouldn't hurt him any.

Gathering up the reins to let the mare know she meant business, Maggie gave them a shake and clucked. The mare's ears pricked happily, and she stepped off down the wagon track at an eager, ground-eating trot.

In the clear air of the Colorado piedmont, the sun dropped behind the mountains with surprising swiftness. As dark blue shadows swirled through the dry grass, swallowing the sloping hills around her, Maggie began to doubt her decision to leave March behind.

Rustlers had killed her mother's cousin and his family. Lawless ruffians might lurk anywhere in this desolate country. And what if she missed the Penny ranch? In the twilight she could still make out the ruts of the road well enough, but in half an hour or less, the light would be completely gone.

She glanced back over her shoulder. Nothing moved on the track behind her. She'd passed through the rocky break in the long hill March had called a hogback and could no longer see the prairie. Maybe she should go back for him, but if she missed him, she might find herself lost for good.

The wagon tilted as the gray mare turned sharply to the right. Maggie whirled around to correct her, only to discover that they'd come around an elbow of hill. The dark shapes of a long ranch house and a large barn and stable rose from the land. The mare's stride lengthened as she turned again, toward the barn.

Maggie heaved a sigh of relief. "Good girl," she called softly. "I should have known you'd get us home."

She grimaced at her own words. The Penny ranch looked anything but homey, lying dark and silent in the gathering dusk. She'd never given much credence to the idea of ghosts, but a tiny shiver ran up her spine at the thought of being alone here.

The barn door stood open, so she drove the mare right in, putting off leaving the uncertain safety of the wagon seat until four walls separated her from the endless expanse of the Colorado plains. A small chorus of horse voices answered the mare's soft nicker, and for a moment all the strangeness and terror of her new surroundings faded from Maggie's mind.

"Welcome to you, too," she called to the invisible creatures waiting in the stable that extended from the end of the barn. Descending from the wagon by herself took a little ingenuity in her long skirts, but the mare waited patiently, happily snuffling the familiar smells of home.

To her surprise and relief, she found a lantern and box of matches near the barn door. The small flame reflected off warm wood, bringing out bright patches of straw on the floor and shafts of gold hay drifting from the hayloft.

It took her less than a minute to find a halter, brush, and curry comb in the tack room. She hung the lantern on a hook in the wall and set to work unharnessing the gray mare.

The smell of horses and hay, the warmth of gray hide beneath her hand, the familiar repetitive motion of grooming, all brought her the first sense of peace she'd had since Stephen had taken her to the train station three days earlier.

She pushed back her fears of how Stephen was treating the horses back home and which ones might be sold before she could return. She pushed back the memory of leering eyes and groping hands in The Golden Rose this afternoon, focusing completely on the task before her.

Harder to banish was the knowledge that at any moment the stranger she'd deserted sick drunk on the road would walk through the barn door behind her.

A creaking stair broke her concentration, abruptly informing her that the horses were not her only companions.

"Who's that? Who's there?" The alien voice came from the blackness at the other end of the barn.

Maggie dropped the curry comb, her heart thudding hard in her chest. She'd assumed no one else lived here at the Penny ranch. But what had March actually said? It was dangerous. There was no one to chaperone her. She'd have to agree that this man in the shadows with his deep, dark voice wouldn't qualify as a chaperone.

She glanced at the barn door, starlight showing faintly in the framed square of sky. Where was March? She could run, call for him. But her pounding heart made it hard for her to breathe.

"I said who's that? Speak up or I'm gonna use this shotgun."

She'd had only herself to rely on for so long, perhaps she

hadn't listened carefully enough to March. Given the choice between risking measles or being killed—or worse—she'd probably have chosen measles.

"I'm Margaret Parker," she spoke up loudly, with all the authority she could muster. "I'm Lucas Penny's cousin. Who are you?"

"My name's Lemuel Tate," the voice said, "an' you look about as much like a relation to Lucas Penny as I do."

Something shifted in the darkness at the end of the barn, and into the light stepped a big black man, at least two inches over six feet tall, and at least seventy years of age. He stood straight and steady, only his shoulders curving beneath the weight of his age, but his close cropped hair and carefully trimmed beard showed few streaks of black through the white. Rheumatism gnarled the hands clutched around his shotgun, and his eyes squinted to focus on her.

Maggie took a breath of tentative relief. She could probably outrun him if necessary, but not the shotgun.

"My grandmother was Lucas's mother's sister," she explained. "I doubt we bear much resemblance to each other. Perhaps you can help me carry my trunk into the house?"

"Where is March?" Lemuel Tate asked, his lips pursed with distrust as he eyed her attire.

"Mr. . . ." Dammit. She couldn't very well admit she couldn't remember March's last name. "He'll be here any minute." She'd been certain of that a few moments ago, when she'd dreaded his arrival. Now she could only pray he hadn't gotten lost or eaten by coyotes or whatever other horrible things happened to people in this godforsaken land.

"I 'spect we can wait for him, then," Lemuel said. He transferred the shotgun to his left hand and came over to inspect the wagon. "I'll jes' put away this grain. You make yourse'f comfortable."

31

Maggie detected no irony or amusement in his statement, but neither did she see anywhere to sit down. Instead, she took the gray mare's halter and led her to the first stall at the stable end of the barn. An armload of hay spilled out of the manger, and a bucket of oats hung beside the door. Maggie held the bucket while the horse ate. Once she'd settled the mare, she made her way down the row of stalls, unable to resist inspecting the other horses.

In the box next to the gray mare, she found a big, muscular bay gelding, his dark eyes regarding her with nearly as much suspicion as Lemuel's.

"Hey there, big fella," she murmured, standing still and close so he could smell the scents of hay and mare on her. "What a handsome boy you are. Thoroughbred from the look of you."

"Watch out for that one." Maggie looked up to see Lemuel watching her, a sack of grain balanced easily on one old shoulder. She was suddenly glad she hadn't tested her theory that she could outrun him. "He'll bite."

"What's his name?"

For a second she thought he wouldn't answer. "Achilles. He was Lucas's horse. Honey in the next stall was Miz Jane's."

The beautiful little Palomino in the next stall showed no hint of Achilles' bad temper. She nuzzled Maggie's hand and tilted her head to have her ears scratched.

Maggie moved down to look at the next horse and felt an unexpected smile curve her lips. "And you must belong to March."

She couldn't quite describe the gelding's color, the yellowish brown of clay mud, as golden. His mane and tail looked uncannily like old straw. She estimated him to be at least a hand and a half shorter than Achilles, but his big, solid

32

bones made the larger bay look delicate by comparison. Even in the dim obscurity of the box stall she could tell he had knobby knees.

If not for the powerful muscles of his shoulders and thighs, he'd have looked like a nag sent to the glue factory. His muscles and his eyes. Set in the big-boned, awkward face was a pair of warm brown eyes that regarded her with gentle intelligence.

"He's not much to look at, but he's been with me six years, sound as the day I got him and smarter than most people I know."

Only her fear of spooking the horses kept Maggie from jumping out of her skin. The hair on the back of her neck prickled. She hadn't heard a single footfall, but from the sound of his voice, March stood no more than a foot behind her.

Her stomach fluttered in fear, but she kept her voice calm. "His face shows good character."

"Mm." She heard March's movements now as he stepped forward to pat the gelding's nose. "I guess I needn't have worried you'd know what to do behind a pair of reins."

She'd expected anger. If he'd come in and knocked her flat on the floor, she wouldn't have been surprised. She didn't know how to react to this wry resignation.

"I don't suppose you'd believe the mare ran away with me?"

He turned to her, and she saw his face again, was surprised by the mesmerizing play of the shadows across it. One corner of his mouth curled up. "Pamela?"

"No, I suppose not," she agreed.

"March! I was worried 'bout you. This gal is with you, then?"

March returned the old man's smile. "More or less, Lem.

33

This here is Miss Maggie Parker, Lucas's cousin from Kentucky."

Lemuel nodded to Maggie without a trace of embarrassment. "Then I shore am glad I didn't shoot you, miss. Since that's settled I think I'll be getting myse'f along to bed—'less you need me to carry in Miss Parker's trunk."

"I've got it, Lem."

The old man nodded again and disappeared into the blackness beyond the range of the lamplight, leaving her alone with March.

"Look, Maggie—Miss Parker, there's nobody here on this ranch but me and Lemuel. I can't even offer you a hot meal tonight, much less a proper chaperone. Let me take you to the Culberts."

The only things she knew about this man were that he had a nice uppercut and he couldn't hold his whiskey. And she remembered keenly what the men in The Golden Rose had thought of the clothes she wore. She knew women weren't safe alone with men. She ought to be begging him to take her to the Culberts.

But however foolish he thought her, she couldn't bear the idea of facing a sick child, praying between his every feverish breath that he'd take another one. Not to mention that she'd barely slept in three weeks, and had been traveling for three days. She wasn't sure she could take another step.

And March looked worse than she felt. Watching him watch her, waiting with the patience of the dead for her response, she could see the skin drawn over his cheekbones, the dark circles under his haunted eyes. Specks of blood darkened his shirt and vest from his fight with Shelby Brennan. He held an arm over his stomach as though to keep it steady.

"You're in no shape to endanger my virtue," she said

34

matter-of-factly. "And I don't care what anybody else thinks of me."

"Miss Parker—"

"Mister—" It wasn't fair. He'd been the one stinking drunk, and she was the one who couldn't remember names. She pushed on brazenly. "You may as well call me Maggie. And you're the one who pointed out it's only for one night."

The lines of exhaustion around his mouth softened again in his ghost of a smile, bringing a beguiling boyishness to his features that made her stomach twist queerly. "I am beginning to have a suspicion of why your stepfather sent you away, Miss Maggie Parker."

"It's not my fault everyone argues with me," she muttered, almost giving in to the temptation to return the smile.

March passed by her to the wagon, again lifting her trunk with surprising ease. "I guess we might as well get you settled for the night. The picture we two make, your reputation is probably safer if no one else sees us, anyway."

March leaned against the front porch railing, his eyes fixed west where the knife-edge disappearance of the stars into blackness gave away the shape of the Rocky Mountains against the sky. Exhaustion weighed him down like a wet wool blanket, and his head throbbed with the aftereffects of whiskey, but he couldn't bring himself to go back into the house.

He'd put Maggie in Lucas and Jane's big bedroom, grateful now that Henna Culbert had descended on the ranch house the day after the deaths, channeling her anguish into a top-to-bottom scrubbing. At least the sheets on the bed were clean.

He supposed the sheets on his own bed in the loft were just as clean. He hadn't thought of sleeping for two nights after finding the bodies, grief and terror of death too fresh on him. When he'd finally dropped from exhaustion, it had been on the floor of the barn. Since then, he'd slept in the hayloft, separated from Lemuel Tate's room by a thin bare wall, where he could hear the unending life-sounds of the healthy, breathing horses. The solidity of the big beasts kept the ghosts confined to his nightmares.

A cool breeze ruffled his hair, but he was too tired even to shiver. After seeing Maggie was comfortable, he'd washed his face and changed out of his bloodstained clothes into a fresh nightshirt. But when he'd looked at his bed, he'd had to escape, so he'd pulled his blue jeans back on and come outside to cleanse his lungs of the taste of death. He thought about getting a blanket and trying to sleep here on the porch. The night had never held any terrors for him, but now the cold distance of the stars was almost more than he could bear.

The faint clank of metal against wood froze him into stillness. The voices of ghosts whispered in his head . . . The sound of a child playing with a toy soldier on the table . . . A phantom moving a bucket of soapy water across the kitchen floor . . . A man impetuously tossing aside hammer and nails to embrace his wife.

When the ghosts left him, March moved swiftly, calmly, with the stealth of a predator at night. There were any number of rational explanations for the sound, but his world hadn't been rational for a long time. The clank of a spur against the hardwood kitchen floor would make just such a noise.

His rifle lay upstairs in his loft bedroom. He'd left his Colt pistol in the hayloft this morning, afraid to take it into town, afraid of the anger that boiled within him. He didn't have time to retrieve it. If an intruder had invaded the Penny ranch, chances were he was no stranger to cold-blooded murder.

March's bare feet made no sound on the hardpacked earth as he dropped from the porch. He padded swiftly down the length of the house, pausing beneath the east window of Lucas and Jane's room. Maggie had left it half open to the night air. March hoped he could enter as silently as the breeze, otherwise he'd probably end up with her little dagger in his chest before he got a chance to explain himself.

The window creaked faintly as he opened it wider. He slipped through, taking a defensive position against the wall, but there was no movement; he hadn't woken her. He crept to her bed. He'd send her out the window to the barn and the safety of Lemuel's shotgun.

He put his hand against the shimmer of white sheet. It still held the warmth of her body, but she was gone.

A brief second of sick fear gripped him, followed immediately by a dizzying wave of relief. He almost laughed at himself. The intruder in the kitchen was Maggie. She'd assured him earlier she was too tired to eat anything; she must have changed her mind. He'd better get the hell out of her room before she returned.

But as the pounding in his heart quieted, he heard the unmistakable sharp creak of the top step of the loft stairs. His body tensed again. He couldn't imagine any reason for Lucas's wildcat cousin to climb up to his room. Had he been mistaken about the intruder?

Eyes and ears alert, he made his way out into the hall and to the stairs. He knew every noisy board in the house and made no sound climbing to the loft.

The faint glow of starlight came through the dormer windows, showing him the outline of the figure crouching beside his bed. She'd borrowed Jane's dressing gown.

"Maggie?" he said softly.

"March?" His name came in a harsh, thin whisper.

Before he could react she was in his arms, her head against his shoulder, her warm body trembling beneath the soft flannel gown. Once again she'd caught him by surprise, throwing his hold on the world completely off balance. He panicked, as mindless as a horse shying at a blown leaf, and yet his arms went around her, trying to stem the trembling. His face dropped into her hair, smelling the dust and sweat of traveling mixed with something softly, intoxicatingly feminine.

He hadn't known how he craved contact with another human being. The warmth of her, the softness of her, so vibrantly alive. He hadn't known he'd died, too, the day his family had died, until now when her life invaded his body, awakening an almost painful need for more. More life, more feeling, more nearness.

Her head turned upward, and his lips found hers in a kiss too unexpected, too desperate to be gentle. She made a sound of surprise, her lips parting to his, her body softening to his touch for one heartbreaking moment.

Then she pulled her head back with a growl, and the sharp tip of a dagger pressed into the base of his throat.

"What the hell are you doing, you son of a bitch?" she hissed.

He found he'd almost become accustomed to her swearing. "Kissing you," he said, his voice hoarse from trying to avoid the blade and from desire. Something wild in him didn't care if she pressed the dagger home.

"*Why?*" She still hadn't raised her voice above a whisper.

"You came up to my room in your nightgown and threw yourself at me." He felt foolish and confused, and he wanted to kiss her again. The blade pressed a little harder as she leaned forward; he could almost see the incredulous expression on her face, even in the dark.

"I was looking for you because there's someone in the house," she whispered, bringing her face close to his to emphasize her point.

He thought he was fast enough to take the dagger from her, but he remained still and relaxed. He'd misjudged her before.

"I went to get myself a glass of water," she explained, "and when I was coming back, I heard someone climbing in my bedroom window."

March cleared his throat, ignoring the pain below his adam's apple. "I was out on the porch," he said sheepishly. "I thought I heard an intruder in the kitchen. I wanted to get you out to the barn before I confronted him. That was me at the window."

Silence echoed through the darkness as she digested his story.

"You expect me to believe that?" The volume of her voice told him that at least she no longer feared an intruder.

"I don't know what to expect from you, Maggie," he said, suddenly more weary than he'd ever been in his life.

He felt the cat draw in her claws and saw the flash of her feral grin. "You couldn't have come in the front door, anyway. I didn't know you were out there, and I locked it."

He might have replied, but the room was swaying. He sat down on the side of the bed to stop it.

"You should be asleep," she told him, softening slightly. "You need it."

"You could use some yourself," he said. "I'll see you down to your room."

"I think I can find it myself," she retorted.

For once he was glad of her independence. He waited until her head had disappeared down the stairs before calling after her, "Be sure to latch your window."

Her angry snort brought a smile to his face as he fell over onto the bed. Lucas's baby cousin. After watching her with the horses this evening, he suspected she wasn't far from the spoiled tomboy he'd expected after all, acting the part of an experienced alley cat to shock her hayseed relatives.

He should feel like a foolish cad, kissing the girl like that. He'd made a promise to Lucas's memory that he'd send her safely back to Kentucky. So far, next to her own willfulness, the only danger she'd faced had been his fault. But he was too tired to be sorry for the kiss.

Good thing she was leaving in the morning. He couldn't get a handle on Maggie Parker. Not too long ago, walking down a dark, dusty wagon track, he'd sworn he'd kill her—if he didn't die before reaching the Penny ranch. He'd been stunned when he'd looked up to see the wagon rolling away, Maggie sitting with her back ramrod straight. She'd never even looked back at him.

The sudden sound in the dark loft startled him until he recognized his own laughter. He lay staring into the darkness. His bed didn't hold the terrors he'd expected. He still couldn't sleep here, but he wasn't afraid to be alone. He'd just rest a moment before taking a blanket out to the porch.

Sleep caught him before he could remember to take off his blue jeans.

Chapter 3

Sunlight brushed Maggie's lashes, waking her with a start of fear. She'd overslept. She'd be late for her chores again, and Stephen would be furious.

In the next instant, she was disgusted with herself for her fear. Her stepfather no longer had any power to hurt her. Years had passed since he had sold Ladybug, and she'd taken great pains never to show too much affection for any living creature again.

Her fingers found the scar on her cheek. If she needed any reminder to hold herself aloof, she had only to read the pity and distaste in the eyes of strangers when they saw her face. Though the men in The Golden Rose had paid it no attention. Maybe she should simply take care to meet only drunks and lechers.

Her eyes flew open, taking in the unfamiliar yellow beams over her head, the thick multicolored quilt pulled up to her chin. She didn't have to face Stephen or her mother at all this morning; she was in Colorado Territory. A strange emotion, something like elation crept over her. It felt almost like . . . freedom.

She pushed the covers away and swung her legs over the side of the bed. The sun already warmed the air around her, but the floorboards chilled her feet. Last night she'd felt sure she wouldn't sleep, lying in Lucas and Jane Penny's bed, knowing they'd been murdered in the next room barely a month ago. She'd stiffened at each movement of shadow, every faint noise.

But this morning the room glowed with warmth. Sunlight poured through the lacy white curtains to gild the handmade furniture with gold. Brightly colored pillows softened the rocking chair and the bench against the wall. Rugs of braided rags offered islands of comfort from the icy floor.

Maggie hopped from rug to rug to reach her trunk. She grimaced at the dust-coated green dress she'd left draped across a chair. She'd leave it there, and March could burn it if he wanted to. She certainly never wanted to wear it again. It had shocked the Coloradans she'd met far beyond her expectations, but she no longer needed to shock anyone to get sent home.

Rummaging through the trunk, she found the plainest, primmest dress she'd packed, her split-skirt riding habit. It might be impractical for stagecoach and train travel, but she wouldn't attract any unwanted attention looking like a scarred schoolmarm. An eccentric scarred schoolmarm, she amended to herself as she pulled on the pantaloons that went under the skirt.

Once dressed, she wrenched her protesting hair into a strict chignon and put on a country bonnet her mother said made her look sweet.

Surveying herself in the mirror, she nodded approval. The high-necked, stone-colored habit and bonnet left her about as attractive as a catfish. She needn't worry about a repeat of the scene at the saloon yesterday. Or the one with March last night.

The red flush that crept into her cheeks surprised her. She shook her head at the foolish chit in the mirror, acting as if he'd kissed her because he'd found her attractive. He'd been drunk and miserable, that was all. A lout, just like the other men at The Golden Rose. Just like Langley.

She let out the breath she'd been holding and unclenched

her fists. She'd tormented herself all the way out here to Oxtail, plotting ways to make Langley pay, make him sorry for how he'd treated her. In truth, he'd already won; she was weak, mortally ashamed of facing him again.

She looked herself in the eye, willing the weakness away. She wasn't afraid of Langley. And she should be angry at herself, not March, for the scene last night. Angry for the foolishness that made her want to believe he found her attractive. Angry for the insanity that, for a fraction of a second, had allowed her to enjoy his kiss, desire the warmth of his lips against hers, the strength of his arms around her. The insanity that even now made her want to tear off the bonnet and let her hair hang loose — thick red hair that caught the eye, and, when she tilted her head, swung across her cheek to hide her scar.

She turned abruptly from the mirror. Langley hadn't damaged her pride so much that she needed to impress a drunken cowhand.

She'd taken March's advice to latch her window, and she'd also lodged the back of a chair up under her doorknob, mostly in retaliation for his having gotten in the last word last night. Moving the chair aside, she opened the door and stepped cautiously out into the hall. Muffled sounds came from the direction of the kitchen. At the smell of bacon and coffee, her stomach growled.

She hurried down the hall. A potbellied stove separated the kitchen from the sitting room, which also apparently served as an office and library. Maggie dragged her eyes from the low bookcase that ran along the rough-hewn wall. She wouldn't be here long enough to explore it.

March stood at the stove, intent on a cast-iron skillet sizzling with frying eggs. Dressed in blue jeans and a red shirt, he looked so casually at home that Maggie felt herself flushing again, remembering she'd spent the night alone in the house with him. He'd taken time to clean himself up this morning. Damp, his hair showed streaks of bronze she hadn't noticed before.

"I hope you're hungry," he said without looking up. "I think I cooked too many eggs. Help yourself to the coffee, and there's bread Henna Culbert brought over yesterday morning."

There was no way to reach the coffee pot at the back of the stove without leaning close to him, so she took her seat instead. He'd set the plain pine table for two, with what must have been Jane Penny's good china, silver utensils, and good white linen napkins.

"There's no butter for the bread, but I did the milking this morning, so the cream's fresh. And there's honey."

At her continued silence he finally looked up at her. She caught the surprise in his face at her appearance before he turned back to the eggs. He lifted the frying pan off the stove and brought it to the table.

"One? Two? More?"

"Two, please," she answered primly, though the smell of food left her faint. She could have eaten all six eggs in the pan. She hoped he didn't hear her stomach grumbling.

With an old, beat up spatula, he slipped two eggs onto her plate. "Coffee?"

"Please." Maggie clenched her hands in her lap, waiting for him to serve himself, set down the pan, pour two cups of coffee, and return to the table before she reached for the bread and the plate of thick bacon.

With as much grace as she could muster, she wolfed down a slice of bread smothered in honey, hoping to forestall further embarrassing comment from her stomach. March seemed content to eat in silence, so she focused on her food.

She couldn't remember ever having eaten anything so good as this plain fare, but then she hadn't eaten much in three days, nothing at all since breakfast the day before.

"I hardly recognize you this morning," March spoke up finally as she reached for her fourth slice of bread.

"That's hardly surprising, considering the condition you were in yesterday," she replied tartly, refusing to let the comment hurt.

He groaned. "Don't remind me."

She glanced up, looking into his eyes for the first time that morning, unsettled by the humor she saw in them.

He rubbed his temples. "I think someone's taken a pick-axe to the inside of my head."

"It can't be all that bad; your appetite doesn't seem to be suffering."

"And it's not so bad I've forgotten the little hellion who stranded me a mile and a half from home last night," he said, his insult so self-effacing, Maggie found she couldn't be properly offended. "You look downright respectable this morning."

"I'm glad you approve," she said darkly, stabbing at her bacon.

"It makes it a little easier to put you on that stagecoach all by yourself," he said, his face settling back into tired lines of responsibility.

"I see." Maggie pushed aside her last bite of bacon and laid down her fork. Her desire to return to Kentucky, to civilization, had sustained her since before she'd even left home, the only thing that had made the journey to Colorado tolerable. Now that no one wanted to hold her here against her will, the idea of returning home—to Stephen's coldness, her mother's spells, Langley's scorn—no longer held as much appeal.

"I'll telegraph your parents to let them know you're returning."

"Fine." She rose to carry her plate to the sink. "I suppose Stephen dying of an apoplectic fit at the shock of me arriving unannounced would be too much to hope for anyway."

They both heard the rider approaching in the same instant—hoof beats galloping down the drive, halting with a great noise of snorting and jangling by the front porch.

"Stay back," March ordered, getting up from the table and running to the door.

As he swung it open, Maggie heard a youthful voice calling, "March! March!"

"Jacob! What's the trouble, son?" March pulled a hat off the rack by the door and stepped out onto the porch. Maggie followed to the doorway, looking out to see a boy of about twelve on a stringy brown and white pinto mare no bigger than a pony. The mare rolled her eyes while the boy waved his arms in excitement.

"Lucifer's got your mares in the barley again, March. You better get over there quick. Pa says if you don't hurry, he's going to shoot the son of a bitch this time."

From the way March discreetly covered his smile, Maggie guessed the boy's father probably hadn't intended his message to be delivered quite so literally.

"Go tell your pa I'll be right there," March said.

The boy nodded and whirled his little mare in a cloud of dust, as full of grave importance as if he were carrying General Lee's orders to James Longstreet during the Battle of Gettysburg.

March turned and saw Maggie in the doorway. "This shouldn't take too long. I'll load your trunk and Lem can drive you down to the Culberts' place. I'll just take you to town from there. You won't even have to go inside

46

and risk the measles."

"What horses is he talking about?" Maggie asked, ignoring the barb. "The ones you herd the cows with?"

He brushed past her into the house and headed down the hall. "Cows?"

"Cattle," she tried, fighting annoyance. "Whatever you call them out here. The ones you raise."

Even with his back turned, she could tell he was trying not to laugh. "We don't raise cattle or cows or any other bovine. I suppose we could herd Daisy, the milk cow."

She followed him into her room and picked up her carpet bag. "I thought everyone in Colorado farmed cows—cattle," she said with enough careless disdain to show she didn't care if he laughed. He hefted her trunk onto his shoulder.

"Well, we don't. We . . ." His voice caught on the pronoun, but he couldn't bring himself to change it. "We raise horses."

She hurried down the hall to open the front door for him and followed him across the yard toward the barn. "What kind?"

"The usual kind, I guess. Head, four legs, tail." Then, as if suddenly realizing how defenseless the heavy trunk he carried made him, he shied away from her.

"Cow horses," he added quickly. "Lucas's gamble. You see, there's plenty of wild horses out there for the taking, but the more ranches there are, the more competition, the better horses they're going to need. And the wealthy ranch owners, they're going to need horses, too. They have money to spend, and don't want to be seen on some spindly Spanish pony, no matter that these old mustangs are the smartest, toughest horses I've ever come across."

He glanced at her, but his eyes looked right through her, fierce with concentration. "Now your eastern horses, American horses, they're big and pampered and need too much food and water, too much shelter from the elements. So Lucas is . . . was . . . breeding a sort of compromise. Our horses aren't as hardy as the mustangs or as handsome as the thoroughbreds—" He focused on her now, and the life in his eyes surprised her into losing a step. "—but they're smart and quick and strong. And mostly well-behaved."

They'd reached the open door of the barn. Lemuel Tate had already hitched Pamela to the wagon. The mare blew them a quiet greeting as March settled the trunk into the wagon bed.

"Except they like the neighbors' grain," Maggie finished his thought.

"If Jed Culbert wasn't the soul of patience, he would have shot Prince and Stormy by now."

"I heard young Jacob out there." Lemuel's deep voice jumped Maggie. The old man loomed into view, leading March's horse. "I've got Balthasar saddled and ready for you."

"Let me go with you," Maggie said, feeling a sudden desire to see the horses that lit March's eyes.

He swung onto Balthasar with controlled grace. "Lem'll bring you along in the wagon."

"You can't tell—" She caught herself with an effort. They were his horses; he really could tell her what to do. "I'd very much like to see your horses. I was raised on a horse farm myself; I've been riding all my life. I wouldn't be in the way, I promise. I might even be able to help."

"Can you rope a horse?" he asked dryly.

"Of course," she lied immediately, wondering exactly what he meant. She could halter and lead any horse she'd ever met, if that's what he wanted. "I'm dressed for it," she reminded him, shaking her split skirt with one hand. "Please, March."

He frowned at her. "You are the most . . ." He turned to Lemuel. "Would you saddle Honey, Lem? She ought to keep Miss Parker out of trouble." He nudged Balthasar forward. "Do you think you can follow the road back to the Culbert farm?"

Maggie nodded.

His mouth remained set in a tight line. "If you can't, you trot right back to Lem and Pamela, do you hear? If you get lost or cause any other trouble, I will tie you up in your trunk until the stage gets here and send you home that way. Do you understand?"

She couldn't fight down her delighted smile. "Yes. I do. Thank you."

He grunted and sent Balthasar into a canter out of the barn and up the drive. She hurried to where Lemuel was saddling the palomino mare.

"Honey's a sweet gal," he told her. "But she ain't been rid in a while, so take care with her. Here, let me give you a help up."

She tried not to notice how his big dark hand dwarfed her boot as he lifted her lightly into the saddle. For a moment she felt disoriented, the heavy Mexican saddle strange between her thighs. She ran a hand over the pommel. She'd seen saddles with horns before, but never ridden one.

"You set, Miss Parker?"

"Yes, thank you," she said, her attention focused on the half ton of grace and muscle beneath her.

"All right. I'll see you at the Culberts' then. If March asks, you jus' tell him Lemuel forgot about the rope."

Even astride Honey, she barely had to bend her head to study his deeply lined face. But she couldn't read his dark eyes to tell if he was baiting her with her ignorance about roping or inviting her into a friendly conspiracy against March.

Not knowing how to reply, she turned away and pressed her heels to Honey's side. In an instant, Lemuel and March receded from her consciousness as Honey sprang into a canter. From Lemuel's comment and Honey's eagerness, she guessed the mare hadn't been ridden since Jane Penny's murder. Traveling, Maggie had felt unpleasantly confined herself the past few days. She leaned forward and gave the mare more rein, grinning at the instant response.

They flew up the drive and around the low hill, hitting the wagon track at full gallop. The sun felt warm through her riding habit, but the air filling her lungs was cool and fresh. Laughing with the sweetness of it, she urged the mare faster, Honey's gait so smooth she thought they must have stopped touching the ground long ago.

As her gaze lifted from the road before her, Maggie suddenly understood the term "hogback." The long, low hill that had sloped up so gradually from the prairie the evening before had hidden its other side from her in the darkness. The west face of the hogback dropped as sharply as though someone had sliced it with a knife.

The top of the hogback was a stone rampart, running north and south as far as she could see. If not for the places where the rock had crumbled away, leaving a gap, the hill would have been virtually impassable.

Honey was flying through a pocket of grassy Eden, tucked between the hogback ridge and the mountain foothills.

The turnoff to the Culbert farm came much too soon. Maggie would have missed it completely if Honey hadn't slowed a little and turned her nose.

"I take it you've been here before," Maggie commented, slowing the mare to a respectable trot as they turned into the tree-lined drive. She patted Honey's neck, which was a little damp from the sudden exercise, but the mare's even breathing and enthusiastic pace indicated her sound conditioning.

As they came over a slight rise, Maggie saw a low-slung farmhouse crouched against the underside of the hogback, but it was the barley field to her right that caught her eye. Out in the far corner of the field ranged a small herd of horses, their long necks reaching eagerly for the ripening grain, apparently unconcerned about the smaller group of human figures waving their arms and shouting.

Maggie and Honey must have nearly caught March on the road, because he seemed to be just arriving at the scene of this little drama. She turned the mare away from the house, onto the path March had followed through the barley.

March slowed Balthasar to a brisk walk as he approached the group of Culberts ineffectually trying to drive away his horses. Young Jake rode his pinto mustang in a snorting, dancing semicircle around the small herd, but other than an occasional curious glance at the duo's antics, the other horses paid them little attention.

Six-year-old Emily saw March first, pulling free from her father's hand to run toward him. Her younger brother, Tucker, wasn't far behind.

"March! March!" Emily shrieked.

March felt a surge of pride as Balthasar calmly stood his ground against this sudden onslaught of flapping skirts and waving hands.

"Me!" Tucker screamed, his sudden tumble over a rock barely slowing him down. "Me! March!"

"No! I'm gonna tell him!" Emily grabbed March's stirrup as she reached him, her delicate features twisted in distress at the thought that Tucker might get to explain first. "March, Prince got the horses in the barley again."

51

"They won't go 'way," Tucker added, his stocky, round body running full tilt into Balthasar's right front leg.

"No wonder you're so fond of that old fellow."

March turned at the voice behind him to see that Maggie had found her way to the Culberts' all right. It should have hurt to see anyone else on Jane's horse, but Honey looked so happy to be out, and Maggie's eyes shone with such amusement at his predicament, trapped by the children, that he could only send her a grin back.

He didn't care if she laughed at him all day if it made her eyes sparkle like that.

His conscience caught him with a guilty tug. When she was out of his sight, he had no trouble thinking of her as Lucas's baby cousin, a precocious brat that her family couldn't handle. But sitting there astride Honey as if she'd been born in the saddle, her stylish bonnet framing those dangerously red curls, and that riding habit molding each curve from her neck to her hips . . . .

"March!" Tucker's screech brought his attention forward. "Listen!"

"Tucker! I'm older," Emily objected.

Jedediah Culbert made his way over to them, giving Balthasar a pat before scooping Tucker up onto his hip. The big, blond man pointed the barrel of his shotgun toward the group of horses.

"That stallion ought to be feeding wolves, not getting fat on my barley, confound his black soul." His booming voice effectively drowned out the children.

"It's Stormy's fault," March informed him. "She's the one with the taste for grain."

"You lay the blame wherever you want, but it's that goddam—" Jed glanced down at where his daughter clung to March's stirrup. "That goldarned stallion that's going to get his rump full of buckshot if he don't get it the hel . . . heck out of my field."

"They're all going to get themselves dead of the colic one of these times, and save you the cost of the ammunition," March muttered as he gently disengaged the little girl's hands from his boot. "Can you point out Stormy for me, Emmy?"

"There she is!" screeched Tucker, bouncing in his father's arms. "Over there, March!"

"Me! He asked me, Tuck!" Emily cried, grabbing her father's free arm. "Lift me up, Pa. March wants me to show him."

"Why don't you point out Lucifer for Pa, Emily," her father asked her, hefting his shotgun with a wink at March.

"His name's Prince," Emily and March corrected him at the same time.

"Darn right," Jed agreed. "Prince of Darkness. Also goes by Beelzebub, I hear, and Old Scratch." He turned to give Maggie an easy smile, including her in the joke. March knew without looking that Maggie smiled back. Jed had that kind of smile.

March took a second to locate Prince. Not nearly as big as Lucas's Achilles, the stallion was still a handsome devil, so dark brown as to be almost black, with the sensitive, intelligent face and easy grace characteristic of Arabian blood. Jacob and his mare were trying to turn him from the barley with little result.

March ignored him. As he moved Balthasar away from the knot of Culberts, he loosened his lariat. He slipped among the horses, none of them doing more than edging out of his way, except for the flea-bitten gray mare who lifted her head at his approach and suddenly dodged behind another horse. Balthasar followed.

"That's a girl, Stormy. Don't make it easy," March murmured, giving up control to Balthasar as he readied his rope. "Give me an excuse to wring your wretched neck."

The gray mare lowered her head and pranced right, then left. Balthasar dodged faster. Stormy whirled to face him and lunged right. March loosed his rope and a loop appeared as if by magic around the gray mare's neck. With a dispirited sigh, Stormy immediately surrendered.

Jacob let out a war whoop, echoed by another boy almost hidden by the barley on the other side of the horses.

"Did you find the break, Wolf?" March called to him, giving a tug on Stormy's neck to bring her in line.

"Right over here, March," the boy shouted back, his dark russet hair the only thing standing out against the pale grain.

"Enough of your tricks, you worthless nag," March warned Stormy, who watched him from the corner of her eye with sly calculation. He called over his shoulder. "All right, Prince. Bring 'em along."

Evidently deciding to save further mischief for a more auspicious time, Stormy followed him meekly toward Wolf and the break in the thick barrier of thorny bushes that served as a fence for the barley field. One by one, the other horses lifted their heads from their quiet munching. Prince snorted and cocked his head in self-importance, turning away from Jacob and his mustang to nip at the nearest horse, a pretty bay mare.

Maggie watched in wonder as, after a moment of what appeared to be aimless confusion, the whole herd of horses turned to follow March and the gray mare. Prince Lucifer flew around behind them, discouraging stragglers.

"What a disaster," the blond man in front of her sighed, surveying the trampled grain. "Well, we caught them before they got out of the corner. And I guess some of it can be saved."

He turned to smile again at Maggie. "Jed Culbert," he

said, crossing to offer her a browned, callused hand. The tow-headed boy on his hip gazed at her with wide eyes. "And this is Tucker."

"And Emily, Pa," the little girl next to him whispered, tugging on his arm.

"And Miss Emily Culbert," Jed added, pulling his daughter's blond braid.

"Maggie Parker," Maggie replied, fighting a moment of panic as the last of the horses disappeared through the bushes behind March, leaving her alone with the Culberts. "I'm Lucas Penny's cousin."

"Is that right?" Jed asked, just as though he and his wife hadn't been expecting her to stay with them the night before. "A real pleasure to meet you, Miss Margaret."

Despite the awkwardness of intruding on a stranger's farm without an introduction, she couldn't help returning his smile. "March said I could come over with him to see the horses."

"And stay to dinner, too, the both of you," Jed offered. "I know Henna planned on taking something over to March and Lemuel, anyway."

Maggie shook her head, his generosity making her shy. "Thank you. But I have to catch the stagecoach this morning."

"Ah, well then, we'll have to settle for having you in for lemonade."

"Lem'nade!" screamed Tucker, clapping his hands.

Maggie suddenly wished she'd waited to ride over in the wagon with Lemuel. She'd never learned the art of light conversation, of making friends easily over tea. She got tongue-tied and distant. She didn't want these farmers to have a chance to think her snobbish or timid or strange.

"But your boy—Daniel, isn't it? March said he was ill . . ."

Jed shook his head. "He'll be fine. The fever's broken. Now, say you'll stay."

"I don't know if there's time. When March gets back . . ." She let the words trail off. It was no use. She was trapped.

"Pa! Pa!" Emily tugged on her father's arm again. She bent him down until Tucker's dangling feet almost touched the ground, but her whisper carried easily to Maggie. "Can I ride with her back to the house, Pa? Honey doesn't mind if I ride her. She likes me."

"Maybe Miss Maggie would rather ride by herself," Jed suggested. "You can walk with me."

"You don't know, Pa. You didn't ask her," Emily said, her whisper even louder as her father rose back to his full height.

"It's all right," Maggie said reluctantly.

"You sure?" Jed asked.

She nodded. She suspected a refusal might induce a scene. And she didn't want anyone to think she disliked children. She didn't dislike them. She simply avoided them until their ages reached double digits. She felt the same way about puppies. Any creature with a reputation for indiscriminate affection made her nervous.

If a horse bit you or stepped on your foot, everyone assumed you'd annoyed it or it had been poorly handled in the past. If a toddler or a puppy disliked you, everyone immediately distrusted your character.

Jed set Tucker down to lift Emily up to Maggie. The girl's bare feet thumped excitedly against Honey's neck before Jed managed to settle her into Maggie's lap. Gingerly, Maggie put an arm around the child's waist.

"Can I hold the reins?" Emily pleaded, squirming to look back up into Maggie's face.

"It's 'may I'," her father corrected, "and no. You hang onto the saddle horn."

"Me, too!" yelled Tucker. "I can ride, too!"

Jed hefted the boy into the air and lifted him over his head onto his shoulders. "No, Tuck, you're with me. We'll race Honey back to the house."

The boy wrapped his arms around his father's forehead, his protest dying immediately. "Run, Pa, run!"

"Let's go!" Emily squealed, grabbing the saddle horn with both small hands. "Make Honey gallop!"

Tightening her hold on Emily's waist, Maggie led Honey into a sedate trot to keep pace with Jed. The children shrieked as the two racers exchanged leads, Tuck draping his hands over Jed's eyes in his enthusiasm. Maggie found herself almost smiling.

As they neared the house, she let Jed get ahead, much to Emily's dismay. At the last minute, she urged Honey forward, halting with a flourish at the front steps.

"We won, we won!" Emily crowed.

"We came in second!" Jed crowed back, bending to slide Tucker over his head.

"If I didn't know better, I'd think I had the Epsom Derby right here in my front yard," a feminine voice said dryly.

Maggie looked up at the farmhouse porch. Even in an old apron, her hands white with flour, the woman in the doorway projected dignity and refinement. Tall and slender, she moved out onto the porch with willowy grace. Cinnamon-colored curls framed her heart-shaped face, which might have been plain if not for her striking amber eyes.

With a lurch in her stomach, Maggie became conscious of the smells of horse and sweat that surrounded her, of her own unexceptional height, of her spinsterish dress and her scar. She could imagine her mother's long-suffering disappointment at the thought that even a frontier farmer's wife could show her up as a coarse, common miss.

"Henna, meet Miss Maggie Parker," Jed introduced her as he lifted Emily to the ground. "Miss Maggie, my wife Henna Culbert."

"Pleased to meet you," Maggie said automatically.

"Likewise, Miss Parker," Henna replied, while her eyes traveled over Maggie in frank appraisal. "Jed, help Miss Parker off her horse."

Maggie opened her mouth to protest that she really had to find March, but the sound of a horse coming up behind them cut off her plan of escape.

"Good morning, March," Henna called, as Maggie submitted to Jed's offer of a hand down. "Your horses all right?"

"They're fine, thank you, Henna," March said, his tone apologetic. He dismounted and tied Balthasar next to Honey along the porch rail. "Wolf and Jake are patching the break in your fence. Mine's fixed for now, and I'll check every inch of it this afternoon, that's a promise. As soon as I get back from taking Maggie to the stage."

"What happened last night?" Henna asked. "We were expecting you to bring her here. We were afraid something had delayed Miss Parker's arrival."

Maggie glanced at March. He seemed to be avoiding looking at her.

"I couldn't bring her over, after all. Maggie hasn't had the measles," he said, rather grimly refusing to give up the use of her first name, despite Henna's hint.

"Where did she stay, then?"

March stared off into the distance. "At the ranch."

"*At the ranch?*" Even raised, Henna's voice remained smooth and cultured. "Have you taken leave of your senses? Did you not even think of the girl's reputation?"

"There was nowhere else to go."

"For heaven's sake, March, you should have brought her

here. You know better. And you should know better, too, child."

A hot flush crept up Maggie's cheeks.

"Measles is nothing to fool around with once you're older," Jed broke in, saving her from formulating a response. "I don't blame Miss Parker for being concerned. If we'd have known she hadn't had 'em, we'd never have suggested she stay here, Henna. And she was perfectly safe with March and Lem."

"That's not the point," his wife insisted. "Think if she was your daughter."

"I know March would take good care of Emmy," Jed said with a grin.

"And I think you know what I mean, Jedediah Culbert," Henna said, her lips tight.

"I reckon I do," he admitted. "But what's done is done, and no one's going to think any the worse of the girl for it. Don't fret about it."

Henna held her husband's gaze for a long moment, then stepped back to open the door. "Why don't you all come in," she invited. "It's too warm to stand talking out on the porch. You needn't worry, Miss Parker. I'm sure Daniel's no longer contagious, but he's resting upstairs, so you're quite safe."

"Pa said we could have lem'nade," Tucker put in.

"Not with those dirty hands," his mother said. "You and Emily run and wash up. Make sure he gets clean, Emmy."

Emily grabbed her brother's hand, and the two ran off around the side of the house.

Henna looked Jed and March up and down. "I guess you boys can wash up inside," she decided.

The men stepped aside to be polite, so Maggie preceded Henna into the house, despite her instinct to turn and run. The walls of the dragon's lair were rougher and grayer than at the Pennys' ranch, the furniture showed the wear and tear of more years and more children, but the white lace curtains, the crocheted doilies on the side tables, the fine silver candle holders above the fireplace all displayed Henna's deft hand.

As the two men disappeared into the kitchen, Henna gestured Maggie toward a chair.

"Don't worry," she said. "If anyone says anything about last night, I'll tell them I stayed out at the ranch with you, and Jed will swear to it, too. Not many people argue with Jed."

Maggie gripped the top of the high-backed chair, too nervous and uncomfortable to sit.

"I don't need you to lie for me," she said, the words coming out cold and hard despite the fluttering in her stomach. "I don't care what anyone says. Least of all a bunch of illiterate cowhands."

Henna stopped short and turned her amber gaze on Maggie. "You don't look dull-witted, so I'll assume you simply don't understand. A girl your age can't stay anywhere unchaperoned. Your reputation isn't something you can retrieve once you've lost it."

The chair back dug into Maggie's palm, but she couldn't let go. "I understand a lot more than you think. I'm not a simpleton nor an innocent."

The other woman's eyes narrowed as she moved a step closer. Her soft voice hid a core of steel. "I see. Well, understand this. March is taking care of you because you're Lucas's cousin, and he wasn't thinking of anything but that last night, I'm sure. So, let me repeat myself. If anyone asks, I'll say I stayed with you last night. And if *anyone* says otherwise, I'll call him . . . or her . . . a liar. Do I make myself clear?"

Chapter 4

March watched Pamela's ears twitch in time to "O Bury Me Not on the Lone Prairie." The sound of his own whistling mocked him with memories of a time, it seemed like centuries ago, before death took over his life. But anything was better than the awkward silence the whistling replaced. Maggie, straight as a statue beside him, hadn't spoken more than two words to him since Lemuel had driven up to the Culberts' house with the wagon.

Hell, she hadn't spoken more than two words to him since Henna had served them all lemonade.

Not that he could blame her. Until Henna had pointed it out, Maggie probably hadn't realized just how bad it looked for her to stay with him at the ranchhouse without a chaperone. He'd put her in a humiliating situation. Sure, she'd been the one to insist on it, but she was young yet. Henna was right; he should have known better.

"Are you going to keep that up all the way to Oxtail?"

Her voice startled him so he almost dropped the reins. He glanced at her, but she stared straight ahead, as though she'd never spoken.

"Keep what up?"

"Whistling."

Not if he could find a way to keep her talking. "You don't like the tune?"

He caught the flicker of her quick glance.

"What tune?" she asked. "If it had a tune, I might not mind so much."

"It's 'O Bury Me Not,' a cowboy tune. I could teach you the words."

Her spine softened a fraction as she turned to look at him. He waited.

"I suppose it would help pass the time," she said finally.

Taking a deep breath, he launched into the song. "O bury me not on the lone prairie. These words came low and mournfully . . ." He sang through the first two verses, then repeated the first stanza again.

"Okay, now you join in. O bury me not on the lone prairie. Try that much."

She looked down at her hands, picked at her gloves. "Could you sing it for me one more time?"

He did. "Okay?"

"Once more?"

He repeated it twice more, for good measure. "Now you try it."

"I can't." She didn't look at him.

"Sure you can," he said. "It's not that hard. If I can learn it, anybody can."

He gulped air to start again, but she stopped him with a hand on his arm.

"March, no." Her voice, fallen almost to a whisper, choked a little. "Please." She let go of his arm, and covered her face with her hands.

Tension shot back across March's shoulders and down into his stomach. He'd distressed her or offended her again. God only knew how.

"What's wrong?" he asked, wincing at the anxiety in his voice. "I didn't mean to upset you."

Green-flecked eyes peeked between her fingers. "March, did . . . has . . ." her voice died away.

"What?"

"Hasn't anyone ever told you you're tone deaf?" All the skin he could see between her fingers fired a bright crimson.

He stared at her. "You mean . . . you . . . ye . . . ye . . . ou . . ." Laughter shook his entire body, wrenching painfully at the empty hole in his heart. He clenched his jaw shut, but the effort brought tears to his eyes.

"It's not funny," Maggie rebuked him, but even through the water in his eyes, he could see her shaking, too. "What are you laughing at?"

"You . . . trying not to hurt my feelings," he managed to gasp out. She punched him, making him laugh harder. "Ow! You're the one laughing at my singing."

"I'm not!" she objected. "I never laugh at tragedy."

The wrenching jolt of a wagon wheel hitting a rock in the road almost threw him from the wagon seat. He grabbed Maggie's arm to steady her, but could not steady himself as the world fell out from beneath him.

He held on to Maggie. He had some idea of breaking her fall with his body, but the distance from the end of the seat to the ground was too short to do anything except land with a bone-jarring thud.

When the world stopped spinning, the silence shocked him. Panic had given him the illusion of great noise. He tried breathing. It hurt, but he didn't think the fall had broken any ribs. The weight on his right arm shifted.

"Are you all right?" he asked, turning his head gingerly to look at her. She was staring up into the endless blue sky.

"I'm lying flat on my back on a dirt road in the middle of nowhere, and I think there's a piece of broken axle sticking into my side. How about you?"

"About the same."

She turned her hazel eyes on him and suddenly they were laughing again. Short, painful chuckles.

"Stop it, that hurts," he commanded. He could feel her shaking next to him, from laughter and from reaction. He had to fight the impulse to tighten his arm around her, to pull her close.

Instead he said, "You should hear Wolf sing."

"The dark-haired boy? How did he get a name like Wolf?"

"It's Wolfgang. His father has a fondness for Mozart." But he didn't want to get into that. "Wolf's a natural musician."

"And you're not." She was trying not to laugh again.

"Jane insisted anyone could learn how to sing. She told me I was getting much better."

"She must have loved you very much."

Silence fell between them, but strangely the mention of his sister didn't bring the expected horror, not with Maggie's warmth against his side.

They lay staring at the sky. A puffy cumulus cloud, innocent as a spring lamb, wandered into March's line of vision. He'd have to keep an eye on that. Could develop into a thunderstorm by afternoon. His gaze flicked to the position of the sun.

"Oh, God. The stagecoach."

He sat up abruptly, wrenching the arm that still lay beneath Maggie.

"Ow!" she objected, rising with him.

He didn't even have to stand to observe the extent of the damage to the wagon. The ever patient Pamela had stopped immediately after the accident, and less than two yards from his face he could see the jagged end of the broken front axle. The other end, with the right front wheel still attached, had rolled off the side of the road into a clump of buffalo grass.

"Damn."

"How much time before the stagecoach comes?" Maggie asked.

"Maybe half an hour. It leaves at noon." He offered her a hand and helped her to her feet.

"I don't think you're going to have this fixed by then," she commented, pointing at the axle with her toe.

"Not likely." He walked over to Pamela, who nuzzled his chest, none the worse for their recent adventure. "Good girl." With practiced fingers, he set about unhitching her from the wagon. "Come over here and I'll help you on."

Maggie stared at him.

"Hurry, we don't have much time."

She didn't move. "What about my trunk?"

"I'll send it on the next stage. We can take your carpet bag. That ought to get you home all right."

As she hesitated, urgency tugged at him. They shouldn't have stayed so long at the Culberts. He should have known this wouldn't be simple, not with Maggie Parker along.

"Are you afraid to ride bareback?" It was a cheap trick, but it worked.

She tossed her head. "Afraid? Of Pamela?"

He bent to offer her a knee, and barely felt the touch of her boot as she vaulted to the horse's back. He pulled her carpet bag from the back of the wagon and handed it up to her lap. Then he unhooked the long driving reins from Pamela's bridle.

"What are you doing?" Maggie demanded, clutching at the mare's mane.

"They're too long," he explained. "She'd trip on them."

"Can't you cut them?"

He indulged himself in a grin. "And ruin a perfectly good set of reins? She knows voice commands."

Using the wagon wheel as a mounting block, he slipped onto the mare's back behind Maggie. He wrapped an arm around her waist and leaned forward. "Gi-yap!" Pamela's ears twitched in surprise, but she gamely responded to this new situation, moving into a slow, teeth-jolting trot. The mare's torso swelled out as round and sturdy as a barrel, but her spine still slammed painfully into March's tailbone.

March didn't slow her down. He *had* to get Maggie on that stage.

As his body eased into the rhythm of the gait, March realized just how closely he'd clutched Maggie to keep her from being bounced off. He could feel the warmth of her back through his shirt, could feel the shallow expansion and contraction of her chest against his arm. He hardly had to bend his head at all to smell the sweet, feminine scent rising from her shoulder.

His body remembered how she'd felt against him last night, for a half second all softness and warmth. The taste of her lips. The sweet life that had returned almost all the way to his heart with the tentative flickering flames of desire.

Just for a few moments, it couldn't hurt to enjoy her nearness, the vibrant energy of her breath, the headiness of her scent . . .

He loosened the arm around her chest, eased himself away from her. He was going to put her on the stage and she would leave and he would go back to the ranch, back to the demons and the ghosts and the deadly emptiness where the only hope was revenge. Any life he felt now would only cause him pain later.

He didn't know why he should fear pain. He'd lived with it forever, it seemed. Gotten used to it. But around Maggie Parker his instincts warned him he could learn to hurt again.

They rode in silence. Maggie almost wished March would start whistling again. The torture might distract her from the way his arm cradled her ribs, from the way his breath tickled the hairs on her neck.

Pamela covered the ground steadily, if not smoothly. Oxtail finally appeared, rising out of the unbroken expanse of grassland. Looking up at the sky, Maggie thought they might reach town by noon.

As they neared the first buildings, March urged Pamela faster. Her sides heaved beneath them as they turned onto Main Street. It was deserted.

March shifted his weight. "Haw!" Pamela turned right, toward the hotel.

"You stay here. I'll go ask the Colonel if the stage has left already." He swung to the ground and disappeared through the double doors of the Grand Hotel.

Maggie clutched her carpet bag, feeling absurdly exposed sitting on Pamela's broad back, she and the mare the only two living things on Main Street. She eyed "the Colonel's" Grand Hotel, admiring his nerve, if not his business instinct. "Grand" certainly described the hotel's facade, three stories of fading whitewash and green trim fronting the more modest two-story building. Quite suitable to a town of several thousand along a main travel route. Neither part of that description described Oxtail.

The doors opened again and March came out, his relief evident on his face. "The stage is late. Could be another hour before it gets here."

Maggie's stomach sank, telling her just how little she looked forward to returning home, back to the routine of anger and recriminations. After Oxtail, even Lexington should seem like paradise. Yet this morning Oxtail didn't look so bad.

She handed March her bag and slid off Pamela's back. March led her up the porch steps, setting her bag beside a white bench.

"Would you like anything to drink while you wait?" he asked. "It's a long leg to the train at Greeley. Especially if those clouds build into a thunderstorm."

Maggie sat on the bench, focusing her eyes on her hands. The fall from the wagon had ruined her right glove. She picked at the torn leather, willing herself into her place of retreat where nothing Stephen did, nothing anyone did, could cause a reaction. Where March's eagerness to be rid of her didn't hurt.

Then she looked back at him. He'd left her already. His eyes scanned the sky, blue reflecting blue as he gauged the gathering clouds.

"You go on," she said, though the idea of waiting alone here in Oxtail twisted her stomach. "I can get a glass of water if I want one. You need to get back to the wagon."

His gaze touched hers briefly. "You sure?" His brow furrowed. "I haven't taken very good care of you while you've been here."

"I'm still in one piece." She had hoped he'd smile, just one more time. She looked back down at her gloves. Hell, she didn't care about his smile.

"Well, I do have to see about getting a new axle."

She nodded. "Good-bye, then."

"Good-bye." Still he stood there, his eyes on her until she was forced to look up at him. "Good-bye, Maggie. I'm sorry you can't stay."

He mounted Pamela from the porch and turned down the alley next to the hotel, out of sight.

Maggie stared after him long after he'd disappeared, searching for an appropriately stinging reply. *I'm not sorry,* she wanted to shout after him. *No one in their right mind would stay in this little dust pit when she could return to civilization.* She couldn't wait to get back to Kentucky, away from drunken

68

ruffians and farmers' wives who put on airs and pretended to be ladies.

Her ears still burned from Henna Culbert's insinuation that she might have stayed with March last night to . . . what? Force him into marriage? Maggie bit the side of her lip until it stung. If she were a gold digger, she'd certainly set her sights a good deal higher than some incompetent wrangler letting his ranch fall apart while he drank himself senseless.

She'd wanted to tell Henna that, but the men had come in from their hand-washing just then. So she'd said nothing, sitting as tongue-tied and miserable as she'd ever felt in the parlors of her mother's fine friends.

No, she wasn't sorry to be leaving Colorado, and surely March didn't think she was. What had she said to him about home? How could he know how bad it was? She didn't need some two-bit cowboy's pity. She had come out here fully intending to be back home within the week, and she'd have managed it even if Lucas had been alive and well and determined to keep her.

Her building fury died. Of course March was sorry. In his mind, she had to go back because his sister's entire family had been murdered. Maggie winced. She hadn't even told him again she was sorry for his loss. And she wouldn't get the chance.

It was funny, that feeling like ice in her stomach at the thought that she'd never see him again.

Maggie sat with her eyes closed, her face turned into the stagecoach side, trying not to smell her fellow passengers. They'd insisted on closing the canvas curtains to keep out the rain, but Maggie considered a little dampness infinitely preferable to slow suffocation. Even the sweat and the sour smells of whiskey and cigars would be bearable if they weren't overlaid with the sickly sweet scent of cologne and perfume.

Rain pounded the roof of the stagecoach, huge wet drops cleansing the short-grass prairie. The thought of the sweet fresh air just outside almost drove her crazy.

Thunder cracked the sky, and she pulled aside the edge of the curtain to look out the window. Huge black thunderclouds blocked the sun, cooling everything on the plains except the interior of the stage.

She wondered if March had made it back to the Penny ranch before the rain had hit. The first drops had fallen as the stagecoach pulled into Oxtail an hour and a half late, and so far it showed little sign of letting up.

Maggie's fingers inched aside the curtain. If she didn't get some air soon, she would be sick, and she suspected her fellow passengers would like that even less than a few raindrops.

As her hand grasped the dust-caked canvas, the stagecoach jerked to a sudden halt, throwing her unceremoniously into the lap of the sleeping miner across from her.

"Pardon me," she mumbled, hastily reclaiming her own seat.

Even so rudely awakened, the miner helped Maggie assist the elderly woman beside her, while a middle-aged man in a black suit pounded the roof of the coach with the handle of his umbrella.

"What are you trying to do, get us all killed?" he bellowed.

"Flash flood, blast you," came the sharp reply from above.

Maggie looked out the window. Ten yards ahead, the stage road disappeared into a shallow wash. Dry as dust the day before, the sudden thunderstorm had transformed it into a broad, angry stream.

"What rotten luck," the voice of the man riding shotgun came down less clearly. "Another delay."

"We'll ford it downstream," the driver replied, anger and

frustration churning in his voice. "Damn if I won't get to Greeley before dark."

"It'll be at least two miles out of our way before we can cross this," the other man objected. "Better to wait it out."

"To hell with that."

The sound of the whip cracked louder than the fading thunder. If their pace before had been breakneck, now it was reckless. The coach rocked as it turned sharply, then the horses broke into a dead gallop along the side of the wash, bouncing and jolting the stagecoach along a side road which was obviously infrequently traveled.

Maggie dug her fingernails into the seat beneath her, fighting down a sudden tingle of fear and the renewed queasiness in her stomach.

"The driver's a madman," gasped the man in the suit, his face paling to match his white shirt.

The dapper young man to the other side of him smiled. "Every day's an adventure out west. You can guarantee it."

The bone-jarring rattling of the coach precluded further conversation, though Maggie could hear the old woman beside her murmuring prayers.

The noise and jolting went on for an eternity. Every few seconds Maggie lost her balance, and each time the next bounce sent her back to her own seat instead of over the old woman or into the miner. But she knew it was only a matter of time before one of the passengers bloodied a nose or broke a neck. She felt an almost nostalgic fondness for the bored disinterest of yesterday's driver.

Then, suddenly as it started, the pace slowed again. After a moment of shock that she had no broken bones and the coach was still all in one piece, Maggie risked another glance out the window.

Beside them, the wash had begun to broaden out across

the plains. A line of cottonwoods and box elders suggested damper, more absorbent soil, eagerly soaking up the water and levelling out the flood. Apparently the driver had slowed to look for the shallowest place to cross.

They'd already started into the water when Maggie caught a glimpse of movement in the dense brush around a stand of cottonwoods. A duck perhaps or an antelope. Then she saw a flash of red.

"Wait!" she yelled, grabbing the curtain and wrenching it open. "Wait! There's someone out there!"

The miner joined her at the window. "Where?"

"Over there by those trees." She pointed. "He's waving a red handkerchief. I don't think he can stand up. See, he's on his knees."

"Driver!" The miner pounded the roof with the heel of his hand. "Stop, won't you! There's an injured man out there."

The stagecoach slowed to a reluctant stop.

"It could be an ambush," growled the shotgun rider.

"Pretty stupid place for an ambush," the driver replied. "Nobody travels this way this time of year." He spit and sighed. "I guess we better see if we can help."

The coach turned back, heading for dry land, blocking the man from Maggie's view, but she could hear his hoarse voice as they drew near.

"Thank God, thank God," he repeated over and over again as the coach rolled to a stop. "I can't believe it. Oh, thank God."

Maggie scrambled down from the coach, unmindful of the puddles that soaked her boots. As suddenly as it had begun, the storm was breaking up. Only a few large drops spattered on her bonnet as she slogged through the mud. The other passengers followed close behind, perhaps grateful for a chance to touch solid ground after their recent wild ride.

The driver had already reached the man under the trees, a thin, fair, middle-aged man painted a dreary gray-brown by dust and mud. He knelt in four inches of water, one hand clutching the red kerchief that had caught Maggie's eye.

Behind him, tethered to one of the trees, stood a horse the color of dead grass, its head sunk almost between its knees, only a faint movement of the chest showing life.

The injured man grabbed the driver's arm, hanging on as though afraid they all might disappear. "I can't believe you're here," he said, the words tumbling out at a feverish rate. "I've been here forever and ever and not seen a single soul. Didn't think I would until I saw Saint Peter."

A hand touched Maggie's arm, and the old woman brushed past, her heavy black skirts swirling unheeded in the shallow brown water.

"What is your injury, son?" she asked, the only one of the clustering passengers to kneel beside him.

"My leg," he told her, patting the leg that twisted under him. "It's broke bad. Can I have some clean water? My canteen went dry yesterday morn."

The shotgun rider tossed a flask to the driver, who passed it to the injured man.

"I ain't going to die, am I, lady?" the man asked. "You got to get me a doctor. I been lying here since my horse gave out. I couldn't get back up on her; I passed out when I tried. Lady, you got to get me a doctor."

"My name's Emmeline Strachy," the old woman told him, pressing a firm hand to his forehead. "I helped nurse the boys at Gettysburg, and I saved youngsters a lot worse off than you. By some luck, you don't seem to have a fever, but I'm going to have to take a look at that leg. You men, stop lolly-gagging about and lift him into the coach."

Having been relegated to uselessness, Maggie turned from

the groans of the injured man to see about his horse. The mare lifted her head slightly and snorted as Maggie approached.

"Ho, there," Maggie murmured, coming up beside her. The mare's neck twitched where she laid her hand on it, but the horse lowered her head again to suck at the water swirling around her feet.

Maggie's free hand clenched into a fist, even as she continued to stroke the mare's neck. If the man with the broken leg had run out of water yesterday morning, it had been even longer since the mare had gotten a drink, standing here in what had, only hours ago, been a dry creek bed. She'd probably not had much to eat either, tethered to this tree for a day or two or three. And from what the man had said, he'd ridden her to exhaustion before that.

Maggie ran her hand up along the mare's brushy black mane, pausing to scratch behind her ears. The mare lifted her head and turned to push her muzzle into Maggie's stomach, snorting again softly.

"Stop it, that tickles," Maggie scolded, biting her lip to keep tears from forming. She moved down the length of the horse, noting her sturdy legs, strong, straight back, and muscular hindquarters. A black dorsal strip ran down her back and zebra markings laced her upper legs. "What a handsome little buckskin you are. I bet it took him a long time to wear you out."

The mare's tail twitched, and she raised her head again, this time above her withers, ears pricking at the compliment. The deep brown eye she turned on Maggie showed an alertness that thirst, hunger and heat should have burned out long ago.

Maggie bent down and wrenched out a clump of grass that waved above the muddy surface of the water. She held out the grass to the animal. The mare's breath cooled the dampness of her wrist, lips as gentle as feathers brushed her hands. But there was nothing gentle about the grinding of broad flat teeth against the soggy brown grass. The mare's jaw paused several times while she chewed, as though gathering strength to continue, but she swallowed the whole mouthful and her lips brushed Maggie's hand again looking for more.

Maggie grabbed the mare's reins, fumbling with the knot that held her to the tree. She stepped away, hardly daring to breathe as the mare tried to follow. One, two, three—all four legs moved forward a step, weakly, stiffly, but without a limp. Another step and another and the mare could reach the grass on her own, tentatively at first, then plunging her muzzle into the water to rip out the stalks.

Slowly Maggie led her back toward the stagecoach, pleased by the growing confidence in the mare's gait.

"Miss?"

Maggie looked up to find herself face to face with the shotgun rider, a painfully thin man with pale blue eyes.

"Miss, we've got that fellow into the stagecoach. A couple of the gentlemen have agreed to sit up top to make room, so you can take your seat. I'll take care of this gal here."

Maggie's eyes focused on his weapon, which despite his title was a sharpshooter's rifle, cold and deadly in his hand.

"You're not going to shoot her."

He shifted his hat farther back on his head. "Trust me, miss. It's the kindest way. We can't just leave her here for the wolves or coyotes to eat."

"But she's not ruined. She'll come back sound, I'm sure of it. We can take her with us."

"Like that?" The driver's voice came down to her from above, vibrating with impatience. "It'd take us two days to reach Greeley. That man in the stage don't have that long if we're going to save his life, much less his leg. And he says his leg was broke when outlaws attacked his supply wagon. If they hadn't thought he was dead, he'd never have escaped. I won't feel safe until we get to town."

"It wouldn't take us that long to get back to Oxtail," Maggie reminded him.

"We ain't going back to Oxtail."

"Why not?"

"Because this stage goes to Greeley, that's why. Now get into the coach and let Jim do his job."

Maggie kept her eyes on the driver, away from Jim's gleaming rifle. "So you're willing to shoot a good horse because she happens to be inconvenient?"

"Yes." He spat tobacco juice in a straight stream to the ground. "And if it wasn't a hanging offense, I'd shoot inconvenient passengers, too. Now get in the coach or get left behind."

Soft breath blew a stray curl from Maggie's ear, and the buckskin mare's chin settled on her shoulder. Maggie crossed her arms over her chest and gave the driver her fiercest glare. "I guess I'm staying behind then."

The businessman in the black suit leaned down from the top of the coach. "You can't do that, miss. There're only bandits, Indians, and wild animals for company out here. This is no country for a lady, much less one traveling alone."

"It won't take me more than three or four hours to walk back to Oxtail." She raised an eyebrow in challenge. "Unless you're coming with me, I guess I'll make it fine by myself."

The young miner leaned over the businessman's lap. "You'll be all right, miss, don't you worry. Even the worst ruffian in the West respects a lady."

Maggie decided not to mention her experience in The Golden Rose the afternoon before. Shotgun Jim had the look

76

of a man who might shoot the mare without her permission and toss her into the coach "for her own good."

"You follow this wash back up to the stage road," the miner continued. "It'll take you right back to Oxtail. You got kin there?"

The thought of March's reaction when she showed up on his doorstep made her quail, but she wasn't going to let anyone shoot her little mare. "Yes. I've just been visiting my cousin there."

"C'mon, Jim," the driver growled. "Leave the little fool. We'll probably have our pay docked for the delay as it is." He turned to the miner. "That carpet bag's hers, mister. Toss it down."

The miner lifted it carefully down to Maggie's waiting arms.

The driver nodded. "All right, let's go."

"Wait!" The door of the coach opened and the elderly Mrs. Strachy gestured to Maggie. "Come here, child."

Keeping a wary eye on Jim's rifle as he climbed up next to the driver, Maggie approached the stagecoach.

Mrs. Strachy fixed her with bright blue eyes. "I've traveled all over the West with my husband, and I travel by myself now he's gone. I've never had a bit of trouble with even the roughest cowboys, but it's been a long, long time since I was young and fresh as you. So, here, you take this. It's sort of a good-luck charm."

Surprised, Maggie put out a hand. The old woman covered it with her own, leaving behind a tiny derringer with a silky smooth mother-of-pearl inlaid stock.

"It won't hurt a fly unless he's close enough to be disrespectful," Mrs. Strachy told her, as practical and prim as though passing along a needlepoint pattern. "If you need to use it, try to hit something vital, like his heart. It doesn't make a very large hole."

"Thank you," Maggie finally managed, wondering if her mouth had been gaping open.

The injured man gasped weakly, "That's a fine horse, ma'am. If you can save her, she's yours."

"Thank you," Maggie murmured again, as the driver's shout rang out from above.

"Stand back! Giddyap!"

His whip cracked, and the stagecoach jolted forward. Maggie watched it rock out into the wash, the receding water not reaching even to the hub of the wheels. In front of the stage, beyond this temporary oasis of water, the plains stretched out to the infinite east. Sunlight slanting beneath the breaking clouds gilded the scanty grass with gold, but the desolate beauty didn't ease the sudden panic Maggie felt as the reality of the stagecoach's desertion hit her.

"My God. They've left me out here all alone miles from anywhere." All alone except for a horse too weak to ride who had about a fifty percent chance of collapsing for good before they ever reached Oxtail. "I suppose just because Stephen says I'm too headstrong, that doesn't mean I'm not."

The mare lifted her chin from Maggie's shoulder and pushed it into the small of her back, snorting again.

"I said stop that." Maggie turned to frown at the mare. The mare looked back, her ears cocked forward, almost as though asking a question. Maggie smiled. "Not just a prankster, but a philosopher, too, I see. A horse of many talents. You're right, of course; we'll never make it anywhere if we don't start walking."

With a show of determination more for herself than the mare, she stuffed Mrs. Strachy's derringer into her pocket, picked up her bag, and led the horse up the wash toward the road.

Chapter 5

Maggie hugged her carpet bag to her chest and suppressed a shiver. She thought wistfully of walking with an arm across the buckskin mare's back for warmth, but each time she tried it, the horse took it as a signal to stop and rest. Even at the mare's top speed, their pace was too slow to bring Maggie much comfort against the night chill.

She'd overestimated the mare's stamina and underestimated the distance back to Oxtail. They hadn't reached town until after dark had fallen, skirting the blazing bonfires and the light pouring from the saloons. The sheer noise and number of men and horses filling Main Street had shocked her. She'd half imagined only ghosts ever actually walked the streets of Oxtail.

Exhausted from the day's heat, Maggie might have risked trying to get a room at the Grand Hotel, but her stepfather had sent her to Colorado without so much as a penny, hoping to lessen the possibility of her escaping from her frontier relatives.

As a result, she and the mare were stumbling across the empty prairie, picking their way toward the Penny ranch. The crescent moon lit the dust of the wagon track with silver to guide them. Stars frosted the night sky from zenith to horizon, transmuting the prairie into an immense expanse of black nothingness. Awe stuck in Maggie's throat at the sheer number of stars, despite her aching arms and feet.

The mare's abrupt halt pulled her gaze back down to earth.

"Don't give up on me now," she begged, coming back to put a hand on the mare's neck. "We're almost there. I promise. Please."

The mare nickered softly, but didn't turn to nuzzle her. Following the faint outline of the horse's head against the stars, Maggie could see the mare's ears pricked sharply forward. She hadn't stopped out of exhaustion. Maggie froze as still as her horse.

In quick succession her imagination brought up images of what might face them: wolves, mountain lions, bears, a wounded bull buffalo. . . . But the little buckskin seemed more curious than afraid. Which might mean she was too exhausted to feel fear, but more likely meant that whatever waited silently in the dark before them was human rather than animal.

Maggie dropped her hand from the horse's neck and slipped it into her pocket. Her fingers clutched Mrs. Strachy's derringer.

The tiny gun seemed little more than a toy in the black of night in the middle of the empty prairie. But neither she nor the mare would get far running. She dropped her carpet bag to the ground, pushing panicky thoughts of her cousin's murdered family out of her mind.

"Who's there?" she croaked. Not that a merciless killer was likely to bother with a reply . . .

"Why, you're Lucas's cousin, Miss Parker." The high, youthful voice came from much closer than she expected.

She jumped back, knocking against the mare's side. "Who are you? How do you know my name?"

"It's Wolf Culbert, ma'am." Out of the darkness before her, a shadow coalesced into the figure of a boy rising to his feet. "We didn't get introduced, but I saw you riding Honey this morning."

80

Maggie remembered a glimpse of dark hair rising out of the sea of pale barley and blond Culberts. Wolfgang. She'd been surprised by March's revelation that Jed liked Mozart. Slowly she unclenched her fist from around the little derringer.

"Wolf, may I ask you a question?"

"Yes, ma'am."

"What in God's name are you doing out here scaring the living breath out of unwary travelers at this time of night?"

The boy's embarrassment was almost palpable. "I'm awful sorry, ma'am, I didn't mean to frighten you. I thought you and the horse would walk right by me. I didn't want you to see me, in case you were a rustler."

She could hardly blame him for that. "That's all right. I guess we scared each other. But shouldn't you be home in bed?"

"It's my turn to wait for Pa. Jake and me trade off."

"Jake and I," Maggie corrected automatically, then bit her lip. She sounded like Mama. "Where's your pa?"

The boy's stance relaxed and he moved a little closer, so Maggie could make out the pale circle of his face beneath his dark thatch of hair. "He goes into town every Friday to get the news. The cowboys get paid Fridays, so they all come into town. They all like him, even if they hate farmers, but Ma doesn't like him to drink."

"I'll bet." Maggie had no trouble picturing Henna Culbert's disapproval.

"Sometimes coming back he misses the turnoff to the farm and ends up at the Penny place and just sleeps in the barn, so Ma thinks something awful's happened to him. So Jake and me—I—take turns waiting for him Friday nights."

Maggie felt an unexpected flash of sympathy for Henna. She'd worry, too. Especially if her neighbors had been brutally murdered the month before.

"I thought you went home on the stagecoach today, ma'am."

"Wolf, you're making me feel like a schoolteacher. My name's Maggie. And I did try to leave on the stage—I'll be leaving tomorrow, instead," she added hastily, fearing what Henna Culbert might think when Wolf told her he'd run into Maggie. "That's not a problem. But the stage driver was going to shoot this little mare, and I couldn't let him do it. So, I brought her back for March. She's smart and tough, and I think she'll make a good addition to his herd."

Wolf moved forward again and held out a hand for the mare to snuffle. "I'll take you along to the ranch, if you like. I don't mind the dark at all."

Maggie looked down at the boy. He wouldn't be much protection, but the company would make the last leg of the walk shorter. "What about your pa?"

Wolf shrugged. "If he comes along while I'm with you, I'll just catch him on the way back." The boy gave a tug on the mare's bridle and she stepped forward. Maggie grabbed her carpet bag and walked alongside, finally able to take advantage of the horse's warmth.

They walked into the enveloping darkness, moving at a faster pace thanks to Wolf's confidence in the path. Maggie saw his face turn toward her briefly. "What's her name?"

Maggie scratched the mare's withers, considering. "I thought I'd call her Aristotle."

The boy cleared his throat. "Ma'am, this horse is a mare."

"Maggie. I know, but she's quite a philosopher." Maggie smiled. "We've had plenty of time for discussing metaphysics on our walk this afternoon."

"But Aristotle is a man's name."

"That's being awfully picky coming from a boy named Wolf."

For a moment she feared her teasing had offended him, but then he said with all the serious thoughtfulness of youth, "I suppose we could call her Ari. Miss Maggie."

March lay in bed staring upward at the ceiling he could not see in the darkness. The muscles in his arms and back ached from more hard work than he'd done for the whole month before. It felt good. It had seduced him into thinking he'd be able to come back and sleep in his own bed again tonight.

He should have gone into town with Jed. Right now he should be well into his act of drunkenness, of helpless despair. But yesterday afternoon the act had become too real. He'd fallen over the edge from drinking to drunk without even noticing. He couldn't afford to let guilt or self-pity weaken him and leave him unprepared when the time came to avenge the murder of his family.

So he lay staring into the darkness, listening intently to the silence, no closer to sleep than he'd been two hours ago. Each time he relaxed enough for his eyes to flutter closed, the ghosts came. Images of blood, of staring eyes. Voices.

"Don't go far from the ranch, March. I've got a bad feeling about these rustlers."

His own laughter. "I know how to handle a gun, or have you forgotten, Lucas? I can take care of myself."

"Still, I want you back here for dinner at noon. You hear me? I don't want Jane worrying about you."

When he peeled his eyes open, when his heart stopped pounding and he unclenched his fists, another ghost haunted him. Flaming hair and flashing eyes. A soft scent of woman, warmth pressed against him, the infinite possibilities of a kiss.

The memory made him hard, and he tried to push it away with guilt, and when that didn't work, derision. He'd acted like a fool, thinking even for a second that a beautiful city girl like Margaret Parker might be attracted to a dusty ranch hand. And it didn't matter, anyway. She was gone. Back to the family that didn't want her.

He could well imagine why her stepfather had sent her away. Everything about her was shocking, from the way she dressed to the way she swore like a cowboy to the way she handled herself on a horse. From the moment she'd stepped into The Golden Rose yesterday afternoon, she'd kept his head spinning too fast for him to think straight.

Fiery as a sunrise, she'd flooded the ranch with life, driving away the ghosts and the horror. He was glad she was gone. He couldn't bear the illusion of hope, couldn't afford the distraction.

He wished he hadn't had to send her back.

If he hadn't been so deep in reverie, he would have heard the soft sound of voices before they reached the ranch house. Instead, the gentle nickering of a horse alerted him to the visitors out front.

As he shoved his feet into his jeans, he thought he heard a woman's voice. Henna? He reached for his rifle and stumbled toward the black pit of the stairs, dread pounding in his veins. If the rustlers had attacked the Culbert farm while Jed was in Oxtail . . .

He jumped from the stairs to the hall floor and ran to the door. As he reached toward the knob, he finally caught the words of the conversation outside.

The woman's voice, muffled. "It's locked."

"There's a window in the loft you can reach from the shed in back." Wolf Culbert's voice. "Logan, Danny, Jake and me—and I—used to get out that way all the time. I can go wake March up for you."

"He might shoot you before you get a chance to tell him who you are." Familiar, but not Henna.

"Nah. Don't worry. You go find a place for Ari in the barn."

"No, thank you. I'm not facing Lemuel Tate's shotgun by myself."

March paused with his hand on the door, wondering if he'd fallen asleep after all. Although, in a dream, that voice would surely be softer, sweeter. He yanked on the door, nearly pulling his arm out of its socket. As the woman on the other side had observed, it was locked.

After fumbling a moment with the lock, he managed to pull the door open with a semblance of dignity. By the faint illumination of the stars, he could make out the two forms that had drawn back from the door to the porch railing. The small, thin figure in jeans must be Wolf Culbert. Across from Wolf stood the slender form of a woman, not much more substantial than the boy.

He waited for one of them to speak, since he could think of nothing at all to say. He recognized the defiant tilt to that prim bonnet.

Maggie stepped forward, her chin tilting even higher. "I had to leave the stagecoach." As though she'd been at a play she didn't like and had left at intermission.

Wolf spoke up earnestly, "I helped her find her way back to the ranch."

"What are you doing here?" he asked, the words rough, but he could think of no others.

He wouldn't have believed Maggie's spine could get any straighter. "I don't have any money to board at the hotel. I had nowhere else to go."

"They were going to shoot this mare," Wolf explained,

gesturing to the large shadow hulking by the stairs. "Miss Maggie walked her all the way back here."

March ran a hand through his hair, wishing he could shake the fog of disbelief from his thoughts. "You left the stage-coach?" he repeated.

Maggie settled her hands on her hips. "No, right now I'm on a train to Cheyenne. You're just having a bad dream."

She backed up involuntarily as he stepped out onto the porch to look at the mare.

"That mare saved a man from a gang of outlaws," Wolf said, coming up beside him. "She went across rocky ground and through rivers to hide her tracks and outraced a herd of antelope. That's what finally threw the outlaws off her trail. Once she stopped, the man she saved was too hurt to go on, so she waited with him. She fought off wolves and survived a week without food or water."

No, he hadn't had a dream this outlandish in quite some time. "I thought Henna warned you about making up stories, son."

"I didn't make it up," Wolf said, stung. "It's true. Miss Maggie told me."

March raised an eyebrow at Maggie. The mare stood with feet splayed wide and her head hanging down so her nose al-most touched the ground.

"Well, she certainly looks the part," he said. He stepped down the stairs and passed a hand along the mare's neck. He could feel the muscles trembling with fatigue. "I can't believe anyone would dare shoot such a noble beast."

Maggie surged forward, nearing him for the first time since he'd opened the door. "Don't you make fun of her! She's been treated badly, but she's got the heart of a bear. She'll come back sound. She's smart and tough and beautiful . . ." Her voice caught and she turned away from him. The mare lifted her head from the ground and pushed it into Maggie's stomach.

March watched her scratching the mare's ear. The dark fringe of her lashes brushed across cheeks made luminescent by the silver moon. Smart and tough and beautiful. He bit down on his lip to halt the words "Just like you."

He took a deep breath of the bracing night air, felt the gooseflesh prickle his bare arms. He had to bring himself back to reality, as impossible as reality appeared to be. She had left the stagecoach. She was standing here in front of him. And he didn't know what to do with her.

"Wolf, why didn't you take her home to the farm?"

"I . . ." The boy stared at him, nonplussed. Obviously Maggie had told him she was coming here, and it had never occurred to him to question her.

"It's all right," March said, as much to reassure himself as Wolf. "Henna will be waiting up for Jed, anyway. Let's settle the mare in the barn—I don't think she's up to more walking tonight. I'll hitch up Pamela and we can ride over to the farm."

"There's no need. I'm staying here." Maggie picked up her bag and started for the door.

"You can't stay here!" The desperation in his voice turned her head. March edged up onto the porch, afraid of spooking her into the house, where it would be that much harder to get rid of her.

"I'm sorry I've made myself unwelcome." She might as well have had a poker for a spine. "But all I'm asking is a bed for the night. I promise not to be any trouble to you."

Beneath her fierce hauteur, he could hear the effort it took for her voice not to tremble. He wanted to strangle her.

"I'm not saying you're unwelcome, and you know it," he growled, still moving toward the door.

Even in the shadows under the porch roof, he could see her lifted eyebrow.

"Then if I'm welcome, I'll be very pleased to stay with you, March. Thank you."

He slammed his fist into the door, ricocheting it closed. "You're going to stay with the Culberts, measles or no measles."

Suddenly, this close to her, he couldn't keep the hard edge in his voice. "It's not proper for you to stay here, Maggie. I won't allow it."

Out of the corner of his eye, he saw her young accomplice slipping off the porch. "Wolf, why don't you take the mare to the barn and feed and water her."

Maggie waited until the horse and boy had crossed the yard before speaking again. Her eyes glittered as she glared at him. "You allowed it all right last night. This isn't about what's proper; it's about Henna Culbert calling you on the carpet."

Not in a million years was he going to admit that the idea of being alone night and day with Miss Maggie Parker scared him a hell of a lot more than Henna Culbert's disapproval.

"Maybe so, but Henna was right," he said. "As long as you're here in Oxtail, I'm responsible for you. I don't want anything I do—or don't do—to hurt you."

Her stance softened slightly. "Oh, for heaven's sake. It's only for one more night. I'll be back in Kentucky before anyone can even think of starting a rumor."

He stared at her. No wonder she seemed so unconcerned. "Maggie, it's not just for one night. The stagecoach only runs through Oxtail to Greeley on Fridays. You're stuck here another week."

"Another *week?*" Her voice squeaked. "Are you sure?"

"I'm sure."

"No wonder you were so all-fired determined to get me to the stage on time." He heard her deep breath, watched her shoulders sag. "I'm sorry. I hope you'll believe I wasn't trying to cause you any more trouble."

She didn't need to try.

"Obviously you don't want me here, and I can't blame you. I've been nothing but an inconvenience. You shouldn't have to pay for my ignorance. I wonder if you would be interested in purchasing Ari, the horse, from me for a small sum."

Once again, her turn of reasoning stumped him. "You want to sell me that broken down mare? Tonight?"

"I had planned to give her to you for your breeding program. She's a sturdy, well-built little mare, as you'll see in the morning, but I find myself in need of funds." Her voice wavered. "I'll sell her to you dirt cheap, just enough to rent a room in Oxtail until next week."

"Would you stop this nonsense!" He was not going to give her a chance to cry. "You are not going back to Oxtail tonight, and you are not going to rent a room there. I'm taking you over to the Culberts."

She whirled on him. "I don't believe you're my father. You're no relation to me at all—isn't that the whole point of this argument? I will do what I please, and I don't give a damn what you think about it."

He pushed himself away from the door, letting the shadows and his anger darken him with danger.

"Damn it, you should be pleased to have a safe place to stay with a good family like the Culberts."

He should have intimidated her. Despite his average height, he loomed over her. The moonlight didn't hide the muscles on his bare arms, hardened from ranch work. She should have agreed with him from self-preservation if not good sense.

"I am *not* going to stay with the Culberts."

"Why are you being so mulish? You heard Henna say that Dan's past being contagious."

"I will not stay with the Culberts," she repeated, as though he hadn't heard her the first time. "Henna disapproves of me. No, Henna dislikes me, and I will not stay a week in her house." Her heard her swallow. "I get enough of that at home."

"Damn, Maggie. You might find you got along better with people if you stopped being so hostile."

"I was not—" she choked in obvious outrage on the words. "I was not hostile," she managed hoarsely. "Henna said . . . she thought . . ." He couldn't tell in the dark, but he thought she might be blushing. "Never mind what she thought. I meant to be pleasant. Jed was so nice. I *wanted* them to like me."

Unable to stop himself, he touched her, the gentlest of caresses against her cheek, his thumb wiping away the dampness. Before she could protest or pull away, he dropped his hand.

"You're exhausted," he said, his own voice husky as he stepped back. "You go to bed. I'll work something out for tonight. We'll talk about it in the morning."

"Damn you all to hell," she choked out, jerking open the door and throwing herself into the house.

If he lived a hundred years, he'd probably never figure her out. And he wasn't sure he'd live through the week.

Chapter 6

March watched as the beams in the roof slowly took shape in the pre-dawn gloom. Wolf's shallow breathing came in a soothing rustle from the other end of the room, though the boy's presence had caused grim dreams of Logan Penny to destroy what little sleep March had managed to find during the night.

With a sigh, he sat up and swung his legs out into the cold morning air. Not even a full night's sleep would have prepared him to face this day.

He'd left his jeans on in case of emergencies. Maggie Parker seemed to have a talent for creating them. So it took him only a minute to dress, pulling on his boots and his old blue work shirt. The light cotton gave no protection against the morning chill, but an hour of mucking stalls and milking Daisy before breakfast would bring more than enough warmth.

He crept quietly down the stairs, trying not to wake Wolf—or worse, Maggie. No sound came from the master bedroom. He breathed a sigh of relief as he escaped through the front door.

The whispering grasslands lay in cold gray obscurity, waiting for the sun to return color to the world. To the west, past Jane's little vegetable garden, past the apple trees, up beyond the rugged foothills, the high peaks of the great Rockies suddenly caught fire, a haunting pink glow promising morning.

The sight caught March by surprise, and he stared at the mountains trying to discern what caused in him that sudden feeling of unease, of difference. Then he had it. It was beautiful. The massive, endless, dark mountains tipped with the sun's fire filled him with awe.

Nothing had held any beauty for him since the day he'd found his sister's family murdered, and suddenly the beauty was too painful to be borne. He turned abruptly and headed toward the stable, gathering the gloom about him like a protective cloak.

The door to the barn stood open wide, and March frowned. He'd hoped to have this time to himself, to lose himself in physical labor. Usually Lem didn't get up until the sun had fully risen, his way of proving to himself he had free choice of when to rise and when to retire.

As he crossed the threshold, he heard the old man's voice. "How's that, Miss Maggie?"

And Maggie's reply. "Thank you, Mr. Tate. This one fits her perfectly."

He saw them standing halfway down the row of stalls, Lemuel's tall, dark form towering over Maggie as together they adjusted a halter on the little buckskin mare, Ari.

Something like fear squeezed his heart, fear that Maggie planned to make good her threat to walk into Oxtail and sell the mare for room and board. And anger, that she'd sneak out before dawn without telling him. As he came closer, he noticed the outfit she wore and had to bite his lip to stop his relieved laughter.

She'd found a pair of Jane's Levis, just enough too long that they puffed up out of her boots like Yorkshire pudding. One of Lucas' old work shirts hung almost to her knees, the sleeves rolled up to her elbows, and over that she wore a stained leather vest. A thick red braid hung down her back beneath her broad-brimmed hat, or he might have been tempted to mistake her for Jake Culbert.

He'd bet his last dollar she wasn't going into Oxtail dressed like that.

"You two are up early," he said, making Maggie and Lemuel both jump. He almost smiled at the identical looks of embarrassment they wore.

"I heard Miss Maggie messin' around down here," Lem explained, "and I wanted to make sure she didn't get herse'f into any trouble."

"And did she?" March asked.

"She shore can muck a stall. I jes' helped her find the wheelbarrow."

Maggie said, "If you'll take Ari out to the corral for me, Mr. Tate, I'll clean her stall next."

Her green eyes sparkled as she looked up at March, and he knew he was going to lose. He didn't know what the battle was yet, but he was going to lose.

He watched Lem lead the mare down the length of the stable, surprised to see the lift of the mare's head, the height of her step.

"All she needs is good food, good water, and a little rest," Maggie said, retrieving a pitchfork from where it leaned against the wall.

"There's life in her yet," March admitted. He watched Maggie attack the mare's stall with strong, practiced strokes, dumping forks of soiled straw into the wheelbarrow. He had found no effective verbal weapons to use on her, so he tried silence, waiting with all the patience a lifetime around horses had taught him.

She broke first, as he'd known she would when he'd seen the excitement in her eyes.

"There's a simple way to solve the problem of my living arrangements for the next week," she said as she dumped the last forkful of straw into the barrow.

Still he waited. He could afford to. He didn't want to know.

"You can take me on as a hired hand."

"Pardon?" He grimaced. Another point for her. Every time he thought there was nothing more she could do to shock him, she did it again.

"Why not? It's the perfect solution." She leaned toward him in her eagerness. "Bachelors hire housekeepers all the time. Widowers hire governesses for their children. It may occasionally cause a raised eyebrow, but it's hardly scandalous. Besides, you need the help."

"I do?"

The question only encouraged her.

"You do. Mr. Tate says there's too much work for just the two of you."

"Lem wouldn't—"

"And lucky for you, I'm willing to work for nothing more than room and board."

She had such a slender, white neck. Perfect for strangling. "Maggie, you can't . . . I'm not going to hire a girl—"

"This girl can clean out a stall as fast as you can. Faster, I bet," she said, her cheeks turning a dangerous shade of red. "And I bet I can ride better, too. Maybe I can't rope, but I can catch any horse you've got, anyway, and I can groom—"

"I believe you!" he exploded finally, grabbing her by the shoulders. It took all his will not to shake her. "I'm not hiring you. I'm not hiring anyone. I could hire a decent cowboy off the streets of Oxtail any day of the week. But I'm not going to get anyone else killed."

Maybe it was seeing her in Jane's clothes, he didn't know. But the thought of anyone hurting her, the way Jane had been hurt, terrified him.

He knew his breathing was ragged and he was squeezing

her shoulders too hard, but he couldn't let go. "Do you understand? The rustlers who killed Lucas and Jane and Logan didn't get what they were after. When they come back, you are *not* going to be here."

Her shoulders raised beneath his hands as she lifted her fists to her hips. "Do you mean to tell me you're sitting out here letting this farm—sorry, this ranch—go to pieces, just waiting for a gang of outlaws to come along and kill you?"

He dropped his hands to his sides. His voice came out a feral growl. "Only if I don't kill them first."

"And what about Mr. Tate? Do you intend to get him killed, as well?" When he didn't answer, she pressed on, her eyes locked on his. "You don't think these killers were common outlaws at all, do you? If they were out here rustling some horses, they'd be long gone by now."

He glared at her. He'd tried to frighten her, and she'd cut right to the heart of his own logic. He hadn't shared his theory with anyone but Lem, not even Jed Culbert, who probably ought to know. He certainly shouldn't risk divulging it to a hotheaded, spoiled tomboy.

And yet, the words came out anyway. "We'd lost a few horses in the weeks before . . . before the murders. Enough to make us think rustlers. But men who would kill a man and his family in their own kitchen aren't after a few ponies. I think whoever's behind the attack wants this ranch and the water rights that are on it."

Simply talking about it made him sick. "I think . . ." A dizzying flash of memory, of blood everywhere, of his sister's lifeless hand clutched around the barrel of a shotgun. He turned from Maggie to the wall, pressing his forehead against the cold, hard wood to stop the vertigo.

"I think they meant for Jane to survive. She couldn't run a ranch by herself. She'd have had to sell. But they underestimated her and had to kill her."

He took a deep breath, pressing his fists against his temples. "I should have been there in that kitchen, but I wasn't. So now anyone who wants this land has to come through me."

He heard her come up behind him and prayed she wouldn't touch him. She didn't. But her voice came soft as a caress to his ear. "If you convince everyone that you can't run this ranch, that you're too overcome with grief even to care what happens to you, someone is going to offer to buy this place from you dirt cheap."

He turned from the wall, away from her, to give himself time to compose his face. "I'm betting on it."

"And until then, they'll probably leave you and Mr. Tate alive."

March nodded grimly, working out the logic one more time. "If I die, the ranch goes to Harry, the last of us. Mother died not long after Harry was born, and Father, well, he might as well have. Harry's in school in Philadelphia. Too far away to be intimidated by rustlers in Oxtail. They'll prefer to have me sell."

Maggie clicked her tongue. "Then as near as I can figure, until someone offers to buy the ranch, everyone sits around and waits. No more dangerous than waiting for the rest of the Culbert clan to come down with measles."

He looked back at her over his shoulder. She grabbed the handles of the wheel-barrow. "I'd better get to work. There's one more stall to be done before breakfast."

Damn it. Her cussedness shouldn't be able to make him smile.

"Do you always get your way, Maggie?"

She grinned. "Almost."

For the second time that morning, his heart quailed at the

sight of beauty. He should tie her to Balthasar's back and drag her over to the Culberts' kicking and screaming. Not for her own good. For his.

"I'll rustle breakfast," he said. "You'll be in charge of dinner."

She stiffened, her eyes narrowing. "I'm not a housekeeper," she objected. "I said I'd work with the horses, not scrub your floors and wash your clothes and do your cooking. I'll do a man's job—"

"That's right," he cut her off, finally allowing himself a smile. "Lem and I share all the chores here, including meals. Except breakfast. Lem doesn't eat breakfast, so that's mine. If you want to do a man's job, you're going to take your share of the cooking. I don't hire shiftless loafers. Is that clear?"

One side of her mouth twitched. "I guess I don't always get my way, March."

"That's 'Mr. Jackson,' miss," he said with a frown. "I don't tolerate familiarity in my hired hands."

"Jackson!" she exclaimed. "Jackson, Jackson, Jackson. Of course! Whatever you say, Mr. Jackson."

He stared after her as she rolled the wheelbarrow out the barn door.

Maggie waved her hand through the black smoke pouring from the oven, biting back tears of frustration. She'd only turned her back for a minute to put coffee in the coffee pot.

She wrapped her dishrag around her fingers and reached in for the loaf pan. Unable to see through the smoke, she banged her wrist against the pan. With a cry, she jumped back, bringing the pan of burning bread with her. It clattered to the floor, a charred mess.

She sank to her knees beside it. She'd felt so natural with the horses this morning. March had let her exercise Honey, the pony Skylark, and even his beloved Balthasar, while he took Achilles out to check fences.

Galloping in the shadow of the somber gray-green mountains that loomed over the ranch like the forgotten fortresses of ancient gods, with the sky the palest blue she'd ever seen, she'd thought for the first time that Colorado was beautiful. She might have ridden on forever, if not for the knowledge that another horse waited for its run, the knowledge she was needed.

Lemuel Tate had told her what work needed to be done, just as though he believed she knew what she was doing. His trust had gone a long way toward dispelling her lingering fear of the big black man.

Wolf had helped her groom Ari, massaging the mare's muscles and brushing her dun coat until it felt as soft as kid leather. From Wolf, she gleaned the information that March had sent the boy back to the Culberts the night before to make sure Jed got home, and then had him come back to act as a stop-gap chaperone. Wolf was to stay with them until Henna came to get him this afternoon. Henna Culbert was the last obstacle to her remaining on the Penny ranch.

She could still hardly believe March had agreed to let her stay. But he couldn't get rid of her now, not after this morning. She hadn't felt so free, so comfortable, so . . . *happy* in as long as she could remember.

She glanced down at the blackened bread pan. At least, she'd been comfortable until she'd entered the kitchen.

She'd felt so clever at breakfast this morning, complimenting March on his biscuits and asking for the recipe. She'd gotten flour all over the clean dress she'd changed into, but she was sure she'd made up the biscuit dough exactly as he'd said, though it hadn't looked much like bread lying in the loaf pan.

98

"At least it's not flat and pasty anymore," she muttered as she managed to get a grip on the pan. "It's flat and black."

She got to her feet and dumped the whole thing into the sink. As she reached for a knife to scrape the charcoal evidence out of the pan, she heard the thunk of boots being knocked against the side of the porch.

She dropped the knife, gave another futile wave of her apron at the smoke, and turned to stir the pot on the stove as March, Lemuel, and Wolf came through the door. She heard them pause on the threshold.

"What's burning?" Wolf asked at the same moment March said, "My, something smells good."

She turned, and three pairs of eyes dropped sheepishly to the floor.

"The bread burned," she said, brazening it out. "But there's plenty of beans and coffee."

"Sounds good," Lemuel said.

"I'll get the coffee," March offered.

But she caught Wolf eyeing the thin wisp of smoke that still rose from the sink.

She brought four bowls to the stove and lifted the lid on the pot. The beans bubbled merrily, but they didn't look as thick as she'd expected, though she'd added salt pork and onions, the way Lily, her mother's cook, did. They'd cooked for nearly half an hour. She must have put in too much water.

"It's a bean soup," she said, ladling out portions into the four bowls.

March set the coffee pot back on the stove and helped her carry the bowls to the table.

Maggie sat down and peered into her bowl. It did look watery, but it smelled all right, thank God. She'd eaten more than March and Wolf combined at breakfast, and she was already starved again. She heard the clink of spoons around her and dipped her own into the soup.

The broth did taste watery. And the beans . . .

"They're hard as rocks," she said, dropping her spoon back onto the table. She looked at the others, frozen in the act of manfully spooning broth into their mouths. "Or didn't any of you notice?"

Damn! She would *not* cry again. She shoved her chair away from the table and ran from the room. She tripped once on the hem of her dress, but made it to the master bedroom without falling. She slammed the door behind her and threw herself on the bed, choking back the tears. So much for feeling useful. She couldn't even cook beans.

She ignored the quiet knock on her door. It opened anyway.

"Maggie?"

She didn't roll over. "If someone doesn't answer your knock, you're supposed to go away," she growled into her pillow. "I could be naked in here."

For once she'd failed to shock March. He laughed. "Next time I'll ask if you're naked before I come in, I promise." He sat down on the edge of the bed.

She turned enough to glare at him with one eye. "Go away."

"Maggie, there's no reason to be upset over a pot of beans."

"No reason?" She propped herself up on her elbow to give him the benefit of a full glare. "Yes there is. Don't treat me like a useless child. You've worked hard all morning and must be hungry, and I've completely ruined dinner. There's not an edible piece of food in that kitchen. You should be furious with me. Go ahead. I can take it."

She knew how to handle anger, disappointment, disapproval. They wouldn't make her cry.

"Lem's going to mix up some more biscuits and a little gravy," March said instead. "And I've sent Wolf down to the cellar for some preserves. We've had disasters in the kitchen before, and we haven't starved yet."

"Well. Good for you." She pushed her face back down into the pillow, damping the tears.

"Have you ever cooked anything before?"

The gentle question gave her enough anger to face him again. "No." She brushed furiously at the water on her cheeks. "Stephen thinks it isn't proper for a lady of society to know how to cook. So, if he ever ranks a place in high society, I'll be prepared. Meanwhile, I can't even cook beans."

"Why didn't you tell me?"

She wished he'd get off the bed. His weight pulled her toward him so her hip knocked against his, and the summer storm color of his eyes so close to hers did something strange to her insides.

"I told you I'd do all the work you'd ask of any hired hand," she said.

He smiled. The smile that transformed the habitual grim set of his face. "Remind me not to ask you to shoe the horses." He tugged on the braid hanging down her back. "You've done as much work as any of us this morning, and the beans will be fine. We'll let them simmer on the stove this afternoon and have them for supper. Besides, you make a darn fine cup of coffee."

He stood and offered her his hand.

She took it, frowning at him. "You don't need to humor me. I never learned to make coffee, either."

He frowned back. "I wasn't humoring you. How'd you make the pot I just poured?"

She let him pull her up so she stood only inches from him. "I watched you make the second pot this morning. I

101

just did what you did."

"You made a pot of coffee, exactly the way I like it, just by watching me do it once?"

She searched his face for the joke, but he was serious. She'd done something right, after all.

"Don't worry, Maggie Parker. We'll make a fine cook out of you yet. Stephen will be horrified."

She tried to back away from that unexpectedly intoxicating grin, but the bed hit the back of her legs.

"He usually is," she said. *Oo, snappy reply.* But she couldn't concentrate on anything besides the sudden realization that the temperature in her room had risen at least twenty degrees since she'd gotten up this morning. And the fact that March hadn't released her hand.

He still smiled at her, as though he didn't even realize his thumb was stroking the back of her hand, the hard calluses as gentle as a feather's touch. "If you don't know how to do something, ask. Okay? I almost broke a tooth on those beans."

She knew it wasn't okay. She'd done something wrong, and he should be angry with her. When he finally figured that out, she had to be prepared, had to have her heart cold and ready in defense.

But his touch seemed to be sending curls of flame up her arm, and all she wanted was for him to let her go. All she wanted.

"Okay," she said, the word coming out in a strange croak.

He stepped back then and dropped her hand. "Okay. Now let's go see if those biscuits are ready."

Maggie dipped the large wooden cooking spoon into the pot of beans. They looked more like porridge than soup now, but they smelled divine. She blew across the top of the spoon, took a deep breath to give herself courage, and tried a bite.

"Hey!" She spun around, wishing there was someone to offer a second opinion, but the men and Wolf hadn't come in yet. "It worked!" she crowed instead, then gave a quick curtsy to the stove. "Thank you, thank you. Oh! The cornbread!"

She snatched her dishtowel from the edge of the sink and opened the oven door. A crown of gold topped the baking pan. She pulled it out, breathing deeply of the smell of fresh baked cornbread.

She'd insisted on making supper, since Lemuel had saved dinner. With unseemly eagerness, Lemuel and Wolf had objected she needn't bother, they'd take care of it, but she'd firmly reminded them that she'd started the beans, and she fully intended to finish them. A doubting Lemuel had given her his cornbread recipe, and March had set Wolf to churning butter to top it, but the final product was all hers.

"And not a wisp of smoke to be seen."

She would set the table and ring the big triangle hanging on the porch. Just like a frontier farm wife. Stephen *would* be horrified.

At the thought, she broke into a whistle, which quickly died as she realized it was one of March's tuneless versions of "O Bury Me Not." She took up "Camptown Races" instead.

The knock at the door came while she was setting napkins on the table. Neither March, Lemuel, nor Wolf would knock. She swallowed her sudden apprehension. A murdering rustler would no more knock than the men would.

She opened the door to find Henna Culbert standing on the porch. She looked cool and dust-free in a quietly stylish yellow cotton dress and straw hat. Maggie would have preferred a rustler.

"May I come in?"

No. "Of course," Maggie said, hastily stepping aside. As

Henna brushed by, Maggie noticed the other woman's careful coiffure, her pristine white gloves. In a futile gesture, she wiped her hands on her apron and tried to push her stray curls behind her ears.

She cast a miserable glance out the door, but the yard remained empty of cavalry. She'd won more battles than she'd lost in her life, using her wits, her will, and sometimes her fists. But force and logic each seemed equally powerless against the omnipotent reign of propriety.

"You're here to pick up Wolf?" she said, deciding the best defense was in not being defensive. She moved toward the kitchen rather than following Henna into the living area. She wouldn't give her enemy the choice of battleground.

"Yes." Henna came back toward the dining table, watching Maggie arrange the silverware. "I suppose it won't shock you to hear I was disappointed you didn't make it to the train yesterday."

"No." Maggie stared down at the tablecloth, searching for a reply, but cool verbal sparring didn't come naturally to her. She'd have to use more direct tactics.

"I'll be staying here at the ranch until the stagecoach comes back through town next week," she said, turning to face Henna. "You and I having words won't change that. I'll be working for my room and board as a hired hand. When the stagecoach arrives, I'll leave for Kentucky, and neither you nor Mr. Jackson will ever have to lay eyes on me again."

"I see." Undoing the hat ribbon beneath her chin, Henna studied Maggie with those uncanny amber eyes. With a faint rustle of lemon-colored skirts, she took a seat. "Please, Miss Parker, sit with me. Perhaps we can talk without 'having words.' "

Against her better judgment, Maggie took the seat across the table, smoothing out her own green-sprigged calico dress.

It was a sweet dress, decked with lace and ribbons, suited to an afternoon tea on a cool patio, not to cooking over a hot stove on an already blazing summer day. It felt sticky under her arms and the skirt sagged limply toward the floor. But nothing else in her trunk was any more suitable.

She didn't dare admit to herself that it hurt to think how little consideration her mother and stepfather had put into their decision to send her out west.

Henna set her hat on the table. "Miss Parker, March has been a good friend of my family's. He and Lucas made it their business to protect our water rights, despite the fact that the Pennys were here first and had first claim to the water. We couldn't grow much of anything without irrigation, so we owe them a great deal.

"You know that Lucas, Jane, and Logan were murdered. But I don't think you can have any idea of what it was like to come into this house and see them lying here."

Henna glanced down at her hat and tucked the ends of the ribbons beneath it, the first nervous gesture Maggie had seen her make. "When Lemuel came back from his errands in town that day, he thought March had been shot, too. He was covered in blood, out of his mind with grief.

"I thought we were going to lose him, too. He couldn't eat, couldn't sleep. I know he blames himself for not being here to die with them." Her eyes focused suddenly, sharply on Maggie. "He's still not himself, and he's very vulnerable right now. He needs his friends. I intend to protect him from further hurt in any way I can."

Maggie thought she could imagine March's grief better than Henna suspected. She had only to look into his eyes to see it stamped on his soul. To see it reflected in the other woman's face lessened her antipathy toward Henna.

"The last thing I want to do is hurt Mr. Jackson," she said, sending up silent thanks that she'd finally relearned his surname. "He's been nothing but kind and generous to me. I only want to spend this week working with the horses and minding my own business. I can't wait to get back to Lexington—the man I love lives there." It wasn't quite a lie if it used to be true.

"I believe you don't mean harm to March," Henna surprised her by saying. "I should have held my tongue yesterday until I got to know you better; you don't have the temperament for deceit. Indeed, it might serve you well to learn to guard your feelings a little better. But all that said, I still must warn you to be careful. You could easily hurt March without intending it."

Maggie opened her mouth to ask what she meant, but Henna had already moved on.

"If you insist on staying here and March insists on allowing it, I think it would serve you better to tell visitors you've been hired as a housekeeper rather than as a stable boy." She tapped a long finger on the table for emphasis. "I, of course, will speak up for you if it comes to that, and I will have Wolf stay with you for the rest of the week. March could use the help, and with Danny feeling so much better, we'll be able to get along without him for a while."

Maggie bit back her objections to the other woman's decisions. At least she herself was no longer a direct target of Henna's battle plans. "That would be fine," she said, "if it's all right with March—Mr. Jackson. Wolf's a very sweet boy."

A gentle smile touched Henna's lips. "He is that." She cocked an eyebrow at Maggie. "He told me quite a yarn last night about a mare you brought back with you. It seems that at one time she belonged to an Indian princess?"

A flush crept up Maggie's cheeks as she remembered March chiding Wolf for her story the night before. "I didn't mean to get him in trouble," she said.

"You didn't," Henna assured her. "He was just repeating what he'd heard. But he does have a tendency to add his own . . . creative flair. I suppose he gets it from his father."

That was a side of Jed Maggie hadn't seen the day before, a surprise, like his appreciation of Mozart. Perhaps Henna's disapproval had scared it away.

"I don't think having an imagination is something to be punished for," Maggie said, careful to keep her voice neutral. If Henna treated Wolf the way Stephen treated her . . .

"Wolf's imagination has proven to be quite useful," his mother said with a certain pride. "He can entertain the other children for hours with his stories. Emily and Tucker will miss him this week. But he has to learn to make clear the difference between make-believe and reality. As long as he tells his stories as stories, there isn't a problem. I just want to be sure that if there's a fox in the henhouse, I don't think he's making it up."

"I'll keep that in mind," Maggie said, appeased. "I tell myself stories to pass the time, and I guess I made up quite a whopper for Wolf last night."

Henna's smile deepened, an expression that transformed her cool beauty into puckish mischief. "I especially liked the part where Ari made her way twenty miles through a trackless wilderness to bring medicine back for a sick child—during the worst blizzard to hit Minnesota in a century."

"It was forty miles," Maggie corrected her. "And she had a bullet in her shoulder."

Henna laughed, a light, sweet sound that tempted Maggie to smile back. She rose instead, taking the coffee pot from the stove.

"Can I offer you anything?" she asked, suddenly awkward that she hadn't played hostess with any grace. "I'm about to make coffee, and I noticed there's tea in the cupboard."

To her relief, Henna shook her head. "No, I've got my own hungry mouths to feed. If you'll send Wolf over this evening, I'll pack him up some clean clothes."

"Of course," Maggie said brightly, though the thought of dirty clothes filled her with sudden foreboding. One more thing she'd have to ask March how to do.

Henna rose from the table, replacing her hat over her coiled braid of cinnamon-colored hair. "You know, you surprise me." She glanced at Maggie while her fingers deftly tied the bow. "I expected Lucas's city cousin to be a spoiled brat who'd never worked a day in her life, but you're obviously not afraid of work."

Maggie decided to ignore Henna's failure to take back the rest of her preconceptions. She didn't care if the woman thought her a spoiled brat, as long as she left her in peace.

She followed Henna to the door and watched her climb onto her waiting buckboard wagon with the dignity of any lady boarding a fancy surrey. When the wagon disappeared up the drive around the hill, Maggie closed the door and sagged against it with a sigh.

"Dragon one, Maggie one. The score is improving."

Chapter 7

Maggie took another stack of flapjacks from the platter. Served with fresh butter and blackberry preserves, sizzling bacon, and scalding black coffee, March's flapjacks made a breakfast fit for the gods. She couldn't remember ever being so hungry in her life or enjoying her food so much.

She felt shockingly scandalous, sitting to breakfast in her work clothes, just like March and Wolf. But they didn't seem to notice, and there hadn't been time to change. Her third morning as a ranch hand, and already she felt more comfortable in this simple kitchen than she'd felt in a long time in the big dining room at home.

Church yesterday had made her a little uncomfortable, with all the good folk of Oxtail staring at her. But, true to her word, Henna Culbert had introduced her as a gentle-bred young lady working as a housekeeper to earn her board, and Maggie had yet to meet anyone willing to contradict Henna.

She rolled her shoulders, enjoying the ache that mucking stalls had put there. As a child, she'd thought of her chores as drudgery, something to be gotten through as quickly as possible to give her more time for riding or reading. Not until her stepfather had decided she must become a lady and give up outdoor work had she realized how much she'd come to rely on her chores as a way to escape disappointment and insecurity in strenuous physical labor.

The girls in Lexington society wrinkled their noses walking past a stable. Even the boys considered mucking stalls beneath them. Langley Fitzgibbon had never touched a curry comb in his life. That's what grooms were for.

She'd been so infatuated with him she'd agreed, letting Stephen banish her from the stables, riding in the carriage instead of on horseback for fear of offending Langley's patrician nose. She'd been a fool. He'd probably laughed up his sleeve at her the whole time.

She'd learned her lesson well enough. It would be a long time before she trusted another man more than she trusted her horses.

"Miss Maggie, are your folks awfully poor?"

She looked up to see Wolf gazing at her with his serious golden-brown eyes. "No," she said, wondering where the question had come from. "My father owned his own horse farm, like the ranch here. My stepfather brought money of his own to it when he married Mama. Why?"

"I've never seen a girl eat that much before."

Maggie suddenly noticed that both Wolf and March had set aside their forks, their plates empty. She narrowed her eyes at Wolf. "You have some learning to do about charming the ladies, young man. Besides, this is only my second helping."

"Fourth," Wolf corrected her quickly.

"Well, maybe my third."

"Fourth."

"Wolf . . ." she growled in warning, trying to ignore March's amusement across the table.

"She's only getting paid room and board for all her work," March said. "She's got to eat plenty to make it a fair wage."

"You couldn't feed me enough to compensate me for the excellent work I do," Maggie informed him haughtily before taking a slow, deliberate bite of her flapjacks.

"And there's plenty more to be done," March said, rising from the table. "Wolf, the dishes are yours this morning."

The boy's face fell. "But March—"

"When you've finished the dishes, find Lemuel and see what he needs help with. He was talking about maybe scaring up a jackrabbit or two for supper."

The boy jumped up from the table, pulling Maggie's plate out from under her fork as she rescued the last bite of bacon.

"I guess I'm finished with breakfast," she said, heaving a woeful sigh for March's benefit. "If there's nothing more to eat, you might as well tell me what you want me to do for the rest of the morning, Mr. Jackson."

"You're with me, Miss Parker." He tossed her hat to her from the rack by the door. "I was thinking I'd bring the colts down from the north pasture and work with them today. After a month of freedom, they're probably wilder than spring hares, and I could use some help handling them."

"Oh, thank you, March!" The eager words escaped her before she thought to hold them back. She pulled her hat down, shading her eyes, feeling like a fool. How could he know she was dying to see the results of Lucas's breeding program? And why should he do something just to indulge her?

But her excitement seemed to please him. As they walked to the stable, he told her about the horses Lucas had sold the year before and about the most promising of the colts he was training now.

"One of the yearlings is a blood bay. He hasn't been separated from his dam long, but he's already showing a steady personality and good intelligence. His form looks good, too. Lucas was already talking about keeping him with us for breeding. But of course, a lot can happen in three or four years."

March lapsed into the silence Maggie had already come to expect when he spoke of his dead family. The confidence left his stride, the life drained from his face, replaced by a grim withdrawal that seemed to pull color from the day.

"And how much can you get for a good, well-trained colt here in Colorado?" she asked, trying to bring him back.

He shrugged, his answer curt. "I don't know. We sold one for two hundred and fifty dollars in Denver last year, I think. I just train them. Lucas took care of the buying and selling."

He lengthened his stride, making her trot to stay with him, and she gave up trying to draw him out.

As they entered the stable, Ari nickered a greeting. Maggie paused by the mare's stall to slip her a cube of the sugar March had put on the table for Wolf's coffee. Ari fixed a longing eye on her and fluttered her nostrils.

"Soon," Maggie assured her. "You'll be flying across the prairie in no time. But for now, you enjoy your rest."

She moved down to Honey's stall and set about saddling the palomino. She half expected March to snap at her to hurry up. Somehow she almost wished he would. Anything to dispel the despair he wrapped so tightly around himself. But he waited quietly, leaning against the stable door, staring out toward the mountains.

She checked Honey's cinch and swung herself into the saddle. "I'm ready."

Still without a word, he mounted Balthasar. She followed him out across the yard, away from the road and through a gate in the wooden fence marking the north pasture. They rode northwest, angling into the foothills, following the fence line.

Despite the sun's building heat, the air had a sweet freshness to it, and Maggie breathed deeply, savoring it. Honey moved like a dancer, letting Balthasar take the lead in a minuet of crossing undulating hills and dodging jagged rocks. A hawk cried, but the only other sounds were the horses' hooves hitting the ground in pounding rhythm.

To Maggie, it suddenly felt as though they could ride on forever without meeting another human being. Miles stretched before them without the shouts of angry voices or the acrid smell of fire. The mountains towered above them, cloaked in the cool green of conifers, unrelenting in their wildness.

As they moved into more rugged terrain, they passed patches of shrubs, and along north facing slopes, even scrubby pines. But not until they reached the top of a rocky ridge did Maggie begin to understand why anyone would want Lucas Penny's ranch enough to kill for it.

March pulled Balthasar to a halt and Maggie stopped beside him, looking down into a gash of color. Cottonwoods and willows splashed their shocking green against the muted gray, saffron, and ocher of a shallow canyon. But in the semi-arid climate of the piedmont, it was the water, still clear and fast in late July, that glittered more precious than gold.

Just downstream, the canyon flattened out briefly into a marshy valley. A group of twelve to fifteen horses stood along the stream bank, dozing lazily in the shade of the cottonwoods or munching contentedly on the only green grass for miles. They ranged in age from gangly colts too young to ride to young stallions and geldings ready to be sold.

"They've all been halter broke," March said, breaking his silence. "They should come along with us fairly quietly. Nero—see that dark bay by the cottonwoods, with the blaze?—he's the most likely to bolt. I'll rope him. You flank them down the valley there, in case anybody else gets any ideas. Okay?"

Maggie nodded, though her heart pounded with excitement and trepidation. She didn't want to tell March she hadn't ever herded anything before in her life. But she reached out a hand to touch his arm. She'd rather admit ignorance than let him down again.

She hesitated, fighting down embarrassment. "You said if I was ever unsure of how to do something . . ."

He turned back to her, and his smile overwhelmed her. That unexpected, delightful smile that chased the ghosts from his eyes and made her heart skip a beat.

"Just put yourself between them and their escape down the canyon, pardner," he said with an exaggerated drawl. "Come on up the streambed nice and easy and follow us home. Don't startle them. If anybody gets an idea to turn tail and run, you discourage him. It's the dirty end of the job, but you're the greenhorn here on the ranch, kid."

"I think I can handle that."

"Then git a move on, Parker. We ain't got all day."

She pulled a face at him and turned Honey back the way they'd come. Riding in a wide semicircle beyond the sight of the unsuspecting colts, she came back to the canyon a hundred yards downstream of them. Honey picked her way down a short trail to the stream bank. Looking up, Maggie saw March still waiting on the crest of the ridge. She waved to let him know she was ready.

He came straight down the ridge, Balthasar's hocks sliding underneath him almost to his forelegs as he scrambled down the steep slope. Almost in unison, the colts raised their heads, shifting from languid rest to attentive concentration with a ripple of youthful muscle.

As Balthasar reached the streambed, March began to whistle gently, tonelessly. One of the younger colts trotted forward, eager to check out Balthasar and apparently wondering what March might have hidden in his pockets. Several more colts dropped their heads back to the grass.

But the one he'd identified as Nero snorted and pranced, edging away as March neared.

Maggie watched March loosen his rope as Balthasar worked his way toward the rebellious bay. Abruptly, Nero leapt into a gallop with a sprightliness March's knobby kneed gelding could never hope to match. But luck was with them, for another colt shied into Nero's path, sending the bay flying down the canyon straight toward Maggie.

She maneuvered Honey sideways to block his path. Her heart raced as the big colt pounded toward them, his eyes rolling wildly with all the melodramatic terror of the consummate actor. Nearly full grown, if not yet his full weight and strength, Nero presented a frightening picture barreling down the canyon, his hooves flashing and foam flecking from his mouth.

"I think it's too late not to startle him," Maggie muttered, nervous sweat making the reins slippery in her hand. "Now don't you take offense at this, Honey."

Taking a deep breath, she stood up in her stirrups and pulled her white lace handkerchief out of her pocket.

"You stop right there, you blasted bronco!" she shouted, waving the handkerchief in a wide arc.

Honey twitched her ears daintily, but Nero seemed not to notice her at all. Maggie waved harder. "Stop, you damn fool!"

She practically jumped out of the stirrups, waving both arms now, and finally her movements made an impression on the charging horse. He skidded to a theatrical stop, slipping down onto his haunches mere yards from where Honey stood quietly, watching him with a disdainful eye. Even as he turned to flee back the way he'd come, March's rope slid over his neck.

Nero reared with a defiant scream and danced out into the cold water of the stream. But caught between the calm of Honey and Balthasar, he couldn't pretend for long that he was facing down a deadly danger. He slowed to a shuffling, snorting prance. His muscles shuddered and he turned a baleful eye on Maggie, but he knew the game was up.

"That was exciting," Maggie managed to say, despite the dryness of her mouth.

March nudged Balthasar forward, skirting Nero. He reached out and put a hand on Maggie's saddle horn.

"Maggie," he said slowly, leaning toward her to emphasize his point. "It's all right to get out of the way of a stampeding stallion. You're not getting paid enough to risk a broken neck. Do you understand?"

His breath sounded ragged, but his eyes fixed hers steadily.

"It's all right," she said, reacting more to the expression on his face than to what he'd said. His tone was calm enough, but she thought just maybe she saw lingering fear in his eyes. "Honey wouldn't have let me do anything too stupid."

The slightest of smiles touched his face. "You do beat all, Miss Maggie Parker. Hell, I should probably be warning Nero about you."

"It won't do him a bit of good," Maggie said, almost daring to share the smile and the warmth behind it. March still leaned toward her, his hand on her saddle. And this time, she didn't want to pull away. Some giddy girl inside her, inspired by adrenaline, by something she couldn't name, suddenly wanted him to kiss her.

Insanity. Wanting March Jackson, an uncouth cowboy to kiss her, the daughter of a Kentucky gentleman and Confederate officer, Brand Parker . . . Her, Maggie Parker, a scarred, dirty tomboy in jeans with a sullied past.

But when he looked at her like that, it didn't matter what he was or what she looked like. Langley didn't matter; he'd never looked at her like that. The realization sent a ripple of fear and of . . . anticipation . . . tingling along her nerves. March looked at her as though she were beautiful.

A rosy flush spread up her cheeks, and her breathing quickened. Against every ounce of sense she possessed, she found herself leaning toward him. She could feel his breath, still irregular, harsh, against her cheek. Her eyes drifted closed . . .

A huge splash sent March whirling back to face Nero. The big bay snorted and churned his hooves, heaving himself out of a deep pool next to a boulder downstream.

"You big fool," Maggie scolded, not sure if she meant the horse or herself. "Watch your step."

"Okay, Nero, that's enough," March said, guiding the colt out of the water. He didn't look back at Maggie. "We'd better be getting these boys back to the ranch. As I said, most of them should follow along with us. If Nero's theatrics scattered any of them, we'll come back and get them tomorrow."

Honey followed Balthasar up the canyon toward the shallower valley. *Idiot,* Maggie cursed herself, tilting her hat farther down over her face. *Damn fool.* Acting like a silly schoolgirl.

She might be young, but she knew better. Kissing men led only to more trouble than she knew how to handle. Bitter experience had taught her that. Love was only an illusion, an unlikely dream—at least for someone with her face and her past.

And for heaven's sake, she didn't love March. It would take an even greater fool than she to love this painfully gracious man with the haunted eyes, who waited patiently for the chance to atone for his sister's death by getting himself killed. If he escaped violence long enough to get her to the stage next Friday, she'd count herself lucky.

No, she couldn't love March Jackson. She'd just have to

be careful not to look into his eyes.

March wiped his kerchief across his brow and replaced his hat. He'd long ago discarded his shirt, but no breeze offered relief against the afternoon sun.

He heard the latch on the gate click and looked up to see Maggie bringing in the next colt for him to work, a handsome two-year-old chestnut he was slowly introducing to the bit. She led the colt over to him, then went to take the halter of the brown yearling waiting by the fence.

"You didn't work him long," she said, patting the brown's nose.

"Too hot," March explained. "If it's any cooler at all in the stable, you might rub him down there."

Usually he liked to perform all aspects of the training himself, including the grooming, accustoming the young horses to human contact, conditioning them to having their hooves and teeth examined, their tails touched, their halters, saddles, and bridles put on and removed. But he'd watched Maggie with the first three colts, and she took care of them with confident gentleness, making the grooming pleasant, but not allowing an inch of rebellion.

She worked naturally with the horses. She seemed to have a knack for soothing equine nerves—very different from her effect on the human species.

"Who do you want after this fellow?" she asked, breaking up his thoughts.

He shaded his eyes to check the position of the sun. They still had time before supper, but he'd get more done tomorrow morning when he could work the colts harder without worrying so much about the heat.

"Bring Nero next, I guess," he said. "He ought to be calmer by now. Then we'll see if we can't find something to do out of the sun."

"Sounds good to me."

He heard the gate click shut after her, heard the hooves of the horse she led pass around the ranch house. The other colts waited in the corral next to the stable, but he always worked them one by one here in the paddock behind the house. They seemed to take offense at being asked to work if they could see their comrades lounging in the shade.

He moved over to the chestnut and ran a hand along his neck. The colt looked back at him, taking in his scent.

"Hey there, old fellow," March murmured. The colt's ears twitched, alert, but calm. A fine young horse with steady nerves, in a couple of years he'd make an excellent cow horse.

Despite his month of freedom, the colt stood calmly while March saddled him. March then showed him the snaffle bit. He'd bridled the horse several times in the past with the colt's nose in a bucket of oats, so the colt took the bit with no sign of balking.

"What a prince among horses," March praised him, scratching behind the colt's ears as he adjusted the bridle. He'd work him on driving lines for a while, then focus on Nero. Most likely, he'd have this young colt gelded and sell him to an enterprising cow hand or someone in a profession needing a good seat for long rides.

Nero, on the other hand, would never make a sensible workhorse, but the handsome colt would bring a pretty penny from some vain businessman, or perhaps a breeder, if properly trained. Nero's speed might make a buyer overlook his lack of judgment. He might enter him in a race or two in Denver before selling him. That is, he might have before Lucas's murder. There was no point in thinking about it now.

"Gee!" March called as he walked behind the chestnut, adding a gentle pressure on the reins to acquaint the colt with the bit. The horse turned left, and March walked him in a circle around the paddock.

March worked him until they both dripped with sweat, more from the sun than the effort. But it felt good to sweat, felt good to have the sun beating on his bare skin, to smell dust and horse and fresh air instead of the stale whiskey and cigarette smoke of The Golden Rose. It felt too damn good. He had to remember not to get used to it.

"March, I've brought Nero."

He pulled the chestnut to a stop and turned to see Maggie leaning against the paddock fence, damp red curls trailing like fire across her cheeks.

"Just let me get the saddle off this fellow," he said, leading the colt to the fence. "I want to use it on Nero, too."

He didn't look at her while he unsaddled the chestnut, but he knew she watched everything he did, ready to learn anything she didn't already know about caring for horses.

Damn her. It was her fault he was out here working these colts instead of in town drinking himself into an attractive target. From the moment he'd found the bodies of his sister and her family, it hadn't mattered if the ranch he'd loved for so long fell down around his ears. All that mattered was finding the killers and making them pay.

It didn't matter if the colts forgot their training, if Honey and Achilles went insane from boredom, if the west fence broke down and Stormy led Prince and the mares right into a rustler's camp.

Yet here he was, working as if it mattered. And the only thing different today from four days ago was the flame-haired troublemaker who'd taken to ranch work like a seasoned hand and had shown an honest interest in his horses.

Beautiful, unattached young women—as few as he met, living near Oxtail—made him nervous, afraid his hands were

120

dirty or his speech might offend them. Much too nervous to think about kissing them. Yet he couldn't help his awareness of Maggie Parker's lips, the way they tilted when she smiled, the way they thinned when she frowned, the way they pursed temptingly when she teased.

Out working, she acted and talked more like a ranch hand than a young lady. She wore jeans and she swore worse than he did. He didn't have a chance to get nervous until he was already much too close to her. He'd have kissed her again this morning, out at the canyon, if it hadn't been for Nero. Without a thought for her sharp little dagger.

No, Maggie Parker didn't make him nervous. She scared the living daylights out of him.

"Jackson!"

The shout came from the direction of the house. March turned from the chestnut colt to see a man in a dark suit striding toward the paddock, a hired hand leading a horse behind him.

"Who's that?" Maggie hissed.

"Alexander Brady," March told her, grabbing his shirt from the rail and pulling it on. "He's what they call a cattle baron. Has a ranch up here and two more in southern Colorado. Probably owns near fifteen thousand head of cattle."

"Oh."

He stepped through the paddock gate and moved forward to shake Brady's hand. In late middle age, the man presented an imposing figure, his bearing giving the impression of more height than he actually possessed, his stocky figure more the result of natural build than excess weight. But it was his sharp eyes and undauntable self-confidence that made the greatest impression on those who met him.

"Jackson. Good to see you," he said. He gestured toward Nero, a large diamond flashing on one finger. "Handsome

121

young stallion you've got there. You know I'm always on the lookout for good horseflesh. Don't forget to give me a crack at your fellows when you're ready to sell."

"Of course, Mr. Brady."

"And who's this young lad you've got working . . ." He stopped, took another look. "Sorry, ma'am. Please forgive my mistake." Brady removed his hat and sent a sweeping bow toward Maggie, where she waited by Nero. "My name is Alexander Brady, and it is a great pleasure to meet you."

She flushed a deep, painful crimson, and March could tell she knew how disreputable she looked in those dirty work clothes. But there was nothing to do about it now.

"Miss Margaret Parker," March introduced her. "She's Lucas's cousin from Lexington, Kentucky."

"Please forgive my attire, Mr. Brady," she said calmly enough, despite the redness of her cheeks. "Mr. Jackson has hired me as housekeeper until I may return home, and my chores include assisting with the colts."

"No need to apologize, Miss Parker," Brady assured her. "The error is all mine." March had heard that Brady's suave good manners never deserted him, and he was ready to believe it. "My daughters have learned to ride cavalier fashion and now refuse to do anything else. One has got herself a pair of those blue jeans. I'm old-fashioned, I suppose, and not used to the new ways, but the day I'm afraid of change and progress is the day I hope they lay me in my grave."

"Your daughters are very lucky."

"Perhaps you can drop by and tell them that some time, my dear," Brady said with a chuckle.

"Mr. Brady, what did you come out here to see me for?" March asked, rescuing Maggie from further geniality.

"Ah, yes." Brady rubbed his palms together. "I came about a horse. This particular horse, as a matter of fact." He waved to the man waiting patiently behind him.

March's eyes narrowed as he closely examined the horse Brady's man led forward. He whistled.

"He's gorgeous," Maggie breathed, coming up beside him.

"Blue-blooded as the Queen of England," Brady said, obviously enjoying their admiration. "I paid a fortune for him, I don't mind telling you. Brought him out here from Virginia."

March stepped forward for a closer look. Pure ebony from his nostrils to his tail, the stallion held his head high, liquid brown eyes taking in every inch of his surroundings. His satiny coat smoothed each well-defined muscle into a sculpture of perfection.

"You're not planning to rope cattle with this one," March observed.

Brady laughed. "No, sir. I'd like to win back his purchase price racing him in Denver, maybe Cheyenne. And he'll make a fine stud."

"But . . ." March prompted.

"But I can't ride the bastard," Brady burst out. "Beg your pardon again, miss. He stands quiet as a lamb while he's saddled, but put a man up on him and he rears. If you stay on, he tries it again five minutes later. And he bolts."

"Toward the stable?" March asked.

"Toward, away, it doesn't seem to matter," Brady said, frowning at his horse in frustration. "If I'd known he was a renegade, I'd never have paid a cent for him. But now I've got him, I plan to make the most of it. You've got a touch with the horses, Jackson. I'm still grateful to you for getting Darcy's spoiled mare to quit nipping. I want you to help me with this devil."

March pulled his hand from the horse's side and stuffed his fists into his pockets. From the horse's calm stance and intelligent eye, he'd bet a bundle this stallion was no renegade. Most likely he'd been ridden poorly by some heavy-handed idiot who'd not only hurt the horse, but had probably had the poor sense to fall off when the stallion reared and to stop riding him altogether when he bolted.

It shouldn't take him an hour to cure the horse of both bad habits. Maybe a week to get him to enjoy being ridden again. But he might not have a week.

"Surely you've got some cowboy who can take care of the problem," March said, stepping away from the horse.

"I don't want some bronc buster touching this stallion," Brady said. "I don't want him injured and I don't want his spirit broke and by God, I want to be able to ride him myself without worrying I'll leave my Emmeline a widow."

March affected an indifference he didn't feel. Somehow Maggie had lured him into working with his own horses, but he couldn't forget the role he had to play for the rest of the world. For all Brady's blustery charm, he was known as a sharp and ruthless businessman. The cold, cruel stab of March's suspicions sickened him, but he had to consider the possibility that the man had come out here to the Penny ranch to size up his receptiveness to an offer on the land.

"I'm not interested," he said.

"What?" He'd forgotten Maggie's inability to leave well enough alone.

"I'll pay you for it, of course," Brady said. "It's worth a good fifty dollars to me."

"I'm not interested," March repeated.

"Reconsider," Brady persisted, sounding almost bewildered. "Fifty dollars is a good sum. I would think you might have use for the money, considering your recent tragedy. You don't want to risk losing your ranch."

The mention of his family's murder helped him set his face

in a sullen frown. "This ranch was Lucas's dream, not mine," he said, pain adding the recklessness he wanted in his voice. "And all he got from it was grief. What the hell do I care what happens to it?"

Brady frowned. "I'll tell you, Jackson," he said grimly, "because I consider you a good man and you've helped me in the past, that there are rumors you're in trouble financially and that you're spending more time drinking than taking care of your property. I have to say, I didn't want to believe it, but your behavior today indicates you're not thinking rationally."

March thought that was probably true enough. "I've given you your answer about the horse," he said, careful not to look again at the beautiful stallion. He entered the paddock and led out the chestnut colt. "For all I care, you can chop him up and feed him to your dogs. Good day, Mr. Brady."

He stalked toward the stable, leaving Maggie and Brady staring after him in stunned silence.

Chapter 8

March heard Maggie enter the barn, but he didn't look up from the saddle he was polishing. He'd worked out much of the frustration from his encounter with Brady by grooming the chestnut colt, and he didn't need Maggie to rehash it. He couldn't have missed her obvious disapproval of his behavior, but she'd had the sense to keep her mouth shut, and he wanted to leave it that way.

He leaned farther over the saddle, breathing in the soothing scents of oil and leather and horse, closing his eyes against her inevitable intrusion. But Maggie stayed down at the stable end of the barn. He heard Ari nicker to her, heard her soft murmurs to the buckskin mare. And he heard her open the unused stall nearest the barn, the one with the squeaky hinge he'd been meaning to oil for months.

"That's it, big fellow. You stay there, and I'll get you a nice bucket of oats."

The hair on the back of his neck prickled a warning. The Lord above help him, he didn't want to know what she was doing. But he found himself straightening up from the saddle he was working on, looking down toward the stable.

Maggie stood by the oat bin, dipping out a ration into a metal bucket. And gazing at him inquisitively from the nearest stall was Alexander Brady's prize thoroughbred stallion.

Involuntarily, his hands clenched into fists. Fury snaked through his veins, bringing a sick red haze similar to what he'd felt when he'd hit Shelby Brennan. She'd gone too far this time. Shock and disbelief held him frozen in place.

126

Though she didn't look at him, she must have heard him turn around. "In all the excitement, I never did remember to ask his name," she said, offering the oats to the stallion. "So I thought we could call him Sandy, after Mr. Brady."

She rubbed the horse's nose as he ate. "You did say Mr. Brady's first name was Alexander, didn't you?"

March couldn't unclench his jaw far enough to speak. He managed a stiff step forward. And another. He stalked within a yard of her, then stopped. He didn't trust himself any closer.

"Thanks to your performance out in the yard, I managed to talk Mr. Brady into quite a favorable deal, I believe," she went on, her eyes still firmly on the horse. "We could make quite a negotiating team."

"I didn't want a better deal!" he finally managed to say, his voice rising from a hoarse whisper to a shout. He stopped, tried again. "I wanted him to take his wretched stallion out of here. I don't want anything to do with Alexander Brady or his horse."

"Then you're a fool," she said, apparently oblivious to his murderous rage. "Sandy is the handsomest horse—"

"Brady might very well be the man who ordered Lucas's murder!" March exploded. "Are you so self-centered that means nothing to you?"

"Mr. Brady is too much of a gentleman to do something like that," she said, her shoulders squared defiantly. "Don't you even want to know what he's offered—"

"No!" March roared. "I don't give a damn what he's offered!" He grabbed her shoulder and wrenched her around to face him, trapping her against the stall door. Her hat tipped off her head, dropping to the floor, removing her last refuge from his anger. And looking into her eyes, darker than emeralds in a face ghostly pale, he saw the fear he thought she

127

couldn't feel. It only fed his fury.

"You think Brady's a gentleman, do you?" he growled. "Let me tell you something, city girl. You can't be truly respected as a businessman in Colorado Territory unless you've done your share of lying, cheating, and stealing on your way to the top. And Alexander Brady is *very* well respected.

"You think you know better than everyone else. Some God-given gift gives you the right to do whatever you want and the rest of us just better get out of your way. Well, out here, you don't know what you're getting into."

"I know you can cure Sandy of his bad habits," she said, standing up to him, though he could feel her tremble beneath his hands. "And that your plan of revenge is a fantasy, just an excuse to drink and feel sorry for yourself. A ranch hand like you, I bet you barely know enough about guns and outlaws to get yourself killed."

He could almost have laughed at that. "You don't know a damn thing about me, Maggie," he said, tasting the bitterness in his mouth. "Any more than you do about Brady. I know a lot more about guns than I do about running a ranch. I don't know the first thing about breeding records or financial ledgers. Like I told Brady, this ranch was Lucas's dream. I couldn't make it come true, even if I wanted to."

"Maybe—Ow!" She broke off her reply, her head snapping back.

March looked up to see the black stallion's ears snap forward in dismay at her cry, the end of Maggie's braid a shocking red flame hanging from his mouth. Maggie's hands flailed upward behind her, knocking against Sandy's nose. The horse jerked back.

"Ow!"

"Hold still," March commanded. He loosened his grip on

her shoulders to reach past her for the horse's head.

"You're crushing me," Maggie objected, pushing against him.

Ignoring her, March leaned farther into the stall. "It's not my fault your hair is so long." He caught the stallion's jaw. It took only a gentle pressure to pry his teeth apart and free the braid. He lifted it out of the stall, safely beyond the horse's reach. "It's a little damp, but I don't think there's any permanent damage."

But Sandy had apparently swallowed the ribbon. The braid had begun to unravel, and silky strands of hair tickled his palm. He no longer pressed against her, but his body burned suddenly from even that brief, innocent contact. Dressed in those awful work clothes, dirt smudged on one cheek, her hair unraveling about her, she made him ache as no woman had in a very long time.

Heaven help him, he couldn't strangle her and he couldn't kiss her.

"May I have my hair back now? Or are you going to have a bite, too?"

Don't tempt me. He dropped the end of her braid and stepped back, running a hand over his face.

"Maggie . . ."

"I'm sorry." Once again the last thing he expected her to say.

"No, you're not."

"Yes, I am." She met his gaze now. Apparently her fear had dissolved as suddenly as his anger had. "You're right. I did what I thought was best for you without giving you anything to say about it. I have no right to interfere in your life."

"A pretty apology. Why don't I believe you mean it?"

"I *do* mean it." But that eager glint had returned to her eye. "I'm sorry I told Mr. Brady you'd train Sandy. But I had such a great idea. I got him to agree to pay you sixty dollars, and, in addition, free stud service on three mares for two years."

He simply shook his head. She couldn't understand how any pretense at plans for a future ripped through him like a mountain lion's claws.

"He may have been bred in Virginia," she said, "but his dam's bloodlines are from the Lexington stallion Boston."

"Is that good?"

"If you knew anything about racing horses, you'd know it was good."

He shook his head again. "Maggie, I don't know what I'm supposed to do with you. I don't have much experience living with women. Ma died when Harry was born, so Jane pretty much raised us, and she always had the last word. Harry got me into more scrapes than I can count, but if I needed to keep Harry in line, there was always the threat of the willow switch out in the shed."

He'd meant it as a joke, but she paled again. Her chin came up. "I'm not afraid of a willow switch!"

She might as well have punched him in the stomach. His gaze caught on her scar, a white lightning gash against the pallor of her cheek, and he cursed his stupidity.

"Your stepfather hits you." Fresh rage coiled through him at the sudden realization.

"No," she denied firmly, turning her head to hide the scar. She crossed her arms over her chest as the bravado left her, and added softly, "Not any more."

He reached out to touch her chin, trying to turn her back to face him, but she shook him off, stepping away.

"Maggie, would you tell me about it?" he asked quietly, pushing away his sudden hatred of a man he'd never met to focus on the woman standing before him. The maddening

hellion with pain in her flashing eyes. The woman he'd come
to . . . care for.

"No."

"Maggie, I would never hit you."

She looked at him from beneath lowered lashes that sparkled with suspicious moisture.

"I never even hit Harry. Harry'd start to cry the minute I
mentioned the willow switch and that seemed like punish-
ment enough. A good thing, because I'm not sure I could
have brought myself to use it."

He thought he might be babbling, but it brought the hint
of a smile to her lips. She turned almost full toward him. "I
believe you. I don't think you'd hit me. Though I thought you
might shoot me when you saw Sandy."

He wasn't going to tell her that the thought had crossed his
mind.

She bent down to retrieve her hat, absently brushing dust
from the brim. "I just don't want to talk about Stephen. I
don't want to think about him. While I'm here, I want to pretend he doesn't exist."

He wouldn't push her. "Okay. You don't have to talk now.
There's nothing more to be done about Sandy today, but
there's plenty of work left before supper. Why don't you start
feeding and watering the horses. I'll finish this saddle before I
help you."

She nodded.

"And do it without any more surprises."

She set her hat firmly back on her head. "Whatever you
say, boss."

He walked back to the saddle he'd been working on. He
could hear her getting out the wheelbarrow for hay for the
horses. In his mind's eye he could still see the scar across her
cheek, her pallor when she'd said she wasn't afraid of being

hit. He wished he hadn't teased her, had added things up sooner.

Usually when one of his colts balked, he'd pushed it too hard or too fast. With patience and gentleness, he could convince a horse to do almost anything. He'd discovered that the principles by which people and horses operated weren't so very different. With time, he might find his way past Maggie's prickly exterior, past her habit of shying away when anyone came near.

But he didn't have any time. In four days Maggie would be gone, and he'd never see her again. He'd be left to work his revenge. Death had severed his connection to eternity, cut his future down to days and minutes. The best he could do for Maggie was let her go.

Maggie wrapped Jane Penny's robe tightly around her to keep out the night chill, then picked up the lamp burning on the table next to her bed. She cracked open the bedroom door, listening intently, but silence filled the house. She slipped down the hall toward the living room, her lamp a small pocket of light in the inky darkness.

She'd worked hard enough today to sleep for a week. She'd even found herself nodding over her mending after supper, listening to Lemuel Tate's deep, rich voice reading from the Psalms.

Evenings were already settling into an easy routine. She and March mended clothes and bits of tack while Lemuel read from the Bible. Or Lemuel would tie flies or cast bullets and sing his favorite hymns and part-songs. Maggie sang the ones she knew, and even March added his voice occasionally, usually a single, unwavering note. But Wolf sang every song, adding a pure, sweet descant or singing the melody while Lemuel harmonized far below.

Sitting out on the porch while the light lasted and then resting on Jane Penny's colorful pillows in the living room after the sun went down, relaxed her muscles and senses into a profound readiness for slumber. But tonight, once she'd made her way to bed, sleep had escaped her.

Thoughts of facing Stephen when she returned home, remembering March's anger this afternoon, imagining him shot down by the men he was trying to fool, all burned in her brain until she felt feverish. But they left her less restless than her memory of having very nearly kissed March out at the canyon this morning. Or the remembered touch of him leaning against her to free her hair from Sandy's jaws. His fury had set her trembling, but it didn't disturb her as much as her body's response to his nearness.

She moved into the living room, pausing as her lamplight played over the bookshelves. She'd wanted to explore them since the morning after her arrival, but she hadn't had a free moment until her insomnia tonight.

She crouched beside the low shelves and read the titles, suddenly remembering how she'd felt when she'd been very young, opening her presents on Christmas. She couldn't discern any rhyme or reason to the books' organization. A treatise on Chinese history stood next to Edwin James' report of Stephen Long's expedition to the Rocky Mountains in 1820. Beside them she found a copy of Dickens' *A Tale Of Two Cities*, an almanac, and then a complete set of Shakespeare's plays.

She moved along the shelves, running the titles over her tongue, the beloved familiar and the tantalizingly new. One thing Stephen could never take away from her was her books, no matter how much he disapproved of her storytelling or how many times she was late with her chores. Mama loved for Maggie to read to her in the evenings, and the only good quality Stephen possessed was his devotion to her mother.

The bookshelf ended against a rolltop desk of polished ash wood. The top had been left rolled up, exposing ink, pens, some scraps of paper, and a black bound ledger. Maggie set down her lamp. She should pick out a book and move to the rocking chair. But . . . she flipped the ledger open with scarcely a pang of guilt. Dead men could hardly complain about anyone snooping into their affairs.

A neat, plain handwriting filled the first half of the ledger. Lucas Penny had scrupulously recorded every monetary transaction he made, from the sale of a horse, to the purchase of oats and a new saddle, to material for a new dress for Jane.

Looking at the money made from selling fillies and colts and from stud fees, the ranch seemed in recent years to have begun to make an acceptable profit. But it appeared that Lucas also received a small pension from his days as a Texas Ranger, which had helped to keep the family in small luxuries.

On the last marked page a new hand had written in a purchase of coffee and another of grain and something almost indecipherable that Maggie thought might be whiskey. He'd put the amounts in the wrong column, and he hadn't bothered to subtract.

Maggie shook her head, reaching for a pen. Her hand paused in mid-air. She'd practically promised not to interfere anymore with March's running of the ranch. On the other hand, if she simply corrected something he'd already done, he could hardly complain that she'd gone against his will.

With a deft flicking of the pen, she inked out March's haphazard bookkeeping and ordered the amounts neatly farther down the page, subtracting carefully as she went.

She clicked the pen against her teeth as she examined the new total. Alexander Brady's sixty dollars would come in handy, but she didn't think March needed to fear losing the ranch for lack of money. He might even have enough to hire a hand or two, which he'd need, especially when the mares started foaling and when he took the young horses to market.

As for the other half of the bargain she'd struck, Sandy ought to foal some very handsome colts and fillies. Not that March planned to live long enough to find out. But if she could find Lucas's breeding records, she could pass a sleepless hour or two trying to figure out which mares the black stallion should cover.

She closed the black ledger and put away the pen, then began rummaging through the lower drawers of the desk. In the bottom drawer she found another black bound book. She set it on the desk and opened it.

From the moment she'd seen Lucas's meticulous account ledger, she'd known he'd put equal care into recording the lineages of his horses. And there they were, gracefully branching family trees, pages of breeding dates and foaling dates, all the information he'd need to plan his next generation of foals.

She noticed with a smile that Prince, Lucas's herd stallion, the horse Jed Culbert referred to as Lucifer, went by the full name Prince Charming.

Going through Lucas's desk, she felt almost as if she were getting to know her cousin. She saw Lucas's pride in his ranch in his attention to detail, his love for his wife and son in the little gifts recorded in his ledger. She'd already learned from Jane's wardrobe that her cousin's wife favored warm colors, russets and reds, oranges and browns, sunflower yellows. And that she had a neat hand for mending and never wasted a scrap of material—Maggie recognized the silks and cottons of Jane's dresses in her quilts and cheerful pillows.

She guessed Jane had named Prince Charming. Guessed

she and her husband had laughed about it. Her first night here, Maggie had been afraid of ghosts. But tonight, she could almost feel the warmth of the Penny family surrounding her. She didn't realize there were tears in her eyes until she brushed them away.

Sometimes she couldn't even remember what her father looked like, but now his image came back in a flash of clarity. And her mother, young and healthy. Her baby brother, his cheeks rosy, his pudgy hand in hers. Her father's death had shattered her family. Stephen could never pick up the pieces. And Langley had managed to destroy her dreams of a family of her own.

No, not Langley. Her own foolishness.

A soft noise from the hall snapped her back from Kentucky and childish dreams. She closed the breeding book and stuffed it back into its drawer. Her heart pounding, she jumped up from the desk and snatched at the first book her hand found on the bookshelf. She hadn't intended to snoop, but she didn't want to have to explain that to March at this time of night.

Of course, she might get lucky and it would be Wolf looking for a drink of water . . .

But it was March's voice that greeted her from the doorway.

"Maggie? I thought I heard noises down here. Are you all right?"

She turned. He stood just at the edge of the lamplight, his pale nightshirt half tucked into his hastily donned blue jeans. He moved into the living room, his bare feet quiet against the floorboards. He must have made noise on purpose coming down the hall, in order not to startle her.

"I'm fine," she said, her panic receding. "I just couldn't sleep. I came in here to get something to read."

Some of the worry smoothed away from his eyes as he neared. He glanced at the slim volume in her hand. "That's one of my favorites."

She looked down at the book and discovered to her relief that it was a volume of the Romantic poets. A treatise on botany would have taken some creativity to explain.

"You like poetry?" she asked, flipping open the book. The inscription on the title page caught her eye. It read, "To March, with all Christmas joy, your loving sister, Jane."

"This ignorant cowpoke's sister made him read every day of his childhood until he learned to like it."

"Then why don't you read something to me," she suggested, turning his teasing back on him. To her surprise, he took the book she thrust at him.

"What would you like to hear, ma'am?"

She made a show of thinking it over, adding to the amusement in his eyes. "Coleridge, I think. Yes, 'Kubla Khan' if you would, please."

It took him mere moments to find the place. He cleared his throat. " 'Kubla Khan,' by Samuel Taylor Coleridge. 'In Xanadu did Kubla Khan—' "

"Wait, let me get comfortable," Maggie ordered. She moved to the sofa and settled herself among Jane's pillows, tucking her feet up under her robe. "Okay. You may continue."

March moved over to the sofa and sat down on the rag rug in front of it, one arm on the cushion next to Maggie's feet.

"In Xanadu did Kubla Khan / A stately pleasure-dome decree," he began again. "Where Alph, the sacred river, ran / Through caverns measureless to man / down to a sunless sea."

As her initial surprise at having bluffed March into reading to her faded, Maggie slowly lost herself in the poetry. March's voice wrapped Coleridge's sensuous words and sinuous rhythms around her, drowning her in mighty fountains, in ancient forests, in the music of a dulcimer, which she heard clearly though she couldn't have said what a dulcimer might look like.

The music played on after he'd finished, mingling with the sound of the wind slipping past the house and her own breathing.

His fingers tapped the book. "It looks like you might be ready for sleep after all," he said.

"That was my favorite poem when I was younger," she said, yawning against the drug of the poetry. "I used to dream of caves of ice and poets drunk on honeydew."

"And what do you dream of now?"

The soft question brought her back to full waking. She pulled her feet from under her robe and put them on the cold, hard floor.

"Nothing," she said, wrapping her robe closer as the chill ran up her legs. "There isn't much point to dreams if they can't come true. Maybe I'm as dreamless as you are."

"I dream," he said, surprising her. He rose and looked down at her, his eyes dark in the lamplight. "I dream every night that Jane and Lucas and Logan will come back, that all of this is some crazy mistake and my life will return to normal. Since the day I came back and found them, I've been living in a nightmare. A nightmare so terrible that I can't wake up." Unpredictably, a wry smile touched his lips. "Sometimes I think you must be a dream, yourself."

"Why?" she asked.

"You're not the Cousin Meggsie that Lucas was expecting. The way he described her, she was a rebellious tomboy, a spoiled brat in pigtails." He paused, his eyes locked with hers. "But you're a grown woman. A woman as soft and sweet-smelling as any I ever met, but tougher to tame than an outlaw mustang. And beautiful. A woman like you doesn't belong in this brutal, violent nightmare."

His words burned like whiskey on new wounds. "Beautiful?" she repeated bitterly, turning her face away.

She felt him sit beside her on the sofa. His hand caught her chin, and this time he didn't let her pull away. He brushed the hair away from her face. His finger traced the line of her scar, from temple to jaw.

"Stop. Leave me alone," she commanded, unable on her own to break the prison of his gaze.

"Do you really think this hides your beauty?" he asked, sounding almost bewildered.

"It's ugly," she said, with the force of certainty. "I've never met anyone who didn't think so. It's the first—and last—thing people see when they look at me. Don't pretend you don't see it every time you look at my face."

He shook his head in frustration, both hands sliding to cup her face. "Don't tell me what I see when I look at you, Maggie. I see courage, and mischief, and beauty. And I see uncertainty, pain, and fear."

He dropped his hands. "I knew a woman once who lost most of her hair, running back into a burning house to rescue her child. It never really grew back. She never complained she was ugly, only said she'd been blessed by God to be able to rescue her baby. You don't think you're ugly just because of that scar. Someone did that to you on purpose. I'd like to know, Maggie, if you'll tell me."

She shook her head, finally able to drop her gaze to her lap. The morning after it happened, all the other children at school had clustered around her, and she'd told them a wolf had attacked her and one of his teeth had grazed her cheek. She'd been about the biggest hero the school had ever seen for two whole days, until Pete Brogan told everyone his dad said there weren't any wolves around Lexington and that she was a liar. Then Mary Lewis overheard her mother telling a friend that Maggie's stepfather had been the one to hit her.

After that, the most she'd ever got was pity. Poor, scarred Maggie. Not even her family wants her.

March's hands reached out for hers, wrapping around them, warm and secure.

"It's not much of a story," she said, focusing on his hands. Had he really said she was beautiful? "I came home from school one day when I was ten to find Stephen Casey, my stepfather, leading my pony Ladybug down the lane away from the house. I asked him what he was doing with her, and he said he was going to sell her. He said I spent too much time playing and reading and daydreaming, and maybe this would teach me not to forget to feed the chickens again."

Even now, eight years later, she couldn't help shaking with disbelief and anger. "I told him I hadn't forgotten the chickens all week. I told him I'd do all my chores on time for the rest of my life. My father gave me Ladybug. She was all I had left of him. Papa was dead. Brian was dead. Mama was sick in bed most of the time . . ."

March held her hands tightly. She couldn't free them to wipe the tears away. "He didn't listen. He told me I'd learn to mind and call him Pa, and maybe this would get my attention, since I didn't seem to pay any heed to anything else.

"I called him a murdering Yankee, the worst cuss word I knew, and grabbed his stirrup. I don't know what I thought I could do to him, but I know I had murder in my eyes. He hit me with his quirt, knocked me to the ground and rode away. I never saw Ladybug again."

"The bastard," March growled. "I've never even hit a

horse with a quirt. To use one on a little girl . . ." His voice ground to a stop.

"Hell, it was almost worth it," Maggie said, half-choking on sudden hysterical laughter. "Mama took one look at my face and told Stephen if he ever so much as laid a hand on me again, she'd leave him. He's never touched me once since then." She shook with dry sobs of laughter or tears.

March wrapped an arm around her and pulled her to him tightly. She rested her cheek against his shoulder, too tired to want to resist.

"He never had any power over me after that," she said, the words muffled by March's white cotton nightshirt. "Once he got rid of Ladybug, he didn't have any hold over me. I've made sure not to care about anything since."

He released her other hand to wrap her with both arms. His heart beat against her ear, and the warmth of his arms stole through her, smoothing away her tension. The red burn of her memories faded, leaving her quiescent.

Yet each nerve in her body hummed to some unheard music, and each beat of March's heart tuned her more tightly. Pressing her palm against his nightshirt, she could feel the imprint of the hairs on his chest. His breath stirred her unbound hair.

An emotion like fear rippled through her, fear he might kiss her. But he only held her, coiling her like a spring. And then she feared he might not kiss her.

He'd told her she was beautiful, but perhaps he meant it only as a kindness. He would gentle a frightened horse or an injured child as simply as he held her now. Perhaps he didn't feel the same rhythm of fire that pounded through her veins. If not, she didn't think she could bear his kindness.

Almost angrily, she moved in his arms, lifting her head from his shoulder to look up into his face. The flickering lamplight shadowed his eyes so she could read nothing there. He had frozen when she moved. Now his hand rose to brush against her cheek. His fingertips wove into the hair near her scar, and she leaned her cheek against his palm.

"You are a dream," he whispered, even as his other arm clutched her more tightly.

"Kiss me," she whispered back.

Chapter 9

He could do nothing less.

He ached with the reckless need to hold her close, to touch her, to assure himself of the flesh and blood existence of his dream, of this angel-demon whose kiss might steal his very soul.

He lowered his lips to hers. She tasted of sunshine and of moonlight, of redemption and damnation. And if he'd only meant to hold her, to comfort her, her soft request had broken every link in the chain of his control.

His hands ran through her hair, down her back, his palms pressing heat through her robe. She eased away from his chest, instinctively inviting him, and his hands slid around her sides, moving up to cup her breasts.

Maggie gasped. His touch set a wildfire deep within her that burned out of control. She trembled from the fierceness of her own desire.

March's mouth left hers to find the soft skin of her neck, even as his hands parted her robe, entering its warmth to brush her breasts through the silky thinness of her nightgown. His thumbs rubbed against her nipples, and his moan matched hers as the soft pink nubs hardened beneath his touch.

Maggie pulled her hands back to the front of his nightshirt, fumbling with the buttons to expose his chest. Light played across the bronzed muscles, and she touched him with her fingertips, running them over the warm skin. She touched him as though she could draw his essence from his skin, draw him into herself to ease the ache of loneliness.

"Maggie . . ." he breathed against the sensitive skin below her ear, lowering his mouth to one of her breasts.

She arched beneath his touch. To know he pleasured her drove him to a need greater than any he'd ever felt before. He wanted to bury himself in her warmth, wanted to make her cry out in ecstasy.

He slid his hand down the gossamer nightgown, over her belly, pausing at the juncture between her legs.

His fingers pressed between her thighs, sliding against the heat building there. Maggie wanted to tell him to stop, to stop torturing her, to never stop the sweet torture of his touch. But she could not find the breath to speak.

He released her to slip his hand down her calf. Finding the hem of her gown, he began raising it up over her legs, but it had caught somehow on the leg of the sofa. Lost to patience, March tugged on the material, then yanked, ripping the gown in two from hem to thigh.

The sound of the cloth tearing split through Maggie's brain like a rifle firing. The world lurched beneath her, throwing her back to Lexington, back to her last meeting with Langley Fitzgibbon.

"Langley, you can't let Stephen send me away. I thought . . . I thought you wanted to marry me."

"Marriage?" Langley's laughter. "To you?"

"But . . . We . . . We've been together. You compromised my honor. You have to marry me."

"Don't try to threaten me. You're a two-bit slut, and if you start making things difficult for me, I'll make sure everyone knows it."

"I was a virgin, Langley! You damn well know it!"

"And who's going to believe your word over mine, Maggie? Everyone knows you're trouble. Don't make a fuss. It was fun,

*while it lasted. And you enjoyed it, don't deny it. No hard feel-
ings?"*

"*You low-down, dirty, son—*"

"*You're best when you're feisty, Maggie. C'mon. One more
time between friends.*"

"*You're not my friend, Langley. I swear, if I get half a chance,
I'll kill you. I'll run you through with—*"

*And then his hands on her, rough, powerful. Pawing her, his
mouth coming down on hers. Her fists striking at him, but without
enough room to do any damage, his arms pinning hers to her sides.
Touching her, hurting her. Pawing at the front of her bodice. The
sound of fabric tearing . . .*

"Stop it! Let me go!" She flailed with arms suddenly free,
hitting his head, his shoulders, choking on fear and rage. She
had to reach her knife, stuck securely in her boot top for
emergencies. But she wasn't wearing her boots. She was in
her nightgown.

"Maggie, hush, don't fight. God, I'm sorry. Please, Maggie."

Not Langley's voice. March. He'd pulled away from her,
catching her hands with his to keep her from striking him.

Not Langley. She was safe in Colorado. Safe with March.

Safe? She shook, her breath coming in ragged sobs.

"Maggie, Maggie, I'm sorry. You're all right. It will be all
right."

He still held her hands. She looked into his face, his eyes
black with worry. His breath came as forced and painful as
hers.

"March . . ." She could barely hear her own whisper above
the roaring in her ears. "I'm so sorry. I'm so sorry."

"No." His voice, firm, commanding, held her together.
"It's my fault. You didn't know . . . what you were getting
into. I shouldn't have lost control."

She couldn't laugh at the irony; she couldn't breathe. All the times she'd said she didn't care what people thought of her burned on her tongue like acid. She couldn't tell March what had upset her, because she couldn't bear it if that warmth went out of his eyes, couldn't bear it if contempt or disgust were all she saw when he looked at her. The contempt and disgust she felt for herself were enough.

"March? Miss Maggie?" Wolf's voice, thin with anxiety, broke the electric silence of the night. "Are you all right?"

Looking over the back of the sofa, Maggie saw the boy standing in the hallway, a dark-eyed wraith in a white nightshirt clutching March's Colt revolver in both hands, its muzzle pointed toward the ground. She pulled her robe tightly around her.

"What's wrong, Wolf?" March asked, dropping Maggie's hands. His voice was low, but controlled.

"I heard Miss Maggie screaming. I thought the rustlers had come back."

"It's all right, Wolf. Miss Maggie . . ." March stopped, looking back at Maggie.

She held her right hand out over the back of the sofa toward the boy. "I'm fine, Wolf. It was just a nightmare, that's all."

Wolf's shoulders sagged with relief. He walked over to the sofa, the revolver now dangling from one hand.

"When I was little, I had nightmares there was a monster hiding under my bed," he said. "Did you walk out here in your sleep? Emmy walks in her sleep, and I have to keep watch for it, 'cause I'm a light sleeper. I found her all the way out behind the chicken coop once."

Maggie shook her head, trying not to smile at the boy's solicitousness. She was afraid if she did, she'd cry.

"I fell asleep reading on the sofa," she explained. "I

couldn't sleep before, so I came out here for a book. I guess I was more tired than I thought."

Wolf nodded solemnly.

"Now that you're satisfied that Maggie's safe," March said, "perhaps you'll tell me what you think you're doing with my revolver."

Wolf looked down at the gun in his hand, as though surprised to see it still there. "When I heard Miss Maggie screaming, I went to wake you up. You weren't in your bed, and I was afraid the rustlers had gotten you, too."

"A gun isn't a toy, son."

"I know."

"If you let your imagination run away with you when you're holding a gun, someone could get seriously hurt."

The boy straightened his shoulders. "I know how to handle a gun," he said, hurt. "It's not cocked, and I know not to point it at anything unless I want to kill it. I couldn't come down here without it, in case somebody was hurting you or Miss Maggie."

March's face softened. "You did just fine, Wolf. But one gun isn't going to be much good against a gang of outlaws. If trouble comes while you and Maggie are staying here, I'm going to need you to sneak out of the house and run for help."

Wolf looked down at the gun. "I'm a good shot, and I'm not yellow. I wouldn't leave you . . ."

"If nobody goes to the barn to warn Lem or gets the news to Jed out at the farm, lots more people could get hurt. It's a dangerous job, but you're the only one small enough and quiet enough to do it. You understand?"

Wolf nodded slowly, his eyes already darkening with plans of just how he'd escape the bad guys and spread the alarm. Maggie bit back a smile of admiration at March's tactics. They worked because he meant every word.

"Wolf, could you do me a favor?" she asked.

"Sure, Miss Maggie. Anything."

"Could you light the other lamp in my room? And maybe just take a peak and make sure there's nothing lurking under the bed?"

He nodded. "You wait here just a minute."

"And, Wolf," March called after him as the boy headed for the hall, "then you put my Colt back right where you found it."

"Okay."

March took Maggie's hand again as they listened to the boy's feet pad down the hall, leaving them behind in silence.

Maggie looked down at her hand, small and pale wrapped in March's browned, callused one. She couldn't pull away. She couldn't even hate the weakness that made her want to ease back into his embrace; emotional exhaustion had drained her.

"Are you sure you're all right?"

She looked up into March's eyes, pools of black ringed with summer blue. She couldn't remember what all right might feel like. If March was living a nightmare since his sister's death, she felt as if she had, in coming here, briefly escaped from one.

"I'm fine," she said wearily.

"You don't need to be afraid," he told her, his voice urgent and tight. "I promised . . . not to hurt you. I can't change what I did tonight. But it won't happen again. I won't touch you again. I promise."

I asked you to kiss me. I wanted you. But she said nothing. Nothing she could say would change her past or take the pain from March's heart. Friday she would leave. Better to leave with as few regrets as possible.

She let him help her to her feet and lead her down the hall.

Soft lamplight spilled from her doorway. She had asked Wolf to check for monsters as a gentle joke, but the emptiness of the room made her shiver.

"I won't come down again tonight," March said awkwardly.

With the fearlessness of the condemned, Maggie put a hand around his jaw and kissed him on the cheek.

"I'm not afraid of you," she whispered. She dropped his hand to enter her room, and it was like relinquishing a lifeline.

March blew out the lamp he'd carried from the living room and felt his way up the stairs in the dark. Making his way to his bed, he fumbled with the buttons of his jeans, shocked to find his hands were shaking.

He could still feel the warmth of Maggie's hands, still taste the sweet depths of her mouth. He wanted nothing more than to bury himself inside her, feel her heat surround him, watch desire darken her emerald-flecked eyes.

How in hell was he going to keep his promise not to touch her now that he knew how it felt, knew how eagerly she could respond? But he had to keep it. Because if he hurt her, if he made her scream again, if he took her body and her reputation without offering anything in return, he wouldn't be able to live with himself.

Only four more days. Only four more days until she was gone and the nightmare his life had become would begin all over again.

Chapter 10

Maggie broke into a fast jog, glancing over her shoulder to watch Ari. The mare followed at an easy trot, her ears pricked eagerly, her feet skimming the bare ground in front of the barn. Maggie took her in a circle left, then right, watching the mare's stride for any weakness.

Maggie came to a halt finally, easily tired under the hot afternoon sun, but Ari still breathed calmly, showing no hint of unsoundness.

"I knew you'd be all right. I told March he'd be glad to have you," Maggie murmured exultantly, stroking Ari's nose. The mare pushed against her hand, blowing gently. "I know, you want to go for a real ride. Maybe this evening, when it's not so hot. Right now, I better see about starting supper. Wolf's spending the afternoon with his family, so maybe I can try some peppers in the stew. It's no wonder that boy's so thin, considering everything he won't eat."

Ari's ears twitched, and she nodded her head, perfectly happy to agree with Maggie as long as she got to walk around outside. But as they neared the stable door, the mare's head drooped, and she tripped over a nonexistent rock.

Maggie laughed. "Now don't look insulted. I promised a ride after supper; you'll just have to wait."

The sound of hoofbeats turned both their heads toward the drive. A single rider approached them, riding a coffee-colored bay.

For once it was the man and not his horse that held Maggie's attention. Not for his size, though he probably topped six feet, or his looks, for she couldn't see much of him behind the broad brim of his hat and the enveloping folds of his black duster. It was the way he held himself that froze her in her tracks and made her wish Lemuel hadn't taken his shotgun with him when he'd gone into town for supplies.

The horse stopped a good thirty feet from where she stood with Ari, and the man dismounted. From the dust that covered his coat and his horse, she'd have guessed he'd ridden quite some ways that day, but no stiffness showed in his stride as he walked toward her.

He moved with a feline grace that made Maggie feel as if she were being stalked by a mountain panther. He walked with a soft step and the wary confidence of a creature expecting at any moment to have to prove himself against another animal's teeth and claws.

As he neared, he removed his hat, and she saw his thick hair matched the rich brown of his horse. His eyes, somewhere between green and gold, fixed on her with the curiosity of a predator who hasn't yet decided whether he's hungry.

"Afternoon, ma'am," he greeted her in a soft drawl. A man's shirt and a pair of jeans wouldn't hide her identity from those keen eyes. "I'm looking for March Jackson."

"He's busy," Maggie said, her voice louder than she'd intended. "I'm not sure exactly when he'll be back. What's your business with Mr. Jackson?"

March had taken the colts back to the north pasture. She didn't know what he was doing or when he'd be back. He had barely spoken to her at all this morning, and she'd been just as glad, since every time she heard his voice, it sent an unwanted, longing shiver through her.

She'd welcomed the thought of having the afternoon to herself. Until this stranger had arrived, she hadn't thought about how alone she really was.

He stopped two long strides from her, his weight balanced for quick movement. "I was hoping to find lodging here for the night."

"Lodging?"

"Yes, for myself and my horse."

"Mr. Jackson doesn't usually take in travelers." She didn't know if that was true, but she didn't think March would mind her saying it under the circumstances.

The man's face softened, though she wouldn't have called his expression a smile. "I think he'll take me, but I don't mind waiting outside until he gets back. May I put up my horse? I'd like to get his saddle off and give him some water."

Maggie cursed silently to herself. There was probably some unwritten, unbreakable code of the West that you had to take in strangers in need, even if they looked like a combination of Jesse James and Mephistopheles. At least if she let him take care of his horse, she could go into the house and get her derringer.

"I suppose you'd better give him something to eat, too," she said reluctantly.

"Thank you, ma'am."

"What's your name?" she asked, before he could turn back to his horse.

He smiled now, a smile that didn't light his eyes. "In the West, we generally wait for a man to volunteer his name, if he chooses to. Mine's Elijah Kelly."

She decided to save her sarcastic comments on that. "I'm Maggie Parker. There's an extra stall in the stable. I'll make sure there's straw in it for him."

"Much obliged, ma'am."

Despite the strong instinct not to let him out of her sight, she led Ari into the stable and settled the mare into her stall. She didn't remove Ari's halter. If the necessity arose, she

152

could ride bareback with the halter.

Then she got a stall ready for Elijah Kelly's horse. She'd put him in Balthasar's stall. That way, when March returned, he'd know something odd was going on.

"I've got to start supper," she told the tall stranger, giving him a wide berth as he led his horse into the stable. "You can sit on the porch if you like, when you're finished."

He nodded. "Thank you again." Then, almost as an afterthought. "March didn't leave you here at the ranch all by yourself, did he? Not after the killings here?"

"Of course not," Maggie lied, her stomach spinning at his words. "Lemuel and Wolf are around here somewhere."

The strange expression that crossed his face at that news didn't fill her with confidence.

She slipped out of the barn and hurried across the yard, her heart pounding, feeling an itch between her shoulder blades as though someone had drawn a target on her back. She'd never fired a gun in her life, but she knew in her bones that the smell of fire and brimstone that hung about Elijah Kelly was gunpowder.

She slammed the front door closed behind her and locked it but felt no relief. A little thing like a locked door wouldn't stop a determined killer. She ran down the hall, skidding through the door into her room. She dug frantically through her carpet bag, trembling fingers closing around the tiny derringer at the bottom.

She slipped it into the pocket of Jane's old leather vest. It bulged. It didn't fit into the pocket of her jeans. Finally, she slipped it under her belt and prayed it wouldn't fall out at an embarrassing moment.

"Okay, now what?"

She scooted to the window. She watched Elijah Kelly walk

out of the stable, his saddle bags thrown over his shoulder, a rifle in one hand and a violin case in the other.

"Maybe he likes a little fiddle music while dancing over the graves of his victims."

She edged back from the window. She'd told him she had to start supper; she might as well start it. For all his alarming mannerisms, if he'd wanted to kill her, he could have done it easily enough before now. If murder was his intent, she wasn't his target. She had to put aside her fear until she could think of a way to warn March.

One thing for sure, she didn't plan to change into her housekeeping dress. She might need all the mobility she could get.

She made her way back to the kitchen and scrubbed up at the sink. She could hear Kelly making himself comfortable in one of the chairs on the porch. She filled a glass with water, took a deep breath, and went to the door. She unlocked it and swung it open with her hip, keeping her hand free to reach for the derringer.

"Mr. Kelly? Would you like some water? There's some leftover bread, too, if you're hungry."

He slouched in his chair, his black hat tilted low over his eyes. He touched his hat brim to her and reached out a hand for the glass. " 'I was thirsty and you gave me drink.' Thank you, ma'am. This will do me fine for now. Don't trouble yourself over me."

Oh, no. Not much chance of that. "All right. If you need anything, call. I've got stew to make."

She locked the door behind her once more. Great. Now she was trapped in the ranch house with a gunman on her front porch and no way of knowing when March would come home.

First things first. She had to start the stew. She didn't want to make Elijah Kelly nervous. She set about cutting meat, chopping potatoes, carrots, and onions, going to great lengths to bang pots and clang the stove door. She mixed up dumpling batter, according to March's instructions. That was a quieter job, so she whistled "Dixie," hoping it would appeal to the southern gentleman resting outside.

By the time she had the stew bubbling cheerfully on the stove, the dumplings ready to go in later, and the mess cleaned up, her nerves had stretched to near breaking. March might want to avoid her, but she felt she knew him well enough to know he wouldn't put everyone else out by being late for supper. Which meant he'd be coming home within the next half hour.

She could keep an eye on Kelly, make sure she was near him when March showed up. She could drill him with the derringer if he tried anything funny. But the derringer held only two bullets, and she wasn't even sure how to tell if it was loaded, much less how to fire it into a killer's heart.

She untied her floury apron and put it away.

"Mr. Kelly?" she called through the window that over-looked the porch.

"Yes, ma'am?"

"I'm going to change for supper. Mr. Jackson should be home any minute."

"I'll be here."

She hurried down the hall until she reached the stairs to the loft. With a nervous glance over her shoulder, she started up the stairs. If Wolf had found March's revolver so easily in the dark last night, she should be able to tell quickly if March had taken it with him this afternoon.

He hadn't. The holster hung over one bedpost, the dark stock of his Colt gleaming in a slanting beam of sunlight.

"Damn." If *her* family had been murdered a month ago,

she wouldn't have gone anywhere without a gun. "Damn! Damn! Damn!"

She couldn't very well let March ride into a potential ambush unarmed. She had to get out of here, and that was that. She pulled March's holster from the bedpost and buckled it around her waist. She couldn't make it small enough to be comfortable, but her hips kept it from sliding off.

Cautiously, she climbed back down the stairs. Her bedroom window slid open without a sound. Awkwardly, she scrambled through. Her foot caught on the sill, sending her tumbling to the ground head first. She lay in the dirt, trying to breathe, trying to hear through the ringing in her ears.

A sound came from the porch. Whistling. "Yankee Doodle."

"Very funny," Maggie muttered, pushing herself to her feet. She took a deep breath, ignoring the pain in her side, and trotted toward the back of the stable. Kelly shouldn't be able to see her from his position sitting on the far side of the porch. As long as he didn't get up and wander around, she'd be fine. She broke into a run.

Bolting around the end of the stable, she moved along the wall to the side door. Inside, soft nickers welcomed her, enveloping her with familiar safety. She could sneak up to Lemuel's room and hide. Kelly would never find her there. And if he did think to come looking, she'd meet him with March's revolver.

Elijah Kelly was no business of hers. She was just a green city girl, thrust into this unpleasant situation against her will. This wasn't her fight or her land to defend. She'd come to Colorado under protest, and her goal since before she'd arrived had been to get back home.

Memories flashed at her. Shelby Brennan's big hands pawing her. March's hand splattered with Brennan's blood.

March shaking his head in exasperation, letting her stay on at the ranch instead of sending her to the Culberts. March holding her last night, telling her she was beautiful. He'd almost made her feel beautiful.

She put a hand on the Colt and made her way down to Ari's stall.

"You're going to get that ride before supper, after all," she whispered. She should be taking Honey or even Pamela, horses she'd ridden and knew she could count on. But she hadn't brought the others in from the corral yet, and she couldn't risk causing a fuss among the horses, trying to halter one.

She looked into Ari's eager eyes, and knew she would have chosen the buckskin anyway. Pamela was barely fast enough to outrun Kelly, much less his bay gelding, and she still considered Honey Jane Penny's horse. From the moment Ari had eaten that first sodden hunk of grass out of her hand, she'd thought of the mare as hers.

"Besides, you used to belong to an Indian princess. You know what to do in these situations." She couldn't even smile at her own joke. She felt sick to her stomach.

She led Ari to the side door, clutching March's revolver in her free hand. No sign of Kelly, though each moment that passed stretched into danger. She pulled Daisy's milking stool from the corner and used it to vault onto Ari's back, the mare's only protest a surprised snort.

Maggie clutched the halter rope and a great hunk of the buckskin's mane in both hands and tried to whisper a prayer. *Please, God, let March be coming in from the north pasture.*

"All right, Aristotle. Let's see what you've got."

March lifted his hat and wiped his damp hair back with his forearm. A swim in the Little Owl River after a long day of working with the colts had refreshed him, but already the dust and heat of the ride back to the ranch made him feel as if he could use another bath when he arrived.

Balthasar snorted and shook his head, bringing a wry smile to March's face. He settled his hat low over his eyes.

"You ready to get home?"

Balthasar rarely displayed impatience, but March had struggled with a reluctance to return to the ranch all afternoon; he wasn't surprised to see it translate into frustration on the part of his horse. He'd had a way with horses as long as he could remember. He could almost feel the telepathic energy that traveled back and forth along the reins.

He forced himself to relax into the saddle, ease his death grip on the reins. He felt Balthasar relax in sympathy. A nudge sent the gelding into a gentle trot.

"No point in trying to avoid the inevitable," March agreed with him. "I have to face her again sometime."

Dread had gripped him upon waking this morning. He hadn't known whether to expect Maggie to snub him or attack him or withdraw in fear and embarrassment. He deserved any and all of them. Shame threatened to drown him when he thought of the way he'd taken advantage of her vulnerability, her need for comfort.

But at breakfast she'd just been Maggie, by turns teasing and prickly, ruffling Wolf's hair as she poured the coffee. March considered all of the Culbert clan part of his own family, but Maggie and Wolf seemed to have developed a relationship just as close in only a few short days, almost as though they sensed a kindred spirit between them.

Knowing more of Maggie's history, March could see better where that kinship came from. They had both found themselves outsiders. Maggie unable to please her stepfather. Wolf too sensitive not to feel different, set apart, in spite of the unconditional love Jed and Henna showered on him.

Maggie had a way of making the boy feel included, needed. It hadn't occurred to March until last night that she might need to be needed as much as Wolf did. Perhaps that was all that had prompted her response to his kiss. Though the memory of the fire in her eyes haunted him.

He hadn't seen that fire this morning. Of course, he hadn't dared to look into her eyes for fear she'd see the burning in his. She'd acted a little shy, perhaps—if such a word could be used to describe Maggie Parker—but she'd shown no indications of hating him.

Which meant that his fear of facing her again this evening had less to do with fear of her reaction to him than of his own reactions to her. Since Jane's murder, he'd only had room in his heart for revenge. Yet Maggie made him forget his plans of vengeance for hours at a time.

Even in the paddock today, working with unruly, intact colts, where lack of concentration could result in a painful reminder of their strength, he'd been unable to keep Maggie from invading his imagination. Just the sound of her voice . . .

"March! March!"

He brought Balthasar to a halt and rubbed a hand across his eyes. No, even his imagination could not have come up with a picture quite so fanciful as the one that appeared on the crest of the next hill. His smile froze on his lips as he realized that something must be very wrong.

Not that it would surprise him to discover that Maggie enjoyed riding bareback without a bridle, her braid flying out behind her like a flame. But she wouldn't let anyone catch her at it. If she needed him for anything less than an emergency, she'd saddle up, and she'd wear her hat.

Instinctively, he patted his hip. No Colt. All he had was his rifle.

Idiot. One more thing that had slipped his mind this morning, thanks to a soft kiss last night.

He sent Balthasar into a gallop, reaching Maggie seconds later. "What's wrong?"

She only shook her head, trying to catch her breath.

"Is it Lem? Has he been hurt?"

She shook her head again. "No, he's not back from town yet. At least, I hope not. March, a stranger came to the ranch looking for you. He's . . . he doesn't . . . I think he might be a gunfighter."

March's fists clenched on his reins. "What makes you say that?"

"First it was the way he moves. And he's dressed all in black. And he smells like gunpowder. He says he wants to ask you for a place to stay tonight."

"Where is he now?"

"I made him stay out on the front porch, then I sneaked out my bedroom window. It might be nothing, but I didn't want to take the chance. I brought you your gun."

He almost smiled, though the thought of the danger she'd put herself in turned him cold. "Only Maggie."

He took the gun belt she held out to him and buckled it around his waist.

"We can circle to the road and go into town for help," she said. "We'll probably catch Mr. Tate on the road."

"You go do that," March agreed, checking the cylinder of his revolver to make sure it was full.

"What do you mean, 'you'? You're not going back to the ranch by yourself to confront this man?"

He didn't have to look at her to know her expression. "Go to Jed Culbert. You should be safe there. I'm not sure who to trust in town."

"You're a goddamn fool, March Jackson!" Her eyes

160

blazed when he finally met them. "Do you lead a double life I don't know about as a quickdraw expert, or are you just planning to get yourself killed and get it over with?"

"I know how to fire a gun." His calm reply didn't turn down the fire in her gaze. But he wanted her mad. Better mad at him and riding to safety than risking danger in a foolish attempt to protect him.

"Maggie, it doesn't take eleven gunmen to kill a peaceful rancher and his family, but that's how many attacked Jane and Lucas. The men who murdered them wouldn't have the guts to face me except as a group. If this man in black is connected to them, he's only here to make me an offer or bring a warning. Most likely both.

"He won't want to kill me. And I'll do my best not to make him have to. Satisfied?"

Her fists clenched in Ari's mane. "I'm glad you find my concern amusing."

"Don't worry about me, Maggie. It'll only bring you grief." At his subtle command, Balthasar surged into a canter toward the ranch.

"Idiot."

Ari turned her head to focus one big brown eye on Maggie.

"No, Ari, I don't know why he'd think I'd just follow orders and go to the Culberts. Anyone that muleheaded needs all the help he can get."

At the touch of Maggie's heels, Ari leaped into motion, no hint of the trauma she'd endured the week before showing in her stride. In spite of Maggie's trepidation about Elijah Kelly, she couldn't help feeling a glow of pride and pleasure in the mare's smooth gait and quick responses.

She held Ari to the same ground-eating canter as Balthasar, following at a safe distance all the way to the gate in the north pasture fence. Only after he'd unlatched the gate did March glance over his shoulder and see her. He scowled.

"You said there wasn't any danger," she reminded him.

"I didn't say there wasn't any danger," he growled. "I said I didn't think this man would want to kill me. Get the hell out of here."

"And let my stew burn?" She sent Ari through the gate.

She heard March curse as he fumbled with the latch behind her. In another second, Balthasar was beside her and March had grabbed Ari's halter.

Maggie dropped from Ari's back to the hardpacked yard. "Help me back through the window," she said, keeping her voice low. "I promise not to interfere with your negotiations with Wild Bill out there. And if he shoots you, I'll hide until help comes."

"You are the stubbornest damn fool . . ."

Unless he wanted to shoot her himself, he didn't have many choices. Still, she breathed a sigh of relief when he swung to the ground instead of reaching for his Colt.

He grabbed her arm and shoved her toward the house, leading the horses with his other hand.

"I'm beginning to think I could spare Lem for the two days he'd be gone if he took you to the train in Greeley," March hissed.

Maggie snorted. "The ranch would fall apart around your ears without me and Mr. Tate."

"It would be worth it."

They reached the house. March knelt, offering her his knee, and Maggie climbed back through the window.

"Now, stay there," March ordered. "I'll leave the horses here. If you hear gunfire, run. Do you think you can manage that?"

Maggie's snide reply died on her lips as she remembered

Elijah Kelly's piercing eyes. "March?"

Impatiently, he turned back to the window. "Yes?"

"Be careful."

Eyes as cold as arctic ice softened momentarily. "I promise."

He slipped around the back of the house, and Maggie realized he intended to come at the stranger from the opposite direction of the noise of the arriving horses. Surely Kelly must have heard them, though he hadn't shown himself from the porch. Maybe he'd gotten tired of waiting and left.

Still, Maggie moved stealthily as she made her way to the kitchen. Whatever March had said, she couldn't stay in the bedroom waiting for shots to be fired.

She pulled the derringer from her belt. It didn't have the satisfying heft of March's revolver, but it looked reassuringly deadly in her hand.

She crept to the porch window, hunching below it. She strained her ears, but no sounds betrayed the presence of either the gunfighter or March. She forced herself to remain hidden. She'd make no move unless absolutely necessary. If the dark stranger threatened March, she'd open the window and shoot him in the head.

The thought made her a little sick.

A creak from the porch broke the silence, the sound of a man shifting in an old chair.

Then, abruptly, March's voice. "I'll be damned."

Chapter 11

"I wouldn't be at all surprised." Elijah Kelly's slow drawl came from just outside the window.

" 'Lije Kelly. You son-of-a-bitch."

"Pleasure to see you, too, March."

March's laughter shocked Maggie's ears. "Damn. I should have known it was you, 'Lije. But it's been so long."

"Too long."

Significant silence. But Maggie had heard enough to realize that March was in no danger from Elijah Kelly. She tucked the derringer back into her belt with shaking hands. Only a fury born of deep humiliation kept her from crying in relief.

Her legs wobbled as she stood, but she made it to the door. Slowly, deliberately, she unlocked it and pulled it open. The two men at the end of the porch turned to look at her.

"I take it you two know each other," she said, with what she felt was heroic calm.

March had the lack of sense to smile at her. "Maggie, this is Elijah Kelly. He's an old friend. He and Lucas and I go back a long way."

"Near ten years, isn't it, kid?"

"Close to it. I . . . Maggie, are you all right? You don't look well. I'm sorry he frightened—"

"You're a friend of March and you didn't say anything?" The words burst from her without warning, directed at the black-clad figure she'd been ready to shoot moments before. "You scared me half to death with that talk about me being all alone here, and all the time you're a family friend?"

Elijah Kelly removed his hat, looking chagrined. "I'm sorry I frightened you, ma'am. But you'd hardly have shown any sense if you'd believed I was a friend of March, not after the trouble out here. I couldn't see March trusting you with his broncos if you didn't have any sense."

"And you, Mr. Jackson," she turned blazing eyes on March, "if you'd mentioned you had friends who looked like villains out of a dime novel, I wouldn't have half killed myself trying to get out and warn you about him."

Elijah's eyebrows rose. "Dime novel?"

"She didn't mean it."

"I did so mean it, March Jackson." She stopped, breathing heavily, unable to think of anything appropriately scathing to add. "If the two of you have had your fun today, you can wash up in the trough like the little boys you are. I've got dumplings to make."

The door slammed with a satisfying bang.

March made a move to follow her, but Elijah put a hand on his arm.

"You might want to give her time to cool off a bit. That one's got quite a temper."

March couldn't stop a smile. "You don't know the half of it. I suspect we're lucky to have gotten off with our lives. Let's wash up, and you can tell me why you're here."

The gunfighter's eyes went flat, yellow as a predatory panther's. "I heard about Lucas and Jane. And Logan."

March felt the familiar constriction of his chest. "I should have been with them."

"And what good would that have done? Lucas knew you'd have been willing to die with him."

In silence they left the porch and crossed to the horse

trough. March worked the pump for Elijah, then they traded places.

Pushing back painful memories with the shock of cold water, March managed another smile.

"I *am* glad to see you. A face from the Texas days, someone who knew Lucas and Jane back then." Sharing the grief with others wouldn't lessen its weight, but it made it easier to carry.

"I bet you weren't half as glad to see me as I was to see you," Elijah said. "I was sure your Miss Parker was going to drill me with that little parlor gun of hers before you got a chance to let her know I was harmless."

"Parlor gun?" He let the "harmless" comment pass.

"The derringer she tucks into her belt."

Elijah had as sharp an eye for guns as March had for horses. Still, March felt a surge of irrational jealousy at the thought that his friend had noticed something about Maggie that he'd missed.

"I was relieved she went to find you instead of taking me out herself." Elijah rubbed the back of his head protectively.

March looked over his friend's disreputable black duster, the silver toes on his scuffed boots, the thick damp hair that needed a trim. "I can understand why Maggie ran for help. You look like the devil himself, 'Lije."

"So much for Henna's theory that I'd be more socially acceptable if I went unarmed."

March had noted the absence of his friend's gunbelt. He raised an eyebrow.

Elijah shrugged. "In my saddlebags. It's a long story."

They'd reached the door of the house, but paused at the sound of a wagon. Pamela trotted jauntily down the drive.

"It's Lem," March said, unnecessarily. The big black man was unmistakable, hunched comfortably on the wagon seat.

"He'll be glad to see you."

"Not so many people you could say that about."

March glanced at his friend, but if there had been wistfulness in his tone, his eyes didn't show it. March ushered him through the door.

Maggie must have heard them enter, but she didn't turn around. While he and Elijah washed up outside, she'd changed into a dark blue silk dress that brought out the fire in her hair. She'd pinned her red curls into a loose chignon at the back of her head that left tendrils dangling down her neck, curling against the deep blue like tongues of flame. The white apron she wore should have given her a domestic, matronly look, but it only emphasized her untamed hair and the trimness of her waist.

March thought about brushing aside a stray curl, kissing the soft skin just behind her ear.

Elijah nudged him.

He cleared his throat. "We've washed up," he said, feeling like a chastened schoolboy. "Is there something we can do to help?"

She glanced over her shoulder, a flash of green in her eyes. "Why don't you bring in Mr. Kelly's things and show him where he's going to stay tonight. By the time you're through, supper should be ready. I heard Mr. Tate arrive, so there's no reason to wait."

Elijah slipped past him to the door. "I don't have much; I can get it." He returned with a pair of saddlebags slung over his shoulder, his rifle and violin case carried protectively in either hand.

March led him up to the loft and pulled out the cot folded under his bed.

"I'll take the cot tonight, you take the bed, 'Lije."

Elijah set his things on the floor. "I'll take you up on that. I can't remember the last time I slept in a bed, especially one without bugs."

March found an old blanket and an extra pillow and tossed them on the cot. He'd have preferred to bed down on the sofa in the living room, but he didn't need the temptation of sleeping alone downstairs with only a short hallway separating him from Maggie's door.

"She's sure something."

March frowned at his friend. He'd forgotten Elijah's annoying ability to read his mind. "Who?" he asked, belligerently enough to discourage most people from continuing.

"Your Maggie. Smart, brave, easy on the eyes. Just what you need."

"Maggie is not mine," March corrected him. "She's Lucas's cousin. She didn't know he'd died when she came out here. She's only staying on until the next stage comes through."

"She's not spoken for? Is that a fact. Then you don't mind if I try a little southern charm on the lovely lady?"

March ground his teeth. There was no mistaking the amusement in his friend's eyes. "It's no damn wonder people are always shooting at you, 'Lije."

Elijah's laughter filled the room.

Maggie poked a fork at the puffy white lumps floating in the stew. March hadn't told her how long the dumplings took to cook, and she didn't want them to be mushy, especially not for her first meal cooked for company. Not that she would have chosen a gunfighter for company.

She heard laughter from the hall and poked again more savagely. She could just imagine they were laughing at her. Climbing out windows, waving guns around, looking like a fool.

"Just call me Belle Starr."

"Pardon me, Miss Maggie?"

Lemuel Tate's deep voice made her jump back, her hand over her heart. He stood next to the door, one hand still on the hat he'd placed on the hat rack.

"Ah'm sorry. I didn't mean to startle you."

"That's all right, Mr. Tate. I just didn't hear you come in." She smiled at the old man, though her pulse still pounded. "I was concentrating too hard on these dumplings. Can you tell me whether or not they're cooked through?"

"Sure can. Stew smells mighty good, Miss Maggie." He moved to the stove and made a show of examining the dumplings. "I'd have to say them dumplings look good enough to eat."

"Thank you, Mr. Tate, you've eased my mind." She pulled off her apron and tossed it next to the sink, then smoothed back her hair before pulling a handful of silverware from a drawer. "As soon as everyone gets here, we can start supper."

Lemuel lifted plates down from the cupboard. "Everyone? I thought Wolf was spendin' the evenin' with his folks."

Maggie wrinkled her nose. "He is. A friend of March's arrived on the doorstep this afternoon looking for a place to stay for the night. You better get down another plate."

She heard boots coming down the hall, but she didn't look up until she heard Elijah Kelly's voice.

"Lem Tate. So, you're still alive, old man."

She glanced over at Lemuel, surprised to see his delighted smile.

"Why, bless my soul if it ain't Preacher Kelly!" Lemuel towered over even the tall Elijah as he gave the man a hearty thump on the back.

The napkins Maggie held fluttered to the floor. Just how

big of a fool had she made of herself? She looked from Lemuel to Elijah to March. "He's a preacher?"

Elijah looked almost embarrassed. "No, ma'am. My father's the minister in the family. It's just a nickname I picked up."

"You should hear him quote the Bible, Miss Maggie," Lemuel said. "He's a proper devil, all right, but there's music in his soul."

" 'For false Christs and false prophets will arise,' " Elijah intoned, " 'and show great signs and wonders so as to lead astray, if possible, even the elect.' "

"If the apocalypse arrives this evening, I'd have to say we'd all be in trouble," March observed dryly. "But I'm still hungry."

The men converged on the table like vultures. Conversation ceased while they focused on supper. Maggie noted with some pride that she was not the only one to help herself to seconds of the stew and dumplings. It was hard to stay angry at folks who took such pleasure in her food.

"I'll take care of the dishes," March volunteered. "Why don't you get your fiddle, 'Lije, and play something for us."

"I play the violin," Elijah said, obviously a worn response to a long-running joke. "And I'll play. If you'll sing for us, March," he added, his face a study in innocence.

"We'll let March tap his foot now and then," Lemuel said hastily. "I'll sing, and so will Miss Maggie. She's got a right pretty voice."

Maggie's cheeks colored at the unexpected compliment. "You're very kind, Mr. Tate, but you and Wolf are the ones with real gifts. It's too bad Wolf's not here tonight; he's so fond of music."

"Wolf?" Elijah asked, intensity coiling around him like a snake.

"Yes, Wolf Culbert," Maggie said, wondering at the strained expressions March and Lemuel wore. "Do you know the Culberts? Their son Wolf is staying here at the ranch this week, as a sort of chaperone for me."

In the cold silence, Maggie heard a raven call in the distance.

"Maggie," March said quietly, setting his dishes by the sink. "Wolf's not a Culbert."

She stared at him. Everything that had happened in the past twenty-four hours had begun to make her feel just the slightest bit mad. But she could have sworn she wasn't this far gone.

"Wolf," she repeated slowly, "isn't a Culbert?"

"No, he's not," March said, still quiet, but fixing her with his gaze. "Of course, you'd get that impression . . ."

"He introduced himself to me as Wolf Culbert!" she insisted.

Elijah's chair scraped sharply as he pushed himself away from the table. "I guess I'd better pay my respects to Henna and Jed before it gets too late."

Maggie opened her mouth, saw March's expression, and changed what she'd been about to say. "You are friends with the Culberts, then, Mr. Kelly?"

He pushed back his thick, dark hair and settled his hat on his head. He didn't quite smile. "I wouldn't put it that way. Henna Culbert doesn't much approve of me."

Maggie didn't quite smile back. "We have something in common, after all."

He gave a short, dry laugh. "I won't ask if you mean you and I or you and Henna. March, thank you for putting me up. I won't be late."

He opened the door on the twilight and was gone.

Lemuel hunched his shoulders and stretched them back,

171

grimacing. "I swear I can almost hear these old bones creak. Jes' as well we don't have music tonight, I guess. Maybe I'll find my bed a little early this evenin'."

"Sure you won't stay and sit awhile?" March asked.

The old man shook his head. "No, I got to take care of this rheumatism, or I'll be laid up all week. See you folks in the mornin'."

"Good night, Mr. Tate." Maggie walked him to the door. "You take care of yourself. March can't do without you."

Lemuel let himself out into the evening, and Maggie closed the door firmly behind him. She turned back to face March, her arms crossed over her chest.

"Wolf's not a Culbert?"

"No."

"Well." Maggie tried to come to terms with her shock. No, not shock, exactly. The first thing she'd noticed about Wolf was his hair, its deep, ruddy brown, dark even compared to Henna's cinnamon tresses, startling against the backdrop of the fair-haired Culbert children.

And Henna had said something about Wolf's father's creative imagination that hadn't quite fit with her image of Jed Culbert's open, amiable steadiness. Wolf seemed more reserved, thoughtful. He reminded her of March that way.

Maggie's stomach took a sudden, sickening swoop. She remembered the casual way March had of calling Wolf "son." No. March was too young, despite the lines of sun and grief on his face. And his dust-brown hair wasn't near as dark as Wolf's. Not March and Henna. Furious, helpless jealousy swirled through her.

"You don't need to look that way at me, Maggie. I'm sorry I didn't think to tell you. Everyone around here knows. Most of the time we just think of him as one of the Culberts, anyway . . . except when Elijah's here."

"And Elijah . . . ?"

"Is Wolf's father."

She struggled to hide her relief.

"I can hardly believe that," she confessed. "Henna and Elijah. I don't see it."

"What?" He stared at her, his eyes wide. "Oh. No, Wolf's mother was a friend of Henna's. She died in childbirth. At the time, Elijah didn't even know she'd been pregnant, so Henna and Jed agreed to take the baby."

He didn't have to spell out the details. Henna's friend had died giving birth to an illegitimate baby, without any family willing to step forward and take the child. Maggie began to understand Henna's concern for her reputation.

Henna would not be pleased that Elijah and Lemuel had left her and March alone for the evening.

She glanced at March, watching his muscles move beneath his faded blue work shirt as he finished clearing the table. She clenched a fist to keep herself from reaching for the same glass, brushing his hand with hers.

"I've heard Wolf call Henna and Jed 'Ma' and 'Pa,' " she said, taking a furtive step away from him.

"I guess it just seemed easier that way." He set the dishes to soak in the sink. "Wolf calls Elijah 'Father.' His mother named him Wolfgang and gave him the surname Kelly. Once he knew about it, 'Lije wanted it that way."

"I shouldn't have said anything about Wolf calling himself a Culbert," Maggie said unhappily. "I didn't mean to get him into trouble again."

March shook his head. "Elijah won't blame him for that. But Henna might not get off so easy."

March took his time drying his hands on the towel, using first one end, then the other. Maggie wondered if he felt as awkward as she did about finding themselves alone together for the evening.

"I'll think I'll work on some mending," she said, glad of the sudden inspiration.

Ranch work was hard on clothes, and Wolf especially seemed to pull a seam or tear a sleeve at least once a day. That ought to give her a safe occupation for an hour or so.

She hurried to her room for a needle and some thread she'd found in one of Jane's dresser drawers. As she made her way back to the living room, she saw that March hadn't left the kitchen. He was checking the fire in the stove, adding wood, though the room seemed warm enough to her already.

A more pressing problem confronted her as she stepped into the living area. The sofa. If she sat on the sofa, March might take it as an invitation to sit beside her. Just looking at it reminded her of March's kiss, the way he'd touched her last night. Desire fired along her nerves, quickening her breathing.

She couldn't sit on the sofa. But if she didn't, he might think she was angry about last night. He'd promised not to touch her again. She'd sat on the sofa the past three evenings. If she didn't tonight, he might think she didn't trust him.

She looked up as March's footsteps crossed to the living room.

"You take the sofa," he said, gesturing that direction. "I'll take a chair. It'll be safer that way."

Her chin notched a little higher. "I told you I wasn't afraid of you."

"The feeling isn't mutual."

Maggie reddened and dropped her eyes as pleasure rushed through her. He wanted her. Even after last night. Her scar and her swearing and her boldness—wilfulness, Stephen called it—didn't repulse him.

Of course, Langley had wanted her, too. She forced herself to think of that as she made her way to the sofa. He'd wanted her body and nothing else. Except maybe power, control. That last meeting, when he'd ripped her dress . . . If she hadn't managed to twist free long enough to get to her knife, he would have raped her.

He would have done it simply because he could get away with it. Who would believe her word against his when her own stepfather called her a shameless hoyden? Langley was the fair-haired son of the richest man in Lexington. It was no contest.

But March hadn't forced himself on her last night. He was being painfully careful not to pressure her tonight. And all she could think about was the feel of his lips on hers, his hands touching her. She'd never felt that way when she'd been with Langley, even though she'd thought she loved him.

She took a hard look at March out of the corner of her eye. She could no longer see the drunken, nondescript cowboy who had rescued her from The Golden Rose Saloon. Lamplight caught his tousled hair, highlighting the glimpses of gold and mahogany in what she'd thought to be a plain mouse brown. The lines that prematurely creased his face spoke of sorrow and sun and hard work, but she saw faded laughter around his mouth and good humor in the crow's feet around his eyes, eyes the color of the Kentucky sky reflecting rolling hills of bluegrass.

Her needle pricked her thumb, and she dropped her eyes back to her mending. When she'd fallen for Langley, she'd been a foolish child, infatuated with his good looks. She'd been in love with the idea of snaring the most eligible young man in Lexington and lording it over the girls who looked down on her and on her stepfather's social climbing. She couldn't pretend it was March's looks that had first attracted her, and she certainly didn't envy his social position.

"So why did you and Lucas and Jane move to Colorado from Texas?" she asked, breaking the strained silence, afraid to examine her feelings for March any more closely.

March pulled the mending basket over, sorting it for her.

"Lucas retired from the Rangers after he took a bullet in his leg that left him with a limp. This wasn't long after the war. Colorado seemed like a good place to start over, live a peaceful life."

He tugged at a seam, grunted when it held. "And Jane wanted to get Harry away from Pa. Pa was never much of a father. He liked drink and gambling too well. But after Ma died, he was too drunk most of the time even to remember he had children, much less to look after them. After Jane married Lucas, Harry and I were pretty much left to ourselves, and I was too young and too wild to look after Harry the way Jane did."

He spoke matter-of-factly, but Maggie knew the pain of losing a parent, of having the other parent fade out of your life. Her own mother's sickness served Lynette much as alcohol had served March's father, as an escape from the harshness of reality.

But she was the one who had turned wild, not March.

"What do you mean, you were wild?" she asked. "What did you do, sneak off for a horse ride during church? Pull the girls' hair in school?"

He shook his head. "I decided I wanted to be a gunman."

"You joined the Rangers with Lucas?" She would have thought he'd been too young for that ten years ago.

"No, I didn't join the Rangers. I robbed a bank."

Chapter 12

He loved the way she laughed. It shook her whole slender frame. Her eyes sparkled with such amusement he had to smile back.

"I can't say anyone else has ever found that funny."

She choked. "You mean you're not kidding?"

He dug back into the mending basket.

"No, I'm not kidding," he assured her.

"Why on earth would you rob a bank?" she asked, leaning forward eagerly.

He should have known curiosity would be her first reaction. At supper in that blue silk she'd looked like a cool, distant stranger, a proper lady. But a lady would be properly appalled by his confession. Not Maggie.

She was dangerous, which was precisely why he was sitting on the edge of Lucas's armchair instead of risking temptation on the sofa.

He wished he'd let the fire die. It was too warm in the room by half.

"I was a stupid kid," he said in answer to her question. He hardly understood the reasons himself anymore. He'd had some crazy idea of proving to his father, or maybe to himself, that at fifteen he wasn't a boy anymore. And he'd had grand notions of providing for Harry, who'd been reduced to wearing March's old hand-me-downs.

Maggie shook her head. "I don't believe it. You don't even care enough about money to balance your account book properly. You wouldn't rob a bank."

"Maybe I shouldn't have said I robbed a bank. I *tried* to rob a bank. The cashier had me pegged for a scared kid the minute I walked in the door. He pulled the gun right out of my hand and dragged me down to the jail by my shirt collar."

If possible, she was even sexier when she tried *not* to laugh. Her smile warmed his soul.

"All right, I believe you. You couldn't have made that up. What did your father say? I almost wish I'd thought of robbing a bank. That would have sent Stephen right over the edge."

"Robbing a bank is a serious crime," he reminded her. "You can be hanged for offenses like that."

She frowned at him prettily. "Well, of course I disapprove of it. Shame on you. Are you satisfied? But you obviously don't do that sort of thing anymore. And they obviously didn't hang you."

He laughed—he couldn't help himself. "No, I guess not. My case never even came to sentencing. My bad luck in my new profession continued. My one smart move was to choose a bank far from home. But I hadn't done any reconnoitering. I didn't know that the day before my attempted robbery a Texas Ranger had ridden into town with the Deane brothers in tow."

Maggie didn't squeal with fear.

"I guess their reputation didn't reach much beyond the Mississippi," March admitted. "But in 1865 everyone in Texas knew of them. The four Deanes had been named after the gospels, but only Luke and John survived the Battle of Vicksburg. They deserted the Confederate Army and headed west, making quite a name for themselves as hell-raisers and gunfighters.

"They were on their way to justice, possibly in the ultimate sense, when I got thrown into Blackwater's one jail cell with them."

"What were they like?" Maggie asked, setting aside her mending and curling her feet up under her blue skirts, caught by his story.

"Charming," March said without hesitation. "The Deanes could have charmed their way out of hell. Their family had owned a small farm in Tennessee before the war, but John and Luke were southern gentlemen to the hilt. They'd only been caught after their last heist because they tried to sweet-talk a hiding place out of a woman whose husband had died fighting for the Union. She set them up in the barn loft, then rode ten miles to turn them in."

"So, what happened?"

"They charmed me," March confessed. "They talked about the freedom and romance of living as an outlaw, and I didn't have enough experience to translate that into the dirt, fear, exhaustion, and debauchery of the reality. They said I had the makings of a true renegade.

"I bought into all of it. And when their gang rode into town and broke them out of jail, I went with them."

She'd hooked an elbow over the arm of the sofa and leaned her chin on her crossed arms. She looked thoroughly at home, nestled across from him, her eyes fixed on his, a faint frown of curiosity hovering around her mouth.

"Then what?"

"I didn't mind the dirt and the hunger and the running all that much," he said. "They gave me charge of the horses when they saw I had a way with them. That was good enough for me. That, and escaping what I saw as the deadening responsibilities at home."

"What made you go back?"

"I saw the Deanes as Robin Hood and Little John, misunderstood gentlemen who robbed from the rich in order to live free of Yankee laws, when the truth was, they were thugs and killers.

"They left me behind at their various hideouts, looking after the horses, sometimes cooking a meal for the gang's return. It was a month after the breakout before they took me on my first robbery. They planned to hold up a stagecoach carrying gold to the bank in Blackwater, that same little town I'd tried unsuccessfully to rob. Poetic justice.

"It started out smoothly enough. We ambushed the stagecoach, and when the driver saw there was no way out, he pulled the coach to a stop rather than making us shoot him."

In those first heart-pounding seconds, the look of enraged terror on that driver's face had told March all he needed to know about outlawry. But it had been too late to turn back.

"The trouble didn't start until they'd unloaded the gold into the pack horses' saddle bags. Then they called out the passengers, an obviously wealthy group of people. Luke went up to one of them, a pretty young woman, and told her to drop her valuables in his bag. She refused. He said he'd do it himself."

The scene remained as vivid in his mind's eye as the day it had happened. The clouds brushing across the hot sun, the rocks baking in the dry creekbed, the rustling of scrubby trees in the wind.

"And?"

Her voice was barely a whisper. The rest of the story must have already shown in his face.

"When he put a hand on her, she gave him a swift knee where it counted, then ripped off his bandanna and spit in his face. Luke shot her in the chest at point-blank range."

Maggie paled, and March cursed himself for starting the story in the first place. He wouldn't relate any more details.

"One of the other women screamed, cursing Luke and all the rest of us. She said the girl was the daughter of Joseph Templeton, one of the richest ranchers in all of Texas and that he'd never rest until we were all six feet under.

"Luke said it was too bad she was probably right. They'd just have to kill all the passengers to ensure there weren't any witnesses."

"How many were there?" Maggie breathed.

"Eight, counting the driver." March remembered the features of every one of them. He could still hear the clicks as gang members cocked their guns. "Luke's order to kill them wasn't even the worst part. It was the pure pleasure I saw on his face at the prospect of murdering those defenseless people."

He saw Maggie's expression and quickly continued, "My horse stood right next to John's and I saw that same bloodlust in his eyes. If I'd been old enough to have any sense, I'd probably have been frozen by horror. Instead, I reached over and grabbed John's collar, dragged him right off his horse."

Used to working with horses, he'd had strong arms for a fifteen-year-old. "He was so surprised, he dropped his gun. I stuck mine against his head and yelled at the others to hold their fire. I told Luke if he didn't let the stage go, I'd blow John's brains out."

Some of the color returned to Maggie's cheeks. "What did he do?"

"Luke ordered the passengers back on the coach, and the driver whipped those horses as though the devil himself was after them. Maybe he was."

"How did you get out of there?" Maggie asked, sitting up again. "The Deanes can't have been too pleased with you."

"That's an understatement. I think any of the others would have let John die without a second thought in order to get to me, but Luke would have killed anyone who tried it. He'd have done anything to protect his baby brother. I made them all dismount, take off their clothes and guns and tie them to their saddles. Then I rounded up the horses and rode off toward Blackwater, leaving John along the wayside."

"You left them there, completely naked?" Maggie gasped, a sparkle in her eye.

"Without even their underwear," March acknowledged, though he couldn't smile, remembering the body of the slain girl lying alone in the dust.

Maggie's eyes narrowed. "And just what happened to the gold?"

"I couldn't keep it. It was tainted with blood. I returned it to the bank in Blackwater. Didn't have any more luck than I'd had robbing the place the first time." Now March could laugh. "I broke into the lobby that night and dumped the saddlebags with the gold on the floor. I slipped back out the door, just in time to run headlong into the town marshal heading home from the saloon.

"I tried to run for it and the son-of-a . . . he shot me."

"*Shot* you?" Maggie burst out. "You really are making this up, aren't you? You had me going, you—"

"The bullet cracked a rib," he interrupted her. "There's still a scar, about the size of a penny."

His eyes dared her to ask to see it. She didn't take him up on it. "So they put you in jail for the rest of your life for dumping gold in a bank. What are you doing here?"

"That bullet was my introduction to Marshal Elijah Kelly."

"He's a marshal?"

"He was at that time, for a couple of months. Good thing he was drunk when he pulled the trigger, or I wouldn't be here to talk about it. Instead of taking me to a doctor, he dragged me to the hotel, where the Texas Ranger assigned to bring in the Deane gang was staying. That Ranger just happened to be my brother-in-law. I don't know who was more shocked, me or Lucas. Probably Lucas; I'd lost a lot of blood.

"Luckily, Lucas knew me well enough to believe I could be idiot enough to break into a bank to return its money. He scared up a doctor, woke up the bank manager to check on the gold, and then he and Elijah took a posse after the Deanes.

"They found the stagecoach with a broken axle about ten miles from town, but all the passengers were safe. And over the next two days they rounded up every member of the Deane gang. I got off with a night in jail and the bank manager even gave me a reward for returning his gold. True story."

"And the Deanes?"

He shrugged, not wanting to darken the mood again. "I don't know for sure what happened at the trial—I couldn't testify, being laid up with a bullet wound. Eight witnesses saw Luke Deane shoot that girl in cold blood. I heard he charmed the jury, but they hanged him for it anyway. Several members of the gang were sentenced to hang for other crimes they'd committed, but John Deane and most of the others got life imprisonment. Most of them deserved to die as much as Luke did. John especially."

"Hanging would have been too easy on them," Maggie said firmly, reaching for her mending.

March watched her move, the quick flashes of her fingers with the needle, the shimmer of blue silk as she breathed. He could watch her forever. Except that led to wanting her. Just one touch, just to tuck back that curl. . . . He found himself straining to hear the sound of Elijah's horse on the drive, Wolf's feet hitting the porch. Where the hell were they?

183

★ ★ ★ ★ ★

Silence stretched into minutes.

Maggie bit back a curse as she pricked her thumb yet again. She simply couldn't keep her mind on the stitches. Better to get March talking again, distract herself from the way his shirt stretched across his chest.

"Were the Culberts farmers back in Texas? Did they move to Colorado with you or later on?"

"Jed and Henna were living in Missouri when Lucas retired from the Rangers and we moved up here," March answered, handing her one of Wolf's shirts. His fingers brushed hers. "It was after Emily was born that they decided to move west. Elijah ran into them on the trail by pure luck. That's when he learned about Wolf. He encouraged Jed to come to Oxtail."

"He thought this would make good farmland?" Maggie asked doubtfully.

"It's good soil, if you've got water to irrigate it," March said. "Though Elijah probably wouldn't know the difference. He just wanted to keep them out of trouble. Ranchers don't take to farmers fencing off the land. 'Lije thought Lucas and I would be able to protect Jed and Henna from harassment."

"And what will the Culberts do when you get yourself killed trying to avenge Lucas?" The words were out of her mouth before she could stop them.

If she'd wanted to back him away, it worked. "Jed and Henna have lots of friends in town now, and other farmers have settled peaceably in the area. They're not in any danger."

She didn't want to ruin the evening, but she couldn't stop. "You think someone's after your land and your water rights, but you don't think they'll cut off the Culberts' water the minute they get the chance? I guess it doesn't much matter to your revenge scheme, since they won't have to kill the Culberts to get rid of them. I guess Jed and Henna can give up their home and move on to new territory without too much trouble. They've only got five kids to worry about."

March stood, knocking the mending basket over. "I see Miss Know-It-All is back. I thought we'd agreed you were going to stop interfering in my life."

Maggie tossed Wolf's shirt onto the pile beside her. "Fine. You're doing such a good job of running things, you obviously don't need my help. Sorry."

"Come on, Maggie, you're never sorry for anything." He crossed his arms over his chest, scowling at her. "What would you do in my place? If I sell out, my sister's murderers will have won. They'll have the ranch and the water rights. If I don't sell, they'll kill me, leaving Harry with the mess, and they'll get the land eventually, anyway. The way I see it, the only alternative is to play along, find out who's responsible, and take them down."

She could feel the acid on her tongue. "I see. You rode with a dangerous gang for a month ten years ago and you think you're some kind of gunfighter."

"No. But I'd rather die with a bullet in my chest than one in my back."

Maggie rose to her feet, frustration boiling in her heart. "You asked for my opinion? You're more likely to die of slow starvation." Her voice rose, ridiculously loud in the silent house. "You want to know what I think of your plan? I think it's stupid! I don't think anyone's after your land. I think Lucas and Jane were in the wrong place at the wrong time, killed by rustlers who didn't give a damn who they were. I think you've made up this whole conspiracy to give yourself an excuse to drink and wallow in self-pity and let the ranch fall to ruin along with you."

The dead emptiness in his eyes frightened her. "Now that you mention it," he said, his voice flat, "I haven't drowned myself in drink nearly enough lately."

He turned and stalked to the door, pulling it open to show the deep indigo sky at the end of twilight. He glanced back over his shoulder. "Don't wait up for me. Wallowing in self-pity can take most of the night."

Then he stepped out the door, not bothering to take his coat or hat.

"Go to hell, March Jackson!" Maggie shouted after him. She turned and kicked the leg of the sofa with all her might. It hurt, even through the stiff leather of her boot. She kicked it again, growling in frustration. "Damn him, damn him, damn him!"

She shook with the desire to throw something heavy through one of Jane Penny's precious glass windows, though she couldn't have said whom she was more furious with, March or herself.

The evening had been going so well. She'd felt as comfortable as though they were friends, able to talk about anything. Except perhaps when his blue eyes caught hers, and she'd felt another kind of pleasure in the evening, a promise, between almost friends.

She should have kept her mouth shut, shouldn't have drawn March's ghosts back into the present. In that moment, she hated the three dead Pennys with an intensity that scared her. She hated the fact that their happy family had been destroyed by violence. Hated the fact that she'd never get a chance to meet March's sister, never know if Jane would really have welcomed her. She hated that their brutal deaths haunted every moment of peace on the ranch.

But most of all, she hated the fact that avenging their deaths was more important to March than living his own life.

He cared more for their ghosts than for his beautiful horses, for his land, for his future.

He cared for his phantoms more than he cared for her.

Not that it mattered. She'd be gone soon. March's life would no longer be any concern of hers. She could go back to civilization and never have to face another blackened pot or Henna's disapproval.

She brushed a hand across her eyes; it came away damp with tears.

The sun hovered just above the horizon, but its sharp rays pierced March's eyes like needles.

"Might as well have drunk myself blind, after all," he muttered grimly, trying to ignore the pounding in his head.

Alexander Brady's black stallion watched him with a measuring eye as March checked the tightness of the saddle cinch one more time. The horse's ears twitched at his tone.

"It's all right, fella. You're not the problem. I just didn't get much sleep last night." He ran a hand along the stallion's neck, gauging the horse's tension level. Less than his own, he guessed.

Despite his words to Maggie when he'd left the ranch house last night, he hadn't had the stomach to face The Golden Rose and another bottle of whiskey. He'd ridden hard out into the night, toward the mountains. But even the cool night breezes and the lonely sounds of the wilderness hadn't soothed him.

He'd returned more confused and frustrated than when he'd left to find the house dark and Elijah and Wolf pretending to sleep quietly in the loft. He'd joined them, lying wide-eyed in the darkness, forcing his shallow breathing into a smooth rhythm.

Thoughts of Elijah's strained relationship with his son, of

death and violence, of Jane and Lucas and Logan, of horses to be trained and supplies to be bought, of revenge and retribution and redemption all wrestled in his brain, all trying to push aside thoughts of Maggie. To push aside his anger and desire and a tenderness that threatened to cripple his need for vengeance, the only reason he had left for living.

He must have drifted off at some point, because a leg cramp had woken him this morning. He'd gotten rid of the cramp quickly enough, but he still had a splitting headache and a crick in his neck. Not the best of circumstances under which to work a dangerous horse, but he didn't want Brady's stallion in his stable any longer than was absolutely necessary.

Of course, he could have sent Sandy back to Brady with a final refusal to work with the horse. But the idea of some bronco buster digging his spurs into the stallion's flawless coat and beating him with the handle end of a whip troubled March as much as it did Brady. Probably more.

Sandy had stood more or less calmly while being saddled and bridled. March had chosen to use a snaffle bit. It left him with less control, but he didn't want to put undue pressure on the horse's mouth. The fact that Sandy exhibited no behavior problems until mounted told March that the stallion had faced his share of harsh bits and heavy hands. He had to learn that being ridden didn't mean pain.

March took hold of the reins, beginning a soft whistle. Other humans might find the sound unnerving, but he'd never gotten a complaint from a horse. He led Sandy around the corral, from a walk to a trot, back to a walk. He wanted the stallion to begin to forget his apprehension at being saddled, to focus on March as a nonthreatening leader.

He'd worked Sandy the day before for about fifteen minutes and then left him saddled in the corral for an hour, getting used to the feel. The best way to avoid a fight with a horse was not to start one. But they didn't have much time together. If he wanted to work through Sandy's problems, he had to start today. He could feel the danger from his family's killers pressing in on him.

You've made up this whole conspiracy to give yourself an excuse to drink and wallow in self-pity and let the ranch fall to ruin along with you.

He shook his head sharply. What did she know. If he wanted to drink himself into oblivion, he didn't need an excuse. The only thing keeping him sober was the belief that he'd be playing right into the murderers' hands if he let whiskey have its way.

"What does she know," he repeated aloud. "That darned female is a more dangerous distraction than all the rotgut in Oxtail."

Sandy bugled loudly in agreement.

March looked up to see what had caught the stallion's attention. Maggie and Ari had just rounded the corner of the ranch house, back from their morning run into the foothills. The two moved together in instinctual harmony, a blend of beauty in motion that caught at his heart.

"Forget it, fella," he said, moving into a walk and turning Sandy's attention back to the corral. "They're more trouble than you and I know how to handle." March started whistling again and broke back into a trot.

He'd worked for another ten minutes before he realized he was waiting for Maggie to come back out of the barn before he mounted.

"See, what did I tell you?" he asked the stallion. "Turning me into a damn showoff. It's time for you and me to get down to business and stop worrying about the ladies."

Gradually, he worked Sandy to the center of the corral.

Without giving the stallion enough warning to get worked up about it, he launched himself into the saddle.

Maggie gave Ari's back one more swipe with the brush. The mare smelled of sweat and the sweet, wild morning. She wasn't even winded. Maggie imagined they could have ridden to California without tiring.

"I'm not going to want to leave you Friday," she whispered to the mare. She didn't want to think about what else she wouldn't want to leave. In the dim silence of the barn, she couldn't get away from the sound of March's whistling.

"I can't take you home, though. Stephen wouldn't let me keep you." She could just hear the comments her stepfather would make about her beautiful buckskin. *Scrawny little Indian pony* would be the kindest. "Maybe you and I shouldn't come back from our ride Friday morning. We could explore the Rockies together, just you and me. Maybe go up to Canada or down to Mexico."

Ari eyed her speculatively.

"Well, no, I don't know how to fight off wolves or Indians. You're the one with the reputation as a hero."

The mare cocked her head.

"All I'm saying is, think about it. Now eat your oats. I'm going to go see how March is getting along with Sandy."

"He said he's going to ride him today."

Maggie almost knocked the breath from her lungs jumping back against the side of the stall.

"Wolf?"

The boy's head popped out of the next stall down. Straw poked wildly from his hair. "Yes'm, Miss Maggie."

"What are you doing in there?"

He rubbed an arm across his eyes and yawned. "I was cleaning stalls. I just meant to sit down for a minute, honest. I guess I fell asleep."

She'd noticed the circles under his eyes earlier. "You didn't sleep much last night, did you?"

He shrugged, and she didn't press him. It didn't take a genius to figure out why he hadn't slept. Whatever had passed between Wolf and his father the night before, it hadn't closed any of the distance that separated them.

Between Elijah and Wolf's awkwardness with each other and the angry words she and March had shared the night before, breakfast had been a grim meal. No one had spoken a word, the tension so thick it hung over them in a blacker cloud than the smoke from the gravy March had uncharacteristically burned.

"You go lie down in your own bed for a while," she suggested. "You can catch up with your chores this afternoon."

The boy shook his head. "No, I want to see March ride Sandy."

"You mean *try* to ride Sandy," Maggie corrected.

"March can ride anything," Wolf assured her.

"I hope so." She wasn't as eager as Wolf to watch the contest between March and the black stallion. Images of March crushed against the bars of the corral or lacerated by powerful hooves refused to be banished from her mind.

On the other hand, if the thick-headed fool took a hard fall on his rear, it wouldn't break her heart.

She latched Ari's stall door.

"I'm sorry I woke you up," she said as she followed Wolf toward the stable door, wondering how much of her foolishness he'd heard.

"I talk to the horses all the time," he said, trying to ease her embarrassment. He glanced at her out of the corner of his eye. "But they've never talked back to *me*."

"I have an active imagination, Wolf," she confessed.

191

"You'll have to help keep me honest."

"You and me . . . you and *I* can keep each other honest," he said with grave generosity.

The words tugged at her heart, and she had to bite her lip against unexpected tears. *Damn.* She was turning into a whimpering crybaby. But she couldn't put out of her head the thought that even if March never spoke to her again, in Wolf and Ari she'd made two more friends here than she had ever had back in Kentucky. All her promises to herself never again to care about another creature had proven about as valuable as a Confederate dollar.

She followed Wolf out the door, blinking furiously against the moisture in her eyes and the brightness of the sun. Wolf tugged her hand, dragging her toward the corral.

"There he goes!" the boy whispered excitedly.

March and Sandy stood in the center of the corral, each of them focused intently on the other. She and Wolf crept up to the fence, not wanting to cause any distractions.

In a sudden flow of movement, March vaulted into the saddle.

Maggie saw the stallion's muscles bunch beneath him. Sandy's ears lay back, his nostrils flared. Unable to breathe, she waited for the horse's explosion.

It didn't come.

With an almost imperceptible pressure from his legs, March urged the stallion forward. Sandy stepped into a walk, tension making his gait choppy, but as long as his legs were extended, he couldn't rear. As they neared the north side of the corral, March leaned right, laying the left rein gently against the horse's neck. Sandy's head jerked up and down, but he turned, continuing his slow walk around the corral.

Maggie risked a quick breath, clenching her hands around the top bar of the fence as she watched them circle. They moved into a slow trot, still circling. Slowly, very slowly, Sandy's ears twitched upward and some of the awkwardness left his gait.

"What's going on?" she whispered to Wolf. "Brady said no one could ride him without him rearing."

"Maybe he's waiting for March to lose concentration," the boy suggested. "March said he thought Sandy was one smart horse."

She hadn't heard footsteps behind them, but Elijah Kelly's black duster caught the corner of her eye as he moved up beside her, Lemuel Tate on his other side.

"I think they're past that point," Elijah said, his soft drawl contrasting with the intensity of his gaze, focused on the pair in the corral. "It just happens that way sometimes with March. I've seen other men use 'scientific' techniques for taming a horse, just as fast and more effectively than most of your cowboy wranglers. But I've never seen anyone with a touch like March."

"Lemuel says he's part horse himself," Wolf added, looking to the old man, who nodded with a smile. "He knows how to talk to them."

"But do they talk back?" Maggie asked, with a wink at the boy.

Wolf grinned. "I wouldn't be at all surprised."

Maggie managed to hold onto her own smile, in spite of the fact that she'd heard Elijah Kelly say those same words in almost exactly that same way the day before on the Pennys' front porch.

She glanced at Elijah, but he was staring straight ahead into the corral. He looked as though he were trying to blend into the scenery, as though afraid if he spoke or moved, Wolf might withdraw into silence again.

If she hadn't known already they were father and son, she

would have recognized it then. The two of them leaned against the fence, arms crossed the same way, Elijah leaning on the top rail, Wolf on the second. Their hazel eyes serious, they concentrated on the rider in the corral, each too sensitive, too aware of the other's feelings to make the first move toward a relationship.

"Wolf!" March's voice broke into her thoughts. "Open the gate for me."

She looked up, catching his eyes for a split-second. Then he turned Sandy toward the gate. Once out in the yard, the stallion might bolt anywhere. But she wasn't going to ask March if he thought this was wise.

Wolf opened the gate, and March urged Sandy out into the yard. The horse's ears twitched with interest. March held him to a trot as they made a large circle between the stable and the house.

The stallion's gait finally began to flow. Muscles rippled beneath his gleaming black coat as he extended his stride, moving like a dancer across the hardpacked earth. Maggie found herself holding her breath again, this time at the sheer beauty of the rider and horse working together.

She swept a critical eye over Sandy's profile, and could find nothing wrong with his conformation or his gait. If March could hold onto the ranch long enough to figure out his rustlers weren't going to return, he'd end up thanking her for the agreement with Alexander Brady. Sandy's foals out of Lucas's mares would be a sight to behold.

She would not think about the fact that she'd never get to see them.

Sandy moved into a canter, his tail floating out behind him like a banner, his nostrils flaring to catch the wind.

"Hey, it's Jake."

Wolf pointed up the drive. It took Maggie only a second to

find the oldest Culbert boy flying up the drive on his stringy pinto mustang. The boy had one hand on his hat, his legs bouncing wildly against the mare's sides as they pounded toward the corral. In a sudden flurry of motion, he skidded the mustang to a dust-raising halt.

"God, no. Not the Culberts."

Maggie turned abruptly at Elijah's hoarse whisper. His face had paled, and she saw his hand reach toward a nonexistent gunbelt.

"No." Maggie touched the elbow of his jacket. The glow of knowledge that ran through her felt almost like . . . belonging. "It's just the horses in the grain again."

"March!" Jake Culbert yelled in a voice loud enough to carry almost from the Culbert farm, "It's those gosh darn horses of yours. They got into the barley again."

Jed Culbert had obviously taken more care with his language this time.

March groaned in frustration. "All right Jakey. Tell your pa—"

But in the moment March's balance shifted off center, his concentration on Jake and the mustang, Sandy made his move. With a sudden explosion of powerful muscles, the stallion bolted straight toward the cluster of people standing beside the corral.

Chapter 13

March felt the burst of rebellion in the change of the stallion's muscle tone, giving him the breadth of an instant to adjust his seat so he wasn't thrown to the ground when the break came.

Given the animal's powerful hindquarters, Sandy could hit full speed in just a few short strides—and he would hit the group of spectators frozen beside the corral less than a second after that.

In the same moment that he saw Elijah throw himself at Wolf and Maggie, March yanked hard on his left rein, wrapping it around the saddle horn for leverage.

As Sandy's head twisted abruptly to the side, the horse lost his balance, skidding and stumbling in an attempt to adjust. March freed his feet from the stirrups, ready to jump to safety when the horse fell, but the black stallion's quick feet somehow kept them upright as they spun into a tight circle.

March could see the surprise in the stallion's eyes. He could bring Sandy to a halt here, if he wanted, safe for the moment from the black's urge to bolt. But Sandy would try it again. March could respect the horse's patience and ingenuity. But he couldn't let him threaten lives by remaining a runaway.

Sharply, he dug his heels into the horse's sides, forcing Sandy to move forward. With his head bent back toward his tail, the stallion could go nowhere but around in a circle.

March pushed him. Sandy lunged in frustrated response. Ignoring the sounds of voices from the corral, the pounding heat of the sun, the strain on his muscles, March kept the horse spinning, around and around, until it seemed his whole world consisted of gleaming black hide and the growing sickness in his stomach. He pushed the horse on and on, just to the point where he felt the stallion's fight drain away.

The moment Sandy agreed to submit to his authority, March loosed the rein from the saddle horn, rewarding him. The stallion shook his head, his muscles twitching, but stood quietly. March hoped the horse's world was spinning as fast as his was.

"I don't think I want dinner. What about you?" he asked, in between quick shallow breaths he hoped would steady his internal organs. He sent the horse into a sedate walk, taking him in a wide circle this time, letting the horse know the appropriate behavior he expected.

Sandy's ears flickered, and he lifted his head. March grinned, just a little. This stallion's spirit wasn't broken, not by a long shot. But the horse was too smart to pick another fight he couldn't win. He pulled Sandy to a halt.

"March, are you all right?"

He looked down into the loveliest pair of eyes he'd ever seen. Cool and clear, dark with concern, they left his brain just as unsteady as the spinning horse had, but for quite different reasons. Maggie placed a light hand on his knee, and he suddenly couldn't remember what she'd asked him.

"You don't look so good," she said. "It's your stomach, isn't it?"

He frowned at her. "My stomach's fine."

"You're green, Jackson."

He'd saved her from the hooves of a rampaging stallion, turned the beast into a gentle saddle horse right before her eyes, and all she could do was comment on his skin coloring. It figured.

"I'll probably live," he grumbled. He looked over at Jake

Culbert. "Tell your pa I'll be over in a minute. See if you can't rope Stormy for me, Jake, give me a head start. I just have to saddle up Balthasar; I don't know that I'd trust this fellow around Prince yet."

"That's just it, March," Jake burst out, finally remembering his message after all the excitement. "I did rope Stormy. Me and Pa and Danny got the rest of the mares out of the barley ourselves. But Prince ain't with 'em."

March's feet hit the ground before the boy finished speaking.

"Lem, take care of Sandy for me." He tossed the reins into Lemuel's capable hands. "Give him plenty of attention, he deserves it." And then he broke into a run toward the stable.

"What should I do, March?" Jake called after him.

"Go back and keep an eye on the other horses," he yelled over his shoulder. "Make sure they don't go too far before I can get them back into the west pasture."

He reached the stable and sprinted the last few yards to Balthasar's stall. Maggie panted up behind him.

"Help me," he ordered simply. Without slowing him with questions, she ran for Balthasar's bridle while he led the gelding out to where he could saddle him.

"What can I do?" Wolf asked, coming up beside him.

March gestured toward Elijah's coffee-colored mount. "Help your father get his horse ready."

He grabbed a coil of rope and tied it to his saddle. Maggie had already bridled Balthasar. She handed him the reins.

"Don't worry, I'm sure Prince just wandered off," she said.

He shook his head as he mounted, his stomach worse than when he'd been spinning Sandy. "Prince is the herd stallion, Maggie. He wouldn't have left the mares. And he wouldn't have let the mares leave him."

He didn't need to say anything else. He could see his own fear dawning in her eyes.

Maggie stared after March until he hit the drive. Then she ran back down the stalls and threw open Ari's door.

"Two runs in one day; aren't you a lucky lady," she murmured. Ari nuzzled her stomach in complete agreement.

Maggie took only enough time to bridle the mare, then led the horse to the nearest bale of hay. As soon as she hit the mare's bare back, she turned her toward the barn door. Let March and Elijah saddle their horses. Since she didn't know a thing about roping, she didn't need a saddle horn. But March needed her to join the hunt for Prince as soon as possible.

And she had an uncomfortable feeling in the pit of her stomach that once they found the stallion, he might need help of another kind, though she didn't know that she'd have any idea how to give it.

Stop it, she chided herself. *You're letting March's defeatism get to you.* For all they knew, the spunky brown stallion had simply decided to kick up his heels and have a run. But she pushed Ari into a flying gallop as soon as they hit open ground.

The Culbert farm looked much the same as it had the first time she'd seen it, nearly a week before. The bright summer sun shone down on waves of golden barley, waves that eddied around a trampled circle near the northwest corner of the field.

Today, however, no horses munched contentedly on the grain, no high pitched voices carried to her on the soft breeze. The cluster of blond heads surrounding March and Balthasar looked confused, subdued, even from a distance.

Maggie sent Ari cantering down the path through the barley. Even Henna's presence, standing straight and willowy beside her husband, didn't prevent her from riding right up into the center of the group. This wasn't a time for personal differences.

"No, I can't be sure," Jed Culbert was saying, his face lined with concern. "I don't think any of the mares are missing, but I don't know them all as well as I know Luci . . . Prince."

"Where'd Prince go, March?" little Tucker asked, his eyes wide as he gazed up from his perch on his father's hip.

"I don't know, Tuck," March answered, with a calm Maggie could tell he didn't feel. "But I intend to find out."

"Maggie!" Emily cried, dropping her mother's hand to run over to Ari. "Maggie, can I help you look?"

"I don't think you can ride with me today, Emmy," Maggie said, surprised that the girl not only remembered her, but recognized her in her work clothes. "I don't have a saddle."

"You can help me make dinner," Henna told her daughter, taking her hand.

Emily resisted her gentle pull, grabbing for Maggie's foot. "No! I want to look for Prince Charming!"

"March and Maggie aren't going to have time to make dinner while they're searching," Henna continued calmly. "Once they find Prince, they're going to be hungry. You and I can make enough for everyone. We'll send Jakey back over to get Wolf and Lemuel."

"Wolf's coming home for dinner?" Emily glanced at Henna, wavering.

"If we get it ready. It will be like a party. But I'll need your help."

"Okay." The little girl let her mother pull her back from Ari's side.

Reflected in Henna's eyes Maggie could see her own belief that they'd all need something to cheer them up once they found the stallion. *If* they found him. For the first time, the thought of rustlers tickled the back of her neck like an evil breeze.

Jed hefted his shotgun and held it out toward March. "Just in case you need it for . . . anything."

"For what, Papa?" Tucker asked.

Neither man looked at him.

"Jed, you might need this," March said, choosing his words carefully around the children. "If his disappearance isn't, um, natural."

The big man shook his head. "Elijah's coming, isn't he? And I've got a .45 in the house. You take it."

March nodded and rested the shotgun across his thighs. "Have 'Lije help Jake take the herd back through my fence into the west pasture. Whatever's happened, Maggie and I can find Prince."

Maggie started. The moment March had taken Jed's gun, she'd expected him to tell her she couldn't come along. Only when she saw the grim expression on his face did she realize he thought neither going nor staying was completely safe. But if Prince was alive and in trouble, March knew he might need help.

For a moment her eyes locked with his. She felt color staining her cheeks, but she didn't care. He trusted her to be able to help if he needed it. The thought flowed through her on a rush of wonder.

Then he broke his gaze away, turning toward a thin, pale boy a little younger than Wolf. She guessed he must be the Culbert boy who'd just recovered from the measles.

"Danny, show us where the break in the fence is this time," March said. "We'd better get started."

"Sure, March." The boy bolted toward the line of brush that formed the field fence, with Balthasar close on his heels.

Maggie followed quickly, determined not to give March a reason to leave her behind.

She didn't see the gap in the bushes until Danny disappeared through it. March's mares had forced their way through a forbidding tangle of vicious thorns to get to the Culberts' barley. Maggie crouched down, laying her face along Ari's neck, her arms tucked close under her body. Branches slashed against her legs and shoulders, but Jane's denim pants and Lucas's leather vest protected her.

"Either your horses have brave hearts or they're the stupidest beasts I've ever met," she said to March's back as they broke through to the other side.

"Tough hides," March answered. "Must be the mustang in them. They'd fight through thorns twice as thick for a taste of fresh barley. If Jed doesn't get himself some barbed wire fencing damn soon, I'm going to do it for him."

Once on the other side of the brush line, she saw the herd of mares and foals standing calmly on a grassy hillside. Jake Culbert and his little chestnut were circling them vigilantly while Stormy, the old lead mare pretended not to care.

March waved the boy over. "Jakey, Miss Parker and I are going out to look for Prince. Mr. Kelly's not far behind us. He'll help you get the horses back onto my property. Do you think you two can handle that yourselves?"

Jake nodded vigorously. "Sure we can, March. Don't you worry about a thing."

"All right, son. I know I can count on you."

The boy's face lit up with pride. He dug his heels into his mare's flanks and they sped off to resume their circling of the herd.

March looked back at Maggie, his face still dark. "Our best bet is to find the break in my fence. I don't know that the herd could have made it here intact without Prince to keep them together. Once we find it, we can work our way back."

Maggie nodded. "I'll be right behind you."

March set off at a gallop toward the northwest, back toward Lucas's ranch. He changed course only once, taking a wide detour around a bare mound of earth pocked by holes that could be fatal to a galloping horse. Maggie glimpsed furry faces studying her from the burrow entrances and watched round, dun-colored bodies flash across the dun-colored earth to safety.

After about a quarter mile they crossed a broad ditch half-filled with water. Jed Culbert's irrigation ditch, Maggie guessed. His grain fields must have contained the best pocket of farmland in the area, or he would never have expended the backbreaking labor of running a ditch so far.

Of course, she knew without asking that March, Lemuel, and Lucas had all bent their shovels and strained their backs right beside him. Ten years ago, back in the eighteen-sixties, this land had been frontier, somewhere in the no man's land between the Great American Desert and the Rocky Mountains.

Out here, far from even the smallest eddy of the white man's civilization, at the mercy of drought and fire, thunderstorm and blizzard, in a country until recently roamed by now dispossessed Cheyennes, Arapahos, and Utes, a neighbor became more precious than gold. In the absence of the web of extended relations a settler left behind, the family around the hill or just over the ridge took the place of aunts and uncles, cousins and in-laws.

Struck by this sudden insight, Maggie began to understand the ties that bound March to the Culberts, Elijah to March, Lemuel to the Pennys. She thought back to her comments to March the night before about his responsibilities to his neighbors and could have bitten her tongue.

If this strange family of March's, this odd assortment of farmers and fighters, adults and children, couldn't help him find his way out of his grief, how could she have been so smug as to think she could give him a stern little lecture and make it all disappear?

They reached the fence line of the Penny property and followed it west. The split rails of the fence, most of them gray with age and dust, spoke of as much labor as the irrigation ditch. Lucas and March must have brought the wood down from the Rockies, not so very far away, perhaps, as the crow flew, but she'd never seen a loaded wagon that could fly like a crow.

March had spoken of Jed getting barbed wire to protect his barley. She wondered if March had considered it for his own property. She'd heard conflicting stories about the danger it might pose to stock. But it was coming to the west, invading prairie and rangeland like a morning glory with vines and tendrils of steel.

Her wandering mind began to settle on more immediate concerns. She'd nearly forgotten how hard riding bareback was on certain areas of her anatomy, not to mention the strain on her leg muscles.

March pulled Balthasar back to a slow canter and waved Maggie up beside him.

"You keep an eye on the fence," he directed. "I'll keep a look out for anything unusual."

She nodded, and they rode on in silence.

The sun shone down without relief, but even worse, it reflected harshly from the dry ground, lit up the dried grasses and glinted painfully from the boulder-strewn mountainsides. The unrelenting brightness burned Maggie's eyes as she kept them fixed on the fence line.

Ari cantered smoothly, tireless despite the heat, but Maggie could feel the horse's sweat soaking through the legs of her blue jeans. She lifted her hat to brush an arm across her forehead. She wished she'd thought to bring water along.

They had moved well into the foothills now, the terrain requiring a slower pace, the scrubby trees and rough ground offering more obstacles to their searching eyes.

Maggie swallowed, her dry throat constricting almost painfully. Just as the thought crossed her mind that she might lose all feeling in her legs from the strain of maintaining her seat, she saw what she'd been looking for. The break in the fence.

With a surge of renewed energy, she looked for March. He'd drifted nearly a hundred yards from her, and she could just see his hat over a small rise.

"March!" she yelled, the sound nothing but a loud croak from her parched throat. She swallowed. "March! I found it! They came through over here."

She pulled Ari to a stop. The top two rails of one section of the fence had fallen away. One appeared to have been split by a strong blow, the other still leaned against the fence on one side, slanting drunkenly toward the ground.

March pulled up beside her and dropped to the ground, examining the fence.

"I saw the trail they made over there," he said, waving back the direction he'd come. "It should be easy enough to follow."

But still he crouched by the fence, his eyes far away.

"What is it?" Maggie asked.

He pushed himself to his feet, shaking his head. "I don't know." He turned in a circle, examining the countryside around them. "From what I saw of the horse tracks out that way, it looked like Stormy made a beeline in the direction of Jed's barley. If Prince had gotten into trouble, wouldn't they have been more upset?"

Lines of frustration creased his face. "And this fence rail
. . ." He picked up the one that had split in the middle.

"It looks like one of the horses kicked it," Maggie volunteered.

"The top rail?" He tossed it back to the ground. "Could
be . . ."

He lifted the unbroken rail and set it into place, then
swung himself back onto Balthasar. The doubt hadn't left his
eyes. "I suppose we should follow my original plan and track
the horses' route to the farm."

"We could split up," Maggie suggested. "I don't have any
tracking experience, but I'm sure I could follow a whole herd
of horses for a couple of miles."

"I don't want you riding out there alone."

For once Maggie felt no inclination to argue. Prince's disappearance and March's reaction to the downed fence had
her spooked. She might not believe in his theory about the
men who had killed the Pennys, but she had to admit she felt
better with March and his shotgun beside her.

"I've got to come back this way eventually, anyway, to fix
the fence," he said at last. "If we don't find anything on the
way back to the farm, I'll search the ranch property this afternoon."

Maggie nodded and swung Ari toward the south. But
March's voice caught her before she could urge the mare into
motion.

"Wait!"

She looked back to see him gazing over the ranch lands.
When he didn't speak again, she urged Ari up beside him.
The bleak look on his face chilled her.

"March, what—"

He pointed upward. A mile or more beyond the line of

fence, two huge black buzzards circled slowly in the uncanny blue of the summer sky.

In the next instant, he'd spun Balthasar around, taking him ten yards from the fence. For a moment too long, Maggie didn't understand what he planned to do.

"March, no! You'll break your fool neck!"

But he'd already started back toward the fence, Balthasar's hindquarters straining for leverage. Too horrified even to close her eyes, Maggie watched them launch into the air. To her surprise, the ungainly gelding cleared the damaged fence with a foot to spare. And he kept right on going.

"Damn you, wait for me!" she yelled after them, but they'd already rounded a clump of brush and disappeared.

Her hands clenched on the reins, aching with her desire to jump the fence after him. Instead, she swung off Ari's back and dropped heavily to the ground, her sore legs almost crumpling beneath her.

"Serve him right if I killed us both trying that jump," she growled to her mare, while lowering the middle rail that March had replaced. "That would make the idiot sorry. Maybe."

She let Ari pick her way daintily over the bottom rail, then replaced the one she'd removed. She tested it for steadiness before climbing up on it to give herself access to Ari's back.

"All right. Let's go find them."

March knew he shouldn't have risked jumping the fence. He knew he shouldn't let Balthasar run this fast over broken ground. But all he could think about were those two buzzards and their lazy circles. Pain squeezed his heart.

He was pushing his gelding as though there might be

something he could do once he reached the birds, but reason told him that whatever had caught the buzzards' attention was beyond his help. And his mind told him it could only be Prince.

He knew what he'd find. Prince had stepped in a prairie dog burrow and broken a leg. Or he'd lost his footing and tumbled down an embankment—up here, near where the Little Owl River entered his property, the canyon cliffs sheered down more sharply than anywhere else on the ranch.

Or, worst of all, he might find Prince the victim of a killer's bullet. The sick mind that could orchestrate the murder of an entire family wouldn't hesitate to kill a horse as valuable as Prince. March prayed they'd shot him between the eyes, that they hadn't just maimed him and left him to a pain-racked, lingering death.

He clutched Jed's shotgun tight against his lap. Whatever the truth, if Prince was still alive, he'd have to be prepared to use the weapon, even if it was the last gun on earth he would have chosen for a mercy killing.

He'd had to leave Maggie behind. He couldn't let her see the result of a shotgun blast on his beautiful stallion, Jane's Prince Charming, the first great horse to come out of Lucas's breeding program eight years ago.

He rode on, past jutting outcrops of granite, over a hill, and down into a cooler valley swathed in Ponderosa pines, a tattered hem of the great tree skirt of the Rockies. The pines reigned over an almost parklike expanse of open forest and dry grasses that merged seamlessly into a small swatch of meadow, a favorite resting spot for the ranch's horses.

Over this open space, the buzzards glided soundlessly. March dismounted and walked out into the shallow sea of grass. Suddenly, Balthasar balked, his ears laid back, his nostrils flaring. In the next instant, March saw why.

There would be no need for the shotgun.

Moving over a low ridge, Maggie caught sight of the buzzards once more.

"Thank God."

She'd drifted too far east, but she couldn't be more than a hundred yards off, if she was still following the right birds. She turned Ari to the left and plunged back into the Ponderosa forest. In the thin shade of the trees, the silence contracted about her, a pocket of sweet-scented peace. Up ahead, she saw a break in the trees and movement. Balthasar.

She'd never known March to do more than ground-tie his reliable gelding, but Balthasar's reins were looped around a branch of a stout pine, and the whites of the horse's normally calm eyes showed as he turned toward her.

Maggie dismounted and quickly tethered Ari to the next tree. Her legs protesting every step of the way, she followed the trail of flattened grass out into the meadow. She caught sight of March's hat, and then March himself, leaning over something lying in the grass.

"March?" she asked, barely able to hear her own whisper.

He turned and rose, putting up his hands. "Maggie, go back. You don't need to see this."

"Oh, God." She put a hand up over her mouth. Even after seeing the buzzards, she hadn't been able to believe they'd find Prince here. Despite March's warning, she moved forward, unable to stop herself.

Her eyes dropped toward March's feet. She saw the trampled earth, smelled the scent of death that had drawn the buzzards . . .

"Maggie, don't." He grabbed her arm, and she stumbled against him.

. . . saw the soil damp with blood, strewn with trampled

grass, specked with . . . gray fur.

She breathed a great, heaving breath. "It's not Prince."

"It's not Prince." He pulled her closer, turning her head away from the scene of death.

"What . . . ?"

"It's a wolf."

She would have sagged against him in relief, but she could feel the tension still straining his muscles. She looked up into his eyes, waiting.

"She must have attacked one of the horses," March said, his expression troubled. "A damn fool thing to do—all my horses are plenty healthy. One wolf against one sick horse, and I might put my money on the wolf, but trying to pick one out of a healthy herd? Even this year's foals are old enough not to be easy prey. Prince must have killed her, protecting the mares. He obviously won the battle, but if she severed a tendon or slashed an artery . . ."

He looked around the meadow. "The question is, where is he now?"

Maggie knew he didn't expect an answer, but it came anyway. A shrill scream of pure equine fury shattered the serenity of the tranquil valley.

Chapter 14

From the other side of the meadow, Ari and Balthasar whinnied in answer.

"They'll be all right," March said, releasing Maggie's arm to get a better grip on Jed's shotgun. "This way."

He sprinted toward the opposite end of the meadow, Maggie right behind him, the aching in her legs momentarily forgotten.

Prince called again, angry and frustrated. The sound led them into the trees and up a rough, rocky slope. March slowed to a walk, then stopped, crouching behind a pair of trees. Maggie crept up behind him.

Through the bars of tree trunks, she saw a flash of shadow. Squinting, she brought the shadow into focus, the broad flank of a dark brown horse. As she watched, the stallion shifted and danced to the side, his hooves flashing against the pale ground.

"He doesn't look hurt to me," she whispered. The unwanted image of rustlers returned. "Is he tethered there?"

March shook his head. "That's what I thought at first, but there's nothing around his neck. You wait here."

Maggie gave him a yard head start, then followed. He couldn't expect her actually to stay behind, she reasoned, so he must have said it just to make himself feel better.

As they neared the stallion, Maggie could see that blood spattered his forelegs, but it must have belonged to the wolf, for it had dried already and Prince showed no signs of weakness as he pawed the ground. Foam flecked his neck and the whites of his eyes flashed, but she could see no trace of any adversary on the ground before him.

He caught scent of them as they neared, and his head shot up, his legs stiff, ready to run or fight. For a second, Maggie thought she heard an injured mountain lion mewing, but Prince recognized the sound immediately as March's peculiar whistle, and he relaxed his stance, turning his attention back to the ground.

"It's just a hole," Maggie said, examining the forest floor more closely.

March whirled on her. "I thought I told you to wait back there."

"I'm obviously in terrible danger," she said, her residual fear turning to sarcasm. "Though I suppose I ought to be frightened to get too close to a horse who can't tell a panther from a hole in the ground."

"That's the wolf's den," March informed her, leaning the shotgun against a tree. His voice turned low and soothing as he approached the stallion, though the words were for her. "There must be cubs in there."

"You think so?" she asked doubtfully.

"Mm. Prince hates wolves . . . coyotes, dogs, you name it. I'm surprised Stormy would lead the mares off without him, but not terribly surprised that Prince would obsess over a couple of doomed cubs."

As he neared the stallion, Prince dodged away, shaking his head. He skirted around March, trying to keep the wolf den in sight.

"Maggie, go back to the horses and get my rope, please. And there's some sugar in my saddle bag. We need to distract him."

Maggie scrambled back down the slope to the waiting horses. Ari and Balthasar nickered a grateful greeting, still unnerved by the scent of the dead wolf in the meadow. She stopped to give each of them a cube of sugar before grabbing March's rope and trotting back up the hill.

He'd begun whistling again, and he took the rope and sugar with only a nod for thanks. Preoccupied by bloodthirsty intentions, Prince hardly noticed when March slipped the lasso over his head.

"I'm going to lead him back down to the others," March said, giving a gentle tug on the rope. "Then see if I can calm him down a little. Watch over the den until I get back. Even if the wolf down in the meadow is the father and the mother's still in the den, I don't think she'll come out. But I'm leaving you the shotgun. Just point it at the target and pull the trigger. The gun will do the rest."

Maggie lifted the shotgun from where it leaned against a pine tree and dutifully placed her hand so her finger could reach the trigger. While March led the reluctant stallion away, she kept her eyes focused on the innocuous dark circle that broke the shadowed carpet of pine needles.

She tried to picture a huge, vicious gray beast with dripping fangs bursting from the den, but she couldn't manage it. She sagged against a tree and pretended she was waiting for Prince to emerge from the hole so she could crack him over his thick-skulled head with the stock of the shotgun.

"You don't need the shotgun. No wolf would be stupid enough to brave that glare."

She'd been concentrating so hard she hadn't heard March return. She turned her frown on him. "I'm beginning to understand why shooting Prince Charming in the head appeals to Jed Culbert so much."

"Prince has his quirks," March admitted, a smile curving one corner of his mouth. "If I weren't so damn glad to see him, I'd probably shoot him myself. But he's smart and he's tough and he sires good colts."

Maggie snorted.

March's grin deepened. Relief had lit his eyes like sunlight dancing on still water, and Maggie looked away.

"Here, hand me that gun."

She passed it to him, watching him fumble one-handed through his pockets. He pulled out a stub of candle and a box of matches she'd noticed in his saddlebags when she'd been searching for the sugar.

"What's that for?"

He lit the candle and returned the match box to his pocket before answering. "Wolf hunting."

Not until he'd crouched down beside the hole and poked in the shotgun did she realize what he meant.

"You're not going in there!"

He dropped to his stomach and stuck the candle into the hole alongside the shotgun. "No one's coming out of that den as long as we're here, so I've got to go in."

"I wasn't asking a question. I was telling you, you're not going into that damned hole," Maggie said. Suddenly the slavering mother wolf, eyes glowing red, teeth yellowed and sharp, came all too clearly to her imagination.

"I've got a shotgun," March said calmly, making her want to scream. "In a hole this size, I'm hardly going to miss anything coming at me. As soon as the candle picks up the glow of their eyes, I'll shoot. Besides, I'm pretty sure the wolf Prince killed was the dam. Only a truly desperate creature would attack a herd of healthy horses. If she had a mate to help her hunt, she wouldn't have tried it."

He wriggled forward, the light of the candle disappearing before him into the darkness. Maggie dropped beside him.

"You think there's only cubs down there."

He nodded, crawling forward.

"Then you can't just shoot anything that moves," she objected, her fear for March diminishing at the thought of a shotgun blast ripping through a litter of baby wolves.

He looked at her over his shoulder. "Why not?"

"You're planning to murder those pups!" she realized abruptly. She stared at March's familiar face with horror. She'd never have thought him capable of such an act.

He pulled back from the hole. "Maggie, I don't like it any better than you do, but I have to kill those cubs."

She shook her head, crossing her arms over her stomach. It burned with acid. A dark shadow fell back over the day, obscuring the joy of finding Prince safe and sound.

"You can't kill helpless babies," she said, pleading, as though the words might somehow make it true. Not March. He couldn't be that cruel.

He swore. "Their mother's dead, Maggie. They won't be old enough to survive on their own. Would you rather have me leave them here to starve to death?"

"We could take them back to the ranch, feed them ourselves."

"Jesus Christ." He slammed the shotgun down onto the ground. "These are not puppies. They won't grow up to be dogs. They're wolf cubs, and they'd grow up to be wolves—if we could even save them, which is not bloody likely.

"They couldn't survive in the wild, and they couldn't be trusted around livestock. The first time they attacked one of my horses, I'd have to put them down, and believe me, it would be a lot harder to do then than now. And I'd have to count myself lucky if they attacked my horses instead of someone else's milk cow or somebody's child."

His eyes begged her to understand, but she could only look away, swallowing the rest of her pleas along with the first welling of tears. After a moment she heard him move again, scooting himself forward into the den. She hadn't felt so bereft and alone since she'd watched her stepfather take Ladybug out of her life forever.

March dragged himself forward, rocks digging into his elbows, the candle flickering feebly before him. The walls of the den pressed in on him, confining his movements, increasing the feeling of danger at entering a wolf's lair. He'd done this once before, in the frigid cold, when wolves, lean and hungry from winter's scanty game, had crept down from the mountains in search of easier prey.

He knew cowboys who gloried in the excitement of a wolf hunt to break the boredom of winter. The big ranches kept wolfhounds or deerhounds to track the beasts down, and the hunters took turns outboasting each other about the number of pelts they'd collected, the biggest packs their dogs had run down, the risks they'd taken facing down she-wolves in their dens.

March hated it. He could remember the face of every wolf he'd killed. He'd heard them described as cowardly, craven beasts, but his experience had shown him only brave, intelligent creatures, caring for their young and each other better than many human families he'd known.

But when it came to choosing between a wolf and his horses, there was no choice. He made a promise to each horse that came into his hands to treat it well and protect it from danger, and he wouldn't turn away from that promise, even to stop Maggie's tears.

The candle burned on ahead of him, but the blackness and closeness of the den created the mental illusion of lack of air. He wriggled forward another foot, cursing the awkwardness of Jed's shotgun in the confined space. He'd assured Maggie there wasn't an adult wolf waiting for him down there, and he prayed he was right. A cornered she-wolf could charge past the end of the shotgun before he got a chance to pull the trigger.

He'd have paid a handsome price to hold his compact, six-shot Colt revolver in his hand at that moment.

His eyes strained for the flicker of reflection that would betray the watchful eyes of the den's occupants. The blackness and confinement distorted his sense of time and space, so he couldn't be sure how far he'd come. Six feet? Seven?

When the candle showed the back wall of the den, he didn't believe it. He kept forward until the end of the shotgun bumped into the crumbling earth. He'd so expected the confrontation at the end of this journey that his heartbeat refused to slow, though no living creature had come forward to challenge him.

He hadn't been wrong about this being a she-wolf's den. He didn't have Prince's sensitive nose, but he could smell the strong odor of wolf, though the dirt floor was meticulously bare.

He knew, with the strength of experience and intuition, that more than hunger had driven the wolf Prince had killed. Only a desperate mother would have taken such a chance. But where were the cubs?

The slightest scrape of claw against dirt sent him rolling to his side, fumbling to swing the shotgun around. The end of the barrel dragged across the floor, catching on a mound of gray fur curled into the far corner.

Teeth as sharp as needles gleamed in the inadequate candle light. A long pink tongue rolled out between them, and a pointed white muzzle stretched toward the den ceiling in a tremendous yawn.

March allowed his eyes to close for a brief second of relief.

Only a cub. And smaller than he'd expected for this time of year.

Quickly, he swept the candle around him, inspecting every inch of the circular den while the wakened cub watched him closely with unblinking silver eyes. When his survey turned up nothing more than dirt and some stray fur, March turned back to the single cub.

The jackrabbit-sized ball of fur, still showing the roundness of babyfat, couldn't have been more than two months old. The cub, who should have been cringing and growling at this intruder in his home, examined him with a curiosity equal to March's own.

He stretched his muzzle forward, poking at the end of the shotgun barrel. March's stomach lurched. It took no imagination at all to know what a shotgun blast at this range would do to the little wolf.

Hardly aware of what he was doing, March let go of the stock of his gun and set his candle on a flat spot near the wall. Scraping up handfuls of wolfy smelling dirt and fluff, he rubbed it over all of his body he could reach—in his hair, over his chest, along his arms, between his fingers. While he rubbed, he hummed.

The cub cocked his head at him.

March broke into the whistle he used to soothe mares and their newborn foals. Slowly, he scrunched himself toward the cub, holding out his hand. The cub raised his head back. March stopped. After a moment, the cub lowered his nose.

"Go ahead, take a sniff."

The cub did, starting at his fingertips and snuffing toward his wrist. With a suddenness that March couldn't counter in those close quarters, the cub grabbed his thumb in his teeth.

March braced himself for the piercing needles to come, but the cub didn't bite down. He let go, then put his mouth around March's front knuckles. He chewed gently, let go, and tried another spot, his eyes closing as he stretched to take in as much of March's hand as he could get.

He let go and sat back, looking up into March's face. He whimpered.

"You're hungry."

The cub answered with a thin, high-pitched whine.

"Sorry I don't taste like much, but I bet I can find something you'll like if you'll let me take you out of here." *He's not a puppy. Wolf cubs grow up to be wolves.* "So, what do you think, fella? Jed might even have a fresh rabbit around somewhere."

He scooted back, turning toward the candle. He'd have to blow it out. Young he might be, but the cub was big enough to cause real problems if he wanted to fight. March didn't need the extra handicap of carrying the candle.

As he reached for the stub of wax, a dry nose bumped his other arm. He looked down into pleading silver eyes. Leaving the candle lit after all, he picked it up and took hold of Jed's shotgun. He wriggled back a foot. The cub followed. Another foot. And another.

His legs reached the freedom of open air. Still the cub followed. He hunched his lower back out of the den opening and blew out the candle, leaving it there. He reached forward, grabbing the scruff of the cub's neck. Pushing off with the shotgun, he heaved himself back out into the daylight, pulling the cub along with him.

The cub struggled now, wiggling to get down. March shrugged out of his shirt, setting down the shotgun and transferring the cub to his other hand to pull off the second sleeve. Then he wrapped the cub in it, preventing him from being able to push off with his strong hind legs or scratch with his claws.

March pulled the bundle to his chest, keeping a sharp watch on the cub's teeth, but the little animal's struggles subsided quickly. While wrapping him, March had seen his shrunken tummy. The cub's ribs didn't show the skeletal outline of starvation, but he was obviously weak from hunger and undoubtedly suffered from thirst as well.

March reached down and picked up the shotgun. Even with care, the cub might not live. He hadn't been able to blow the little wolf to bits with Jed's gun, but a wolf was a wolf. The responsible thing now would be to take him down to where the horses waited, find his hunting knife, and humanely take the poor beast's life.

But even as he thought it, he knew he couldn't do it. Even without Maggie's accusations of murder.

Maggie.

He swung around in a quick circle. She was gone. She'd left him to do his bloody task alone. He'd probably find her back at Jed and Henna's.

He started down the steep slope toward the meadow, clutching the cub to him with one arm, using Jed's shotgun for extra balance with the other. He'd have to give the gun a good cleaning when he got back.

"March?" The sharp, worried voice came from below, among the trees.

"Yes, it's just me, Maggie."

She was scrambling up toward him, her eyes big and green, clutching the wickedly curved hunting knife from his saddle bag.

"You son-of-a-bitch." She came to a halt, panting for breath. "I didn't hear your shotgun go off, and you were down there so long. Why didn't you answer me when I called?"

She'd gone for a knife when he hadn't returned, planning

220

to come down after him.

He knew it was the wrong time to smile, but her concern did strange things to his heart. "I'm sorry; I didn't hear you."

"I shouted and screamed," she said, obviously not accepting his explanation. She'd nearly caught her breath now, and climbed a little closer. "I ought to use this knife on your rotten hide, March Jackson, you—"

She froze, her eyes moving from his offending hide to the bundle at his chest. The bundle whimpered.

"There was only this one cub," March said defensively. He could feel his skin reddening at being caught in his sentimental weakness. He made his voice gruff. "If I'd had my Colt, it wouldn't have been a problem, but Jed's shotgun was just . . ."

Maggie's hand on his bare arm silenced him. The cub's forehead crinkled in concentration gazing up at her, trying to decide if she was a threat or might have some food.

"You can let him sniff your hand," March said, giving up his bluff of toughness. "I don't think he'll bite."

Maggie shook her head. Her fingers on his bare skin sent sparks flickering up his arm, and now, as she leaned closer to the cub, the swell of her breasts pressed against him.

"Really, it's all right," he said. "We'll need to get him used to human scent."

"Puppies . . . make me nervous," she mumbled, tilting her head so her hat shielded her eyes from his gaze.

"He's not a puppy," March reminded her.

Her head came back up, and he could see the smile playing around her lips. "I don't want to frighten him."

"Wolves are like people in some ways. They like to be touched." He honestly hadn't meant that husky note to creep into his voice. Perhaps she hadn't noticed, for she didn't pull away.

Instead, she reached a tentative hand toward the cub. His long tongue wrapped around her fingers. He nibbled at them.

Maggie laughed. "That tickles."

March stared straight down at a spot between the cub's ears. He would not think about what Maggie's reaction might be if *he* tried nibbling her fingers.

"He's hungry," he said. "We'd better get him something to eat and drink, or I might as well have shot him. I've got some jerked beef in my saddlebag, and a canteen of water."

Maggie glanced at him out of the corner of her eye. "Is there anything you don't carry in your saddlebags?"

"You don't want to be caught out here without food and water, whether it's the middle of summer or a blizzard in January."

She shook her head and laughed, turning to lead the way back down to the horses. March found himself resisting the urge to reach out and pull her bouncing braid, any excuse to touch her.

As they crossed the little meadow and neared the horses, Prince whinnied loudly, rolling his eyes at March. Ari swung abruptly away from him, stopping only when her rump hit a tree. Even faithful Balthasar snorted questioningly, though he stayed motionless as March came up beside him.

"It's all right," March murmured, patting the gelding's neck. "I may smell a little like wolf, but it's just me."

Maggie cleared her throat.

"I didn't want to mention it," she said, stroking Ari's nose to calm the mare. "But you smell a *lot* like wolf."

He could feel a flush creeping up his neck. "There's worse things to smell like."

"Lots worse. But I'm not sure the horses think so."

Holding the cub and shotgun with one arm, March rummaged through his saddlebag until he found the package of jerky. He tossed it to Maggie, then untied his canteen from his saddle.

"We're not far from the river," he said. "You can feed our little friend while I rinse off some of this smell. That might make the ride back to Jed and Henna's a little easier on the horses."

She glanced doubtfully at where the cub's head poked out of his shirt, then toward Prince who was snorting and pawing at the ground.

"I suppose it's worth a try."

"Here, you can do it. Just eat a little bit," Maggie begged, holding the strip of jerked beef out toward the silver and gray cub. After she'd unwrapped him from March's shirt, he'd drunk eagerly, if a little clumsily, from the edge of the stream March called Little Owl River. But so far his attempts to gnaw at the jerky had proven woefully unsuccessful.

He tried again, tugging at the strip in her hand. He chewed on it with one side of his jaw, then turned and tried the other. Finally, he dropped back on his haunches and stared up at her, his eyes asking her what he was doing wrong.

"Please, please eat," Maggie pleaded. The cub answered her tone of desperation with a tiny whine.

She glanced toward the stream. Some long ago flash flood had left a nest of boulders at this bend in the small canyon, creating a deep pool of shimmering clear water, almost precisely the color of March's eyes. March himself stood waist deep in the pool, plunging his head under, rubbing out the remnants of dirt and wolf scent. He flung his head back, shaking water from his hair.

Maggie tried and failed to swallow her envy. She'd drunk most of the water from March's canteen while the cub lapped at the stream, but though that had taken the edge off her thirst, she still felt hot and sticky from their long morning ride. She longed to plunge into the depths of that cool, cleansing pool.

Anything to wash off the fear that sat in her stomach, the fear of her own inability to do something so simple as feed a starving baby.

"March!" When he glanced back at her, she gestured at the cub. "He won't eat."

As March turned and came toward her out of the pool, other thoughts replaced her fantasies of a swim. His tanned skin, glistening with water, would be nearly as cool to the touch as the stream. Droplets ran down his chest, tangling in the curly hair that veed toward his waistband. His sodden jeans clung to him, shaping the muscles of his thighs.

She glanced away, hoping her thoughts didn't show. She wished he would put his shirt back on. He crouched down beside her. If only she could lean her hot cheek against that cool, damp chest . . .

". . . have to chew it for him."

She caught the end of March's sentence as he tugged the piece of jerky from her hand.

"What?"

He tore the strip in two and handed half back to her. "We have to soften it for him. He's used to fresh meat; this is too tough."

Maggie looked down at the dried meat in her hand, then toward the wolf cub. His pleading eyes frightened her. What if they couldn't help him and he starved?

"He won't eat it with our spit on it," she said in despair, shoving her piece of jerky at March.

He caught her arm as she tried to scramble to her feet.

"Your horse killed his mother," she said, tugging against his hold. "You do it. You make him eat."

"You're the one who wanted to rescue a whole den of wolves," he said. "Chewing a little jerky is too disgusting for you? I'm not asking you to let him chew it for you, for heaven's sake."

She sat back down hard, the energy she needed to run lost in his accusing eyes.

"It's not that," she whispered. "What if we chew it and he still won't eat it?"

"He'll eat it."

"How do you know?"

"I know. Don't you trust me?"

Maggie Parker didn't trust anyone. She knew better. Trust led only to betrayal. Even her beloved father had betrayed her, getting himself killed and leaving her to the mercies of a hard, uncaring stepfather.

"Maggie?"

Slowly, almost imperceptibly, she nodded and held out her hand. He placed a piece of jerked beef in her palm.

"Be sure to chew until it's nice and soft."

He tore a chunk of jerky off with his teeth. She tried to copy him, but discovered that trying to bite into jerked beef was similar to biting into boot leather. No wonder it had given the cub so much trouble. She got a better grip with her teeth and pulled hard. The jerky tore with a satisfying rip, and she pushed the wiry piece of meat back to her molars.

March finished softening his piece first. Maggie quit chewing, holding her breath as he handed it to the cub. The little wolf grabbed hold and tugged, landing in a surprised thump on his bottom as a bite pulled easily away from March's hand. He flung his head from side to side, as though to subdue his suddenly aggressive meal, then chewed it with huge, noisy clampings of his jaw.

He swallowed, paused, licked his lips, and looked expectantly back at March, who obligingly offered him another bite.

Maggie felt the sting of tears in her eyes, but when March glanced up at her, she scrunched her face in disgust, making him grin.

"Your turn."

She set to chewing her jerky with renewed fervor.

Once they'd found something the cub could eat, he turned out to be nearly insatiable. Maggie chewed and chewed until her jaw ached.

"How much do you think he weighs?" she asked March at one point.

"Somewhere between fifteen and twenty pounds, I'd guess."

"He must have eaten nearly his own weight in jerky by this time."

"Quit talking, and keep chewing."

Finally, March offered him a piece which he simply sniffed and licked politely, looking up at March's face to see what happened next.

Maggie hastily set down the fresh strip of jerky she'd pulled from March's oilskin package. "Is he full?"

March laughed. "You sound so hopeful."

"I'm desperate," Maggie corrected.

March offered his piece one more time. The cub lowered his forelegs to the ground and daintily settled his muzzle on top of them, his gaze traveling from March to Maggie and back.

"Time for a nap," March concluded. "I don't blame you, little one. It's been a hard day. I wouldn't mind joining you."

"Oh, no," Maggie said, rising to her feet and dusting off her jeans. "We've probably already missed Henna's dinner, and I'm getting hungry."

"We've got some jerky left."

"There's no force on earth that could compel me to eat the rest of this jerked beef. I'd sooner starve."

March's low, genuine laugh warmed her. She couldn't remember seeing him this relaxed since she'd arrived in Colorado Territory. Perhaps finding Prince safe and hale had dispelled some of his obsession with rustlers. Whatever it was, she suddenly didn't feel quite so eager to return to the Culbert farm and all the things that reminded March of violence.

"I just want to jump in the river one more time before we go." He stood up beside her.

"That's not fair," Maggie objected.

"What's not fair?"

"That you get a swim, while I have to stand here broiling."

"Join me."

She crossed her arms over her chest, glowering at the challenge in his eyes. "In case you hadn't noticed, I neglected to bring a bathing outfit. Or do you have one of those stashed in your saddlebags, too?"

"Just come in as you are. You'll dry long before we get back to the Culberts'." He gestured at his jeans, which showed only a few damp spots from his previous swim.

Maggie glanced from March to the beckoning blue water. Who could possibly object to her cooling off with just a short dip in that quiet, safe little pool, completely, modestly clothed? Maybe Henna Culbert could, but she'd never know.

Maggie sat on a rock next to the wolf cub, who'd dropped off into that limp, dreamless slumber that only very young creatures seem able to achieve. She pulled off her boots and her stockings, the coarse sand of the small beach hot against her bare feet. She unbuttoned Lucas's vest and set it on top of her boots; the water would wreak havoc on the leather. She glanced down at the stained, worn vest. *Not that anyone would notice.*

"Are you ready, or are you just going to sit there all day?"

Maggie held out a prim hand, and March helped her to her feet.

She smiled at him sweetly. "I guess I'm readier than you are." She dropped his hand and dashed toward the pool, plunging into the cold, clear water.

Chapter 15

March laughed at Maggie's high-pitched shriek as she splashed up to her neck in cold, pure water straight from the ice fields of the high Rockies. The noise stopped for a second as her head dunked below the surface, then began again as she broke back out into the sunlight.

He followed more slowly, making his way in up to his knees.

"That's cold!" Maggie yelled unnecessarily, spinning to smile up at him from near the center of the pool.

"Too cold for a pampered city girl?"

She laughed, a sound that sparkled more brightly than the sun on the water. "I'm not the one standing over there afraid to get his knees wet."

"I guess I just don't have your impetuous nature," March said haughtily.

She swept her arm across the surface of the pool, splashing him with a fan of water.

"Witch!" he shouted trying to dodge aside as she splashed with the other arm.

"What's wrong, you afraid of a little water, March?" She moved toward him, a wicked gleam in her eye.

March knew she intended to drag him kicking and screaming into the pool, but as she rose up out of the water, he forgot his intention to play along. Every day this week he'd seen her wearing Lucas's old work shirts, but always with that ugly leather vest on. It hadn't ever occurred to him that of course she wouldn't wear a corset to work with the horses.

Now, he couldn't help but notice her lack of undergarment. The river water had melted Lucas's shirt against her skin, and it clung to every curve, nearly transparent in its saturation. He could trace the rosy peaks of her nipples, hardened to nubs by the cold.

Suddenly he needed the concealment of the water to protect him from more than the sun. He plunged past Maggie into the heart of the pool. Cold water flashed shock waves across his skin. The glacial touch of the mountains rippled over his shoulders, banishing the heat of the sun. But the icy water seemed to have no effect on the heat that burned inside him, sparked by one glimpse of a red-haired water sprite.

He heard her laughter when his head broke the water, sweet and light, as life-giving on his barren soul as this river across his land.

"Oh, March, this is wonderful."

He turned. She'd come up behind him, her eyes shining. Underwater, her shirt billowed out, obscuring her figure, but not his memory of it. Her hands flickered beneath the surface, and he saw she was trying to untangle the end of her braid.

"The ribbon's knotted," she said, seeing his glance. "I wanted to untie it and get all the dust out of my hair."

"Why don't you let me?" He took the end of the braid from her fingers and turned her from him. If she faced away from him, she couldn't see the desire in his eyes.

The water tightened the faded yellow ribbon. He poured his concentration into the knot, slowly reasserting control over his body . . . until the ribbon came free and tendrils of red hair began to flicker over his hands like fire.

She sighed, stretching her arms out to the side and gazing up into the sky as he sorted out her hair.

"I wish I did have a bathing dress," she said. "These blue

jeans are too heavy for a swim. Better yet, I wish I could feel the water over my bare arms, like you. Nothing between me and the water."

March closed his eyes and counted to ten. But all he could see behind his closed lids was an image of bare legs and arms flashing through clear water, lithe as a mermaid.

"Do you ever do that?" she asked, turning back toward him. The freed strands of hair slipped through his hands and floated about her in a red cloud. "When you're out here all by yourself?"

If he could have formed a coherent thought, he might have blushed. "You mean swim, um . . ."

Her cheeks bloomed red as her hair. "Oh, I'm sorry. I don't . . . Did I really say that?"

She disappeared under the water. He followed, catching her arm and bringing her back to the surface. He even managed a smile.

"It's all right, Maggie, you didn't embarrass me."

"Oh . . . good." She wouldn't look at him.

"I do sometimes come out here and swim—" He cleared his throat. "—without the encumbrance of clothes. If you'd like, I could go wait with the horses while you—"

"No!" She turned even redder. "That's all right. Maybe we should be getting back, anyway."

"Fine. I'm just going to swim across to the rocks and back." And hope the exercise and the cold water kept him from embarrassing himself when he stepped back onto land.

Maggie watched him slip under water, his arms pulling powerfully toward the far side of the pool, and wished the sand beneath her feet would part and pull her down into oblivion.

It was bad enough that she could so easily imagine March

here alone, his bare skin flashing bronze through the water, as natural as the river and the animals that shared it. But to have *said* it . . . He must think her a shameless hussy.

And maybe she was. Instead of retreating to the bank to pull her boots back on, she stood locked in place, unable to take her eyes off his movements as he touched a gray boulder and pushed off for the return swim. She didn't move until he'd passed her, then she followed him toward the shore.

He turned to look back at her. "You sure you're ready to leave?"

She nodded and followed, her clothes heavy as they cleared the water's surface. She saw March watching her as she neared, and couldn't quite interpret the strange expression on his face. She looked down the front of her shirt, the shirt Lucas had worn thin from use, thin enough that the water had . . .

March's hand on her arm yanked her toward him with such force that they both lost their balance, tumbling together into the shallow water at the pool's edge.

March's body cushioned her fall, one arm coming around her waist as they hit the sandy bottom. Maggie's head went under, and in her shock, she forgot to hold her breath. For one second, fear and water threatened to choke her.

Then she found herself back in the air, gagging and sputtering, too desperate for breath to break free of March's hold.

"What was that for?" she demanded, furious, as soon as she could speak. But she knew. Or, more importantly, she should have known. He was a man. One glimpse of her chest in Lucas's shirt, and all that gentleness, that veneer of respect, had flown right . . .

"Snake," March said, his voice as water-choked as hers.

"What?" She paused in her plan to slam her elbow into his throat.

"Snake." He raised his free hand to point across the surface of the pool to where a dark ripple crossed the river, as supple and gleaming as the water itself.

"Oh." Panic of another kind gripped her. Suddenly the water's buoyant density seemed like a heavy trap, holding her to mortal slowness while death skitted along the surface like a beam of light. She scrambled with fists and feet to get a purchase on the sand.

"Maggie, it's all right. There's no danger."

March could tell his words hadn't gotten through to her when her hand pushed hard into his stomach. He tightened his hold around her waist.

"Maggie!" He grabbed a flailing hand with his free arm. "It's just a watersnake. He's harmless."

She stopped moving, but her muscles didn't relax. "Are you sure?"

"Yes." He took a deep breath into the sore spot in his abdomen. "I'm sure. I just caught a glimpse of it behind you and thought it was a cottonmouth, but it's not."

She didn't need to know that he'd never seen a cottonmouth in Colorado. When he'd seen that lithe, dark body slipping toward her through the water, he'd panicked, a holdover from his childhood in Texas. But he couldn't tell Maggie that without admitting to his fear—hell, his terror—of snakes.

Besides, she might think he had ulterior motives for grabbing her like that. Where their bodies touched, heat mocked the cold touch of the river, and he couldn't pretend, even to himself, that he wanted to let her go.

She relaxed a little against him, trying to catch her breath. Tendrils of red hair floated across his arm, wrapped themselves over his shoulder, caressed him with flicking tongues of flame.

Only the faintest thread of memory connected him to his promise not to touch her. Only strength of will kept his hand still against her ribs. "I'm sorry. I didn't mean to scare you."

Perhaps he'd failed in his struggle to control his tone, for her body stilled, suspended between the thudding of his heartbeats.

"Maggie." The tattered rags of his voice hung in the shimmering air. "I promised not to hurt you."

She moved then, turning in his arms, only to freeze again when her thigh brushed across the front of his jeans.

March threw back his head, dunking it under water, stifling the groan that rose in his throat. He forced himself to unwrap his arm from her waist, then came back up for air. Opaque hazel-green eyes in a pale face held his gaze.

"I didn't promise not to want you," he told those accusing eyes. Yet maybe that was enough to hurt her. He looked away. "Stay here and wait with the wolf cub. I'll see to the horses."

"It would be faster if I wrapped him up and came with you."

March gritted his teeth until his jaw ached. Why didn't she move away? "I'd like a little time to . . . get control of myself."

Maggie's hand found his cheek and turned his face back toward her. The flatness had left her eyes, replaced with a damp, dark green of questions and magic.

"I do trust you, March," she whispered, her voice full of wonder and fear.

"Maggie, move away from me, please."

Instead, she lowered her mouth to his, lightly, tentatively, her lips whispering across his like butterfly wings.

His hands dug into the sand beneath him, but it slipped through his fingers, leaving him nothing to hold firm to. He could find no solid ground on which to brace himself against the swirling pull of sudden, aching desire.

"Maggie . . ."

She heard the plea in his voice, but she could not find the will to save herself, much less March, from the whirlpool that engulfed them. She turned until her fingers found his bare shoulders, hanging onto him as a life raft against the tide of need and fear and bright, coiling emotion that threatened to drown her.

He shuddered beneath her and his hands found her sides, pressing against her ribs, neither pulling her close nor pushing her away.

She turned her face, pressing her cheek against his, her nose inches from the water. She could hear his ragged breathing against her ear.

"I'm sorry, March," she whispered, the words tearing at her heart. "I can't . . ."

"It's all right," he said, though his voice had become a low growl of desire. "I wouldn't ask you to. But you have to leave me, Maggie. You—"

"No!" She tightened her grip on his shoulders. "I meant . . . I can't bear this any longer March. I don't want to leave. I want you to . . . touch me."

His hands left her sides to find her face, tilting her head back until his gaze could lock with hers. "You don't understand."

She frowned at him, though she knew her voice shook. "I understand perfectly well. I'm not a child. I want you."

"Damn you, Maggie Parker. You don't mean that."

She flushed up to the roots of her hair. "Yes, I do. But only if you want it, too."

In answer he pulled her mouth down to his, his lips bruising against hers. She dug her fingers into his shoulders, answering the questions his mouth asked hers with kisses of equal fire.

His hands left her face, running down her back, pressing her against him. The frigid water should have chilled her by now, but at every point where their bodies touched she felt heat rippling between them.

His hands worked up under her shirt, caressing her bare skin. She groaned, and his tongue found her open mouth, testing her, tasting her. He pushed her from him just far enough for his hands to find her breasts. Fire and ice rippled over her skin, making her shake.

Abruptly March's hands moved to her sides, turning her from him.

"No," she objected, resisting.

"Maggie, you're turning blue." Amusement rippled in his voice, but couldn't hide the desire threading through it.

Maggie relaxed, letting him position her until he could lift her free of the water. He carried her up onto the beach, laying her down gently on the warm sand. He knelt beside her, and his hands found the buttons of her shirt, inch by inch exposing her skin to the rays of the sun. But it was the heat in his eyes that banished the last of the chill from her body.

His fingers traced from her breasts to her belly and back again, but his eyes never left hers.

"You are so lovely," he whispered.

And in that moment she believed him, for the feelings that flooded her had a beauty all their own.

She tried to sit up, but he put a hand on her shoulder, restraining her.

"You said you wanted me to touch you. Will you let me?"

His eyes were dark with desire and promise. She couldn't very well speak when even breathing seemed beyond her, but she managed to nod.

He brushed her lips with his, then began to explore every inch of her bared skin with his hands. He caressed her with his palms, his knuckles, his fingertips, sensitizing, relaxing, teasing. And he followed each touch with his mouth, nibbling, kissing, stroking.

When he pulled one breast into his mouth, she cried out, clutching at him, tangling her fingers in his hair.

March heard her cry, felt her writhe beneath him, and his own tentative grasp on control deserted him. He wanted to bring pleasure to this woman beyond anything she'd ever known. And yet, the simple knowledge that she wanted him, that his touch did pleasure her, spun him past all conscious thought.

He swept his hand across her belly to the waistband of her jeans, fumbling awkwardly with the buttons and the water-logged denim. Finally he had to turn and use both hands.

"Here, let me." She sat up beside him, shrugging out of her shirt before reaching for his hands.

"I've got it," he said, slipping loose the last button.

Her fingers wrapped around his and she brought them up to her chest. He looked back at her. She flushed again. "May I . . . touch you, before . . . ?"

He managed a slight smile. "I'm not sure I would survive it, but if it's what you want . . ."

She nodded.

He closed his eyes and let her fingertips gently push him onto his back. The sand burned his bare skin, but he hardly felt it compared to the fire that flowed from her touch. Slowly, gently, she explored him as he had her, following the outline of his muscles with her fingers, tracing his skin with feathery kisses, as though she brushed him with flower petals.

She stretched out over him, her breasts brushing his bare chest as she nibbled the sensitive skin of his neck.

He reached for her, needing to touch her, needing to feel her solidity and warmth. He almost feared to run his work-roughened hands along her soft, pale skin. But her fingers, too, had the hard calluses of ranch work and he could have wanted no other touch.

Maggie moved her fingers through the hair on his chest, following it down across his stomach to his blue jeans. She, too, had trouble with the soaked denim, stretched tight by March's desire. He groaned as her hands pushed and pulled the stubborn buttons.

The sound nearly stopped her breathing as a surge of heat rippled through her. The knowledge of his need fed her own, making the task at hand even more difficult, but also more enjoyable. She pressed and rubbed with her hands, reveling in her ability to arouse him as he did her.

Suddenly his hands circled her wrists and he pulled her forward on top of him, so her whole length stretched against him.

"Witch," he breathed against her mouth before kissing her once more, deeply and thoroughly.

She could feel his heat burning into her wherever they touched, but it wasn't enough. Not nearly enough. She moved against him, all sense, all control abandoned.

"March, please . . ."

"Yes."

He rolled her onto her back and reached for her jeans. She helped him pull them off, along with her underclothes. He touched her, his hands gentle after the harshness of the wet material. He slipped a hand between her thighs, feeling the warmth and dampness there.

She cried out again, and March watched passion darken her eyes, unfocus her gaze. Her lips parted as she struggled to breathe. She pushed at his hand.

"March, hurry, please."

He couldn't have said how he got out of his jeans, for the next thing he knew, he was lying beside her, bare flesh to bare flesh, touching her with the wonder and knowledge of a lover. Heaven help him. He was about to become her lover.

Somewhere in his head, he knew the thought should frighten him away. But all his heart could feel was an overwhelming awe that she should allow him to love her, an overwhelming tenderness that he was afraid he could not express, even in this most intimate of acts.

He raised himself over her, spreading her thighs, his greatest need rubbing against her hottest flame.

"Are you sure?" he asked again, not certain exactly what he was asking, not sure if he meant the words for her or for himself.

"Yes." Though she couldn't have said what question she was answering, for it was an answer her conscious mind could never have given. Only her heart knew what she truly meant, who Maggie Parker truly was in that moment.

Then he came into her, and nothing else mattered but the mingling of their bodies, their need, their souls.

She thought she heard him ask if he was hurting her. She answered in the only way she could, pulling him to her, arching to meet him, needing all of him without reservation.

And he gave it, driving into her with a cry muffled against her mouth. She clung to him as heat whipped and coiled within her, shocked by the explosion of feeling her body was capable of, knowing by instinct alone that if she let go of him, she might never find her way back from wherever it was that he was taking her.

He drove into her again and again. And then, without warning, the building storm hit her full force, tearing her from the outside world with the strength of a hurricane, pulling her down with a powerful undertow, then tossing her back onto the beach with the gentleness of a spring shower.

The echoes of her cries rang from the sides of the little canyon, and then March's joined them as he buried his face against her shoulder and shuddered within her.

For a moment that stretched forever, yet not long enough, absolute silence surrounded them. Then Maggie once more heard the murmuring of the stream, the hushed whisper of an afternoon breeze in the trees, the sweet sound of a bird calling.

March shifted, moving his weight off her. His hand stroked her neck, her hair, her face. His fingers stilled against her cheek. He shifted up on his elbow to look down into her eyes.

"You're crying," he said, his voice shaken. "Did I hurt you? Why didn't you say anything?"

"No, I'm not crying," she said, wanting to reassure him, but not knowing how to explain. "You didn't hurt me."

"I can see your tears."

And she could feel more welling as she gazed up into his eyes, still dark with spent passion. "That's not . . . they're not from pain. That was . . . it felt . . . Oh, March, I didn't know it could feel like that."

The worry eased just a little from his face. He brushed his hand down her side, warm skin against warm skin. "Neither did I."

She believed him. She could have believed in almost anything just then.

"You're sure I didn't hurt you? I know that does . . . with women . . . sometimes. I wanted to be gentle, but I don't think I was . . ."

All the blood drained from Maggie's face, and suddenly

240

even March's body and the touch of the sun couldn't warm her.

March meant that it often hurt women *the first time*.

Her first time, with Langley, it had hurt. The pain and the blood had shocked her, made her understand why women spoke of wifely duty when she had expected so much more. And now, with March, she'd found out just how much more there could be.

But he'd expected her to be a virgin. It should have occurred to her, before she'd let things get this far, that once they made love he would know she was not. She had disclosed to him her most painful secret, the biggest mistake of a lifetime of mistakes, the one that precluded her from ever having a family of her own.

But March was still acting as though his opinion of her had not changed. Perhaps he was too drugged from their passion to recognize the signs yet. Or perhaps he didn't know the signs. Perhaps he'd never made love with a virgin. He didn't strike her as the type to seduce young innocents and then desert them.

She could encourage his misconception of her. It would be easy to pretend she felt a little pain, to feign shyness and virginal regret.

But she couldn't lie to him, wouldn't profane what they had shared. And she would not hurt him with a regret she couldn't feel. If this one afternoon was all he could give her, she would not destroy the gift with recriminations and remorse.

She raised her head to brush March's lips with her own. "Thank you."

"Oh God, Maggie." He braced her head with his hand and kissed her hard, brushing her lips with his tongue. She opened to him, meeting him, teasing him, as the heat flooded back into her limbs.

A piercing whine scattered the embers of returning passion. A cold nose bumped Maggie's cheek, then a warm, rough tongue lapped across her mouth and March's.

"Ugh!" she sputtered, pushing at the furry muzzle poking anxiously at her face.

"Blaah," March agreed, turning his head sharply and wiping his mouth with the back of his hand.

The cub's tail perked up and he licked at Maggie again, taking their strange noises as signs of approval. A heavy paw, surprisingly big for such a small animal, dropped on her head, the better to hold her still for her unwanted bath.

"Get him off me!" Maggie ordered, unable to save herself as a result of a sudden attack of laughter.

"I've got him."

The paw lifted from her forehead, and she turned to see March holding the cub pressed to his chest while the little creature struggled to lick his chin.

March's gaze met hers over the cub's head, and his eyes also were filled with laughter. "You don't suppose he's hungry again?"

"No!" Maggie answered decisively. "I think he just wants to play." In the quiet of the summer afternoon, her own stomach sent out a loud growl. She blushed. "It *is* well past dinnertime."

March bent his nose down for the cub to snuffle. "I think you and I had better get her back to the ranch house, little one, before roast wolf starts to sound tasty to her."

The cub's long, pink tongue curled around his nose. March snorted and pulled his head back.

He glanced back at Maggie with a small smile, but the laughter had left his eyes.

Maggie put her fingers up against his lips.

"Don't say anything," she said. "Let's just go back to the

farm and leave this afternoon the way it is. Later, we can say
. . . what needs to be said."

He took her hand in his and squeezed it, all the answer he
could give.

Then he smiled again, a soft version of the smile that made
her heart tremble. "All right. But before we go back, why
don't we take one more swim—now that you're dressed for
it."

Chapter 16

Maggie shifted awkwardly, trying to get comfortable in Jane Penny's sidesaddle. She'd wanted to change into something ladylike before returning to Henna Culbert's house, but she missed the easy feel of riding astride, of guiding Ari with barely a thought.

She'd ridden like this many times in Kentucky, in this same green-striped poplin dress, with the toes of her boots peeking out from beneath frothy white petticoats, but this afternoon everything seemed new, strange, uncanny. The very sky had a different color. She wondered if it had always been this perfect pale blue and she'd just failed to notice it before.

She glanced at March. He rode ahead of her, his back straight, one arm curled in front of him around the young wolf cub. She struggled to think of something to say to him before they reached the Culbert farm.

Silence had descended between them the moment they'd left the river to return to the horses, and it had followed them all the way back to the Penny ranch.

Maggie hadn't minded the quiet. She didn't know that she could have spoken if she'd wanted to, her heart was too full. But once they'd changed into clean clothes, the cocoon of peace around her had slowly evaporated.

They were returning to the world of society and rules and disapproval. Back to a place where she was a scarred, sullied hoyden and March was a grieving wrangler bent on vengeance. A place where their pasts cut off their future.

After her father died and her mother hid away in illness,

she'd learned not to need anyone, not to depend on anyone. But in the newness and wonder of the emotions she felt, and in the shadow of a sorrow she didn't know how to avoid, she needed March to help her face this return to reality. Fear of that need choked her so she could not speak it.

They rounded the hill of the Culberts' drive, and her chance to speak disappeared. The farmhouse door slammed open as Wolf ran out onto the porch, little Emily close on his heels.

"It's them!" he shouted back over his shoulder. "March and Miss Maggie. They're back."

Ari followed Balthasar into a canter toward the porch, though Maggie would have been happy to delay their arrival.

"Did you find Prince?" Emily asked, running forward to grab March's leg as soon as Balthasar came to a halt.

"Emmy, let them come inside before you start bothering them," Wolf scolded, taking her hand and pulling her back. Unlike his sister, he was old enough to know that their news wasn't likely to be what Emily wanted to hear.

"It's all right, Wolf," March said, a smile breaking across his face. "We found Prince and he's alive and well and back where he belongs."

"You found him! I knew you would!" Emily yelled. She tried to clap, but found her right hand still held by Wolf, so she thumped the boy on the stomach instead.

"Emmy!"

"They found Prince! They found Prince!" she shouted, pounding him some more.

"Ack! Emmy!" Wolf grabbed his stomach and fell with a heavy thud to the hard packed earth. "Ugh," he mumbled breathlessly. "Emmy, you killed me."

Emily's eyes widened and she dropped to his side.

"Wolf?"

He groaned in answer. Maggie choked on a laugh.

"Wolf? Wolfie are you okay?" Emily grabbed his shoulders and shook him with all her six-year-old strength.

"Hah! Got you." Wolf grabbed her with one hand and tickled with the other. Emily's shrieks pierced the late afternoon calm like a rabbit's death cry.

Maggie almost missed the sound of the front door being thrown aside again as Jed came out onto the porch, Elijah and the two older boys behind him.

"Wolf! Emily! Stop that blasted noise!" Jed's deep bear's roar brought instant silence to the front yard.

Emily recovered first. "Wolf tickled me!"

"Emily hit me," Wolf countered in a wounded tone, making Emily shriek with laughter again.

"Quiet!" As the echo faded, Jed turned to March. "Am I to understand from all this levity that you found your infernal stallion?"

March grinned. "Sorry, Jed."

"Too much to hope for that anything could rid us of that malevolent son of Satan." Jed smiled broadly. "But I guess we have his sorry hide to thank for getting us all together for supper. You must be starved. Danny and Jake can take care of your horses. You two come on in."

"I'll get Balthasar," the thin boy, Danny, said, reaching for the reins.

"I'll take Ari," Wolf said, scrambling up from the dust to take the mare's reins.

"Pa said me," Jake objected, pushing past him.

"I was here first!"

"Pa!"

"Let go, Jake!"

Maggie swiftly slipped from the saddle. She thought Ari was sensible enough not to spook at the boys' antics, but sit-

246

ting sidesaddle she wasn't going to take any chances. Still, she was rather pleased by the fact that quiet, serious Wolf could hold his own in a Culbert shouting match.

"Out of my way, Wolf!"

"I said, let go!"

"Boys!"

"Jed, it appears you've got three new visitors to feed, not just two," Elijah's soft drawl brought silence as effectively as Jed's roar.

"What?"

"March has a puppy," Emily exclaimed in wonder. She pointed to March's chest as he swung himself to the ground.

Jed glanced sharply at March. "That's no puppy."

"That's a wolf cub," Jake said.

Both he and Wolf dropped Ari's reins and engaged in another brief shoving match as they crowded up to March. Ari turned her head to Maggie.

Maggie shrugged. "I'm sorry. Everyone knows men are fickle."

"Where'd you get it, March?" Emily asked, reaching up a hand toward the white muzzle.

"Emily, get away from there!" In two long strides, Jed Culbert was off the porch and pulling Emily up to his chest. "That's a wild animal."

"We couldn't leave him alone. I'm sorry," March said. "He's friendly enough, and too small to be dangerous."

"Not for long," Jed observed, his normally cheerful face dark with censure.

"He's just a baby, Pa," Wolf said, his eyes locked on the cub's face. "We could teach him not to be wild."

"Wolves aren't dogs," Elijah volunteered. He pushed himself off the porch railing and dropped down to the group standing below.

"So we've heard," Maggie growled warningly, seeing the panicked look Wolf shot him.

"They don't make good pets," Elijah continued, as though he hadn't heard her. "Their instincts are to survive in the wild. They can't help that."

He held his hand up to the cub's nose. A strip of pink wound around his fingers. The cub whined hopefully.

"I could teach him," Wolf said. Maggie could hear in the boy's low, desperate voice that he was pleading for the animal's life, and Jed was the judge, though she and March had found the cub.

She knew, suddenly, that March had brought the little wolf with them to the farm because he couldn't keep him, not on a ranch where the crown prince was a wolf-hating stallion. So he was straining a long, true friendship, because he couldn't bear to consign the cub to death unless absolutely necessary.

"You can't teach a wolf not to kill chickens and calves," Jed said, his voice full of understanding for the boy. "That's just his nature. And what if Tuck or Emmy pulled his tail one day while he was sleeping?"

"He wouldn't hurt them," Wolf said, balling his hands into fists. "I *could* teach him. They'd be like his own brothers and sisters."

"I did know one case," Elijah interrupted, "where a fellow domesticated a wolf, more or less successfully." He rubbed a hand over the cub's head, pushing aside the blanket March had wrapped him in.

"Elijah . . ." Jed growled.

"Trained her to kill coyotes that came after his chickens. Even convinced her not to eat his cat." He lifted the cub from March's arms, examining his scruffy silver and white fur. He didn't look down at Wolf's pleading eyes. "I won't say I thought she was completely tame, but she was loyal as a shadow to that man. He told me that the trick was that he got her respect. She thought he was her pack leader."

"Maybe we could train him to keep horses and cattle out of the barley," Wolf suggested with a sidelong glance at Jed. "Might save us enough money to pay for his keep."

Maggie looked up in surprise to see Henna standing in the farmhouse doorway, Tucker on her hip. Her voice was neutral, but Jed's expression showed he knew he was outnumbered now.

"Next time I go into town, I can find out if anyone's got a bitch with a litter they want to get rid of," he said. "Henny, I don't want some full-blooded wolf living in my house . . ."

"I don't think you've got to worry about that," Elijah said. He held up the cub in one hand and pointed with the other. "Look at this little fellow's ears and the way his tail is set. I'd say his papa came from the wrong side of the barnyard."

"What's that mean, Pa?" Emily asked in a stage whisper.

"It means he's half puppy after all, Em," Wolf said with a significant glance at Jed.

"Wolf . . ." Jed warned.

Elijah looked down at his son's face. "I'll take him, Jed, if the trouble's too much for you."

"No!" Henna's voice came sharply from the porch. They all turned to stare at her. "What I mean is, how could you take care of a puppy, with the life you lead? That's nonsense, Elijah. He can stay here with us, if Wolf can teach him to behave."

"I can help," Emily piped up eagerly.

"I'll make him a box for a bed," Jake offered.

"Sure," Danny said. "He can sleep up in the loft with us."

"Pa?" Wolf turned to Jed.

Jed glanced at Henna, then back at the boy. "You've got a

month," he said. "If he's house trained and doesn't bite after a month, we'll keep him." He looked grimly at his wife. "But if he once gets out of line after that or ever bites somebody, I'm going to put him down, and there's going to be no argument."

Elijah held the cub out to his son. Wolf looked up at him, his eyes expressing the gratitude he couldn't speak. "Would you show me how to take care of him?" he asked.

For just a second, Elijah shifted in Maggie's eyes from a hardened gunfighter to an awkward father.

"I'd be pleased to," he said. "Let's start by taking him out in the yard for a minute. We wouldn't want him to get off to the wrong start by making a mess in Henna's kitchen."

"No, sir, we wouldn't," Wolf agreed, returning his grin.

They headed off toward the corner of the house, while the rest remained behind in a strained tableau.

Jed sighed. "Jake, Danny, take care of those horses like I asked you." He glanced at March. "Damnation, Jackson."

March took the shotgun from his saddle as Danny led Balthasar away. He handed it to Jed. "I just couldn't shoot him with this, Jed."

Jed took the gun by the barrel. "I'm giving you fair warning, March. If you show up on this farm in the next year with so much as a prairie dog pup, I'm not going to have any compunction about using this shotgun to put you out of both our misery."

"Actually, Jed, I was thinking it's just about time for Danny to have a horse of his own. Britta's little bay foal looks like he's going to be a handsome fellow." March risked a grin as he stepped up onto the porch. "He's just about the age I can take him away from his dam and—"

Jed thumped him on the back so hard Maggie thought she heard his ribs creak. "Damn thoughtful of you, March. One of the things I like about you. Always willing to help out a neighbor. You were saying?"

March laughed. "Maybe some other time, Jed. Maybe some other time."

"This is 'Lizbeth," Emily said proudly, handing her doll up to Maggie for approval.

"She's lovely," Maggie murmured. She held the doll at arm's length, making a show of admiring the brown muslin dress that matched Emily's own. Several white chips marred Elizabeth's perfectly coiffed porcelain hair, and one of her fingers was missing, but she was only more beautiful for being loved.

"She has lots of dresses," Emily said. "I'll show you, okay?"

"All right," Maggie agreed, hiding a smile. In the half hour since she'd finished helping Henna with the supper dishes, Emily had brought in a parade of toys, thrilled to share them with someone new.

"Now stay right here," the little girl said, patting the side of Maggie's chair. She trotted off toward the rear of the house, glancing back once to make sure Maggie was following orders.

"You don't have to spend all evening entertaining Emmy," Henna said, settling into the rocker next to her. "She's perfectly capable of playing by herself."

"I don't mind," Maggie said, surprised to find it was true. To her, Emily still seemed a much stranger species than the wolf cub Elijah and Wolf were playing with by the fire, but she no longer feared the child would judge her and find her lacking. Emily really did like everyone. At least, anyone who would sit and listen to her talk.

"She's certainly enjoying the attention," Henna said.

"Sometimes it can get a little crazy around here. The boys never seem to slow down."

Even as she said it, Tucker grabbed her knitting bag, and Henna engaged in a brief tug-of-war to get a thick brown sweater out of his hands. From outside the house, Maggie could hear the hoots and calls of Danny and Jake as they played. She gathered from the occasional word she could make out that Danny was a sheriff and Jake a notorious criminal calling himself "Kid Culbert".

"Tuck, go play with your father." Henna turned the little boy around and gave him a shove toward the other side of the room where Jed, March, and Lemuel were engaged in a heated discussion about crop rotation.

Maggie let her eyes wander to Elijah and Wolf, two dark heads focused intently on the pale creature playing before them. The cub grabbed Wolf's hand and growled. Elijah gripped him by the scruff of his neck and shook him down.

"No! Say it like that, Wolf. Let him know who's in charge. His mother wouldn't hesitate to let him know when he'd gone too far. You can't, either."

Henna's voice brought Maggie's attention back from the cub. "I owe you an apology."

"For what?"

Henna's knitting needles clicked along steadily as she glanced at Maggie with her penetrating amber eyes. "For what I said to you last week. You're nothing like I thought you were."

Maggie could hardly remember who she'd been a week ago. "You were only trying to protect March."

Henna shrugged, focusing back on her sweater. "Yes. I care a great deal for March. He's faced a lot of hardship for a man his age, but it hasn't made him hard or bitter. He gives unselfishly to his friends and to strangers. I'm a selfish woman, myself, and I don't want to lose him. I've been afraid lately that I would."

"Since the Pennys were murdered," Maggie supplied.

"It devastated him. It devastated all of us. But it did something more to March. It changed him somehow. He blames himself for their deaths, because he wasn't there at the ranch when it happened. It's been eating him alive, hollowing him out until I could hardly recognize him when I looked into his eyes."

Maggie nodded, remembering her argument with March of the night before. "When he talks about Jane and Lucas, all he thinks about is revenge. He forgets about the ranch and how much it means to him."

Henna's needles paused, and she looked back at Maggie. "After their deaths and before you arrived, he didn't lift a hand around that ranch. Lemuel Tate did what he could but, as you know, he doesn't ride, and the horses suffered for it. March spent most of his time in town, in The Golden Rose, and Lemuel says when he was home, he hardly seemed aware of his surroundings. He barely ate. He never slept."

Maggie's memory supplied the image of March being ill by the side of the road, sick from alcohol and rage. Her stomach clenched.

"There must be something that will bring him out of it," she said, but it was more of a question than a statement. "We just have to figure out what it is."

"But we already have, Maggie."

Maggie looked up, startled by Henna's use of her given name. "What do you mean?"

Henna laughed, that light, curiously youthful laugh. "I mean you, Maggie."

"What about me?"

"The March Jackson sitting over there talking with my husband is not the same March Jackson who wouldn't come to my house for supper a week ago because he couldn't sit down long enough to eat a meal. Since you arrived, he's not only eating, he's cooking again. He's socializing with his friends. He hasn't spent a single night at The Golden Rose. And, most important, he's working with his horses again. I don't think that's a coincidence."

Heat burned Maggie's face, touched off by the warmth in Henna's voice and the rush of pleasure at the thought that her words might be true. She glanced at March, catching his smile at something Jed had said. She'd watched him surreptitiously all evening, memorizing his face, the way he sat, the way his fist clenched in his intensity when he made an important point.

"Maybe it's been good for him to have to look out for a greenhorn," she said, looking down at her own callused hands.

"Coyness does not become you, Miss Parker," Henna said. Her needles clicked smartly, sounding annoyed. "He smiles again. The life comes back into his eyes when he looks at you."

It was too much, too much to think about, too much to feel. Maggie's mind fluttered desperately for a way to change the subject, like a moth trying to escape a cat, but she couldn't escape Henna's words.

"And I've noticed the way you watch him, too. Normally I'd say I don't know you well enough to mention any of this. In point of fact, under normal circumstances, I'd judge your speech, the way you dress, the way you ignore conventions to be nothing but trouble March could do without. But these are not normal circumstances."

She glanced a sharp eye at Maggie. "March needs you. I

hope you are considering staying on here in Colorado Territory for a while."

Maggie's stomach flopped over, and she had to breathe deeply to hold back the sudden sting of tears. She'd made a bargain with herself that she wouldn't think about any of that until tomorrow, that she'd enjoy today for what it was and pay for it later. But it seemed her balance was going to be called due sooner than she'd planned.

"I've got a stagecoach to catch on Friday." Her cold tone didn't deter Henna.

"What's one more week?" the woman asked. "I know Oxtail isn't the sort of society you're used to, but you might find that the freedom of the frontier appeals to you. I'm simply asking you to give it a chance."

Maggie swallowed hard. She would not let herself think of staying here, with Ari and Wolf and Lemuel and the horses and the rejuvenating hard work. She wouldn't think of long days riding through the foothills, of peaceful evenings on the ranchhouse porch, of swimming in clear mountain pools. She wouldn't imagine what it would be like to spend her life with March, able to love him without reservation, without the fear of losing him to ghosts.

"March wouldn't let me stay," she said, the words thick in her throat. "He thinks staying here would put me in danger."

As if in echo of her thoughts, a screech came from the back of the house. Then Tucker's voice. "I'm the marshal!"

"I'm not playing with you!" Emily shouted back. "Go away! Play with the boys!"

Another time, Maggie might have smiled. "March thinks someone's willing to kill again to get his ranch. He won't let me stay."

Henna snorted. "There's more than one way to miss a stagecoach. He's no match for the two of us. Give him time, and he'll realize you're perfectly safe here."

Maggie shook her head. "I can't stay."

She would be leaving her heart behind; she couldn't deny that to herself. But a week ago, she hadn't even known she had a heart to lose. She could learn to live without it again.

"Why not? Why can't you stay?"

Because I can't live a lie with March and I can't tell him about Langley. Because March deserves a respectable woman with a stainless past and an unscarred face. Because I love him too much.

"I just can't."

"For heaven's sake, Maggie—"

A tug on her knitting cut off Henna's fierce whisper. The little wolf cub had dug his sharp teeth into her sweater.

"Hey, let go of that. Let go." Wolf grabbed the cub's jaw and pried it loose from the thick brown wool.

The cub wriggled free and grabbed for the sweater again.

"No!"

At Wolf's sharp tone, the cub cringed down, his eyes looking up at the boy, pleading.

"Let go!"

Reluctantly, the cub opened his mouth, letting the sweater sleeve drop back to Henna's skirt.

"Good boy. Good boy." Wolf scratched the cub under the chin and the cub licked him enthusiastically. "That's it. Good fella."

"What are you going to call him, Wolf?" Maggie asked, relieved by the interruption. "He needs a name. We already have a boy named Wolf—we don't want to get confused."

"How about Fang," Jed offered dryly from across the room. "Or Killer."

"Silverfur!" Emily piped up. Maggie turned to see the girl standing in the doorway clutching a handful of doll dresses. She held Elizabeth, newly clothed in elegant burgundy silk, in the other hand. "He's Silverfur, 'cause he's got silver fur."

"Apollo had wolves," March continued, "and didn't he turn into one once? Apollo's a good name."

"In Norse mythology, Loki's son Fenris was a wolf," Elijah said. "His children devoured the sun and brought on the twilight of the gods."

"We could call him Silver for short," Emily said.

"Loki," Wolf said slowly, ruffling the cub's neck.

"Loki," Jed mused, "wasn't he a devil?"

"A rather unpleasant trickster," Elijah admitted.

Jed nodded. "Sounds like a perfect name to me."

"No! Call him Silver, Wolf," Emily commanded.

Wolf shook his head. "His name's going to be Loki. What do you think, boy? Is that a good name? Loki."

"No! No, no, noooo!" Emily stamped her foot, her face scrunching up in frustration.

"Emmy," Henna snapped impatiently. She started to rise, but Wolf held out his hand to his sister.

"Come here, Em. Come pet him."

"No!"

She swung around sharply, turning her back on him.

"All right, if you don't want to play with us . . ." Wolf said, drawing the words out in a tantalizing singsong.

"No!"

"Emmy, pway with me!" Tucker's voice rang out from near the front door.

"No, you go play with Danny and Jakey."

"They won't pway with me." The little boy came trotting past the coats in the short entryway. "I'm the Marshal, Emmy. Put your hands up."

It wasn't until he came fully out into the lamplight that Maggie saw the gleam of metal in his hands.

"Tuck?" she asked, confused, not quite believing her eyes.

"Put your hands up, mister," he commanded Emily's back. "I'm takin' you in."

"Don't call me 'mister,' " Emily said, whirling back around. She tilted her chin haughtily. "I'm Miss Emily Culbert."

"Hands up or I'll shoot you, mister," Tuck said, coming closer.

Maggie finally found her voice, the words ripping in panic from her throat. "Tucker, put that down. Now!"

Henna looked up from her knitting. "Oh, my God!" The sweater fell to the floor. "That's a gun!"

Oblivious to the shouts, Tucker raised the Colt to eye level, needing two hands to lift the heavy gun. "Put 'em up, Emmy."

"Tucker!" Jed shouted, leaping to his feet, but he couldn't jump forward, afraid of startling the boy.

Emily, two years older than her little brother, understood the screams of the adults. She froze in place, all the color draining from her face, leaving only the dark pools of fright in her eyes.

"Emmy," Tucker said, with four-year-old exasperation. "Put up your hands."

"Do it, Emily," Jed whispered harshly, moving slowly toward his son. But the little girl remained unmoving, the doll and dresses dangling from her limp hands.

"Emmy, move!" Wolf shouted, launching himself toward his immobile sister.

The sudden movement startled Tucker. Maggie felt her mouth open in a scream as the little boy's finger closed on the Colt's trigger.

Chapter 17

Wolf's body hit Emily and the two fell to the ground in a flutter of brightly colored doll dresses. For a moment there was no sound at all.

"It's not loaded." Elijah Kelly's voice, cold and shaken skittered across the booming silence. Emily began to cry. "That's my Colt. It's not loaded."

Jed grabbed his son, pulling the gun from his grasp and tossing it to the floor. He pulled the child to his chest, his face ashen, his lips moving in silent prayer.

"Get out." Henna's voice, a low, keening hiss shook her frame as she rose from her chair. She pointed a long, trembling finger at Elijah. "Get out of my home. How dare you bring your instruments of death into this house?"

He pushed himself to his feet, moving an uncertain step toward her. "Henna, I would never bring a loaded gun into your home."

"How dare you?" Red fury transformed Henna's pale, austere features. "How can you stand there defending yourself when my son could have killed my daughter!"

"Henny, don't," Jed said, his own voice not yet steady. "When Prince disappeared, we all thought it could be rustlers. Elijah only brought his guns to protect us. It's not his fault."

Henna whirled on him. "Just whose fault is it?" she asked, her voice rising with anger. "Who is it who comes in here in those black clothes, acting like some kind of knight errant who can go where he pleases and be damned to his responsibilities? Who is it who fills my children's heads with the idea that the quickdraw is some kind of art form, that being an outlaw is some kind of romantic adventure? *Just whose damn fault is it?*"

Maggie reached out a hand, afraid Henna might fall to pieces before her eyes. She never would have thought her capable of such language.

"Henny, please," Jed begged, but Elijah shook his head.

"It's all right," he said, stooping to pick up his Colt. "I'm leaving."

"Get out," Henna said again, as if the fierceness of her voice might have the power to push him through the door. "You are no longer welcome here. I never want you to set foot in this house again."

Elijah moved to the entryway, taking his hat and duster. March rose quietly from his chair and followed his friend out the door.

Maggie stood rooted in place, torn between the lingering terror on Henna's face and the shock she saw in Wolf's eyes where he sat on the floor next to a quietly sobbing Emily.

Jed made the decision for her. "Wolf," he said, shifting Tucker to his hip in order to reach one hand down to the boy. He pulled Wolf to his feet. "Let's go." He led the boy out the front door without a backward glance at his wife. Lemuel followed.

"Mama."

Henna bent down and scooped Emily into her arms, burying her face in the girl's honey-colored hair. Not sure what to do, Maggie followed them down the hall toward the back of the house where a tiny room had been formed from a portion of the hall and the master bedroom. Inside, there was just enough space for the girl's bed and a small chest of drawers.

Henna laid Emily down, sitting on the bed beside her. The girl clung to one of her mother's hands while Henna stroked Emily's forehead with the other.

"It's all right, sweetheart," she murmured, though Maggie could see the strain across her shoulders as Henna willed herself not to shake. "Everything's fine. You're not hurt."

"Is there anything I can do?" Maggie asked.

Henna looked up at her. "Tea? And there's some whiskey in the far left cupboard. About a teaspoon in Emmy's tea. And a couple of teacups for you and me."

Maggie hurried back down to the kitchen, glad to be moving. The sight of that gun, its dark stock gleaming between Tucker's pudgy hands, had chilled her. True or not, death seemed much closer out here in Colorado than it had in Kentucky. She could still see the meadow this morning, the mangled body of the wolf, Prince's bloody hoofprints. The idea of Emily's small, fragile body broken by a bullet from Elijah's gun . . .

She shook her head, clenching her eyes. She wouldn't think about it. Wouldn't think about what March had seen when he'd come home to find his sister, Lucas, and their son all murdered. She wouldn't think about March planning to face down a gang of killers by himself. With the adrenaline of fear still pumping in her blood, that image seemed all too real.

When she finally returned to Emily's room with the tea tray, Henna turned to her with her finger over her lips.

"She's already asleep," she whispered, rising from the bedside. She leaned over to press a kiss against her daughter's forehead before coming out into the hall. "I think she was more overtired and overexcited than really frightened. By morning, she'll think it was all just an adventure."

She led Maggie back to the living room, moving without

her normal willowy grace. Maggie set the tray down on the end table next to Henna's rocker. When she lifted the teapot, Henna waved her away. The graceful, refined mother of five took the whiskey bottle and sloshed a liberal amount into two of the teacups, handing one to Maggie.

"I'm afraid I'm not as naturally resilient as my daughter," Henna said, sinking into her chair and taking a large swallow from her cup.

Maggie emulated her, clenching her eyes at the fire that burned her throat.

Beside her, Henna laughed, a shaky, rueful noise. "I really went overboard this time, didn't I?" she said. "Made quite a scene. 'You are no longer welcome here!' " She drained her teacup, stifling the hysterical edge to her voice.

"Nobody blames you," Maggie said. She reached out a tentative hand to touch the other woman's arm. "I probably would have done the same. Your children were in danger. You had every right to be upset."

Henna shook her head, pouring herself another cup of whiskey. "Jed blames me. Treating Elijah that way. Elijah would give his life for those children. Damn his black soul to hell."

She reached over to top off Maggie's cup. Maggie took another sip. The liquid fire burned away some of the tension in her muscles.

"I don't know that much about Elijah's past," she said, picking her words carefully. "But he doesn't seem evil to me. At least, he seems to have a strong sense of loyalty to his friends, and he obviously cares a great deal about Wolf. March told me he used to be a town marshal at one time. Is he really an outlaw now?"

"Elijah Kelly does what he damn well pleases, inside or outside the law, I don't think it matters." Henna glanced at

Maggie with a bitter smile. "There, I'm not being fair again. He has his own code of honor, which is more than can be said for a lot of men."

"March was an outlaw once," Maggie said softly. "You don't hate him."

"He told you about that?" Henna raised an eyebrow as if Maggie had just confirmed something to her. "Well, you're right, I don't hate March. And I don't hate Elijah for his profession, either."

"Oh, of course, Wolf's mother." Maggie blushed at Henna's sharp look. "I'm sorry. When Elijah arrived at the ranch, March had to tell me Wolf was his son. You must hate him for deserting your friend."

Henna took a deep breath and another long sip of whiskey. "Annabel knew exactly what Elijah was. She had no business falling in love with him, and even less business having a baby. I really believe if he'd known she was pregnant the damn fool would have married her. No, I don't hate him for that, either."

She turned in her chair, hunching one foot up under her like a little girl. A smile haunted the corner of her mouth. "You want to know why I really hate Elijah?"

Maggie turned in her own chair, resting her chin on one hand. "Why?"

"Wolf." She laughed, but tears glittered in her eyes. "Every time that man rides into town, every time he shows up on my doorstep to see *his son*, I think it's finally going to happen. He's going to get some flash of guilt, some consciousness of his responsibility. Every time he comes, I think this will be the time he takes Wolf away with him. Elijah may be Wolf's father, but Wolf is *mine*. He's mine, and I'm terrified I'm going to lose him."

"Oh, heavens," Maggie whispered.

"It's the one thing I can't explain to Jed. I don't think anyone can understand."

"I understand what it's like to lose someone you love," Maggie said. "And to be afraid."

Henna nodded. "Thank you. I believe you do. But there's just something about it being your child . . . You'll understand when you hold your own children in your arms."

The sudden lump in Maggie's throat almost choked her. She swallowed it down with the last of her whiskey. "That's never going to happen."

She stared down into her teacup. Where had that confession come from?

"Of course it will," Henna assured her, reaching over with the whiskey bottle. "I can't tell you how you feel, though it certainly looks to me as though you care about March. But whatever the case, you will eventually fall in love and—"

"I won't have children," Maggie repeated bitterly. "Not with March or anyone else."

"Oh." Henna looked her up and down, compassion filling her eyes. "Is that why you think you can't stay? Is it a physical problem?"

"No." Maggie shook her head in frustration, making the room spin unpleasantly. She stopped, trying to regain her focus on Henna's face. "No, it's not physical. I can't marry anyone. I don't deserve March. You were right about me all along. I wasn't—" no, she wouldn't put it that way, "—I'm not a virgin."

Tears of shame and regret filled her eyes, but she wouldn't turn away from Henna's censure. Stephen had always told her she'd eventually have to face the consequences of her actions. Maybe he'd been right, but she'd prove she could face them with courage.

Henna stared at her for a long minute. Then she began to

laugh. "Is that right?" She shook her head, a strange mixture of sorrow and mirth choking off her speech.

Maggie watched her in concern. "Henna, how much of that whiskey have we drunken? I mean, drunk?"

"There's a swallow left," Henna answered. Before Maggie could object, she'd divided it evenly between their two cups. "Oh, God, Maggie, I guess March didn't tell you quite everything about me and Annabel."

She laughed again, though the amusement had left her eyes. "I wasn't judging you last week when I said what I did, Maggie. I wanted to protect you, and, more important to me at the time, to protect March, from judgment by others. Sweet heaven knows I don't have the right to judge you. I wasn't a virgin when I married Jedediah."

"You weren't?" Shock dispelled some of the whiskey smoke floating through Maggie's mind.

"My God, no. I was a prostitute."

"You don't have to leave the territory, Kelly." Jed spoke roughly, frustration evident in the set of his jaw. "She was just upset. She'll be over it by morning."

March leaned against the barn wall, watching his friend silently saddle his scruffy bay. He'd seen that look on Elijah's face before, his lips thin with suppressed tension, his eyes locked on the simple task of threading his latigo strap. March couldn't have given a name to the emotions that emanated from him, something worse than failure, more painful than shame.

"Elijah, Henna's going to feel rotten tomorrow about what she said," Jed continued, filling the quiet that hung thick in the barn. "Stick around, won't you? We hardly get a chance to see you as it is."

March could almost hear the words Jed didn't speak. *For*

God's sake, think about your son. But Elijah didn't so much as blink.

March glanced at Wolf. The boy sat in a pile of hay, his arms wrapped around Loki, who'd finally fallen back to sleep. Wolf watched the grownups with unreadable eyes.

Jed shifted Tucker on his hip. "She had quite a scare. We all did. She just needs some time to cool off."

"Then I'll give it to her," Elijah finally spoke, giving one last tug on his cinch. "If that's all I can do right tonight, at least it's something."

He led his gelding out of the barn into the starlit evening. "I'll just go by the ranch and get the rest of my things. Thank you for the hospitality, March."

"You can't mean to leave tonight," Jed objected. He turned to gesture helplessly at March. "Tell him he can't leave tonight."

March shook his head. He knew his friend well enough to know he couldn't stop him from leaving. And that it might be a very long time before he saw him again.

He held the bay's reins while Elijah swung into the saddle.

"You know you're always welcome at my place, 'Lije," he said.

His friend nodded.

"Father?" Wolf's quiet voice startled them all. He stood near the barn door, the sleeping wolf cub draped awkwardly in his arms. "How am I going to train Loki without your help?"

Elijah's flat eyes softened momentarily. "You're doing just fine, Wolf. And I'll be back now and again to see how he's progressing."

March wondered if even Elijah really believed that. The gunfighter tipped his hat to them, then dug his heels into his gelding's sides, setting off up the drive at a brisk trot. They watched until the darkness swallowed the last trace of his star-thrown shadow.

"Wolf, it's past your bedtime," Jed said finally, turning back toward the house. "Tuck's asleep already. I'd better take him up."

"I've got to go back with March and Miss Maggie," Wolf said.

Jed gestured toward the barn. "Lemuel's hitching up the wagon. Why don't you get settled with Loki."

"Yes, Pa."

March watched the boy trudge toward the lamplit barn. "I'm sorry for all the trouble we've caused you today, Jed."

Jed let out a short bark of laughter. "If it isn't one darned thing around here, it's another. That's just the life the good Lord gave us."

He clapped March on the back with his free hand. "At least I can be sure that when I die it won't be from boredom."

As Lemuel guided Pamela down the drive toward the ranch house, March glanced over his shoulder at the passengers riding in the wagon bed. Wrapped in a quilt Henna had lent them, Maggie leaned against the side of the wagon, her mouth slightly open in sleep. She had one arm around Wolf, who slept with his head against her side. Loki lay curled between them, his silver fur gleaming in the light from the rising moon.

"A shame to have to wake them," Lemuel's voice rumbled beside him.

"It's been a long day," March said. "We should all sleep well." Though he didn't believe for a minute he'd sleep himself.

He took a deep breath of the night air, drinking in the shimmering scent of dried grasses, the distant taste of cool water, the silver smell of a breeze touched with starlight. If he had ever felt so fully alive in any day of his life, he couldn't remember it. If he fell asleep, tomorrow would come, and he could think of nothing tomorrow was likely to bring that he wanted to receive.

He climbed down from the wagon seat and touched Maggie on the shoulder. She shrugged and let out what sounded suspiciously like a snore.

"I thought Wolf maybe ought to sleep in the barn tonight," Lemuel said beside him. "That little cub shouldn't have to climb all the way down from the loft if he gets a mind he needs to get out."

Wolf's eyes blinked slowly as he sat up beside Maggie. "There's an empty stall next to Ari's." A yawn shook through his body. "I could put some hay in there. Loki'd like it. It'd be like a den."

"All right, son. Why don't you take Loki for a run around the yard first, though." Henna wouldn't like her little chaperone deserting him, but March doubted Henna would approve of many of the decisions he'd made today. He was going to regret them himself, once he let himself think about it, but even if he could change them, God help him, he wouldn't do it.

He brushed his fingertips along Maggie's cheek. Her eyelids flickered.

"There you go. Open your eyes."

She groaned and scrunched them tightly closed. "Go 'way."

"You only have to wake up enough to walk to your room."

Wolf had pulled himself upright, and now Loki awoke, scrambling to his feet with an air that suggested he was afraid he might miss something.

"Here, Loki," Wolf whispered loudly, climbing down the

opposite side of the wagon. "Come here, boy."

The cub's ears pricked. With a mighty shake he rid himself of the lingering effects of his nap. Then he bounced forward, right across Maggie's lap.

"Umph," she objected, pushing at the offending bundle of fur. Distracted by her efforts, Loki turned from his destination to lick her hands. "Go away."

Instead, Loki planted his big feet on her chest, the better to reach the source of the complaint with his long, happy tongue.

"Ugh! Ptttht!" Maggie sat up sharply, sending the cub sprawling onto his back. He sprang to his feet and squeaked, delighted by her response to the game.

"I've got him." Wolf climbed up on one of the wagon wheels. He grabbed Loki by the scruff of his neck and hauled him out of the wagon bed. "I'm sorry, Miss Maggie."

"You've got to teach him to be more friendly, Wolf," she grumbled.

"Good night, Miss Maggie," he replied, wisely ignoring her sarcasm.

"I'll take care of the horses, March," Lemuel said as he untied Balthasar and Ari from the back of the wagon. "You're goin' to have your hands full."

Maggie had managed to get her feet underneath her, but as she tried to stand, she stepped on her skirts and tumbled sideways. "Ow."

"Don't move," March ordered. He swung himself over the side of the wagon into the bed. He was not surprised that she didn't listen to him and tried once more to struggle to her feet. He managed to grab her arm and steady her before she fell over the side.

"I can see how 'don't move' could be misunderstood as a suggestion to stand up," he said. "But believe it or not, I really meant not to move."

"Leave me alone. I'm fine." She shook her arm to free herself, but stopped suddenly as she started to sway. "Mostly fine," she amended. "I just can't seem to get my balance. Your wagon isn't stable."

"I don't think the wagon is the problem," March told her. He guided her to the end of the wagon and eased her down to a sitting position. "How much whiskey did you and Henna drink?"

She watched him intently as he hopped to the ground. "Are you telling me I'm drunk?"

"I'd never tell a lady she was drunk." He reached for her waist and lifted her down, holding her steady until she found her balance.

She gazed up at him, her eyes reflecting the silver glint of moonlight. He had meant to let go of her waist, but her warmth held him there.

"Am I going to be sick?" she asked gravely.

He hoped the darkness hid his smile. "Do you feel sick?"

"No." She shook her head emphatically, then swayed again. "At least, not when I don't move."

"I think you'll be all right. Let's get you to bed." It seemed perfectly natural to put an arm around her to steady her, to lift her arm up to his shoulder so she could hold on to him.

He led her toward the dark ranch house, and as they reached the porch steps, dizziness swept him, as though Maggie's intoxication was contagious. For a brief instant he felt what it would be like to have a home to return to again. How it would feel if he could claim Maggie as his own, swing her into his arms and carry her laughing and protesting through the front door of *their* house. To have someone to share his heart with, so that it might be whole again.

"March?"

"Here we go. Watch the stairs." He wiped an arm across his eyes, fighting the strange blurriness that shrouded them for an instant. But he couldn't brush away the yearning.

They stepped into the house, and a deeper, velvet blackness enveloped them. March didn't bother to stop for a lamp. He led Maggie down the hall to her room, the darkness intensifying the sound of their footsteps, of her skirts swishing softly against his leg, of her breathing.

He opened the door to the master bedroom and helped her across to the bed. But when he moved away, she caught his arm. "Don't leave yet."

"I'm just going to find a match," he said.

"I don't mind the dark."

He touched her hand. "Then why don't you want me to go."

"I don't want to be alone."

Moonlight glowed behind the curtains draping the windows, but though he could make out vague outlines in the room, he could see nothing of her face. But her voice sounded small, almost lost in the big room.

"I'll stay until you fall asleep," he promised. A voice in his head warned him to leave. His very presence compromised her. But it was a little late for that, after this afternoon.

"Could you help me with my buttons?"

He sat down beside her on the bed, and she turned her back to him so he could reach the tiny ivory knobs. He smelled river in her hair and the faint tang of whiskey from her breath. The skin beneath his fingers picked up the faint touch of moonlight like a moth's wings.

He wanted her again. With no lessening of that aching desperation he'd felt, it seemed, since the kiss he'd stolen the night she had arrived. He brushed the back of his hand across her bare shoulders. She sighed, and he felt himself harden in response.

"There, that's all of them."

"Oh." She stood, wobbled, and he rose to steady her once more.

She was exhausted and tipsy. The last thing she needed was for him to seduce her again. He put a firm mental hold on his desire and helped her to step out of her dress.

"I can get it," she said when he reached for her petticoats. So he sat back on the bed and listened to the whisper of cloth as it slipped to the floor.

He folded back the covers and guided her to the side of the bed.

"You'll stay with me?"

"I promised, didn't I?" he said, then bit his tongue. He'd also promised not to touch her. He hadn't hurt her, thank heavens, at least not physically. Just remembering the way she'd melted around him in her pleasure made his breathing stop. Impossible as it seemed, she'd wanted him, maybe as much as he'd wanted her.

But that didn't make it right. If she hadn't hurt today, the pain was now inevitable, beyond his ability to avert it. She had to leave Friday. He had to keep her safe, to protect her from outer danger and his inner demons. The pain of her leaving might very well kill him, but if he failed her the way he'd failed Lucas and Jane and Logan, it would kill his very soul.

He would not have offered a life of hard, continuous ranch labor to a woman bred for running a household of servants and taking her ease of an afternoon by having tea in the sitting room. But he couldn't fool himself into believing Maggie wanted to return to that life, to the rigid code of social conventions and the petty cruelties of her stepfather.

He could tell himself she was too lovely, too delicate to run about in blue jeans, her face smudged with dirt, her hair coated in dust, a curry comb in one hand and a pitchfork in the other. But the purpose that lit her face when she worked with a horse, the smiles she flashed him across the corral when their eyes met, told him clearly enough how she felt about hard work. And he could only imagine her disbelieving laughter if he ever told her he thought she was delicate.

She loved the ranch. He would never have expected it, but he couldn't deny it. She loved the horses, especially Ari. She loved the land, so different from the rolling bluegrass hills of her home. She loved Wolf, and seemed to have developed a sincere affection for Lem.

And deep in his heart, though he didn't want to acknowledge it, though he wouldn't have wished it on her for the world, he knew she cared for him. The knowledge could shatter his heart.

"March?" Her whisper broke through his thoughts. "Would you hold me?"

She'd slipped under the covers, her head and shoulders a dark patch against the white pillows.

He could not have refused her, even if he'd wanted to. He pulled off his boots and pushed aside the covers to lie beside her. Even as he opened his arms, she slid into them, a gesture of dependence he wouldn't have expected from his sharp-edged Maggie.

He held her close, soaking in the warmth of her skin through her thin chemise, breathing in the scent of her. He sensed it when she fell asleep, relaxing into the peaceful darkness before dreams. He brushed her hair with his lips.

"Weave a circle round him thrice," he whispered, "And close your eyes with holy dread, / For he on honey-dew hath fed, / And drunk the milk of Paradise."

He wouldn't sleep. He didn't want to sleep. He wanted to remember every moment of holding her for the rest of his life.

Chapter 18

Maggie stirred the pot of beans slowly, letting the disturbed heat waft the smell up to her nostrils. Almost done. She could put the cornbread in the oven now. She still hadn't mastered the knack of yeast bread, but even Lemuel said her cornbread was among the best he'd ever tasted. Of course, it was his recipe.

She smiled, but the movement crinkled her eyelids, letting moisture spill down her cheeks. She wiped it away impatiently. She wouldn't think about this being the last dinner she'd cook in Colorado. She wouldn't think about leaving tomorrow. Just imagining it was more pain than she could bear.

"But I have to leave," she whispered, trying to feel the strength of moral resolve that had filled her yesterday evening. *Why?* A dark voice asked inside her head. "Because March deserves better." *Because you're a coward,* the voice hissed back, accusing.

She clanged the lid back on the pot, frustration boiling through her. The same argument had ground through her mind since Henna Culbert's impossible revelation the night before.

"That is the magic of the West," Henna had said, the words coming like religious truth from her lips. "That's its allure. What makes men and women risk the backbreaking labor, the drought and flood, the loneliness, disease, and privation? They risk it because in the West, the mistakes you made in the past are in the past, forgotten. If you choose to live outside society's parameters, you are kin to your neighbors, for the rules of Eastern society don't apply. If you work hard, mind your own business, and give a helping hand to others, you're anyone's equal, no questions asked.

"March lives by that code. He won't judge you for your past. He's never judged me. Give him a chance, Maggie. Give yourself a chance."

Henna's words tempted her, heaven knew they did. But Maggie couldn't forget the rules. She knew exactly what her chances for marriage were in Lexington if Langley ever so much as made a sly comment about her to a friend. And she knew how she would be treated if she did marry into the Lexington gentry and her husband found out she wasn't a virgin.

March wouldn't beat her. She believed that with all her heart. Nor would he cast her off in humiliation. That's not what frightened her.

Yes, he might accept Henna's past, might not question her previous choice of occupation. But what a man accepted in a friend was very different from what he might accept in the woman he loved.

Loved?

She shivered, despite the warmth of the day and the heat of the stove. That's what this was all about, wasn't it? She wanted to stay here on the ranch because March made her feel wanted, needed, loved. And she couldn't stay, because she loved him too much to risk his disgust when she told him the truth.

You can't stay because you're a coward.

She almost cried with relief when a knock at the door interrupted her thoughts. She tossed aside her apron and hurried across the kitchen.

Alexander Brady stood outside the door, impeccably dressed in a dark suit with striped trousers and a black bowler hat, which he tipped respectfully to Maggie.

"Good afternoon, Miss Parker. It's a pleasure to see you again. I thought I would stop by to see how March is getting along with that stallion of mine."

"Please, won't you come in, Mr. Brady. Mr. Jackson should be in any minute." She stepped aside to let him enter, glad she'd changed into a dress and put her hair up for cooking. "Would you like a glass of lemonade?"

"I'd appreciate that mightily, thank you," Brady said, taking off his hat as he crossed the threshold. But as he stepped into the kitchen, he stopped. "I'm sorry. It looks as though I dropped in just in time to disturb your midday meal."

Maggie wondered what sort of formality accompanied meals at the Brady household—probably much the same as in Stephen's and her mother's home. Strange, she couldn't quite think of it as her home anymore. Maybe she hadn't in years.

"That's all right," she assured him, crossing to get a glass for the lemonade she'd already made for dinner. "It's the only time you can be sure of finding March within hailing distance. Dinner's only beans and cornbread, but you're welcome to join us if you care to."

"I thank you for the invitation," Brady said, "but I can't stay long. I have some business in town, and just thought I'd stop in and ask about Brady's Mount Bishop's Honor as long as I'm in the area."

It took Maggie a second to realize the elaborate name referred to Sandy.

She handed Brady his lemonade. "I think you'll be pleased. I watched March work him this morning, and he behaved himself beautifully."

The man's mustache twitched in evident satisfaction. "I had no doubt of it. Jackson's the best horse man in the county. Probably the territory."

276

He took a long swallow of his lemonade, then set it on the table. "But before he gets here, I'm glad to have a moment to talk with you."

"With me?" She remembered March's comments about Brady's shrewd business practices. If he thought he could back out of their agreement now that March had worked through Sandy's problems, he was going to have to think again.

"Indeed, Miss Parker. I'm afraid I have an apology to offer you."

Maggie eyed him sharply. Despite his lack of height, his breadth of shoulder made him an imposing figure, and she was sure he knew how to use that impression of strength to his advantage. But in the past week she'd faced half-wild colts, a gunfighter, and a wolf. She wasn't about to be intimidated by a rancher.

"Mr. Brady, if this is about the deal we made—"

"What? No, no." He waved her words aside. "You struck a hard bargain, but if it means that stallion wasn't a wasted investment, I can't complain. No, this is of a more personal nature. I have learned that one of my employees acted toward you in a totally inappropriate manner."

That took her aback. "Pardon?"

"Shelby Brennan," Brady said. "As I understand it, he'd been drinking at The Golden Rose, and offered you the worst kind of disrespect."

"Oh." The sound was forced from her lungs as though she'd been punched. Even after a week, she could still smell the stench of the big man's breath, feel his huge hands pawing at her. She put a hand on a chair for support. "That man . . . he works for you?"

Brady nodded. "He does. He's a good worker, and he's not generally a troublemaker, but he's a damn—pardon me, miss—a darned fool when he drinks. But that's no excuse for showing disrespect to a lady."

"Disrespect?" Maggie repeated, her mouth dry. "That drunken oaf thought I was a . . . a prostitute! God knows what he would have done if March hadn't stopped him."

"Quite right," Brady said. "Completely inexcusable behavior. I hope you'll take my word that he's been properly chastised. I've docked him a fortnight's pay, and he won't get another day in town until the end of the season."

And if Brennan had dragged her upstairs and raped her? Would he have gotten docked a month's pay? "You didn't fire him?"

Brady's eyes widened. "Brennan's a good worker. It isn't easy to find a man with that kind of strength and knowledge of cattle. Even docking his pay, I risked him leaving to hire on with one of my competitors. I thought you'd be pleased to know he'd been punished."

"You have daughters, Mr. Brady. Do they know you have a man like that on your payroll?"

"Miss Parker, if any of my men so much as looked at my daughters in a disrespectful manner, I'd shoot him through the head. But on the other hand, none of my daughters would patronize a saloon, certainly not unattended."

Maggie felt nausea pool in the pit of her stomach. She'd followed the advice of the stagecoach driver to enter The Golden Rose and thus cast a shadow of doubt on her virtue. So much for the moral forgiveness of the West.

The front door swung open and March stood framed in the light. Maggie forced a tight smile to her face. "Mr. Jackson, Mr. Brady's come by to ask you about San—about his stallion."

March hung his hat on the rack before taking the man's hand. "Mr. Brady. You've got quite a horse out there."

Brady laughed, a sound that no longer sounded quite so genial to Maggie's ears. "Tell me something I don't know, Jackson. Miss Parker here seems to think you've made progress with him?"

March nodded. "He's not a vicious horse, Mr. Brady. He just hasn't been handled well in the past. I could keep him a few more days, just to make sure, but I think you could ride him in reasonable safety now."

Brady's small, dark eyes sparkled. "Wonderful! I don't have your touch, but I'm something of a horseman myself. I'd like to try riding him home this afternoon. He'll make quite a sight in next year's Fourth of July parade in Denver, won't he? That will be something. Or maybe I'll take him to the Centennial Exposition in Philadelphia." He rubbed his hands together in anticipation. "Wonderful. Now, Jackson, I have another piece of business I'd like to discuss."

"No." March held up a hand. His quick glance at Maggie warned her not to interfere. "I've helped you with your stallion, but I'm not interested in training any more problem horses. I told you how I felt on Monday. That hasn't changed."

"That brings me precisely to my point," Brady said. He eyed March up and down. "You said some things the other day that led me to believe you might be considering leaving the ranching business altogether. I want to know if you really meant it."

March didn't move, but Maggie could see the tension that suddenly gripped his muscles. He crossed his arms over his chest. "What if I did?"

"That's a mighty fine piece of land you've got out there. The economy isn't what it once was, but I've recovered a bit from the panic of seventy-three. I might be interested in acquiring land with a good set of water rights."

Forced calm settled over March's face like a mask. Maggie hoped Brady missed the fury in his eyes. "Is that right? You prepared to make me an offer?"

Brady's teeth glinted beneath his mustache. "I might be. Say five thousand dollars."

"That's nowhere near what this place is worth."

Brady shrugged. "You may be right there. But I don't need the house or the barn, and I'm not interested in paying for what I don't need. It's just an offer."

"And if I say I won't sell for that price?"

"I don't think anyone's going to offer you more. But you're welcome to ask around."

"Maybe I'll just hang on to the place."

"Well, that's up to you, Jackson." Brady glanced around the kitchen. "It just sounded to me like you didn't want to stay on here. Can't say I blame you, after the murders. Too many memories. Five thousand would give you a chance to start again somewhere else."

Brady waited a long minute. "Think about it."

March nodded, and Maggie could see the effort it cost him to remain calm. "I will."

"Good." Brady nodded to Maggie and placed his bowler back on his head. "Good afternoon, Miss Parker. I'll be back for your answer, Jackson."

Maggie waited until the front door closed behind him, then she turned to look at March. His gaze met hers, cold and grim.

A chill crept over her heart. Her internal debate no longer mattered. Nothing between herself and March mattered any longer. They both knew it. He'd found his sister's killer, and only death remained in his eyes.

Chapter 19

Silently, Maggie helped Wolf put away the dishes they'd washed. The sun burned orange over the mountaintops to the west, but twilight had already invaded the kitchen. Or perhaps it was just the darkness in her heart.

She glanced toward the living room. Lemuel sat thumbing through his old, worn bible, his fly-tying materials on the end table beside his chair. Beyond him, March sat at the rolltop desk, hunched over the black ledger book, but he hadn't moved in minutes, Maggie was sure.

Since Brady's departure at midday, Maggie didn't think she'd heard more than two words spoken among the members of the household, and she could feel the beginnings of hysteria catching in her throat. She couldn't stand much more of the silence, the dread.

Even Wolf, who knew nothing of Brady's offer, hadn't responded to her feeble attempts at conversation over supper. He moved in his own bubble of silence, speaking only to Loki, in a tone so low she couldn't make out the words.

Just as the urge to throw a plate across the room, just to see if she could get a response, became almost too great to bear, the sound of a horse's hooves coming down the drive broke into the thick layer of gloom fogging the house. Shakily, Maggie set the plate down on the counter, breathing a sigh of relief.

March scraped his chair back from the desk with an oath. "Undoubtedly trouble at this hour. I'll see about it."

281

He grabbed his coat on his way out, slamming the door behind him.

Maggie hurried to the window overlooking the porch, pushing aside Jane's curtains. She saw March drop his coat and begin running toward a figure on horseback. She heard cries, but couldn't make out the words. Beside her, Wolf drew in his breath, then ran for the door himself.

The figure dropped from the horse's sidesaddle in a swirl of brightly patterned blue and white skirts. March caught her in his arms, and she wrapped her arms around his neck, planting kisses on his cheek. Her stylish straw hat fell back from her face, revealing gleaming dark hair and flawless white skin.

Involuntarily, Maggie touched her own face, knowing the white of her scar stood out sharply against the color the sun had put in her cheeks this past week. A cold iron band contracted around her heart as she saw the joy on March's face as he clung to the young woman, the love that shone from her eyes, even from this distance.

Why had it never occurred to her that there might be another woman in March's life? Simply because he'd never spoken of one? And why would he?

Her fingernails dug into the windowsill. This woman was everything Maggie had never learned to be. Her every movement spoke of grace and refinement. White gloves covered slender, expressive hands. The latest dress fashion looked as though it had been designed just for her shapely form.

Lemuel moved up beside her.

"Do you know her?" she managed to ask.

"Why, bless my soul." She could hear the smile in his voice. "Ain't this a surprise. Shouldn't be, I guess, knowing her."

"March seems awfully fond of her."

She felt Lemuel's pause. "That he is."

"She's a lovely woman."

"So that's how it is." One of Lemuel's huge hands came down to rest on her shoulder. "She's just a child, Miss Maggie."

Maggie eyed the woman's curves doubtfully. "Oh? Just how old is she?"

"Why she's . . ." The old man shifted. "Why I guess she must be sixteen by now."

"That's not that much younger than I am," Maggie snapped. "A perfectly marriageable age."

Lemuel laughed. "I wouldn't let March hear you say that. He's mighty protective of his baby sister."

"His *sister?*" Maggie turned to face the old man, looking up into dark eyes warmed to chocolate by humor. "She's . . . I . . . You played me like a hooked fish," she accused, trying not to gasp like one.

"Why, how's that, Miss Maggie?" he asked, his face a mask of innocence.

And Maggie could say nothing without admitting to the terrible jealousy that had gripped her heart for those few shameful moments. Lemuel winked at her. She glared back, following him to the door.

If the mere thought of losing March to another woman could affect her that way, what about the possibility of losing him to Alexander Brady's violence? All afternoon she'd thought of nothing but the fact that March would insist on her leaving tomorrow, now that his theory about the rustlers had been confirmed. Since when did she let someone else dictate what she was and was not allowed to do?

A woman's cry cut off her thoughts. "Lem!" The big man stepped through the door to meet March's sister.

"Hello, child." He wrapped his dark arms around her, and

in that moment, as she clung to the big man, Maggie could see the child he'd referred to. Then she stepped back, and though her eyes glistened with tears, she became once more a refined lady as she glimpsed Maggie.

"This is Miss Margaret Parker, Lucas's cousin," March introduced her. "Maggie, this is my sister Harriet."

Only reflex enabled Maggie to take the woman's offered hand. "You're Harry!"

The woman smiled, and suddenly Maggie could see the resemblance to March in the way her mouth curved slightly higher on one side, the way her blue eyes, darker than March's, warmed with humor. "You were expecting a brother."

Maggie returned the smile, but March cut off her reply. "Harry, we weren't expecting you at all. How did you get here?"

"The train," she answered, matter-of-factly. "And then the stagecoach from Greeley. Once I got to Oxtail, I went to the Grand and borrowed a horse from Colonel Treadwell. My trunk's still at the hotel, since I couldn't bring it out on the horse."

"No," March said, his words slow and deliberate. "That's not what I mean. I mean, what in . . . heaven . . . are you doing here?"

In an incongruously unladylike gesture, Harry caught the middle finger of her right glove between gleaming white teeth and tugged sharply, pulling it off. "I knew you must have sent for me, March—" She repeated the procedure with the other glove. "—so I assumed Old Witch Danforth must have ignored it. I was forced to take matters into my own hands."

"I didn't—" March paused. "Just what do you mean by that? You ran away again?"

"Oh, no. I didn't run away. I've been expelled."

Maggie recognized the look on March's face. He'd used it on her on more than one occasion.

"What did . . . No, don't tell me. I don't want to hear it. It isn't going to work. You'll be back on that stagecoach tomorrow, and you'll apologize properly to Mrs. Danforth when you get back to Philadelphia."

"I ran her drawers up the flagpole," Harry said. "I don't think she's going to take me back."

"Simple, but effective," Maggie murmured appreciatively. "I wouldn't have thought of it."

"No, you'd probably have gone directly for setting the damn school on fire," March growled, but Maggie thought she'd effectively diverted him from wringing Harry's slender neck.

Harry smiled sweetly. "Don't worry, March, I'm properly 'finished'. At least as far as school is concerned."

On that note of victory, she walked through the open front door into the living room. And stopped so abruptly that Maggie nearly ran into her. Maggie saw her shoulders begin to shake, but before she could reach for her, Harry crumpled to the floor.

The exasperation deserted March's face as he dropped beside his sister. She turned to him, burying her face in his chest, sobs racking her slender frame. "Oh, God. They're really gone, aren't they? Oh, God. Oh, God."

The raw grief in her voice tore at Maggie's heart so she had to turn away. She felt a brief flare of anger at March for not sending for his sister immediately after the murders occurred, for not including her in his grief so they both might heal faster. But she knew why he hadn't. And after Brady's offer this afternoon, she had to agree with him. Harry wasn't safe here. Especially not as March's sole remaining relative and heir.

"Miss Maggie." Lemuel touched her shoulder. "I'm thinkin' maybe Wolf could use some help in the stable."

Maggie nodded, grateful for the thin excuse. She followed him out into the evening, leaving March and his sister to their sorrow.

When she returned to the house much later she found March alone in the living room, staring blankly out the window.

"I put Harry in your room," he said. "I hope you don't mind having to share."

"No, of course not." She moved toward him, wanting to comfort him, but she had no words. She wanted to tell him he couldn't leave Harry alone, that he should take Brady's offer and start over somewhere else. But she knew he couldn't do that. And in that understanding, her deep, unacknowledged anger at her father for dying in an unwinnable war flickered and went out.

She reached a hand toward March, but he brushed it away. "Go to bed, Maggie. Please."

If her heart hadn't been so heavy, she might have been angry. But instead, she turned and walked away, down the hall to her room. She cracked open the door. By the faint illumination of the three-quarters moon, she crept into the dark room, searching her dresser drawer with her fingers for her nightgown.

"It's all right. I'm awake."

The quiet voice came from the far side of the bed. Maggie could make out Harry's pale face, outlined by the dark hair pooling around her pillow.

"You've had a long trip. You should get some sleep," Maggie scolded. She paused halfway through undoing her buttons. "Damn. If I spend too much more time with Henna

Culbert, I'm going to turn into a mother hen."

Harry laughed, though Maggie could hear the echo of recent tears in the sound. "Don't swear, young lady. It's vulgar and unattractive."

Maggie laughed too. "I'm afraid I'll never make it as a lady."

"Me neither." Harry sat up, scrunching her pillow behind her. "I'd die of boredom. I know Jane and Lucas loved me, but I'll never understand why they couldn't see I'd rather be skinned alive and left for the vultures than go to finishing school."

Maggie shrugged into her nightgown. "My stepfather never bothered to send me to finishing school," she said around a mouthful of hair pins. "He thought I was hopeless. You obviously weren't." Thinking of the headmistress's underclothes, she added, "You *look* like a lady at any rate. I envy you that."

Harry snorted, a distinctly unladylike sound. "Fat lot of good that'll do me out here," she said. "Why does a rancher need to know what side of the plate the knife goes on? I think Jane was just hoping I'd meet some rich man who'd take care of me for the rest of my life, like she always thought Mama should have been cared for." She made a sound of disgust. "I'm not a soft easterner like Mama, even if I do favor her for looks."

"So you didn't meet any men who caught your fancy?"

"Those city boys? Bite your tongue. I had to ride all the way from Greeley in the stagecoach with one of them. He kept telling me what beautiful eyes I had and asked if he could sit next to me. I told him I was looking forward to getting home to my father's cattle ranch and helping with the annual castration of the male calves. That quieted him down."

Maggie pressed a fist to her mouth to stifle her laughter.

She'd feared March's sister would be offended by her looks and lack of refinement. Apparently she needn't have worried.

Harry hugged her knees up to her chest. "I'm sorry," she said in a more somber voice. "About Lucas. Losing your cousin."

"Don't be," Maggie said, then grimaced as she realized how the words sounded. "I mean, I never met him, except once as a child, and I don't really remember that. It's only over this past week that I've started to learn how much I missed, not knowing him. And Jane and Logan. From what March has said, your sister was a very special woman."

Harry nodded. "She was more like a mother to me than a sister, being so much older. We didn't always agree on things. I was more like March than Jane. I wanted to be a cowboy when I grew up." She laughed a little. "I think that's probably what got me sent away to school."

Maggie thought of the blue jeans she'd borrowed all week. "But Jane worked around the ranch," she said, setting aside her hairbrush.

"Sure," Harry agreed. "She loved the horses as much as Lucas did. But she was happier cooking and sewing and looking after Logan than mucking stalls or riding the fence line in zero degree weather. And she thought I was too delicate for that sort of work. I guess because Mama was so delicate."

Her own mother's frail health came to Maggie's mind. If she'd had a younger sister, perhaps she'd have been overprotective, too.

"And now March doesn't want me here, either."

The pain in Harry's voice wrenched Maggie's heart. She climbed into her side of the bed, pulling her own knees up to her chest.

"Of course he does," she said, responding more to Harry's tone than her words.

"No, he's furious that he can't send me back to that awful school, and right now he's trying to think up somewhere else he can pack me off to, the sooner the better. I know he is."

Maggie had no answer for that, since it was undoubtedly true. "He loves you very much," she said instead.

"Right. He loves me so much he didn't even send for me to come to my own sister's funeral. He hasn't written me once. I suppose I should count myself lucky he even bothered to telegraph me that it had happened. I got a longer note of sympathy from Elijah Kelly than from my own brother."

It didn't take much to imagine Harry's grief and loneliness, her feeling of abandonment trapped a thousand miles from her family.

"I don't know that he could have written to you," Maggie said, remembering the March she'd met her first day in Oxtail. "He's been trapped in his own grief. But he hadn't forgotten about you. He only left you in school because he needed to know you were safe. From the way he's talked about you—"

"From the way he's talked about me, you thought I was a *boy,*" Harry interrupted savagely.

"He hasn't been able to talk about Jane, Lucas, or Logan, either," Maggie said, her own temper flaring. "Every time someone mentions them, something dies inside him. Do you think that means he didn't love them? At least when he talks about you, it brings life back to his eyes."

She braced herself for Harry to tell her to mind her own business. Instead, she heard only the young woman's quiet sobbing. Shame engulfed her. Once more she'd said exactly the wrong thing.

"Harry? Harriet? I'm sorry. I didn't mean . . . I'm sorry."
She wondered if Harry could hear her through her weeping.

"I didn't want to upset you. I just don't want you to think March doesn't love you. There's nothing worse than to feel unwanted in your own family." She knew that well enough. "He just wants to protect you. He's been so sure those rustlers will come back—"

"More than a month later?" Harry asked, her voice choked with tears.

"Yes. Even more so now. March doesn't think the people who killed your sister's family were rustlers at all. He thinks they were hired by someone who wants this land."

"Why?"

"The water rights."

"Does he know who?"

Harry's hiccuping sobs had given way to sniffles. Maggie thought about March telling her to stop interfering in his life. She plunged on anyway. "He thinks so."

"Do you have a handkerchief?"

Maggie pulled one from the pocket of her nightgown.

"Thanks." After a long moment, Harry spoke again, her voice no longer sodden with tears. "All right. Tell me."

Maggie did, from March's theory about the strange behavior of the killers to her own doubts about his reasoning to Brady's offer on the ranch that afternoon. Harry listened quietly, and Maggie couldn't tell whether it helped her to know they might find out who had killed her sister or not. When she finished, they sat quietly for a minute, side by side, each lost in the incomprehensibility of murder.

"Why didn't March tell me about this?" Harry finally asked.

"He wants to protect you," Maggie said again. "He doesn't want to hurt you by bringing up their deaths. And maybe he's afraid that if you know the truth, you might not be willing to leave him here alone."

"Of course I'm not going to leave!" Harry exclaimed indignantly.

"Of course not," Maggie repeated faintly, barely refraining from hitting herself alongside the head. "This time March is going to string me up for sure."

"Don't worry about that. I wouldn't have gone anyway," Harry assured her. "This is my home, and I'm not going to let anyone send me away again."

"But you're not safe here. Do you have any other relatives, Harry?"

The young woman shook her head. "Pa died a couple of years ago. We heard it from one of Lucas's old friends in the Rangers. If he or Mama had any relatives left back East, they didn't keep in touch with them, and certainly didn't tell us anything about them."

Maggie swallowed, thinking about March staring out into the night, agony in his eyes. Brady's offer had only firmed his cold resolution. His sister's arrival had brought the despair.

"Harry, as long as you were in Philadelphia, you were relatively safe. But with you here, there's less reason for Brady to negotiate with March. If he kills both of you, who gets the land? I don't know, but I'd guess it reverts to public land, and it probably wouldn't be too difficult for Brady to get his hands on it."

"Especially with his political connections," Harry put in.

Her words did not improve Maggie's mood. "You have to go. You have to get out of range of those killers."

Who knew Harry had returned to Oxtail? She'd borrowed a horse from the colonel who ran the hotel. Maggie glanced toward the window. Surely Brady couldn't have had time to organize a raid for tonight. But the thought chilled her bones.

"You can come home with me," she said, the thought coming to her in sudden inspiration. "March wants to send me home on the stagecoach tomorrow. I'm sure my mother would be happy to welcome you." Stephen might be another matter, but he could hardly object to taking in such a demure young lady as Maggie was sure Miss Harriet Jackson could pretend to be.

"He wants to send you away? But you weren't planning to go." It wasn't a question.

"What makes you say that?"

"The way you said it. The way you talked about me leaving. With all the danger you keep talking about, why would you rather stay here than return home?"

Maggie couldn't hear any hostility or suspicion in Harry's voice, but that didn't mean it wasn't there. Perhaps schooling in the art of polite, artificial society could be useful after all.

"There's not much to return to," she said. There seemed little point in lying. "My mother loved my father and my brother. After they died, there wasn't much love left for me. And my stepfather and I have never gotten along—to put it mildly."

"It must be pretty awful to prefer facing down murdering rustlers on a remote, struggling horse ranch to going home," Harry commented.

Maggie caught herself before her fingers could find her scar. "It is."

"Mm. And that's the only reason you want to stay?"

"It's enough of one."

"If you say so." Harry didn't sound convinced. "But you want to take me back there with you."

"You'd be safe."

"So would you. But you'd rather be here."

Maggie wondered why Harry hadn't been expelled from school long ago. "I think there's less risk for me than there is for you, and I don't want to see you get hurt."

"You mean you don't want to see March get hurt."

Maggie couldn't answer, and after a moment Harry burst into laughter. "I thought so. Well, if you and I leave, who's going to look after him? If you get on that smelly old stagecoach tomorrow, you're getting on it alone. I told you nobody's going to send me away from my home again, and I meant it."

Maggie clenched her jaw to hold back the tears that threatened behind her eyelids. Maybe Harry had felt exiled from home. Maybe being sent away to school had hurt her feelings. But it hadn't changed the fact that she knew this ranch was her home, that she could talk about it with such passionate possessiveness.

Harry belonged here. She didn't. Perhaps the house in Lexington wasn't a "home." But she had even less of a claim on this ranch and its people. Her mother's cousin Lucas was dead. She had no other connection to this land. No other connection but her heart's blood—and to the outside world that meant nothing.

"Maggie?" Harry's voice sounded softer, tentative.

"Yes?" She didn't open her eyes.

"I didn't mean that exactly the way it sounded. It just felt like, I don't know . . . I don't like feeling cornered. But if you just wanted to get rid of me, you wouldn't have offered to go with me. Sometimes I don't think before I speak."

Maggie couldn't quite manage a smile. "I know how that feels."

"If you care about March, you're all right as far as I'm concerned."

She turned to look at Harry's pale face. "You, too, Harry."

"Are you staying?"

Staying? In a place she didn't belong, among people she'd known for no more than a week? In a land of dead grass and dust and sudden death, where neither the animals nor the land nor even the people had been tamed? Staying, only to wait for bloodthirsty hired guns to attack the ranch? Facing insurmountable odds with only an embittered ranch hand and an old man to protect her?

"Of course."

The cool night breeze that brushed across the porch made the hair on March's arms prickle. He thought about going in to get a blanket. Despite the fact that he sat with his rifle across his lap and his Colt within reach in the holster slung across the back of his chair, he didn't really expect trouble tonight.

Hell, even if trouble came, he couldn't head it off by himself. It was that feeling of helplessness more than imminent danger that made his heart skitter in his chest like a mouse in the wall.

Harry.

He couldn't stop his heart from being glad to see her. But her arrival had brought back the ghosts with vivid, shocking strength. He could hear his fears rustling in the darkness. Death's wings, silent as the owl's, swept past the house, and he could feel the eddy of air they left in their wake.

He longed for that one long taste of whiskey that would settle his heartbeat, press the knowledge of murder and death beyond the edge of consciousness.

No, not whiskey. He longed for warm, strong limbs wrapped around his, for a mane of thick red hair to bury himself in, for a sweet voice to tell him there was life left in the world and he could find it if he just held on to her.

Why had Maggie come to him now? He'd always feared death. Even in those horrible hours after he'd found the bodies of his family, when the anguish and the guilt had made him wish he'd died, too, a part of him had felt a horrible relief that he was still alive.

Now, paradoxically, the thought of death no longer frightened him as much. If he could find light and hope and . . . love . . . after the deaths of those he loved so much, then who was to say he wouldn't find peace of another kind after his own death.

But now he no longer *wanted* to die. She'd taken the protective shell of his despair from him; he cared once more. Once more he had more to lose than he could bear.

And Harry.

March rose from his chair and moved to the porch railing. He imagined he could smell his horses, the scent of sweet water, even the tang of the forest-clad mountains. He loved this land. And he had loved Jane and her family with all of his heart. But if he couldn't find a way to guarantee safety for Harry and for Maggie . . . He would take Brady's offer before he got them killed.

He only hoped his land and his ghosts would understand.

Chapter 20

Maggie stood at the window, her hands torturing her handkerchief, watching Lemuel Tate load her trunk into the back of the wagon. Her carpet bag and Harry's valise waited beside the door.

She glanced at March, willing him to carry them out so Lemuel wouldn't have to make another trip, but his usual painful good manners seemed to have deserted him. He stood near the stove, staring at the kettle as if the heat of his gaze might bring it to a boil.

Henna or I could just as well make the tea, she wanted to tell him. But she didn't think he'd hear her. Still, with him there, she could only wait silently while Henna and Harry made strained conversation and the time slipped away.

She glanced toward the table, and Harry's blue eyes caught hers, worry in their depths. Maggie shook her head. She couldn't think of a way to get March out of the house.

She and Harry had sat awake long into the night devising a plan to miss the stagecoach. Perhaps the late hour had befuddled their brains, for in the bright light of morning, the plan seemed poorly thought out, especially since it relied on their ability to prevent March from riding into Oxtail with them. Still, Maggie felt sure they could manage it with Henna's help. But they needed to fill her in on the details. Soon.

"March?" Henna's voice dispersed her feverish thoughts of hitting March over the head with the teapot.

March's head snapped up. "Hm? Sorry, Henna, did you say something?"

"Do you know where Wolf is? Is he avoiding me deliberately?"

Maggie could see the effort it took March to focus on Henna, to set aside his troubled thoughts. In that quick, unguarded moment of reorientation, she saw something strange flicker in his eyes. Fear—or maybe even hope. Something that didn't belong in the eyes of a man longing to get himself killed. Something that belonged in a man who had something left to fight for.

And something in her heart answered, a little flame she'd hardly known existed. It burned away the hurt she'd felt when March had enthusiastically agreed to her suggestion that Harriet return to Kentucky with her.

"I'm not sure where Wolf is," he answered Henna. "Probably out in the barn playing with Loki. He's trying to get him accustomed to horses—and the horses to him. He probably didn't even hear you arrive. Why would you think he's avoiding you?"

Henna shrugged, a delicate gesture. "I haven't seen him since I ordered Elijah out of the house. I'm afraid he might not understand why I was so angry, or that I didn't mean Elijah can't ever come back. He doesn't see his father often enough as it is."

Maggie could see what it cost her to admit that.

"That's true," March agreed, "but it's not all your fault."

"Of course it's not!" Henna said hotly, only by force of will bringing back her calm exterior. "But I'd like to talk with Wolf about the other night. Perhaps you could find him for me?"

Maggie started when March glanced sharply from Henna to her. She thought his eyes narrowed, but he said, "Of course. I'll be right back."

Maggie didn't dare breathe until he'd actually closed the

door behind him, and she heard the tread of his boots on the porch stairs.

"Well?" Henna asked, glancing from Maggie to Harry and back. "I've gotten rid of him. Now tell me what you two are plotting."

March crossed the yard with deliberate strides. There was no point in circling back to the house to eavesdrop. They'd probably posted a lookout at the window to watch for him.

He muttered a low, exasperated curse, which had the disconcerting effect of making him smile. He'd known Maggie was up to something when she offered to take Harry to Lexington with her. She'd found the perfect ally. Harry would jump into any half-baked plan head first.

But Henna? He would have expected her to talk some sense into the two younger women. She could talk sense into a rattlesnake. Since Maggie arrived, though, nothing had happened exactly as he'd expected.

Never mind. He'd get Maggie and Harry on that stagecoach today, and make darn sure they caught the train in Greeley. He planned to send Lemuel all the way to Cheyenne with them.

Not only would his sister and Maggie be safe, but it would also get his old friend out of the line of fire. Lemuel was handy with his shotgun, and he'd be more than willing to die to avenge Lucas Penny's murder, but he'd fought more than his share of the world's fights in his long life. He deserved to end his life in peace, not hatred.

March entered the barn door and walked toward the stable, finding Wolf in front of Ari's open stall. The boy had Loki pinned to the ground, the cub's huge feet waving in the air, while the buckskin mare sniffed daintily at them both.

Wolf heard footsteps and glanced up.

"Hi, March."

March crouched down to rub Loki's belly. The cub grabbed his hand with his teeth in greeting.

"Loki! No!" Wolf pried the wolf's jaws open and shook him. "I'm trying to teach him not to do that. It would scare Emmy and Tuck."

Not to mention Jed, March thought wryly. "He's liable to scare a lot of people without meaning to."

"Ma and Pa'll get used to it."

March tickled the pads on Loki's feet. The cub swatted at him and wriggled to his feet, leaping in ecstatic play at March's face. March wondered if it were really possible for the little beast to have gained five pounds and an inch of tooth in two days.

"That's a lot to get used to," he murmured. Then, seeing Wolf's face, he changed the subject. "Henna's here. She'd like to see you."

Wolf's expression tightened. "All right." He got to his feet, digging a lint-covered cube of sugar from his pocket to give Ari. Then he dragged Loki back from his exploration of the mare's ankles and shut the stall door. "I knew Ari wouldn't be afraid of him. She's not afraid of anything."

March glanced from the horse to the boy and suddenly understood why Wolf hadn't come into the house to greet Henna. His throat tightened. He wasn't the only one whose heart would bleed when Maggie rode out of their lives.

"I'll tell her you're finishing your chores," he offered. "You can come in when you're ready."

Wolf shook his head. "No, I'm coming."

March held out his hand, and the boy took it. Together, they walked to the door, Loki trailing behind them.

For a moment, the bright morning sun dazzled their eyes.

At a sound from the drive, they turned their heads in unison. The pounding of hooves. Through the brightness, March saw a horse, pushed hard. The man on its back carried a rifle in his hand.

The front door slammed open with a crash that had Maggie jumping from her chair. Her two conspirators looked up from beside her with guilt written all over their faces. But their chagrin went unnoticed by the men who burst into the room.

The long, wicked barrel of a rifle stopped Maggie's heart, until she saw Elijah Kelly behind it. On his heels followed March, Wolf, and Lemuel, showing the same confusion and anxiety she felt on her own face.

"What's wrong?" she asked March, but it was Elijah who answered.

"What isn't?" He propped his rifle beside the door. His naturally fair skin looked pale, and she could see a sheen of sweat on his forehead.

"Elijah," Harry breathed beside her.

On the other side of the table, Henna leaped to her feet. "I thought I told you never to set foot in my house again!"

"Henna!" March warned, and she had the grace to blush, remembering she'd said she'd make peace with the gunfighter for Wolf's sake.

Elijah dropped his hat pointedly on the rack. "But this isn't your house, is it, Henna? If you can't stand my presence, you'd better leave, because I've got business here, and I don't have time to argue with you."

"Whatever your business is, it'll have to wait," March said, glancing at the clock on the bookshelf across the room. "Maggie and Harry have a stagecoach to catch."

"Harry?" The gunfighter's eyes settled on the woman beside Maggie. He actually smiled. "Why, Miss Harriet, you've grown into a lovely young lady."

Harry laughed, running over to give him a quick hug. "I don't think March will agree with you on that."

Elijah put a hand on each of her shoulders and looked her in the eye. "I'm not going to ask what you did this time. Will it happen again?"

Harry actually blushed. "Not likely," she said faintly.

Elijah frowned. "That bad?"

"Worse," March put in.

Elijah shook his head, with a wink for Harry. "I guess she's your sister, through and through."

Then his gaze hardened again. "But March, Harry and Maggie aren't going to catch that stagecoach."

"They have to," March said. "I can explain it to you later, 'Lije. They're not safe here. They're going to Kentucky."

"They're not going by stagecoach," Elijah said flatly. "The stagecoach isn't coming."

Maggie felt a guilty second of relief. She hadn't been looking forward to dumping poor Lemuel along the side of the road into Oxtail as she and Harry had planned.

"There's no time to explain," Elijah continued, "but you're right that the women aren't safe here. We've got to send them to the Culbert farm."

"But what happened?" Maggie asked.

"You don't want to hear it. Wolf, you help Harry and Maggie with their bags."

"We're not going anywhere without an explanation," Henna said, her quiet voice laced with steel.

"And I'm not giving one," the gunfighter growled back. His face twisted in what looked like physical pain. "Just get the hell out of here. And hurry."

"We're going," Maggie said, cutting off Henna's reply. "If

it's that important, we'll leave."

She gave Harry a tug and Henna a sharp glare, drawing them by will alone toward the door. "Is there anything else we can do?"

Elijah shook his head and winced. "Just stay put at the farm."

"Understood." Maggie pushed Henna through the open doorway and pulled Harry out after her. Wolf followed reluctantly with the two bags.

They descended the porch steps and crossed the yard, but as they neared the wagon, Henna stopped and turned on Maggie.

"All right, what's the plan?"

Harry and Wolf looked up. "Plan?"

"Plan?" Maggie asked innocently.

"You don't think I would have let you railroad me out of that room if I didn't think you had a plan, do you?" Henna asked. "My original assessment of you wasn't far off the mark, Margaret Parker. You have a devious mind. Now talk."

Maggie flushed, more from pleasure than embarrassment. She almost felt like they were friends, now that Henna could tease her.

"All right. When I first met Wolf, he told me there was a way to sneak into the loft, that he and Logan and Danny used to do that sometimes."

"Wolf!"

The boy met his mother's eyes. "We climbed up the woodpile, but there's a ladder in the shed . . ."

Henna didn't quite manage not to smile. "Every mother's dream. A son who's a natural housebreaker."

"What are we waiting for?" Harry asked impatiently. "Let's go."

★ ★ ★ ★ ★

As the front door closed behind the women and Wolf, Elijah sank into a chair at the table as though all the strength had drained from his legs.

" 'Lije, are you hurt?" March asked the question he'd been holding back.

The gunfighter shook his head, wincing at the movement. "Headache. Do you have a glass of water?"

"Sure." March moved to oblige his friend, almost tripping over Loki. The cub had taken to hiding in one of the kitchen cupboards when the noise in the house overwhelmed him. He must have hidden there during the excitement of Elijah's arrival.

"You think it's safe now?" March asked. Loki smiled up at him, his tongue hanging out one side of his long mouth, but trotted right past March to push at Elijah's boot.

"Hey, little one," Elijah murmured, reaching down to scratch the wolf's ears. "Normally I'd hide out when Henna was around, too."

Elijah reached down to grab the cub by the scruff of his neck and pull him into his lap. Loki placed two huge paws on his chest and enthusiastically licked his face.

"I'm the one who spared your life and spent an hour chewing jerked beef for you," March said to the cub. "You ought to save that affection for me and not waste it on the likes of him."

Elijah chuckled and tilted his chin so Loki could finish his cleaning job. "He knows your first love is horses, March. Besides, we fellow outlaws have to stick together, isn't that right, little wolf?"

March didn't need to be reminded of Loki's unsuitability for farm life. He handed Elijah his glass of water.

"Thanks."

March took a seat opposite Elijah, and Lemuel sat beside him. "Now tell us what happened to the stagecoach."

"It's gone," Elijah said simply. He lifted Loki off his chest and set him gently down onto the floor. The cub settled himself under the gunfighter's chair.

"What do you mean, gone?"

"I mean it's gone, destroyed. The murdering bastards killed the driver, the shotgun rider, and all six passengers. Then they set fire to the stagecoach. While it was still hitched to the horses, I might add. Quite a mess."

"Outlaws ambushed the stage?" Lemuel asked in disbelief.

"They got away with about a thousand dollars in silver."

"Why would they kill the passengers?" March asked. "Did they resist?"

His friend shook his head. "One of the passengers was a woman and three of the men were unarmed. It appears the outlaws shot the shotgun rider, stopped the coach, disarmed the other two men and then shot the driver and the passengers in cold blood. Maybe they were angry there wasn't more money in the cargo. I don't know."

March's stomach churned. "The bastards. Killing helpless people. What sort of monsters are they?"

"Now we get to the reason I came back," Elijah drawled, leaning back in his chair. His eyes were the flat eyes of a killer, but March thought his face looked even grayer than when he'd arrived. "I've been to Denver recently, and there's a man in Cheyenne I don't want to run into, so when I left here the other night, I thought I might find myself some of that healthy mountain air you Coloradans are so proud of. I was in the saloon in Dead Man's Claim last night, having a taste of your not-so-healthy Colorado rotgut, when a gentleman there offered me a very intriguing proposition."

"Which was?" March pressed. Now that the women had left, Elijah seemed to have forgotten his insistence on haste in the interests of creating a good story.

"Which was, he would pay me a handsome sum if I would join him and his friends in a virtually risk-free bit of out-lawry."

"Attacking the stagecoach," March guessed.

"No." Elijah's eyes narrowed. "Murdering you."

Chapter 21

In the silence that followed Elijah's words, a detached part of March's brain registered a scuffling noise that might have been coming from the loft. Mice. No, too loud. Rats. He'd have to bring one of the barn cats into the house.

Lemuel broke the silence. "Kill March?"

"Why you?" March added. Though he was sure there were more important questions to ask, they wouldn't come to him at the moment.

"The gentleman approached me in the saloon because he thought I looked familiar." Elijah's smile was positively malevolent. "I told him I was John Wesley Hardin."

"Why *March*," Lemuel asked, with what March thought was an admirable recognition of the central question.

Elijah roused from his slouch with a catlike shake and leaned forward on the table. "It wasn't a coincidence that this man thought I looked familiar. I helped put him in jail. And so did you, March. It was John Deane."

"John Deane's in prison in Texas."

"Parole."

"But he's a killer!"

Elijah shrugged. "He wasn't convicted of killing anyone, but his brother was. What got John Deane through ten years of prison was his desire for revenge on everyone involved in Luke Deane's capture, conviction, and hanging."

March's skin grew cold. "Lucas . . ." he breathed.

"Deane and his new gang started their killing in Texas. They murdered the judge that passed the sentence against

Luke Deane. So far they've killed two of the jurors. One of them had a wife and four kids. All dead. They even found the hangman, killed him and his brother."

March couldn't find the air to breathe. "Lucas, Jane, Logan . . . Why didn't Deane come back for me sooner?"

"I gather John was rather pleased you weren't home when they killed Lucas." Elijah's hooded eyes reflected March's impotent fury. "He wanted to give you a chance to suffer the loss, as he suffered his. You're the one he holds directly responsible for his brother's death. You're the big prize in his fantasy of revenge."

March pushed himself away from the table, giving his body room to breathe. If he couldn't take in air soon, he was going to be violently sick. He'd made a mistake when he was hardly more than a boy, and ten years later that mistake had cut a swath of death from Texas to Colorado, costing innocent people their lives. Costing his sister, his nephew, and his best friend their lives.

"I should have put a bullet through that bastard's brain when I had the chance." But the words were no more than a whisper.

He could feel his heart pounding as it had when he'd leaped the porch steps that overcast afternoon a month ago. He had hardly registered that the front door was ajar before he burst through it. The smell of blood had overpowered him, though his eyes refused to acknowledge the scene before him. They were all dead. ". . . all dead."

"March!" Elijah's hand on his arm washed the red from the floor, from the walls, drawing him back to the present. His friend's eyes glittered strangely. "You saved eight lives the day you stopped the Deanes from killing those stagecoach passengers. And who knows how many other people lived because Luke was hanged and John's

307

been in prison for ten years."

March clenched his fists, felt them trembling. "And if a hundred people had to die, for Jane, for Lucas, for Logan to still be alive . . ." He didn't need to finish the sentence.

"Lucas had been hunting the Deanes since their jail break—your jail break." Elijah tightened his grip on March's arm until it hurt. "He was a damn good Ranger, March. He would have gotten them with or without you. That's what he did. What he thought was right. And he would not have wanted any less from you."

"I know that." But it didn't lessen the pain or the wrenching regret.

He allowed Elijah to lead him back to the table. Elijah sank as heavily into his chair as he did.

"That man mus' want March awful dead to try to hire you to help him, Elijah," Lemuel observed quietly.

"There's something not right about him," Elijah agreed. "I've seen it happen to killers before. It's as though . . . as though killing gives him an illusion of power. He creates death, so he thinks death can't touch him. He can do anything, and he might as well do it big. Right now he's got eight of the most ruthless killers in the territory on a very thin leash by promising them a share of the gold March took from him, but he doesn't have sense enough to see the danger."

"I counted the tracks of at least ten or eleven horses when the ranch was attacked," March said.

"A couple of unfortunate gunfights reduced the number, according to the bartender in Dead Man's Claim." Elijah's eyes were glittering again. He took a long drink of water. "That's why Deane tried to recruit me."

March attempted a smile. "Thanks for turning him down."

"He couldn't afford me. Besides, I have information he

doesn't have. I know you returned that gold to the Blackwater bank, remember. You don't have enough money to be worth robbing.

"Another thing—he's heard about your drinking and other reckless behavior. He bought it."

"So when do they get here?" Lemuel asked, once more turning the conversation back to practicalities.

Elijah pulled his duster more tightly around him, though March thought the air in the house had warmed considerably since his arrival. "After that business with the stagecoach, I'd say they're going to have to do it soon. Deane can't keep those desperadoes in check much longer."

He finished his water and handed the glass to March. "Another glass?"

"Sure." March took the glass, noting with surprise that his friend's hand was shaking.

Eight desperate gunslingers. Nine, if you counted Deane, and March knew that John Deane had been as good with a gun as he needed to be.

He wasn't going to have time to get Lemuel out of town now, but he and Lem together didn't stand a chance against that number. Even with Elijah's expert help . . .

Turning back from the sink, he saw Lemuel eyeing Elijah suspiciously. The old man reached out a big hand toward the gunfighter's forehead. Elijah dodged it.

"The fever," Lemuel accused.

"No. I don't have the fever." Elijah didn't meet March's eyes as he took the glass from his hand. "Not yet, anyway. Now sit down and listen to me."

Lemuel crossed his arms over his chest. "You ain't been takin' your pills."

"I lost them," Elijah said, as though such a thing happened every day. And, March reflected, when it came to 'Lije and his malaria pills, it often did. "Don't look at me that way, Lem. It hasn't killed me yet."

"But it could *get* you killed one of these days," March reminded him. "Damn it, 'Lije—"

"I meant to get some in Denver. I forgot." The gunfighter frowned like a surly truant schoolboy. "I'll take care of it as soon as the bullets stop flying, all right?"

"You can take care of it now," March said. "Jane kept a bottle ready for just such an occasion."

"Our mother hen," Elijah said with a little smile. But March couldn't smile back. "Where is it?"

"Jane's dresser in the bedroom." March put a hand on his friend's shoulder. "Sit down. I'll get it."

"I can get it," Elijah insisted with surprising savagery, pushing himself to his feet. "I know what you're thinking, March, but I'm not an invalid. You're not going to send me away, and I'm not going to let you down."

March said nothing. There was nothing to say. He watched Elijah set down his glass of water. It sloshed on the table. He met his friend's eyes, and neither of them had to ask the other what good a gunfighter was who couldn't hold a glass of water without spilling it.

Strange, Maggie thought, that she felt almost as much relief as fear at finally knowing the nature of March's enemy. No more wondering, no more vague suspicions and spirit-draining fears.

At least it wasn't Alexander Brady. Despite his attitude about Shelby Brennan's treatment of her, she would have had a hard time wishing death on a man with a wife and daughters. Especially a man with such an eye for horses.

She sighed raggedly. It would be better if it had been Brady. Better to face a bunch of wild cowboys than a gang of killers. And these were killers March had no choice but to face. They wouldn't make an offer on his ranch and let him live. From what Elijah had said, John Deane would hunt him to the end of the earth if he had to.

Maggie shifted in her position on the wagon seat between Harry and Henna, holding Pamela to a quick trot on the road to the Culbert farm. Wolf sat on her trunk in the wagon bed behind them "keeping a lookout for outlaws."

"Nine desperadoes," Harry breathed beside her. "Against three men."

"Two," Henna corrected. "Damn Elijah's black heart. One time we could actually use a gunfighter, and he's forgotten to take his quinine pills."

"Three. Elijah can still fight," Harry defended him. "He's not going to forget how to shoot a gun just because he's sick."

"Two. Once the chills stop, so he can actually aim a gun again, the fever will start. Have you ever seen him when the fever comes, Harriet? Well, I have. He won't even be able to sit up, much less quickdraw John Deane."

"Regardless," Maggie put in, forestalling Harry's heated reply, "We agree that March and Mr. Tate don't have the experience Mr. Kelly has. What kind of a chance do they really stand against nine ruthless outlaws?"

She didn't expect an answer, but a little thing like insurmountable odds couldn't sidetrack Henna's cool logic. "They have the advantage of being inside the house. And there's not much shelter, other than the barn, for Deane and his gang to mount a siege from."

"And they have the advantage of surprise," Harry said. "Deane's expecting March to be totally unprepared for his attack, but Deane will be the one who's walking into an ambush. Thanks to Elijah," she added pointedly.

Maggie wondered what March would think of his baby sister's impassioned defense of his gunfighter friend.

"This really isn't good country in which to mount an attack on armed defenders," Henna mused, glancing around them at the empty short-grass prairie. "It's no wonder Deane hired so many desperadoes to kill a pair of horse ranchers. Still, attacking in broad daylight . . . He could count on surprise the first time, but is he really foolish enough to do it again?"

"Elijah said Deane had heard about March's bitter drunk act," Maggie pointed out. "It's obviously convinced Deane he'll be an easy target."

"Maybe they're planning to attack after nightfall," Harry suggested. "That would take care of cover."

"That would probably be the wisest course," Henna said. "If you had to attack someone in their home. On the other hand, if you could lure your victim out into the open around here, there would be no place for them to run to."

The hairs on the back of Maggie's neck prickled. She gave Pamela a slap with the reins. "I wish you wouldn't say things like that, Henna."

The older woman put a hand on her arm. "Stop the wagon."

That was the last thing on earth Maggie would have chosen to do at that moment, but she pulled Pamela to a halt. Perhaps her nervousness had communicated itself through the lines, because the normally unflappable Pamela shook her head and kicked a front hoof at the ground.

They sat in silence, nothing but the wind in the grass disturbing the quiet morning.

Maggie finally hefted the reins once more. "Now that you've pointed out just how exposed we are out here, I'd rather keep moving."

"No."

"What's wrong, Ma?" Wolf asked from behind them, his voice unconsciously imitating the sudden low tones of the adults. "I don't see anything."

"But they're coming," Maggie said. Her knuckles whitened on the black leather reins she clutched in her fists. "We've got to get to the farm, Henna, and get Jed's help. And then I'm going to ride to Oxtail and see if I can't find some bored cowboys who will welcome an afternoon's excitement shooting outlaws."

"What if that's what they want us to do?" Henna asked, her amber eyes scanning the road ahead of them. "What if John Deane really did recognize Elijah?"

The goose bumps spread from the back of Maggie's neck down her arms as a chill wind touched her heart.

"He'd have killed him," Harry said. "Elijah helped capture his brother. He'd want him dead, too. Besides, it would be surprising if he recognized him after all these years. Elijah didn't live with the Deane gang like March did."

"And he wouldn't want to warn March he was coming," Maggie added.

Henna's gaze met hers for a long moment. "If he's heard about March's drinking and neglect of the ranch, he must surely have heard March has a lovely young cousin visiting him . . ."

Maggie didn't like where Henna's line of reasoning was leading.

". . . And if there were any women or children at the ranch, March would surely send them away if he knew Deane was coming. One thing John Deane knows for sure about March is that he'll go to any lengths necessary to protect innocent people."

"The chance to take a hostage that could bring March out into the open . . ." Maggie couldn't finish the thought, frozen by the image of March, Lemuel, and Elijah cut down in a bloody ambush.

Henna finished it for her. "The chance to take a hostage would be worth the risk of warning March he was coming."

"Deane's crazy," Harry said. "The way he attacked that stagecoach—he's out of control. He couldn't come up with a devious plan like that." But Maggie saw her glance over her shoulder, her blue eyes wide and dark.

"We've got to get to the farm and fast," Maggie said grimly. "If he's got enough sanity to have someone waiting for us on the way into Oxtail, we'd better get off the road."

"No!" Henna said again. "Not the farm. We've got to go back to the ranch house."

"The farm's closer. We don't want to be in March's way."

"They could be watching us at this very moment," Henna said, straining her voice to keep it low. "Jake, Danny, Emily, and Tucker are all at the farm. I'm not going to lead killers to them." She reached over the back of the seat for Wolf's hand. "We're already in danger. We can't take it to them."

Maggie remembered what Deane's men had done to Logan Penny. They wouldn't hesitate to kill more children. "Harry?"

"I won't be in the way," Harry vowed. "I'm a better shot with a rifle than March is. I'm probably better with a rifle than Elijah."

"I know a thing or two about pistols," Henna said. She glanced at Maggie. "It came in handy at one time in my life."

Great, Maggie thought. If they put a gun in her hand, she'd be more likely to shoot herself than an outlaw. But she could get them back to the ranch.

"All right, get in the back," she ordered. "Wolf, scoot down and let your ma and Harry climb over."

"I don't need to hide in the back," Wolf objected. "I can

sit with you and watch for desperadoes."

"Sit!" Maggie ordered in the firm voice she used for recalcitrant horses. "I'm not trying to protect you from outlaws. I just don't want to be worrying about you falling out."

The moment Harry and Henna cleared the back of the seat, she stood up on the seat rest. "Giii-yaaap!" she hollered. Calm, patient Pamela lunged forward like a panther springing. Maggie hauled on the reins, bringing her around in a tight circle that made the wagon rock and scraped the wheels against the side of the bed.

"Hang on," she called behind her and snapped the reins. Pamela broke into a run toward the ranch. The act of flight itself seemed to lodge Maggie's heart in her throat. Her blood pounding in her veins, she urged Pamela forward, driving the solid mare to her greatest speed.

She fought the urge to look behind her, the quickest way to lose her balance and break her neck. If the outlaws had been watching the wagon, she'd know about it soon enough. They'd have to try to catch the women before they reached the ranch.

She slapped the reins again. Even without a loaded wagon behind her, Pamela could never outrun a gang of outlaws on fresh horses, but the game mare would give them all she had until they reached the safety of home.

"I don't see anything," Harry called, over the noise of the protesting wagon. "We're not being followed."

Maggie's shoulders sagged with relief. They hadn't gone far enough down the road for the waiting outlaws to notice them. If outlaws had been waiting for them at all. She could slow the wagon—no sense in risking another broken axle.

But as she prepared to rein Pamela in, the distinct sound of a distant rifle shot rent the air.

She heard Wolf shout. "A rider! He's chasing us!"

"Where?" Henna's voice. "I don't see it."

"There! You can see the dust swirling."

"I see it!" Harry yelled. Then, "He's gaining on us. Fast!"

Maggie couldn't bear it any longer. She turned her head. Already Wolf's cloud of dust had grown into the figure of a man on a dark horse galloping through the break in the hogback. Her muscles froze. The lurch of the wagon hitting a dip in the road brought her sharply around, but she could hardly see Pamela ahead of her. The image of that dark rider behind them filled her vision.

And I saw, and behold, a pale horse: and he that sat upon him, his name was Death; and Hades followed with him. But what was the name of the rider on the black horse?

She felt as though her back had broadened to a target the size of the barn wall. If God weighed her soul, would he find it wanting? She didn't particularly want to find out today.

"I think there's more men behind him," Harry called out, and Maggie wished she'd kept that information to herself.

They hadn't come more than a mile from the Penny ranch. Why did the trip back suddenly seem to be taking hours?

Then she saw the drive to the ranch. They were going too fast to turn safely, but she didn't dare slow down.

"Hang on!" she yelled again, and then they were taking the curve around the low hill, the ranchhouse appearing like a vision from heaven before them. The wagon rocked wildly around the turn, challenging her precarious balance, taking all her concentration and skill. They hit a bump, and she felt both right wheels leave the earth, but then they hit solid ground again, and Pamela fairly flew the last hundred yards to the ranch house porch.

March was at the door before the wheels stopped moving. "What's happened?"

Maggie dropped the reins, surprised to find her arms shaking from terror and exhaustion.

"Someone's coming," Henna answered for her. "We've got to get everyone inside. They're right behind us."

"The farm?" March demanded, and Maggie could see his fear for the children.

"They passed it chasing us."

Lemuel reached the wagon and lifted Henna down. Wolf and Harry jumped after her.

Maggie tried to move, but her knees buckled, and she sank to the wagon seat.

"Maggie." March lifted her from the wagon seat. "Good girl," he murmured, clutching her close. "You got them all home safe. I won't let anything happen to you."

And she believed him. Against all sense, against the fear that had nearly paralyzed her. "You better not," she muttered against his ear. "You'll never find another woman who will put up with your atrocious singing."

And there on the porch, with John Deane and a gang of ruthless killers bare minutes away, he dropped his mouth to hers and kissed her.

He broke the kiss to meet her gaze. "Maggie, I love you."

To hear him say the words . . .

"March, I—"

"Whatever happens, I want you to know that," he continued. "You've brought my heart to life again. I *will not* allow any harm to come to you because of me."

Then other hands touched her, taking her from March's arms. He was passing her to Lemuel Tate.

"March!" She grabbed his shirt, making him stop for just the seconds it took to tell him, "I love you."

And then she was in Lemuel Tate's arms, the old black man carrying her as though she were made of feathers, not bone and flesh. March leaped off the porch, his hands deftly

317

working the traces holding Pamela to the wagon.

"I see him!" Harry screamed from her position at the porch window.

"March, there's no time to get to the barn," Elijah Kelly warned. The gunfighter was leaning against the door frame, and as Lemuel carried her past, Maggie could see the flush of fever on his cheeks.

"I can't leave her hitched here; they'll shoot her," March said, glancing up the drive to where the rider had just appeared. The last of the traces dropped to the ground. He swatted Pamela's flank, and she trotted across the yard, making her own way toward the barn.

March swung himself up over the porch railing, and the others jumped aside as he dove through the doorway. Henna slammed it shut behind him.

He could hear the hoofbeats as the rider raced down the drive.

"Get away from the window," he ordered Harry, grabbing his rifle from where he'd set it by the door.

Pulling both Colt revolvers from the holsters slung across his hips, Elijah moved with him to the window over the porch. With the stock of one Colt, the gunfighter smashed through the glass, sending it splintering to the porch. "Better than having it blown in on us," he explained.

March nodded, taking a crouching position on the right side of the window across from his friend. At the same moment, they both risked a quick glance out at the rider.

"What's he doing?" Elijah asked, bewilderment evident in his voice. "He's not even slowing down. He's going to make a wonderful target out there in that empty yard."

He raised his right hand, leaning his wrist against the now empty window frame. March knew he was using the support to keep his hand from shaking, but he didn't comment. He wasn't even sure how his friend had managed to get up off the sofa where he'd settled after he'd taken his quinine. He wasn't going to ask. Elijah would fight beside him as long as he could, and there was no point in speculating on how long that might be.

March raised his rifle, sighting down the barrel at the approaching figure. The man was dressed in black, carrying a rifle across his lap, his tailored coat flapping behind him, his face shaded by the rim of a black . . . bowler?

Chapter 22

March raised his eye from his rifle sight. The approaching rider's beautiful black stallion had taken on a stunning familiarity.

"Don't shoot," he commanded, rising to his feet. Elijah didn't so much as twitch, though his Colt had a hair trigger.

"March!"

He heard Maggie's sharp cry of fear as he ran to the door. He turned to find her trying to shake off Henna's restraining hand.

"It's all right," he said, hoping that was true. "It's Alexander Brady."

"Thank God," she breathed, and let Henna pull her back behind the sofa.

It didn't occur to him until he stepped out the door that Brady's name shouldn't have eased her mind. *How the hell?* . . . The rats in the loft. Well, he should have known.

"Jackson!" The rancher's ragged voice barely reached him, though he could tell the man was trying to shout. Brady pulled Sandy to a skidding stop in front of the porch. "Men on horseback. Not a half mile behind me."

"Get in the house," March told him, taking Sandy's reins. "I'll take this fellow to the barn."

Brady nodded and swung heavily to the ground.

"I can take Sandy to the barn," Wolf said from March's elbow.

March looked down at the boy and up at the empty drive. "Fast. Loosen his cinch and that's it. We'll take care of the horses when we get a chance." *If* they got the chance, but he wouldn't say that.

He followed Brady into the house. The rancher paused inside the door, taking in Lemuel's shotgun, Elijah's pistols, Maggie and Harry's pale faces.

"Well, Jackson, it looks like you're prepared for a skirmish, and I'd have to say that's probably a damn good idea. Pardon me, ladies."

Maggie hurried forward. "Can I get you a glass of water, Mr. Brady? Maybe you'd better sit down."

Only then did March notice the rancher's labored breathing and the redness of his face beneath his whiskers.

"Water would be lovely, Miss Parker." Brady took off his hat and sat in the armchair she'd indicated.

Maggie handed him a glass. "You gave us a scare, Mr. Brady. What's wrong?"

"I was hoping you could tell me." Brady loosened his bow tie and took a sip of water. "I was riding out here to see if you had an answer for me on my offer, Jackson. I was nearly to Jed Culbert's farm, minding my own business, when I thought I saw movement off that low ridge behind the hogback.

"I'd brought this along—" He held up the highly polished carbine he carried "—and thought maybe I'd get lucky and bag myself an antelope."

"Could you just tell us what happened," Elijah growled from his spot by the window. "We could die of old age here."

Brady started, not used to being spoken to in such a manner. But he didn't waste time taking offense. "Well, I rode out to see what was what, and damn me if it wasn't a whole nest of ruffians waiting out there in the grass like a pack of cowardly wolves.

"One of the sons-a . . . pardon me. One of them took a shot at me. At me!" The indignant outrage on Brady's face might

321

have made March smile under less dire circumstances. "Thank providence I had Bishop's Honor with me—"

"You named your gun?" Elijah asked, incredulous.

"He means Sandy," Maggie told him, in a tone that clearly told the gunfighter to keep his mouth to himself, fever or no fever.

March caught his friend's eye, and despite his obvious suffering, Elijah grinned. "You know, being a gunfighter used to bring a lot more respect than it does these days."

"Sandy?" Brady asked.

"You didn't tell us your stallion's name," Maggie explained. "So I decided to name him after you."

Brady's face lit up with pleasure, and he sat a little straighter in his chair. "Well, well. And not a bad name, is it? Better than that da—darned thoroughbred hoity-toity name he's been stuck with. Sandy. I like it."

Elijah shifted from his lookout position, opened his mouth, glanced at Maggie and shut it again.

"You were saying?" March prompted Brady.

"Right. It's a good thing I had Sandy with me. He's already proven worth the investment. He ran like the wind. Those outlaws never had a chance of catching us."

"How far behind you did you say they were?" Elijah asked.

"Maybe half a mile."

The gunfighter shook his head. "They should be here by now. They've realized they've lost the element of surprise. They must be rethinking their strategy. The only real cover for miles is the barn."

"The barn?" Henna gasped. "My God, Wolf . . ."

But at that moment the door swung open and Wolf darted in, his eyes shining with pride at the successful completion of his mission, a pride that was somewhat injured when Henna grabbed him and pulled him tightly to her chest.

"Ma!" The boy wiggled free. "I took Sandy to the stable, March, and put Pamela in, too."

"Thank you, son."

"What do you want me to do now?"

A movement from the window caught March's eye. Elijah looked on the brink of collapse, his breathing too quick, too shallow.

"Go spell your father, Wolf. We need you to keep a sharp lookout through that window."

"I'm fine right where I am," Elijah growled.

"Sure you are." March moved to his friend's side and took his arm. "But we need your guns, not your eyes. You're going to rest on the sofa until Deane makes his move."

Elijah opened his mouth to object, but as he tried to stand, his legs gave way beneath him. He slumped against March.

Henna hurried over and wrapped his other arm over her shoulder. "Try not to be a damn fool, Elijah. Come over to the sofa."

"Maybe just for a minute," he agreed weakly. "But we're going to need more lookouts. They could come from any direction, and—"

"And we'll take care of it," March said firmly, steering his friend to the sofa. Elijah settled heavily onto the cushioned seat. Harry moved forward to adjust a brightly colored pillow for his head.

"Maybe a damp cloth?" she said, her voice gentle with concern.

March frowned at her. His sister had always had a bad case of hero worship for Elijah Kelly. She was getting too old for that now.

"You take the lookout in the loft, Harry."

Her momentary disappointment brightened as she glanced toward the door. "I'll take your rifle."

His gaze locked with his sister's. Her eyes shone the color of blue violets, bright in her china pale face, so much like the mother she'd never had a chance to know. He would do anything to protect her. Which meant he had to give her the rifle. There was no point in pretending. Either they would kill John Deane or he would kill them. Deane wasn't going to let anyone walk out of the ranch house alive, even if it meant killing women and children.

Harry was a better shot with a rifle than he was, anyway. "Take it."

She retrieved it from its place by the door. "I wonder what Headmistress Danforth would say about one of her students shooting it out with desperadoes." She grinned. "I'd even be willing to look at her sour face again, just to see her expression when I told her."

"Move."

Her face sobered at the grimness in his voice, and she trotted down the hall toward the stairs.

"If Elijah will let me borrow one of those Colts, I'll take the bedroom," Henna offered.

The gunfighter's hands moved reflexively to his hips.

" 'Lije?" March could give up his own revolver to Henna and use Elijah's rifle, but he felt more comfortable with the Colt.

Elijah flipped one of his revolvers from its holster, his hand fitting smoothly, comfortably on the grip. He glanced at it, then up at Henna, his eyes full of questions he didn't ask. He grasped the gun by the barrel and handed it up to her. "Careful, it's loaded."

"I should hope so," she said, her voice tart. "Don't worry, I know how to use one of these."

"I wouldn't have given it to you if I thought you didn't."

Their eyes locked for a moment, then Henna followed

Harry's path down the hall.

"I've got the window in the kitchen, March," Lemuel said, moving in that direction.

"And I'll take the one next to the desk," Brady offered, pushing himself up out of his chair.

March nodded and moved to stand with Wolf at the window overlooking the porch. "I'll hold the gun, you keep the lookout," he said, not wanting the boy to feel displaced. "You've got better eyes than I do."

Harry, Henna, Lemuel, Brady, and himself. Five against nine. Six, if Elijah could rise from the sofa when the shooting started. March glanced at him. It didn't look likely.

And Maggie. She hadn't offered to take a gun, which meant she didn't know how to shoot one. A week ago she would have pretended she did. A little pride flickered in him that she knew they needed their limited weapons in the hands of those who knew how to use them. But there were only six pairs of hands . . .

Not enough.

March forced his grip to relax around the stock of his revolver. He didn't want to have a cramp when Deane attacked. No, they didn't have enough firepower, and they didn't have Deane's gang's expertise.

But they were cornered, run to earth like a badger to his hole. March wondered if John Deane had ever faced a cornered badger.

He leaned his forearms on the window frame, letting his gaze scan the empty countryside before him.

"Come stick your hand in my den, you son-of-a-bitch," he muttered and settled himself to wait.

Maggie sopped the old rag she held in a bowl of tepid water and wrung it mechanically. She couldn't see that it was doing Elijah much good, but it gave her something to do. She settled it across his forehead, feeling his heat without even touching his skin.

Suddenly he raised his hand and swiped the rag from his face. It plopped softly on the floor.

"Mr. Kelly—"

"Miss Parker, I appreciate your efforts, I very much do." His weakness thickened his southern drawl. "But I think you and that rag are going to drive me right out of my mind."

Maggie swallowed her first reply, reaching down to retrieve the rag. A cold nose and warm pink tongue pushed against her knuckles. Loki. She scratched his cheek, then lifted the rag and soaked it once more, pressing it firmly against Elijah's neck.

"I don't care if it drives you crazy, Mr. Kelly. It might help your fever, and we need to do everything we can to keep your fever down."

"The malaria's going to run its course, and there's not one thing you or I can do to change that." He slammed a fist into the back of the sofa with frustrated strength. "I feel so goddamned helpless!"

Maggie thought of the little derringer in her skirt pocket. She just might be able to kill an outlaw if he walked up close enough for her to get a good shot at his eye. "I know how you feel. I don't even know how to load a gun, much less fire it."

Elijah shifted on the sofa to look up at her. "That's simple enough to fix. Go get my rifle, and I'll show you how to load that and a revolver. You can reload for March when the time comes."

Maggie didn't hesitate for a second. Anything was better than the dreadful waiting. She fetched Elijah's rifle from beside the door, then came back and scooted her chair forward so she could watch his demonstration.

"It's too bad we don't have more weapons," he said, rolling out the cylinder on the revolver. "Having someone to reload for you is almost as good as having another gunman." He worked the rod alongside the revolver, sending the cartridges flipping out onto his palm. "Here, put these back in."

She took the cartridges in one hand and held out her hand for the gun. Elijah let go before she could grasp it firmly, and it slipped through her fingers to the floor. She grabbed for it with her other hand, sending cartridges spinning across the polished wood.

"Damn!" She scrambled after a cartridge that had slid under the sofa, reaching it a split-second before it would have disappeared down Loki's gullet.

"That's all right," Elijah told her. "There, there's one on the edge of the rug. That's it."

Heat stained Maggie's cheeks. Such a simple thing as loading a gun, and she couldn't manage it. "Maybe I should reload for Deane and his men. It would even up the odds."

"Don't worry about it, Maggie. I did that once getting ready for a duel. I almost died of embarrassment before the idiot who challenged me had a chance to take a shot."

Maggie laughed, in spite of herself. "You're just saying that to make me feel better."

"No. I wouldn't make up something like that," he swore, solemnly placing a hand over his heart.

"I can better that story," March offered, coming over to hand Maggie two cartridges that had rolled all the way to the window. "You know the day I took John Deane hostage? When I checked my Colt before going into town to return the gold, I discovered I'd forgotten to load it that morning. I'd been holding an empty gun to that killer's head."

Maggie swatted at him, careful to keep her fist closed over

the retrieved cartridges. "You don't expect me to believe that."

He smiled, and the warmth in his eyes melted her insides. "This is the West, Miss Parker. You never question an honorable man's story."

Elijah lifted his gun from the floor and handed it back to her. "Go ahead and try it again."

Gripping the revolver firmly by the stock, Maggie slipped the cartridges in one by one. "There," she said proudly, snapping the cylinder back in place.

"A little practice and you'll be able to do that in under five minutes," Elijah said, softening the comment with a wink.

Maggie flushed again. "Pretty sorry work for the daughter of a decorated officer, isn't it?"

"I knew about as much about guns as you do when I signed up in 'sixty-one," Elijah said.

"You fought in the war?" She felt as though she should have guessed. Many Civil War veterans had brought their guns West.

He gave a half-mocking salute. "Captain Elijah Kelly, at your service, ma'am."

"Maybe you knew my father." A silly statement. The Confederate army had spread all over the south. "He died at the battle of Franklin, Tennessee. Lieutenant Colonel Brand Parker."

Elijah made as if to bolt upright, but sagged back onto the sofa instead. "Your father was Firebrand Parker?"

This time Maggie's blush came from pride. "Yes."

"Your father's bravery was well known. He had a reputation as a good officer and a decent man."

"You never met him then?" she asked, trying not to sound disappointed.

"No, indeed. I feel fortunate never to have had the pleasure. And I suppose that's as high a compliment as any, that the opposing army's officers hated like hell to hear they would have to face Brand Parker."

Rarely did Maggie find herself unable to speak, but she had to work her jaw several times. "You fought for the Union?"

Elijah nodded.

"But . . . you're a southerner!"

"South Carolina," he agreed.

"How could you?" she asked, sitting back in her chair. "How could you betray your people like that?"

The silence in the room became almost palpable, though Elijah didn't seem offended by her question.

"My father was a Methodist minister," he reminded her. "The Methodist Church takes a dim view on slavery, and my father being the sort of man he was, he preached against the evils of human bondage most Sundays and frequently in between. Needless to say, my brother Malachi and I were not the most popular boys in Charleston. Neither Mal nor I felt much compunction about signing up with the North. Mal's still in uniform. He's a captain with the Seventh Cavalry."

Maggie straightened in her chair. "My father wasn't fighting for slavery. He didn't believe in owning people. He was fighting for states' rights." Freedom from outside control was a goal she could appreciate. "The states joined the Union voluntarily, and he thought they should have the right to leave it if they chose. Letting the federal government take power that didn't belong to it was a higher price than he was willing to pay for peace."

"The end of slavery was worth any price."

She had forgotten Lemuel standing quietly by the kitchen window. Glancing over at him, she thought for the first time that he looked old, not because of his grizzled hair or stooped shoulders, but from the ancient spirit that darkened his eyes. For a moment she didn't recognize him as the same man she'd known that morning. And, in fact, he wasn't quite the same man she'd thought she'd known.

"You were a slave."

His eyebrows rose, and she felt a twinge of shame at not having suspected that before.

"I'm sorry, Mr. Tate. I didn't . . . It never occurred to me—"

He smiled the imperturbable smile that did belong to the friend she'd come to know over the course of the week. "Miss Maggie, if more folks was like you, they wouldn't have needed that war to begin with."

Maggie didn't know how to respond. Ten years after the end of the war, she couldn't forget the cause that had fired her father's heart, for which he had given his life. She couldn't forget the southerners fighting on their home soil for their rights and for their families. She couldn't forget what that maniac Sherman had done to Georgia, couldn't forget the destruction of an entire way of life . . . a way of life that had enslaved men like Lemuel Tate, had enslaved their wives and their children, treating them no better than domestic animals. A lot worse than March would ever think to treat one of his horses.

She had never known any slaves. But was that an excuse for ignoring the fact of slavery? It wouldn't be to Lemuel, a man it seemed she knew very little about, yet a man she had felt respect and affection for, a result of the respect and care he showed for her.

"You're wrong, Mr. Tate," she said finally. "If there had been more people like me, nothing would ever have been done to end slavery. I'm sorry, Mr. Kelly, for questioning you for doing what you thought was right."

"That's all the Lord can ask of any of us," Lemuel said. "To do what we think is right. And I've never seen you do any less, Miss Maggie. There was plenty of folks who knew slavery was wrong and never said anything about it. I don't see you ever doin' that."

Maggie risked a frown. "Are you saying I can't keep my mouth shut, Mr. Tate?"

He grinned. "I've just noticed you don't mind sharing your opinions. That's all."

"That's real insightful, Lem," March said, rising from his crouch by the sofa. "It took me a whole five minutes of knowing Miss Parker here to figure that one out. What about you, 'Lije? 'Lije?"

At his tone, Maggie turned to see the gunfighter collapsed on the sofa, his eyes half closed, his mouth half open, the muscles of his neck showing rigid against the skin.

"Mama, what's wrong with Brian? Why won't he wake up?"

"Hush, girl. Leave your mother alone."

"No! Mama!"

"Stephen?"

"I'll take care of it Lynette. Sally, take the child downstairs. Make her be quiet."

"No! You can't make me! What's wrong with Brian? What's wrong with my brother? Brian! Brian, wake up!"

" 'Lije!" March put a hand on his friend's shoulder.

As if in a dream, Maggie felt her hand move toward him. The gun she still held slipped from her fingers, but she didn't hear the sound it made as it hit the floor. She could barely hear her own voice.

"He's dead."

March turned, caught her expression, and grabbed her arm above the elbow. His fingers dug into her skin, but the strength in them steadied her.

331

"No, he's breathing." He shook her a little. "He's breathing, Maggie. He's just passed out."

She watched the gunfighter's chest. The movement of his fine white shirt was so slight that it might have been her imagination. But March wouldn't lie to her.

She must have forgotten to breathe herself, for the air she sucked in came as a relief to her lungs. "Sorry," she managed, despite the constriction in her chest.

March's fingers relaxed, but he didn't release her arm. "You stand watch with Henna in the bedroom." March's voice, practiced in the ways of calming frightened animals, stretched a lifeline to her heart. "I'll keep an eye on Elijah."

"No." She wouldn't let the others down, wouldn't let March down, not for all her fear. "I'd be useless to Henna, but I'm not useless here. You need to be at the window with your gun."

He ran his hand up and down her arm, his eyes searching hers. "It's all right to be frightened, and it's all right to take a break. Wolf can watch the window."

She shook her head. "I want to be doing something to help. I'll get some fresh water and see if I can't cool him. I'll get a glass, too, and make him drink some when he wakes up."

She stood, and March rose with her. Though only his fingertips touched her, she could feel his presence with every nerve ending in her skin. A black pit had opened inside her, and only his touch, his scent, his voice prevented it from swallowing her. Could she memorize his features in these few precious seconds?

He raised a hand to her face, gently cupping her jaw. "Don't worry about Elijah. He's come through this before."

Racing back to the ranch house in the wagon, she had feared for her life. Yet even that elemental, primitive emotion paled compared to the thought that March might die that afternoon, might be killed before her eyes, might lie as still and unresponsive as Elijah Kelly now did, never to return to her.

"If Elijah can live through this fever, I'm sure I can," she said.

March brushed his thumb across her cheek. "I forgot. You're not afraid of anything."

"That's right."

She looked into his eyes and read there the words he'd spoken to her earlier.

I love you.

And she would not have traded them for all the sterile safety of a loveless soul.

The blast of a gunshot exploded the fragile peace between them.

Chapter 23

March heard screams, and for a heartstopping moment he thought Maggie had been hit, but it was Henna's voice, ringing down the hall, "Here they come!"

A rifle blast exploded even closer, but this time he could tell it came from inside the house. Alexander Brady's shoulder jerked from the power of his carbine's recoil.

The rancher whooped in triumph.

"I hit one of the bastards!"

March didn't wait for him to apologize for his language. He reached Brady's side just as a bullet exploded the raised window pane, hailing splinters of glass down on them.

"Get down!" he shouted. Using the window frame as a shield, he risked a glance outside. Four horses bore down on them, two from each side of the barn, flanking the confused horse in the middle whose rider dangled limply from one stirrup.

More shots from the bedroom. A rifle blast from the loft. Bullets peppered the sturdy walls of the ranch house. March returned the fire, focusing six quick shots on the nearest target. The man jerked twice, but didn't fall.

From the safety of the barn came another rifle shot. This one tore through the wall just inches from his shoulder. Another shot toward the loft. Another toward the master bedroom.

When March risked another glance out the window, the riders had turned back toward the barn, leaving only the one man dead behind them, but the one he'd hit had trouble staying in his saddle. Two down. Only seven to go.

"March!" Maggie's voice by his shoulder. Too close.

He turned to shout at her to get back, but she thrust Elijah's rifle into his hand.

"Give me your Colt," she said. "Fast."

With his nostrils filled with gunsmoke, he could hardly bear the sight of her, her eyes so intent, her face white with determination. This bright flicker of life should have no part of death and gunfire.

He took the rifle and passed her his revolver.

"March, what can I do?" Wolf's voice carried loudly in the sudden absence of gunshots.

"Stay by your window!" March ordered sharply, glancing back at the boy. "You, too, Lem. If that ridiculous charge wasn't a distraction—"

But another rifle shot cut off his words. It came from the loft, but March thought it was directed west rather than east toward the barn. Harry'd had the same thought he had.

"I see them," Lemuel shouted, his words punctuated by the roar of his shotgun. "They're comin' through Miss Jane's apple trees. On foot."

"They'll use the training paddock for cover," March guessed. "Brady, you keep that rifle trained on the barn. I'm going up to the loft and see if I can help Harry pick them off from up there."

He took his loaded Colt from Maggie. She wouldn't collapse in an emergency. He loved her strength as much as her softness.

He touched her hand. He wanted to keep her safe, which meant he'd have to let her use that strength.

"Maggie, you take Elijah's other revolver and go to Wolf's window. If anyone gets anywhere near the porch, cock it and fire it."

"March, I promised to tell you if I didn't know how to do something. I'll shoot at anything you want, but unless it's a barn, I probably won't hit it."

He seriously questioned his sanity, that he could smile at a time like that. "Don't worry about hitting anything, sweetheart. Just keep them back until someone can come help you."

She nodded. "That, I can do."

Lemuel's shotgun fired again, followed closely by Harry's rifle. Return fire belched back at them. March heard the gut-twisting sound of splintering wood. He grabbed his rifle. "Remember, everybody, keep low."

And then he was running for the stairs.

Maggie forced herself to move. She turned toward the sofa just as another rifle shot rang from the barn. The tug on her skirt startled her, but she didn't have time to stare at the sudden quarter-sized hole in the fabric. Brady's gasp of pain was more important.

She whirled back to the window to see the rancher slumped awkwardly to one side.

"Mr. Brady!"

"Get away from the window." He waved her back, his voice sounding strong enough. His right hand grasped his left arm, and she saw red between his fingers.

"You're hit."

"I said, get back!" he ordered, and she found herself stumbling back in response. He lifted his fingers from his arm, examining the blood. "It's just a flesh wound. Not even on my shooting arm. I'll be all right. You can fix me up when this is over."

She didn't have time to argue. She had to trust that he knew enough to judge he wasn't going to bleed to death. She continued on to the sofa, scrabbling her hand around on the floor until her fingers hit the barrel of Elijah's Colt revolver.

"Miss Parker." She hardly recognized the gunfighter's voice, the fever had so distorted his whisper. His clear hazel eyes had taken on the dry yellow cast of dying grass.

"Lie back," she ordered, taking a moment to grab her damp rag and press it against his forehead.

"Give me my gun and get me to the window."

When she tried to stand, he grabbed her arm, but she had no trouble dislodging his grip. She pressed his hand back down on his chest. "Everything's all right, Mr. Kelly," she lied with all the confidence in her power. "The fever's giving you bad dreams. Just lie back, and you'll feel better in no time."

She didn't wait to see if he listened to her. Grasping the gunfighter's revolver tightly, she ran in a low crouch over to Wolf at the porch window.

"Nothing yet," he hissed, his voice thin with excitement and fear.

Maggie took up a position across from him and looked out, letting her gaze scan the yard for movement. With the sound of gunfire splitting the air all around her, the eerie emptiness of the view choked her with dread.

"There's one coming around the paddock," Lemuel's bass roared through the noise. His words apparently reached the loft, for Maggie heard two almost simultaneous rifle shots. "He's trying to reach the house!" Lemuel shouted again, then let loose with his shotgun, drowning all other sound.

"They're coming from the barn again!" Brady yelled.

"Stay here, Wolf," Maggie ordered, cocking her Colt. "Yell if you see so much as a jackrabbit." And she dashed across the living room toward Brady.

"Got another one!" Brady shouted.

A bullet sang past Maggie's ear, sending her sprawling forward. Just as it occurred to her how stupid it was to run with a loaded gun, her fist hit the floor, the Colt along with it. By some miracle, it didn't go off.

More gunfire, and shouting. The sound of glass shattering somewhere down the hall. She heard a woman scream.

"Henna!" She had no breath left to shout. She pushed herself up from the floor and tried again. "Henna!"

But rifle shots tore the sound to shreds. She couldn't have said how in all that noise she managed to hear Brady's soft grunt.

Still scrambling to her feet, she watched Brady's slow fall to the floor, the rifle slipping from his hand as he raised it toward his chest.

"Mr. Brady!"

She dropped to her hands and knees and scuttled to his side. He grabbed the hand she reached toward him, pushing her forward.

"Stop the sons-a-bitches," he gasped. "Kill 'em or we're all dead."

Another shot nicked the splintered window frame, punctuating his words. Maggie looked down into the rancher's white face, and she didn't see the man who refused to fire Shelby Brennan. She saw a husband and father whose life was spreading across his pinstriped waistcoat in a crimson stain.

"Hurry, girl," he commanded. He pushed her again, his fingers leaving red spots on her sleeve. "I'm not dead yet, but I will be if you don't get that gun blazing."

This isn't even his fight.

She turned away and wondered if this was how Elijah felt before a gun battle, this detachment, as though someone else were in control of her body.

She reached the window, and stuck the gun over the

frame, pulling the trigger once, twice. Only then did she lift her head for a glance outside. A rifle shot from the loft hit a rider halfway between the barn and the house. She watched him fall.

Another outlaw's horse collapsed, screaming, caught by rifle fire from his own ally in the barn. Maggie gripped her gun in both hands, straightened her arms, and fired. Her first shot went wide to the left, her next to the right. Her third shot finally hit the horse, putting it out of its pain. And her fourth caught the outlaw full in his shoulder.

Another man, the only one still risking the cross fire between barn and house, caught the wounded man up on his own horse, carrying him out of harm's way. But Maggie felt certain that particular outlaw wasn't going to be firing a gun again any time soon.

She flicked open the cylinder of her gun and began to reload.

March's eyes scoured the length of the paddock's board fence, searching for the man he knew would be creeping along it looking for a way to break to the house. The gunfire from below no longer caught his attention; he was focused fully on the fence. He couldn't leave his position, so he had to trust the others to hold theirs.

Beside him, Harry fired. Toward the apple trees, he guessed. She'd hit one of the four sneaking up on them from this direction, and Lemuel's shotgun had taken care of one that had crept too close to the house. One man had made it behind the paddock, the man he was looking for, but they didn't know where the other had gone.

Harry could be shooting at crows for all they knew, and they couldn't afford to waste the ammunition.

"Harry, the west window," he said, waving in that direction. "It sounds like they're making another attack from the barn."

He heard the rustle of her skirts as she moved, but didn't take his eye off the paddock. He knew every knothole in the fence, but hadn't seen a flicker . . .

A shadow. The sun, making its relentless way toward the mountains, had found the outlaw for him, sending a slender finger of betraying shadow beyond the end of the fence.

He made a quick guess at the sun's angle, sighted and fired. The brightness of unweathered wood showed where his bullet had struck the fence. The shadow jerked back. He fired again. Another hole in the fence. Had he hit anything?

"March!" The panic in Harry's voice snapped his head around. Strands of dark hair marked his sister's face like wounds. "The barn. They've set fire to the barn."

March's heart froze even as he turned back to his window. The sight of a motionless hand in the dust beyond the paddock fence hardly registered.

The barn. Balthasar, Ari, Sandy . . .

John Deane hadn't set fire to the barn as a ploy to draw his victims from the safety of the house. No fool would step into gunfire to save a handful of horses. No, this could only mean that Deane had decided the ranch house was too heavily defended to take at the moment.

Burning the barn, killing precious animals, could only be meant as a message, one more way to hurt March before Deane returned another day to finish the job.

No, no fool would cross the no-man's land of the ranch yard to try to save horses. Even the best of horses could be replaced eventually.

"Harry, get back over here."

Still she crouched, poised by the window, staring out toward the barn, her nostrils flaring like a horse's at the scent of fire. "Oh, March . . ." Her whisper came like ashes falling from the sky.

"Harry, now."

She seemed to hear him finally, turning to catch his gaze.

"There's another man out there behind us somewhere. I need you to keep an eye out for him. I'm going downstairs."

Her eyes widened as she moved toward him. "No, March, you can't try to get to the barn—"

"Do you think I'm that much of a fool?" he asked. Not giving her time to think about the question, he grabbed her arm and pulled her toward the window. "Stay here until someone comes up and tells you it's clear. I think they're probably retreating for now, but we can't take any chances."

He left her, running for the stairs without waiting for her answer. His mind's eye could already see nothing but black smoke billowing from the roof of the barn. His imagination could already hear the screams of his horses.

"March!" A stranger's voice from the bedroom door halted him at the foot of the stairs. No, it was Henna's voice, as sharp and fragile as broken china. She had her revolver stuck in the waistband of her skirt, and her hands were covered with blood.

"Are you hurt?" He ran to the door and grabbed her arm to pull her down out of sight of the window, but she shook him off.

"No, no. No." The denial came out in sobs, and she sucked in a breath to steady herself. "It's Elijah . . ."

He followed the direction of her pointing finger.

The gunfighter's body lay on Jane's rag rug. With his white shirt clinging damply to his ribs, he looked thin and vulnerable. March couldn't see what expression had crossed his friend's face when the odds finally caught him; blood hid his features from view. So much blood.

"Elijah!" March stumbled toward him, but didn't drop beside him. If he did, he might not get back up.

A whimper made his heart catch in his throat, but it hadn't come from Elijah. Loki lay pressed against the gunfighter's back, his ears flattened along the back of his head.

March turned on Henna. "How did he even get in here?" he asked, shocked by the fury in his voice. "He couldn't even get off the couch."

Henna shook her head. Tears stained her cheeks. "I don't know. I don't know, March. I was shooting at them, out there—" She waved at the window as though there might be some question of where the enemy had come from. "I ran out of bullets. God, I ran out of bullets!

"I turned to go back to the living room to get some more, when I heard the window break." Her voice shook. "One of them must have sneaked around the side of the house. He was coming in. I could see his gun. He had it pointed right at me. He was *grinning*."

March could see the scene clearly through her eyes. His hand clenched on his own gun.

"I thought I was dead," she whispered, staring at the window. "Then he was diving into the room. I heard shots. One went right past my head. I couldn't move. I think I was screaming. A hand grabbed me, pushed me out of the way. It was Elijah. I think that must have been when the outlaw shot him. I don't know. He shot back, though. A gun from his boot. He killed the bastard."

She pointed toward the end of the bed, and for the first time March noticed the leg sticking out from the end of it.

"March." Her hand touched his arm, and it trembled. "He saved my life."

The smell of blood and fear and pain overcame him and he gagged. He stumbled to the door, trying to breathe.

"Take his gun," he told Henna. He had no time to comfort her. No time at all. This was the end. One way or another. "Stay here if you think you can. If not, join the others in the living room. They're not going to get away with this, Henna, I swear to you."

As he entered the living room, his eyes took in Alexander Brady stretched out on the floor, his eyes closed, a red rag pressed to his chest. He took in Wolf's white knuckles, clutching the frame of his lookout window. He saw the total concentration on Maggie's face as she kept her eyes on the barn, the steadiness in the hand that held her revolver.

But when she glanced at him, her face dissolved in anguish. "The horses . . ."

"They're not going to die." He knew the madness of the words, even as he said them. But he'd left sanity behind a lifetime ago when he'd found his sister's body on her kitchen floor. And just because he was a madman didn't mean he didn't have a plan.

He reached the door before she reacted to his statement. "No, March. Don't. You can't go out there."

"Deane is not going to do this to me any more. It ends today. You stay here, Maggie. I need you safe." He moved his gaze to Wolf, to Lemuel. "You should all be safe in the house, for the time being. But keep your eyes open."

He opened the door and dove through it, not giving himself time to think, focusing on the angle of his roll, on the splinters digging into his palms, anything but the gunmen gathered behind his barn. He reached the wagon, its sturdy bulk between him and the guns beyond.

In his mind, the shelter offered by the wagon had seemed more solid than it did in reality, his legs exposed beneath the bed, the wagon sides not as high as he would have liked. But at least he could be certain Deane's rifleman could no longer snipe at him from the loft of the barn. The thick black smoke escaping from the window of Lemuel's bedroom assured him of that.

Perhaps it was that reminder of his friend that kept him from pulling the trigger as he whirled on the footsteps behind him.

"Goddamn it, Lem, warn me next time."

The big man hunched beside him, his head just below the level of the wagon sides. "We push on three?"

"Get back in the house, Lem. There's no time to argue. Go back."

"You can't push this wagon to the barn by yourse'f and still have a hand free to shoot," Lemuel said. "Everything I own is in that barn. 'Cept this." He hefted his shotgun. "I aim to make sure I get some good use out of what I got left."

March didn't even bother to raise his gun at the next set of footsteps. "Maggie, get the hell—"

"Somebody's got to get those horses out while you two are blowing holes in people."

"One . . ." Lemuel said, shifting to get a good grip on the wagon, one hand on the side, one on the back. "Two . . ."

"Maggie, Lem, listen to me—"

"Three!"

The wagon lurched forward, and there was nothing he could do but throw his shoulder against it and push, praying the thin boards would shield them. Their best protection came from the fact that Deane and his men could not possibly have expected them to try something so stupid. That, and Harry's withering rifle fire covering them from the house loft.

March knew every step of ground between the house and the barn. Never had he realized there were so many of them. Each foot of empty space suddenly became its own separate desert to cross. Even as the wagon picked up momentum, enabling them to move into a crouching jog, he knew they couldn't possibly push fast enough.

By unspoken consent, they angled toward the end of the stables, enabling them to keep the wagon between themselves and the barn. This meant moving toward the line of fire, since no outlaws remained inside the barn itself. But as the eternity of each second passed, not a single bullet was fired at them. Harry's wild shot that hit the wagon tree didn't really count.

As they reached the shelter of the stable wall, Maggie broke away, running back toward the main barn door. March waved Lemuel after her.

"Go around the other way," he said. "I'll take this direction."

He ducked under the wagon bed and crawled to the wall before trotting to the northern corner of the stable. He could hear the flames clearly now and no longer needed his imagination to supply the fear of the horses. He heard Lucas's stallion, Achilles, scream, a bellow of fury and terror.

He tried not to picture a rain of fire and hay falling on the stalls, forced himself not to see Maggie dashing into the barn, beneath an inferno that only waited to burn through the loft floor before collapsing on her and the horses.

He reached the corner of the stable. He stood with his back pressed to the wall, gathering his strength and his nerve.

A rifle shot passed not three feet from his head, singing by the corner in front of him, a gift from Harry.

"Now or never."

He spun forward under the cover of Harry's shot, his Colt ready to fire. The moment froze in time while he took in the scene before him. No need to shoot. There was no one waiting on this side of the barn. No one alive, in any event.

He pressed two fingers to the neck of the man lying on the ground before him just to make sure. Definitely dead. One of the men they'd hit hadn't lasted long after making it back to shelter.

How many did that make now? Six? Seven? Eight? At the most, three outlaws left, more likely two . . . *if* John Deane had told Elijah the truth about the strength of his gang.

And why should he do that?

March continued past the dead man, sacrificing silence for speed. His footsteps could not be heard over the howling of the fire, anyway.

He reached the next corner. Clearly Deane didn't expect him, so he risked a quick glance.

Two men stood arguing in the shadow of the barn, both obviously wounded. One had a makeshift bandage around his head and his right arm hung bloody and useless from his shoulder. The other looked about to topple, the wrapping about his ribs unable to hide the red stain on his chest.

Their arms flailed, and he could see their mouths moving, but could only make out snatches of sound, no clear words. Neither man matched his memory of John Deane's lanky, aristocratic bearing. But after ten years, he couldn't be sure.

Where were their horses?

Following the direction of their waving arms, he suddenly understood their argument. In the distance he could see the forms of running horses, all saddled, all riderless.

The fire. The idiots had set fire to the barn without thinking to move their own horses to a safe distance. The blaze had spooked them. He almost choked on his own humorless laughter. Deane's sadistic vengeance had finally turned on him, paralyzing him with his own poison.

Without horses, the short-grass prairie would offer the outlaws up to their enemies as target practice.

March's hand tightened on his gun, and he prepared to step out into the open. He didn't have Elijah's skill at the quick-draw . . . The image of his friend's bloody body stopped all rational thought. He didn't need skill. He had no intention of entering into a duel with John Deane. Once he determined which of the men before him was Deane, he'd kill him. Period. If the other man held his fire, he'd let him live.

He stepped out from the corner of the barn, his stance wide, pleased to find his hands remained steady.

The outlaws must have caught the flicker of movement. They turned toward him, their mouths dropping open in surprise. In that second, he suddenly knew for sure that neither of the men was John Deane.

He felt his heart turn cold and die. Deane's horses had spooked. What remained of his gang needed transportation. Would he wait around to be picked off by March and his friends when he had access to a burning barn full of horses?

Maggie.

He saw the flicker of movement as the man with the shattered ribs went for his gun. March knew he'd moved too late as he heard the roar of the blast, but it was the outlaw who fell, a huge hole in his chest.

The other outlaw drew his own gun with his uninjured arm, whirling on the danger from behind, but March's shot cut him down before he could fire. Lemuel raised his smoking shotgun in acknowledgement.

"The barn!" March shouted, but he knew Lemuel couldn't hear him. "Deane!" he shouted, hoping his friend could read the name on his lips as he waved at the barn. Then he turned and ran back around the corner, a prayer stuck in his throat.

He reached the side door to the stable and threw it open. The sudden dimness blinded him. He heard flames and screams and the pounding of hooves against wooden walls. Even if he dared call Maggie's name, she'd never hear him. He stepped forward, feeling his way toward the first stall.

A noise, sharp and sudden, broke free of the general roar. A gunshot? The cracking of the timbers above his head?

Then a sharp pain exploded behind his ear and he heard nothing more.

Chapter 24

Maggie's first thought upon entering the barn was surprise at the lack of light. She could hear the fire roaring like a beast above her head but could not see it. Tendrils of flame writhed on the barn floor between her and the stables, devouring wisps of hay and straw, but they only seemed to emphasize the darkness of smoke and fear.

She couldn't stop to let the noise and stench of destruction overwhelm her. She ran, more by memory than by sight, to the line of stalls. She reached the first, and almost concluded it was empty before she heard the striking of iron-clad hooves against the wall. Sandy's head appeared over the door, blacker than the smoke, his teeth and eyes glinting white as he screamed.

No matter how many times she heard it, in no matter how many contexts, the scream of an angry stallion struck something elemental in her spirit, firing her pulse, readying her to run. Echoes of the sound, fierce with terror, rang from the stalls further down.

Maggie swallowed and bent down to grab the hem of her skirt. She had never had to face this worst nightmare, fire in a stable, before, but she'd heard enough stories about panicked horses refusing to leave their stalls not to throw open Sandy's door.

She wrenched the seam along the back of her skirt open, then ripped a long strip around the bottom. Sandy still wore his full bridle, and she grabbed it, pulling his head down with all the strength in her arm.

She spoke to him, not sure he could hear her, not sure what she said. But his eyes rolled back down to focus on the source of her voice, and for a moment he froze, though she could see the trembling along his neck.

With a flick of her wrist, she slid the strip of fabric from her skirt over his eyes. He started, but she hung on to the reins with her other hand. The instant he stopped to assess the situation, she let go the bridle and tied her makeshift blindfold under his jaw.

Only then did she pull open the stall door and give a tug on the reins to lead him out.

His ears flattened at the roar around him. His nostrils flared, testing the smoke. But he could no longer see the flames dropping from the ceiling, no longer be startled by the twist of a burning rope fragment on the dirt floor.

Maggie didn't have time to be gentle. She could feel the fear of the other horses behind them. She tugged Sandy forward with short bursts of strength, toward the blessed square of light at the barn door.

A darker flicker showed in the light, then slipped into the barn.

"Maggie?"

"Wolf!"

She reached out her hand to the boy. "What are you doing here? You could have been killed running across the yard."

"The horses needed me."

And so did she. Maggie thrust Sandy's reins into the boy's small hand, praying he'd be strong enough to hang onto them.

"Get him out into the yard!" she yelled. "Give him a smack in the direction of the mountains. We'll have to hope he doesn't turn back. Meet me back here for the others."

Then she was running back into the hell that had once

been that safest of havens, a stable. She ripped at her skirt as she ran.

The next stall held Daisy, the milk cow. Maggie almost left her, desperate to free the horses, but the cow's gentle brown eyes ripped at her heart. At the door, Wolf took Daisy's rope silently and passed back the blindfold Maggie had used on Sandy.

Then Pamela. The big gray's desire to stay in her stall tested Maggie's strength, but by the time she got her to Wolf, the mare followed with some of her normal docility.

Honey was next. Even in terror, the little palomino showed her calm spirit, and Maggie managed to take both her and Logan Penny's quiet old pony at the same time. Once more she traded lead ropes for a blindfold.

And back again into the smoke and the noise. A noise like a pistol shot made her jump, just in time to avoid a burning chunk of wood that struck the ground beside her. She didn't dare look up. At any moment the ceiling might give way to the flames that were lashing at it from above. She could only keep moving.

The stalls she came to now were closer to the side door of the stable than the main door of the barn. She didn't want to take the horses out that way, for fear they might run to the familiar safety of the corral and be trapped if the fire jumped to it. But time was a luxury she couldn't afford.

She took quick count of who was left. Achilles, Balthasar, Ari . . . and then only empty stalls.

She put a hand on Achilles' door. Only a sixth sense warned her to move, and she barely pulled her fingers away before the stallion's jaw clamped down on the stall door. Bits of wood tore away beneath his huge teeth, and Maggie started shaking.

Her first night here Lemuel had warned her Achilles bit.

Then it had been a bad habit to be wary of, now it might cost the stallion his life.

A tearing sound, like the rending of the fabric of the world, ripped through the bass roar of the fire. Maggie watched in horror as a red hole opened in the blackness of the stable ceiling, raining a ball of fire into the stall she'd so recently rescued Sandy from.

No more time.

She flung open Achilles' door and jumped aside. It was the only chance she could give him.

Another explosion, and fire dripped like blood into Achilles' stall, scoring his flanks. The huge stallion, metamorphosed into a raging monster, knocked her back against the wall as he plunged past her, toward the open stable door.

Open? She hadn't opened it. New fear danced around the terror of fire.

Achilles' body jerked as he leaped to avoid a dark object on the floor and then he was out into the sunlight.

"Balthasar!"

The gelding looked at her, his wise eyes nearly blank with primal panic. If he dissolved into screaming hysteria . . . she probably would, too.

She flung open his stall door. "Balthasar, forward," she ordered. She had seen March drill verbal commands into his colts, surely he would have done the same with his own horse.

"Forward! Walk!"

She could see the gelding focusing in on her words, shutting out the noise and the flame to serve her. He'd had to overcome instinct before, for March; could he do it for her?

And then he moved, coming toward her, his nostrils flaring, his sides heaving with distress.

"Forward!" she shouted again. And as he came abreast of

352

her, she swatted him hard across the rear, sending him flying toward the door.

That left only Ari.

Maggie had to wipe away the sweat dripping into her eyes and found herself choking as she felt her way toward Ari's stall. Any moment the whole building would dissolve into an inferno. But she couldn't leave Ari.

Only a few more seconds, she prayed. *Only a few more seconds.* A mantra to pull her through the smoke and the fire.

She reached Ari's stall and fumbled with the latch. She put out a hand and grabbed the mare's reins.

Reins?

A rough hand grabbed her arm, wrenching her back. She stumbled over black cavalry boots. A hand in the small of her back sent her sprawling to the floor.

She rolled away instinctively, unable consciously to catalog this new danger until the sharp thwack of a bullet next to her ear reminded her of the gunmen who had started this fire. She jerked away, turning onto her back, fumbling for the derringer in her pocket.

But it was much too late.

The man standing above her had his long, deadly pistol aimed straight at her forehead. Something predatory in his stance reminded her of Elijah, but the burning rage in his pale green eyes bore no resemblance to Elijah's cold stare.

Tall, lanky, the man stood with almost casual poise while bits of fire dropped around him. Hair the color of frost-tipped wheat brushed his ears beneath a gray felt hat.

Handsome. Graceful. There was no question in her mind that the man about to kill her was John Deane.

"Coward," she spat at him, desperate for a word to wound him, for any way to show her contempt for a man she knew only by his deeds. "Killing women and children. You didn't

353

learn that in the Confederate Army. You must have learned it from the Yankees." *Forgive me, Elijah, Lemuel.*

The convulsion of his features gave her a grim satisfaction, but it didn't take him long to recover.

"My dear, I consider shooting a smart-mouthed bitch like you a service to humanity."

She didn't find his smug smile charming. She wanted to send his soul to hell and see if the devil found him amusing.

"You're a dead man," she hissed. "March is going to kill you, and I only hope he takes his sweet time doing it."

"March?" Deane cocked his head. "Our Mr. Jackson is a friend of yours? Ah'm so sorry. I don't think Mr. Jackson is in any condition to be killing anyone."

He waved toward the barn door. Though the barrel of his gun had nearly hypnotized her gaze, she glanced the way he'd pointed.

"Oh, God . . ." Despite the smoke, she could make out an arm, the curve of his head. "March!"

Achilles had jumped the body lying there. Had Balthasar? The thought of the ungainly gelding planting his sharp hooves on March's chest . . . But he was dead.

The knowledge screamed through her like a lightning strike, burning out her heart and leaving only a hollow shell behind.

"You killed him."

Deane cocked his head again. "I don't know. I think I just saw him twitch. Maybe that blow to the head is wearing off. After I shoot you, I'll have to make sure I finish the job."

He was shifting his gun back into alignment with her head. If March was alive, she couldn't leave him to John Deane's mercy, but she had no chance against a man with a gun. Even as her mind was sending the message to her muscles to move, he'd already flicked his finger into position, already pulled the trigger . . .

At first she thought the noise of the fire or perhaps the roar of the blood in her veins had drowned out the shot. But then she heard Deane's curse as he flipped out the cylinder of his gun.

There in the burning barn, with fire curling the edges of her skirts and a killer mere feet away, she burst into laughter. It rocked her so hard she couldn't manage to struggle to her feet.

"You're out—" She choked on the words, had to try again. "You're out of ammunition!"

With a savage snarl Deane threw the gun at her. She dodged, but it caught the side of her head, effectively stopping her hysterical laughter.

She scrambled upright, fighting her skirt and petticoat. A tongue of flame fell from the ceiling to her shoulder, and she beat it out with her hand before reaching into her pocket for her little gun.

Deane was yanking Ari out of her stall, more by sheer physical strength than anything else. Maggie wondered briefly why he'd chosen the little buckskin mare. Surely Sandy or Achilles would have better suited his vanity. But maybe he couldn't handle a panicked stallion. From the way he manhandled Ari, she guessed Deane wasn't much of a horseman.

When she finally had the derringer in her hand, Ari stood between her and Deane. He was mounting from the right —presumably an outlaw's horse, like a cowboy's, couldn't be too particular about which direction its rider came from in a life or death situation.

Maggie raised the derringer, taking aim, but Deane ducked his head below the mare's back. Was he checking the cinch or had he seen her gun? She could prevent his escape by shooting Ari . . .

No, she couldn't. She wouldn't.

Deane swung into the saddle. Her finger jerked on the trigger, and she saw the flash as her derringer fired. She fired again.

Deane didn't even twitch. He dug his heels into the mare's sides, sending her pounding toward the door, toward March.

As Maggie ran after them, she saw movement from the form on the ground. March's arm slid across the earth. He *was* alive, and John Deane intended to trample him with her mare.

"March, stay down!" she shouted, knowing he couldn't hear her in all the noise. If he would just stay still, she knew Ari wouldn't step on him. She *prayed* Ari wouldn't run over him. Normally, the canny little mare would never have put her foot on suspect ground, and if she recognized March's body, she would surely jump over him. Surely she'd jump over him now.

But these were not normal circumstances. Maggie could feel the heat as a physical entity lashing at her, the smoke as a flame-eyed beast wrapping itself around her throat to strangle her. She could no longer hear the roar of the fire, it had overwhelmed her senses and she ran in silence.

Whatever Ari had experienced in her life, she had never faced the raging belly of a beast like this one. And she did something she never would have done under normal circumstances.

Instead of leaping over March's prone body. . . . She stopped. Virtually in midstride, she came to an abrupt halt, sending John Deane flying over her lowered neck to land with a graceless thud just beyond March's head.

Maggie reached them a second later. Ari turned to her, her

nostrils flaring, her eyes questioning. Maggie threw her arms around the mare's neck and kissed her.

"Yes, you did right. You did just right. Now get the hell out of here."

March had pulled himself to his knees, and the mare stepped past him. In the smoke and the fear, her normal agility deserted her, and she stepped hard on John Deane's outstretched ankle.

March heard the man's scream of pain even as a wave of blackness threatened to send him back to his knees. He tried to breathe deeply and found himself choking on ashes and heat.

"March, I've got you."

He heard the words. They must have been only inches from his ear to make it through the roaring in his head—or was that the fire? He felt the hand on his arm. Looking down, he saw it, blackened with soot, but no less familiar.

"Maggie." He grabbed her hand and pushed her toward the door. "Get out. I'm all right. I'm coming."

But first . . .

He looked down on the body of his nemesis, the evil that had haunted his life, the man who had done his best to destroy him and all he loved. Now that he saw him, he had no trouble recognizing John Deane. Even after ten years, the handsome features, the killer's eyes, the arrogance of his gray tailored coat and hat remained the same. The rigors of prison and grief hadn't lined his chiseled face, though perhaps he carried a little more weight behind his belt.

The fear and hate that flickered in the pale eyes caused the blood to pound in March's temples. He had never felt such a primal desire to kill. He watched Deane turn to crawl toward the door, dragging a broken ankle behind him. He savored the iron taste of blood and death as he followed the devil out into the sunlight.

March still held his Colt in his hand, and he cocked it, slowly, deliberately. He waited until the man turned to face him before he spoke.

"I don't want to shoot you," he said, hardly recognizing the cold, rasping voice that came from his throat as his own. "I want to hit you with this gun until there's nothing left of your face. I want you to bleed and hurt and cry before I let you die. But that would be wasting too much time on you, you worthless son-of-a-bitch."

Deane's mouth twisted in a sneer. "I consider it an honor to die pursuing vengeance for my brother. Everything I did, I did for—"

March pulled the trigger. Outside, away from the heart of the inferno, the report made a satisfying boom. The bullet kicked up an explosion of dirt from the hard earth of the yard.

March stared down at Deane's white face. White, not red. At this distance he couldn't possibly have missed his mark, yet he had. He noted with a strange detachment that all the bravado had left Deane's expression. The man's skin twitched in conspicuous terror.

And so it should. Deane should be made to feel some inkling of the terror he had perpetrated on Jane, on Lucas, on Logan. March felt the bile building in his throat. After a month of imagining his revenge, it was finally in his hand. He could take righteous vengeance on the evil that had destroyed his family.

He barely managed to turn away before he threw up. Fighting the spinning in his head, he uncocked his gun and thrust it into its holster.

He heard a sound behind him, an attempt at laughter. "What's the matter, Jackson, not enough of a man to finish the job?" But he hardly heard the words, only the soullessness behind them.

He looked back at Deane and no longer felt the hate that had sustained him for so long. Instead, he felt the heart-wrenching grief of his loss, for the first time unfiltered by guilt and plots of vengeance. For the first time, he knew he would survive it, and he knew he would have the love of his sister and her family with him as long as he had a heart to feel it.

"I guess I'm just not coward enough to shoot a helpless man," he said. "Though I don't expect you'll be thanking me for any favors when the noose is around your neck."

Then Maggie was in his arms, and he was pulling her close, closing his eyes against the flood of relief and joy that bathed him. He ran his hands over her back, feeling her warmth, her life. She pressed against him, and he felt her tears touch his neck.

He buried his face in her hair.

"Oh, March."

"Shhh. It's okay." He held her tighter. Given his choice, he'd never let her go.

The sound of running footsteps told him he wouldn't have a choice.

"March! Maggie!" It was Henna's voice, panting with exertion.

"It's all right," he said. He pointed his boot at Deane. "This is the last of the bastards. There's nothing we can do for the barn. We'd just better get out of the way."

The relief he expected didn't show in Henna's face. "Where's Wolf?" she asked, pressing a hand to her heaving side. "I saw him run over here."

"Wolf!" Maggie choked. He felt her stiffen beneath his arm. "He was helping me get the horses out. I haven't seen him since I passed Pamela to him. He must have stayed outside with her." But it was a question, not a statement of belief.

"Find the horses. See if he's with them," March directed, already turning away.

The doorway winked black and red, an eye of hate in the monster of fire before him. He pulled his kerchief from his pocket and pressed it over his nose and mouth, though what good he expected it to do him in that cauldron of smoke he couldn't have said.

March plunged recklessly through the open door. The assault on his senses almost drove him back again. The smoke blinded and strangled him; the noise made his eardrums ring.

Flames flickered up the sides of the stalls now. Burning timbers littered the floor, fallen from the stable ceiling and from the roof of the barn itself. He could feel the skeleton of the building preparing to give way around him, but at least the scattered pools of fire offered him enough light to pick his way toward the main floor of the barn.

"Wolf!" The name, ripped from lungs full of smoke, burned in his throat. If Wolf hadn't already escaped this death trap, he wouldn't be able to hear March's cries. But he yelled anyway, unwilling to accept the alternative. "Wolf!"

He kicked aside the stall doors, searching any dark corner into which a frightened boy might crawl to hide. He reached the main floor of the barn without discovering any creature, alive or dead. Wolf must have had sense enough to get out of the barn. He'd better follow, and fast.

"March?"

He almost didn't hear the sound, so deafened were his ears. But the young voice hit a note higher than the surrounding roar.

"Wolf?"

March's burning eyes caught a flicker of movement

360

through the smoke. He struggled forward, barely jumping aside in time as a fiery beam fell past him to explode in sparks against the floor.

He reached out blindly and caught Wolf's hand, prepared to pull him toward the door.

"March! Here! It's Mr. Tate!"

Shifting his weight, March let the boy change his course, pulling him toward the still form lying on the ground.

"Oh, God, no." The words, prayer more than blasphemy, tore from his throat as he dropped beside the old man. Another body lay beyond him, a stranger lying in an unnatural heap. Flames ate at the outlaw's clothes. March looked away.

"That man tried to take Pamela from me," Wolf shouted into his ear. "Mr. Tate tried to stop him and he hit Mr. Tate in the head with his rifle. I grabbed Mr. Tate's shotgun—" The boy's voice dissolved in a fit of coughing.

March squeezed Wolf's hand, using his other palm to feel Lemuel's chest. It rose beneath his fingers.

"Grab his other arm!" he bellowed, taking Lemuel's right hand. The big man had lost some of his bulk of muscle as he aged, but he still outweighed March by at least forty pounds. Even with Wolf's help, Lemuel would have been hard to move, and March's head spun from the aftereffects of Deane's blow. He could hardly breathe, but he pulled desperately, knowing three lives depended on it, for Wolf wouldn't leave them.

A brush of fresh air, sucked in by the voracious flames, whipped past him, almost too sweet for his lungs. Then other hands gripped Lemuel's body, Henna helping Wolf, Maggie grabbing the unconscious man's feet.

They tumbled into the sunlight, stumbling across the yard until Wolf's legs collapsed and he sank to the ground. March fell beside him, his lungs screaming for air. He heard Henna

361

comforting her son, heard Maggie murmuring to Lem as she unbuttoned his shirt and tilted his head to help him breathe.

A change in the sound of the fire made him open his eyes. As he watched, the whole building shuddered, as though taking a last dying breath. Timbers screamed, and with a last explosive roar, the fire gloried in its own ruin. The barn collapsed, falling in on itself with a sound as loud as two trains colliding, spewing ashes and smoke up into the clean blue sky.

Long, hot hours under the late summer sun, blisters and hope, laughter and curses, all burned to the ground in barely twenty minutes.

Lemuel's groan pulled his eyes away from the destruction.

"Lie still, Mr. Tate," Maggie said, wiping her black hand across his black brow. "You've got a nasty lump on your head."

"Wolf?" he asked, his voice gravelly from pain and smoke.

"I'm here," the boy said, pulling away from Henna to show Lemuel his soot-streaked face. "But I lost your shotgun. I fired it at that man that hit you . . . Then I guess I dropped it somewhere. . . ."

"You saved my life, Wolf," the old man said solemnly. "That's a good sight more precious than my shotgun any day." Lemuel turned his head and caught March's gaze. "What about Deane?"

March scrambled to his feet, his pulse rising once more, but his eyes quickly found the injured outlaw. Deane had managed to drag himself some twenty yards from the burning barn, but now lay sprawled on his stomach on the hard dirt, obviously in no shape to cause further trouble.

Lemuel shifted himself up into a sitting position, following March's gaze. "You shot him," he said with satisfaction.

March shook his head. "Ari's the hero. She took care of

him while I was flat on the ground. Smashed his ankle pretty good, I think."

Lemuel squinted. "That bloodstain on his back—that's not from a bullet hole?"

March frowned at the dark patch marring Deane's gray coat.

"My derringer," Maggie said suddenly, fumbling in her pocket and pulling forth the tiny weapon. "I didn't think I'd hit him."

She looked down at the gun, and her hand shook as she shoved it back into her skirt pocket. "Not a bad shot in a smoky barn, aiming at a man on horseback. Elijah will be proud of me."

March lowered his eyes, and Henna turned her head away.

Maggie rose, looking from one to the other, and her blood froze. She didn't want to ask, didn't want to know, especially not with Wolf there . . .

But the boy had picked up on the sudden tension as quickly as she had. "What about Father?" he demanded looking up at Henna, then over at March. "What happened? Is he hurt? Where is he?"

Henna reached a hand toward him. "Wolf, listen to me—"

"No!" He pulled away, turning toward the house. "Father?" He started to run.

"Wolf! Stop!" Henna ran after him, but the boy easily outpaced her.

"March?" Maggie asked. She saw the grim shake of his head.

"One of the outlaws made it to the bedroom window. Elijah stopped him from killing Henna, but he shot 'Lije in the head."

"March, I'm so sorry." The words meant nothing, but he must have heard the grief and compassion in her voice, for he took her hands in his and held them tight.

"Me, too," he said, his voice thick. He cleared his throat. "But right now we've got to get Lem and Brady to the doctor, and John Deane to the jail. And then there are the horses to . . ."

She freed a hand from his and placed it against his jaw. His eyes met hers, their blue depths reflecting the pain and grief he couldn't express.

"I guess we'd better get to work, then."

He nodded. "Thank God the wagon didn't burn. I thought we'd left it too close to the barn."

"We did," Lemuel said, pushing himself onto his knees. "I moved it before catchin' sight of Wolf in the barn."

"Don't get up," Maggie ordered, but Lemuel already had his feet under him.

March dropped her hand to grab Lemuel's right arm, and she took the other. The old man leaned heavily on them for a moment, then stretched himself upright.

"Now jes' let me find Pamela—"

"I'll get her," Maggie said firmly. She waved toward the north pasture gate. "She's standing right over there with Ari and Balthasar. It won't be any trouble."

Lemuel turned to March. "Then I'd best help you get Mr. Brady into the wagon."

As they turned toward the house, the sound of pounding hoofbeats once more disturbed the summer afternoon.

"Well," Lemuel said. "If it ain't the cavalry."

Maggie felt her legs quiver in relief as she recognized Jake Culbert's little mustang, the boy clinging to her back like a burr. Behind them rode Jed Culbert, his big frame sitting like a sack of grain on the bare back of a solid-boned chestnut who, except for the color, might have been Pamela's twin. Maggie guessed Jed stood behind her with his plow more often than he rode her.

Trailing a discreet distance behind the two Culberts was a man on a pretty bay mare. He sat with the studied grace of a man riding an Irish hunter. Despite the breakneck pace Jake and Jed had obviously set, he looked as though he'd just ridden up from a pleasant afternoon jaunt.

Maggie felt she should know that arrogant form, those patrician features, those rosy cheeks and that strawberry blond hair. But the thin-brimmed top hat, the shiny black boots, the elegant cut of the man's coat and trousers seemed so absurdly out of place in the dusty ranch yard that it took her a moment to recognize the man wearing them.

"Langley." Her throat closed in rebellion on the name. She felt March glance at her.

It couldn't be. Langley Fitzgibbon might visit Colorado in her nightmares, but in reality he was in Lexington, Kentucky, a thousand miles away. He despised the uncivilized frontier, as he called it. He would never leave the comforts of Lexington to travel west—east to Philadelphia, to New York, to Europe, perhaps. But Oxtail, Colorado? Never.

Yet the apparition seemed disturbingly solid as the three horses halted before them.

"We saw the smoke," Jed said, swinging down from his sturdy mare. His eyes traveled from the smoking ruins of the barn to the house's shattered windows to John Deane's bloody jacket. "What the hell is going on here?"

"Outlaws," was March's one-word explanation. "We need to get Lem and Alexander Brady to the doctor—if it's not too late for Brady. And John Deane, I suppose, before we take him to jail."

Jed nodded, his expression grim. "Henna—is she still here?"

"She's all right, and so is Wolf."

365

"Then let's get moving," Jed said. "Jakey, you hitch Lily here to the wagon. I'll help you get the injured settled, March."

Maggie felt a new sense of wonder at the way these neighbors worked together. Jed would save his questions until they'd done what needed to be done.

"Is this the Penny farm?" the other man put in, the one who looked—and sounded—so much like Langley Fitzgibbon. He hadn't dismounted.

"Oh, right." Jed waved a hand at him. "This fellow came to the farm asking after Lucas's ranch. When I took him out to show him the way, I noticed the smoke. I'd been fixing the pump in the kitchen—I guess with all the noise the boys were making, we hadn't heard the shots. Just thought you'd had a fire. I hightailed it over here, and this gentleman trailed along."

"You're Lucas Penny?" the man asked, his position on horseback emphasizing the length of the nose he looked down while sizing up March's singed hair and soot-ruined clothes.

"I'm his brother-in-law, March Jackson. And you are?"

"My name is Langley Fitzgibbon. I am here to collect Miss Margaret Parker and take her home to Kentucky."

Maggie suddenly understood. Stephen, her mother, the right Reverend Zebedee Chalmers—they'd all been wrong. She wasn't on a path to hell. She'd already arrived.

Chapter 25

March's grim face grew even grimmer. "That's something for you to discuss with Miss Parker at a later time. Right now, we could use your help."

Langley's only movement was a widening of his eyes. "Mr. . . . Jackson, is it? This . . . *homestead* is obviously no fit place for a young lady of breeding. I consider it my duty to remove Miss Parker from danger immediately. If you will simply tell me where she is, we will be on our way."

If Maggie could have broken out of her paralysis, she would have laughed. Langley didn't recognize her. He'd seen only her blackened hands and face, her ruined dress, and never once seen who wore them.

Typical.

She wondered for a fleeting moment if she could stay invisible. If he never noticed her, maybe he'd just leave. But that was folly. Langley Fitzgibbon was too big of a mistake ever to escape from, ever to live down as Henna had led her to hope she might.

He'd ruined her and humiliated her. He'd tried to force himself on her. And now he was here to take her away from March, to destroy the one true source of love she'd found in this world since her father died.

She'd wasted the second shot from her derringer on John Deane. She should have saved it for Langley.

Lemuel and Jed had passed March up the stairs and into the house to get Alexander Brady. March paused with his hand on the rail to frown back at the elegant man on horse-back.

"Mr. . . . Fitzgibbon, is it? If you don't intend to make yourself useful, you can get the hell off my ranch. Miss Parker will send word to you in town if she decides she wants to see you."

"I don't think you understand," Langley replied, drawing himself up like a snake about to strike. "I came here at the express wishes of the young lady's father to bring her back home, and I will not leave until I carry out my duty."

"I don't think *you* understand," March growled, his hand leaving the railing to curl into a hard fist. "I told you to get off my land."

Langley's eyes narrowed, and his nose tilted down slightly. "I understood this property belonged to Miss Parker's cousin, Lucas Penny, Mr. *Jackson*. I don't like your attitude, and I don't like this hellhole. Now fetch Miss Parker, or I'll get down and do it for you."

March shook his head, a humorless smile playing about his mouth. "I've had enough trouble for one day, mister, but I swear you're getting on my nerves. I can't promise that if I have to hit you, I'll know when to stop. I don't know who you are, and right now I don't really care—"

"I'm here in the stead of Miss Parker's father, and that ought to be enough for you," Langley snapped. "Show some respect for your betters, you filthy cowboy. Miss Parker's father—"

"*Step*father," Maggie broke in, her own temper frayed beyond salvaging. "For God's sake, Langley, stop that stupid posturing. You're making a fool of yourself."

Both men turned to stare at her, but she kept her gaze on Langley. She couldn't meet March's eyes.

"Margaret?" Langley asked.

368

And despite the appalling nature of the situation, she laughed, though it came out more as a strangled gargle. Langley had never called her Margaret in his life. He must be finding the West an extremely disturbing place to lose the charming, easy attitude he usually employed so successfully with lesser mortals.

She wanted to rant and rave and scream. But she didn't have the energy.

She just shook her head, the laughter still on her lips. "Langley, what are you doing here?"

"Maggie, are you hurt?" He finally swung his long legs down from the mare. He moved toward her, but then glanced down at his spotless pale kid gloves and changed his mind. "What have these barbarians done to you?"

"They tried me for a witch and burned me at the stake," Maggie snapped. "What does it look like they did to me, Langley? They housed me and fed me, and I helped rescue their horses from a burning barn. Are you staying at the Grand Hotel in Oxtail? Then go back there, and I'll come and talk to you later."

She would rather have thrown herself on the fiery remains of the barn than meet Langley anywhere, but she thought the words might get rid of him for the moment. No such luck.

Langley looked at her with an expression she'd never seen before on his face, mystified confusion. "But Maggie, I've come to take you home."

"You mentioned that."

The ranchhouse door opened, forestalling Langley's reply. Jed and Lemuel lurched out, Alexander Brady's body stretched between them. March hurried to help support the stocky rancher's midsection.

"Jake?" Jed called.

"Coming, Pa." The boy had hitched Jed's mare to the

369

wagon, and now carefully led her up alongside the porch.

"How is he?" Maggie asked. She wanted to run to Brady's side but felt trapped by Langley's presence. His reminder of who she used to be made her fear she no longer belonged in this new world she'd fallen into.

"Unconscious," Jed said, grunting as they swung Brady up into the wagon bed. "Probably best that way. Don't know beyond that. He's lost a lot of blood, but if the bullet had pierced his heart, he'd be dead by now.

"Shall we try Deane now, Lem?"

The black man nodded, and they turned to cross the yard.

Langley's attention swung back to Maggie. "You came to me begging me not to let Stephen send you out here."

Maggie's face burned with the memory of that humiliating day and with the knowledge that she hadn't told March about it. She still couldn't look at him. She couldn't bear to see the questions flickering in his eyes, what he must be thinking of her, even before he knew the worst.

"So don't play games with me, Maggie," Langley continued. "I know you too well. What is it? Are you still angry with me?" His tone indicated he was not amused that she chose to waste his time in that manner. "Perhaps what I have to say will change your mind on that score, as well. I'm here because I've asked your father for your hand in marriage, and he's agreed."

Maggie choked. Out of all the fevered explanations her imagination had put forth and discarded as to Langley's reasons for coming to Oxtail, that one had never crossed her mind. Relief that he hadn't brought bad news about her mother—the explanation she'd most feared—gave way to baffled disbelief.

"You're joking."

"Maggie, what's gotten in to you?" He stepped closer, so

that his height pressed down on her, but he still didn't deign to touch her with his elegant gloves. Exasperation snapped in his eyes, and something else. She almost thought it might be fear. Fear of the violence and death around him? Of being so far from home, his domain, where everyone bowed to him as a sort of feudal prince? "I wouldn't joke about something like that, Margaret. I know what I said to you before, but I didn't mean it. I want you to be my wife."

A couple of weeks ago—another lifetime ago—she would have given almost anything to hear those words from Langley. Langley Fitzgibbon, the handsomest, wealthiest, most eligible man in Lexington—hell, in all of Kentucky —asking her, scarred, socially inept Maggie Parker, to be his wife.

Now those words conjured the image of her stepfather's hand, reaching spectrally across a thousand miles to wrap its iron grip around her throat.

"What did Stephen offer you, and why?"

Langley stepped back as if bitten. "What do you mean?"

Maggie raised her eyebrows. "Something changed your mind about my marriageability. What was it?"

"Margaret, when you left, I discovered you'd taken a piece of my heart—"

"Horse manure."

He glared at her. "Very well. If you've no wish to be a lady about it. Your father came to me with a proposition concerning the land he owns contiguous to mine—to my father's—that will be quite beneficial to both of us."

"That's all?"

"He's offered Nomad to us as a wedding present."

Maggie's jaw actually dropped. Nomad was her stepfather's most promising young colt. Stephen had already begun making wagers with other horsemen on the long-legged gray's chances in next year's running of the state's new derby.

She didn't need any further explanations from Langley to piece together what had happened. Langley had let his tongue run loose about her, as he'd threatened to do, and her stepfather had caught wind of the rumors. He might not have the Fitzgibbons' old money style or social status, but Stephen Casey had spent enough money in the right circles to build up significant behind-the-scenes political power.

He must have brought that power down on Langley's head and thrown in the land and the horse to sweeten the threats. Obviously, part of the deal had included haste. Perhaps Stephen feared she might not fit into her wedding dress if they waited too long.

It had never occurred to her that she could go to her stepfather to ask him to force Langley into marrying her. Even if she'd thought of it, she wouldn't have believed Stephen would have done anything about it.

Why *had* he done it? For her mother? For his own honor? For a connection with the social standing of the Fitzgibbons?

She shook her head. It didn't matter.

Stephen had rescued her from shame and dishonor. Marriage to Langley offered her things she'd rarely even allowed herself to dream of—a secure position in her community, the assurance of being accepted everywhere she went, the knowledge that dressmakers' jobs depended on seeing she looked stylish and ladylike. As Mrs. Langley Fitzgibbon she'd never have to face another slight of her reputation or respectability.

"So get your things, and let's get out of this place," Langley said, stepping aside with a grimace of disgust as Lemuel and Jed carried John Deane past him.

"I'm not going anywhere," Maggie told him, her heart pounding with a heady taste of freedom. The freedom of a pigeon released for a hunter's target practice, perhaps, but the look on Langley's face almost compensated for the coming pain. "I wouldn't marry you if my only other choice was General William T. Sherman. I'm staying right here, and you can tell Stephen he needn't worry about me ever darkening his doorstep again."

She felt March move up beside her, offering silent support. When Langley left, she'd tell him everything. He might no longer welcome her here on his ranch, but she wasn't going back to Kentucky. She'd survive. She had friends now, friends who would help her. Even March would help her, no matter how his opinion of her might change. She'd never go back. Not for Langley, not for Stephen, not for respectability.

"Have you lost your mind?" Annoyance was quickly replacing confusion in Langley's voice. "For God's sake, Maggie, this is neither the time nor the place for a scene. You can throw a tantrum when we reach the hotel, if you must. My aunt is waiting there for us, to chaperone you home. Now let's go."

"Go to hell, Langley." Maggie articulated each word with care.

"I've had enough of your little games, Margaret." Langley yanked off his gloves and stuffed them in a pocket. "You're coming with me."

Before his hand could reach her arm, he jerked it back with a cry of pain. Maggie turned in surprise to see March replacing his Colt in its holster. He'd brought it down across Langley's knuckles with enough force to break the skin. Langley was shaking his injured hand, hissing through clenched teeth.

March spoke for the first time in minutes, the violence in his eyes belying his calm voice. "I believe the lady told you to go to hell, mister."

"And what business is it of yours?" Langley snarled. "Step

aside, cowboy, or I'll bloody the rest of my knuckles on your teeth."

Remembering the way March had downed huge Shelby Brennan, Maggie doubted he'd have the chance. But this was her fight.

"It's all right, March, I can handle him," she said, flexing her fingers. "He already knows what I can do with a knife."

Langley blanched, but he didn't step back. " 'March,' is it? That's awfully friendly." He looked March up and down. "I can't say your taste in 'friends' has improved, Margaret. Though you two certainly look a matched pair this afternoon."

She hadn't eaten since breakfast, so the sudden lump in her stomach had nothing to do with food. Maggie's throat constricted, and she fought to keep back tears—not of self-pity, for only she could be blamed for her mistakes, but of grief. She'd given her heart to March mere days ago, and now she was about to lose both it and him.

Her shoulders sagged. "Langley, please, just go."

March's hand touched her arm. "I think you'd better go, mister. If you try to lay another hand on the lady, you won't get it back. She's welcome here as long as she wants to stay."

"So you're her white knight, is that it?" Langley forgot to tilt his nose up as he said it. "I suppose you even fancy you're in love with the little witch?"

March's lips smiled. His eyes did not. "A man of perception, I see."

"Poor fool." Langley shook his head in mock regret. "I hate to have to be the one to break the news, but it's better you find out now, I suppose. Miss Parker isn't the pure white lily in distress she'd have you believe. To be blunt, she's no longer a virgin. I had that little pleasure myself. You're just next in line."

Maggie stood paralyzed between the desire to dig Langley's eyes out with her fingernails and the urge to crawl into a hole and die.

"Let me see if I understand this," March said beside her, his voice poisonously pleasant. "Given the opportunity to compare the two of us, Miss Parker has expressed a profound preference to remain here with me rather than return with you. And you think that should bother *me?* I find it distinctly complimentary, myself."

A rosy flush spread across Langley's naturally fair skin, from his neck to his hair line. He opened his mouth, but no words came out.

Maggie risked a glance at March, but his gaze was fixed on Langley. "I think you should leave," he said again, still not raising his voice. "Before I take offense at the way you've spoken to the woman I intend to ask to be my wife."

Maggie's eyes widened. He couldn't mean it. He must be saying it to save his dignity.

Langley's face turned a deeper shade of purple. "Your wife?" He looked at Maggie. "God, Margaret. All I can say is, you got what you deserved. And as for you, cowboy, as far as I'm concerned, you're welcome to the little slut."

March's hand dropped from Maggie's arm, but Langley must have seen the murder in his eyes, for he ducked under March's first swing and dodged around the body of his borrowed mare.

March tensed, but a voice from the porch stopped him cold.

"Do you want to waste your energy, March, or shall I plug him from here?"

The southern drawl hit him harder than any punch Langley Fitzgibbon might have thrown. He turned to stare at the figure on the porch. The ghost, pale as death, had a black

375

duster draped over his shoulders. One arm was slung over Jed Culbert's shoulder, the other he steadied on the porch railing, his revolver aimed almost casually at Langley's heart. Wolf hovered beside him like a shadow, Loki clutched in his arms.

" 'Lije?" The name croaked from his throat.

" 'He who has died is freed from sin,' " Elijah quoted. "I guess God didn't think I deserved to be freed just yet. God and Loki. I could have gone peacefully into the great beyond if that damn wolf hadn't kept licking my lips."

"Harry heard him muttering at Loki, and just about died herself," Jed said. "But she managed to bandage up his head. The bullet grazed his skull, but didn't go any deeper. Still, we'd better get him to the doctor. The fever's left him for now, but I don't like the thought of it coming back after he's lost all that blood."

March muttered a prayer as he moved toward the porch to help Jed get his friend to the wagon. But Elijah stopped him with a wave of his Colt.

"Plug him?"

March turned back. He'd completely forgotten Langley Fitzgibbon in the joy of seeing Elijah alive.

He shook his head. "No, he's mine."

Langley's flush had given way to a greenish pallor. The sight of Elijah's gun, or perhaps the grisly bandage—or perhaps something he'd seen in March's eyes—had drained him of all his dignified bravado. March would have let the pompous ass ride off if Langley had only insulted him. But Langley had hurt Maggie.

It didn't take much reasoning power to put the facts together—Maggie's fearful reaction when he'd first tried to make love to her, Langley's arrogant possessiveness, the fact that Maggie had never mentioned Langley's name. Maggie's comment about her knife implied she'd given as good as she got. Having faced her little dagger himself, he didn't doubt it.

But that didn't change the violence that curved his fists. He didn't know that if he once hit Langley, he could keep from killing him.

Langley saved him the trouble of finding out. With speed, if not grace, the other man swung himself up onto the mare, digging in his heels even before he'd properly gotten his seat. He grabbed the mare's mane as his foot flailed for the far stirrup. Struggling desperately to find his balance, Langley Fitzgibbon galloped up the drive, leaving behind only a cloud of dust.

"That looks like the man I rode in the stagecoach from Greeley with." Harry's voice came from the ranch house doorway. "What's he doing here?"

No one answered, and Maggie could only shake her head. She remembered the girl's comments from the night before about the sort of man she would never marry. Not only could Harry play the role of a lady with an ease Maggie could never hope to match, but she was also a better judge of character.

Maggie glanced at March and found the sight of him almost painful. Even in his ruined work clothes, his face streaked with dirt and soot, with his wonderful thick, soft hair singed almost to his skull by the fire, his strength, his courage, his gentleness and integrity shone through.

She watched March climb the steps to the porch. Harry had taken Elijah's gun and put it back in its holster, and March moved her and Wolf aside to take the gunfighter's arm.

"You realize," Elijah told March and Jed as they helped him to the wagon, "that I'm only agreeing to go to the doctor because Henna threatened to shoot me herself if I didn't. That woman is a powerful persuader."

"Tell me about it," Jed said. He climbed onto the wagon seat and took the reins from Jake. "Wolf, you want to come along?"

The boy nodded solemnly and climbed up beside him, still holding Loki like a shield. Jed took another quick look around. "Where's Lem?"

"I'm comin'." The old man walked slowly out the door and made his way to Jed's side. Another of Harry's white bandages showed brightly against his grizzled hair. "March, you got a lump, too. You oughta come with us."

March shook his head. "I'll be fine. There's too much to do here." Something about his tone of voice forestalled the arguments Maggie expected.

"I'll pick up some hay in town," Jed offered, "and bring it over this evening. If the weather stays clear, you ought to be able to keep the horses in the corral and paddock until we can get that barn rebuilt. I'll send word to the Larimer County sheriff. He should be able to get somebody out here to pick up the bodies pretty quick."

"Thanks, Jed."

Jed shook his reins, and the wagon rolled off, taking its load of injured toward town.

"Henna's already started cleaning up the blood and glass," Harry said when the wagon had finally disappeared around the curve in the drive. "I thought I might start a little something on the stove so we don't all pass out from hunger when the excitement wears off."

Maggie could see the struggle it took March not to tell his baby sister to rest. "Thanks, Harry. That's a fine idea. Maggie and I will get the horses coralled, then we'll be in to help."

Harry nodded and slipped back into the house.

The horses. For the first time in her life Maggie had forgotten there were horses to be cared for. And then, of course, would come windows to be boarded, floors to be cleaned, food to be cooked and eaten. They'd have to do something with the outlaws' bodies so they wouldn't putrefy or attract scavengers before the sheriff's men arrived. Then they would have to bathe and change and sleep, necessities she could already feel her body crying out for.

A thousand and one things to do to drag out her agony, to prolong the time before she and March could talk, before she would see the disappointment and disapproval in his eyes.

Aristotle first. She could get Ari, Balthasar, and Pamela to the corral without any trouble, and Honey and the pony shouldn't be too hard to round up. Let March worry about Sandy and Achilles.

Her feet weighed much more than she remembered as she lifted one at a time to make her way to the north pasture gate where Ari waited with Balthasar and Pamela. Ari nickered softly at her, and when she nickered back, the mare moved forward to meet her.

"Maggie?"

March's voice stopped her, but she didn't look around. If she saw his face now, she might give up entirely and be of no use to anyone. Ari reached her and pushed her nose over Maggie's shoulder to nuzzle her hair. Maggie leaned forward to press her cheek against the buckskin's warm neck.

She heard March's footsteps falter and stop. "Maggie . . . ?"

She could only shake her head. "I'm sorry, March."

"No, don't. I'm sorry." She could feel the emptiness between them like a weight. "I shouldn't have said that, about marrying you, in front of everybody."

She pressed her face into Ari's neck, but that couldn't stop the tears. "It's all right, I understand—"

But he kept talking. "I didn't mean to embarrass you, or

pressure you. I wanted to get rid of that son-of-a-bitch, and when you said that, about staying here, I thought it meant, well . . ." He paused in frustration, unable to find the words. "I shouldn't have assumed. Just because you said you loved me earlier, I shouldn't have expected . . . anything."

Maggie couldn't be sure she'd heard him correctly, her blood was pounding so loudly through her head. What was he apologizing to her for?

"I meant what I said, Maggie. You're welcome here as long as you want to stay, even if you can't . . ." His voice trailed off.

She lifted her face from Ari's neck and turned just enough to glance at March.

"I was going to tell you about Langley, when all this was over." She turned fully toward him, gathering her courage about her like a cloak. "I hope you can believe that. I didn't mean to deceive you. I just . . . Your love felt so right, so good. I wanted to keep it, for at least a little while. I'm sorry."

He shook his head. "What about Langley? You don't love him. You *don't* love him."

"No." Maggie grimaced. "I thought I did once, but . . . when he and I . . . The other day—at the river—I knew then, what love really was. I didn't mean it to go that far, and after it did, I just couldn't tell you. That I wasn't a virgin."

March stepped toward her, and Maggie forced herself not to step back.

His fingers touched her shoulder, moved to her cheek as his eyes searched hers. "You thought I thought you were a virgin?"

Maggie blinked. "You didn't?"

"Maggie, there are . . . signs."

"I didn't know that you'd ever made love with a virgin!" The words burst out as a strange explosion of relief and fury.

His mouth relaxed, ever so slightly. "I haven't, I guess, but that doesn't mean I haven't heard about it."

Maggie's limbs lost their strength. Only the gentle pressure of March's fingers on her jaw kept her upright. "You've known ever since we made love? You knew this morning when you said . . . that you loved me?"

"Maggie, I don't know everything about your past. But there's nothing in it that can change how I feel about who you are now."

"But my honor—"

"Your being a virgin or not has nothing to do with the honorable, brave, beautiful woman you are. The fact that you once loved Langley Fitzgibbon might make me question your sanity—" He smiled at her in a way that almost broke her heart. "—but never your honor, or what I feel for you."

She stepped into his arms and wrapped her fingers in his hair as he bent down to meet her lips with his. As he held her tight against him, she could feel their bodies melting into even closer harmony.

"Does this mean you weren't offended by my mention of marriage?" he asked, his voice hoarse as he pulled back to watch her reaction.

She shook her head, hardly able to speak around the emotions pounding through her. "Does this mean you're not going to continue plotting to send me home by the next available stage?"

"A lot of good that's done me so far." March brushed her hair back from her face. "I said once that you were too lovely, too vital to belong here in my life. But I'll be damned if I'll let anyone take you out of it now."

Maggie let her fingers trail down his jaw. "Then I guess you're stuck with me, March Jackson."

"You'll marry me?"

"Of course. Somebody's got to take care of you."

She bent his head down to hers and kissed him as thoroughly as he had kissed her.

"Why, Miss Parker," he said when she paused for breath, "I'll be mighty happy to have you take care of me anytime."

Maggie smiled slyly. "There's much more to taking care of a cowboy like you than a mere kiss or two."

March smiled back, a slow smile that burned all the way down to Maggie's toes. "Is that right?"

"Definitely."

"Well, it seems to me that if I need all this care, you should get started right away. You're going to be busy."

"Is that right?"

"Definitely."

He kissed her again, and for the first time, standing there with her hair a mess, her face covered with grime and streaked with horse sweat, she felt truly beautiful.

A soft puff of air in her ear broke the moment.

She pulled back from the kiss. "March?"

"Yes?"

"I do promise to take care of you, but I'm afraid I'm going to have to take care of the horses first."

March frowned at the dusky muzzle nibbling at Maggie's ear. "I've just asked you to marry me, and already you're leaving me for Ari?"

Maggie laughed. "March Jackson, I love you more than I've ever loved another human being. Now you're expecting me to love you more than my horse, too?"

Epilogue

Maggie stood with a hand on the porch railing, the light pressure of March's arm around her shoulders still new and wondrous to her. Her other hand rested on Wolf's shoulder as he watched his father swing gracefully into his saddle.

"You know you're welcome to stay here as long as you like," March said.

"We can always use another hand," Maggie put in.

Lemuel added from March's other side, "Especially one as doesn't let us pay him."

Elijah shook his head. "I appreciate your kindness in putting up with me this long, but it's time I was leaving. Don't worry, I'll be sure to abuse your hospitality again, soon." He looked at Wolf. "I promise."

Maggie swallowed the rest of her objections. He still looked pale, but otherwise he seemed healthy enough. Certainly he'd recovered faster than Alexander Brady. She'd visited the rancher with March only two days ago and found him still laid up in bed, a much thinner, frailer man than the robust cattle baron that had entered the gunfight at the ranch a fortnight ago.

But though his healing remained slow, his forceful personality had still resonated in his voice as he spoke with her. And he had survived. John Deane hadn't even lived long enough to hang. His ankle had gangrened, and the doctor hadn't amputated soon enough. She didn't like thinking about it. She didn't like being glad about death.

Elijah had recovered quickly, despite his malaria. And his

pale skin couldn't be attributed merely to weakness. Out working the horses or picking beans in the garden, he never forgot his hat the way March so often did.

She looked up into March's tanned face, seeing the tracing of lines around his eyes and mouth. They no longer echoed his heart's grief, only the long hours he spent in the sun. He might weather quickly, but he'd never look old with those warm blue eyes that glowed whenever he caught her watching him.

"Goodbye then," March was saying. "We'll be looking for you, 'Lije."

Elijah nodded again. "Goodbye. Tell Harry goodbye for me."

Maggie doubted it was a coincidence Elijah had chosen to leave while Harry was in Oxtail with Henna, but she couldn't blame him for it.

"And take care of that lovely lady you've got there," Elijah added. "I believe I told you she was just the woman for you, so you'd better be sure to keep her happy."

March's hand squeezed Maggie's arm. "I'll do my best."

"Goodbye, Mr. Kelly," Maggie said.

" 'Bye, Preacher," Lemuel added, giving a sly grin at Elijah's grimace. The gunfighter gathered up his reins, and his horse snorted in readiness.

"Goodbye, Father." Wolf's clear voice carried despite its restraint.

Elijah paused, and even his coffee-colored gelding fell still. "Goodbye, son. Be good, and take care of Henna and Jed and the young ones."

"Yes, sir."

Elijah turned his horse, and nudged him into a brisk walk up the drive.

A gray form lying quietly at Wolf's feet suddenly rippled

into motion. The three-month-old wolf-dog bounded out into the yard, shook himself thoroughly, then broke into an easy trot after the figure in black.

Wolf leaped after him, but the cub's seemingly effortless lope was faster than the boy could hope to run. "Loki! Loki, come back here!"

Elijah heard and pulled his horse to a halt. Loki reached him quickly, sitting several feet from the gunfighter's stirrup. Wolf jogged up beside them and reached for the wolf's leather collar.

Elijah swung down from his horse and scratched Loki's chin. "It's all right, little one. I'll be back." He looked at Wolf. "He's gotten used to watching over me these past couple of weeks. I should have sent him back to the farm to stay with you. You'll have to hold him back until I'm out of sight. It might even be best to lock him in the house until I'm gone."

Wolf looked down at the young cub whose eyes traveled with curiosity between the boy and his father. "He wants to go with you."

"He'll be all right. He'll get used to the farm fast enough and hardly remember me by next week."

Wolf crouched down and scratched Loki's ears. The cub licked his cheek. "No, he won't. He should go with you."

The gunfighter stepped back. "No, Wolf, he's your dog. He . . . loves you. I wouldn't take him away from you."

Wolf stood, releasing Loki's collar. "I know he loves me." Maggie heard more in the words than their simple meaning. "But I think Pa was right. A wolf doesn't belong on a farm. He should be traveling, like you."

"But Wolf . . ."

The boy looked up at his father. "I have a whole family here, and all my friends—Miss Maggie, March, Mr. Tate. You don't have anybody. You need him more than I do. I

385

want Loki to go with you."

For once, Elijah had nothing to say. He raised his hand, let it fall, raised it again, and finally let it rest tentatively on Wolf's shoulder.

His voice was low, and Maggie couldn't hear what he said now, nor Wolf's reply. But she saw the quick embrace before Elijah once more mounted his horse and kicked it into a trot up the drive. Loki stood, looked back toward the porch, licked Wolf's hand, then trotted after the horse and rider, his lithe form moving like the touch of the wind over the ground.

When Wolf started slowly up the rutted drive after them, Maggie made a move to follow, but March held her back.

"Let him go. He'll be all right. He just needs some time alone."

Lemuel cleared his throat. "I think I'll jes' go check in on the horses and see about fixing that old saddle we got from the Colonel."

He climbed down the porch steps, and Maggie watched him cross the yard toward the new barn and stable he and March and Jed and a handful of Oxtail neighbors had raised together. Bounty money from some of the dead outlaws had covered the cost of the materials, with enough left over to replace most of the lost tack and Lemuel's belongings.

"It's going to be quiet around here without Elijah and Loki," March said, pulling Maggie a little tighter against his side.

"I miss having Wolf live with us," Maggie said, watching the boy walk out of sight. "I don't suppose Henna would let us abduct him."

March lifted her hand from the porch railing to turn her toward him. He pulled her up against his chest. "No, I'm afraid not."

He bent his head down and kissed her, his mouth moving

slowly against hers. The tip of his tongue touched her lips, and she opened to him, sighing as she melted against him.

"There is something to be said for not having guests in the house," March murmured, his mouth still touching hers.

Maggie bent her head back to look up into his eyes. They glinted with amusement, and something more.

"In the middle of the morning?" she asked, feigning shock.

He grinned, pulling her hips tight against his. "If you miss Wolf so much, maybe we ought to get to work having some children of our own, Mrs. Jackson."

He worked his hands from her hips up her sides until the heels of his palms pressed under her breasts. She wondered if she'd ever be able to control her response to his touch.

I hope not.

Before she could reply, her husband swung her up into his arms, as strong and gentle as though she were a precious new-born foal. He planted his foot against the ranch house door, and it swung open on a room that still smelled like the peach cobbler she had made for breakfast.

He said, as he had every day since their wedding in Oxtail, "Welcome home, Mrs. Jackson."

And Maggie knew with all her heart that she had indeed finally found her way home.